GABRIEL ZAVALA

DON'T GET CAUGHT

RECLUSE

RECLUSE

GABRIEL ZAVALA

Book Cover by MiblArt

First edition 2024

www.authorgabrielzavala.com

"Prisons do not disappear social problems, they disappear human beings. Homelessness, unemployment, drug addiction, mental illness, and illiteracy are only a few of the problems that disappear from public view when the human beings contending with them are relegated to cages."

Angela Davis

PROLOGUE

JUNE 17

NOTHING COULD HAVE PREPARED Detective Amelia Mayman for the dispatcher call she received that night. Murder was always the worst call a detective could receive, even for a seasoned captain such as herself. But from what the dispatcher said, this was more than a homicide.

It was something far worse.

Hurry, she thought.

The gas pedal of the police car pressed deeper into the floor, racing into midnight.

The dim, stark, brick buildings watched Amelia and the rest of the racing police cars with an unwelcoming eye. This didn't surprise her. This was East Haddam, after all—an overrun criminal *correctional* city. It seemed like every other day, there was something new to be solved, which kept her constantly on edge, wondering what new pieces of a puzzle she'd have to put together.

But this was big.

Her long, dark fingers tightened on the wheel, not knowing what she might find waiting for her tonight with the St. Judas Cathedral now coming into view. A glorious monument stuck in the unholy barbarity of this isolated town.

Evil, she thought. That's what was waiting for her inside.

The hot tires scorched the pavement as they parked at the foot of the towering cathedral, an unshakeable dread prickling up her back like a spider.

The flashing blue and red sirens and the screaming of the ambulance ruined what should have been a silent Sunday night in East Haddam, Connecticut.

No time to waste.

From the witness tip phoned in about half an hour ago, she tried to imagine the vilest scene with every shade of red to maroon splattered along the floor inside. The gruesome picture painted by the dispatcher was the most barbaric act she'd heard in her long career.

Maybe it could have been prevented if the state had given the Haddam Police Department more funding to run more city patrols in East Haddam. But they didn't. The state government left the correctional city mostly unsupervised, leaving it to rot away.

Crimes like *these* would have never occurred in Boston, where she used to work.

Amelia stepped out of the car, gazing at the cathedral in front of her, dreading to infiltrate inside. She bit her bottom lip. A glass of vodka waiting for her back home saved her depleting peace.

The car doors slammed as, one by one, the police hurried to the scene. The cathedral's stained windows now flashed the panes of Mary with red bloody lights. *Of course, something this fucked would happen here.* Ever since the Safety First Act passed, the inmate citizens had been running the town to hell.

Unlawful.

Now, as captain of the East Haddam patrol, she was determined to restore order back in the correctional city.

Amelia's body armor squeezed tightly against her torso, a pistol loaded and ready by her side. The eyes of all the scattered units turned to her, waiting for her word, her order. But even she didn't know what that would be. She wasn't aware of the situation inside the cathedral. Would there be a hostage?

The Haddam Police Department instructed the priests not to enter the cathedral until after their sweep, which meant only the victim should've been waiting inside. And maybe the killer.

"Amelia! What's going on?" an officer said.

Amelia's eye twitched at the towering cathedral sitting like a sleeping giant. She folded her arms. "Not sure yet. From what the dispatcher said." She paused. The image she created flashed through her mind again. "I won't believe it 'til I see it for myself," she finished. It was the type of scene that would only happen once in a lifetime one would only imagine, but would never have to face it in reality.

"What the hell does that mean?"

She gripped her pistol, turning to the other officers.

"Nothing good. Let's secure all exits immediately! My team will take the front entrance!"

Police units swarmed around the building to every entrance and exit the building had. If the killer was still inside, they couldn't escape because of the large perimeter now secured.

Amelia and her unit stood at bay at the cathedral entrance, a magnificent pair of ornate wooden doors.

"On my signal," she said.

Whatever was inside, she was ready for.

She mouthed the words: *One. Two. Three.* With a loud burst, they slammed the doors open, rushing into a dark abyss.

Amelia was met with a repugnant smell that spread around like a disease. There was something there lingering in the pitch darkness of the nave, the type of uncertainty like waiting for someone to jump out at you. She covered her nose with her arm, stepping deeper inside the shadows.

Then, each of their flashlights flicked on, looking for anything—a body, movement, an explanation. Amelia's flashlight shot into the air like a spotlight, a strange array of ropes and—blood. Her eyes widened at the full scene.

A vile, spine-chilling sight.

The image she created in her mind was real, and it was right in front of her. A nightmare that, in fact, she was now living in. She remained coldly stiff. The blood dripping from above to the floor made her ears want to curl themselves. A haunting sound that would make anyone go mad.

"Holy Mary Mother of God. Don't tell me that's—" a policewoman whispered.

"It is," Amelia said. She shined her light on the woman's face. *Oh my God, how is this possible?* The spectacle of blood on her carcass struck Amelia with a shivering terror. "That's our victim."

Amelia couldn't take her eyes off the young woman's strung-up, dismembered, and brutally slaughtered body. She'd seen nothing like it before in her career. Only someone with the darkest of minds could've done something on this scale.

The woman was strung up in the air on what looked like a web made of bloody ropes and cables. Hanging from the nave, her detached limbs and other body parts were scattered along the web.

Amelia held her breath. The killer made deep slashes on her torso and legs. The dripping of tar-like maroon blood counted every second the poor woman had been trapped in her perilous state.

The winding man-made web trapped the woman like a spider had devoured her, spitting out what it didn't like.

Amelia's trembling eyes narrowed on her appearance. Scarlet blood stained her once pale face and tangled brown hair. Every aspect of her had been drained blue and became lifeless.

But this seemed fresh, perhaps not even twenty-four hours since she was murdered. How could someone have done something this elaborate? This wasn't some amateur they were dealing with or someone who wanted the quick rush of murder. No. The killer planned this.

Amelia's breath caught in her throat as she focused closer on the woman's face.

A silver piece of tape concealed the woman's mouth. Written with sharpie, blackened words blazed across the tape.

BUG

The rest of the police units secured the entire building now. No one else was there. The killer was long gone by now. She took one last look at the woman before sending paramedics inside.

Amelia imagined how, just days before, the woman was smiling and alive, not knowing she'd end up like this just a few days later—an eaten *bug*.

Evil, Amelia thought.

That's who had done this.

1

LUKAS

JUNE 16

A MIRROR CAN REFLECT everything about a person, Lukas thought. It showed the real him staring back, the full story he tried to hide. The one others try to read.

In the dingy bathroom of SuperShine carwash, Lukas Retter lifted his stained navy shirt over his head and tossed it to the floor. Thin pink scars of his past wrapped around his frail body, his ribcage beckoning to push out further so that he might look bigger. Too many scars to count, some longer than others—always kept covered. A discolored red scar stretched across his abdomen as he traced it with his pasty finger.

Three hissing lightbulbs above the mirror flickered off and on. The cracked, rusted mirror read the story to him. A tale of stolen childhood and freedom. And somehow, the story hadn't ended yet. He wasn't *free*. Moving from one prison in his childhood to now a bigger one: East Haddam. *False freedom*. Just a bigger cage.

Power. He flexed his short biceps. *That's what we all want in this world*, he thought. *To feel like we have control over our own lives, to make others bend to our will.* At SuperShine, Lukas had no power, ordered around like some kind of pet.

He glimpsed at the time on his phone. It was now noon. He must've lost track of time spent picking at every aspect of himself.

The bathroom banged with heavy fists.

"Goddamn it, Lukas! That's twenty minutes now!"

Ian Addams continued to shout his name. He was the owner of the carwash, yet he was always too busy doing *paperwork* in his office instead of helping around like he should've.

"One second!" Lukas called back.

Lukas quickly uncapped his capsule of OxyContin medication and popped a small white tablet in his mouth. Twice a day, all for the pain. The flaming throb in his head that wouldn't go away.

With the pounding on the door relentless, Lukas threw his shirt back on and flung the bathroom door open to reveal an annoyed Ian. A curly-haired brunette man, his round body inching inside the doorway with his greased Hawaiian shirt. The same look of contempt smeared on him.

"You take twenty minutes to shit? What the hell do you do in there?"

"I'm taking my medication," Lukas said.

"Of course you are. Look, there's two cars waiting outside. Mateo's doing one, so you get the other, alright? We gotta keep the customers happy, Lukas. You can't be doing twenty, fucking, drug, jerking off, shits or whatever it is you do," Ian said, tossing him a dirty sponge and plastic bucket.

"Right."

Outside the carwash, a tall wooden lamp post where the same missing person's flyer had hung for two months now.

Cassandra Holland

Age: 19

The flyers bought nothing but a quick glance of sympathy from pedestrians, hoping she'd turn up but not *really* expecting her to be recovered. Still, every day, her picture hung, her empty smile displayed to every car that pulled into the carwash. He was sure drivers never gave more than a passing thought about her black-and-white face. But wherever she was, she had to be in East Haddam. No one ever got out. The patrols made sure of that.

Swish, splash, the soaking sponge glided across the door of an old orange Hyundai. The car could use a fresh coat of paint. It was peeling off bit-by-bit. June brought nothing but a trail of sweat down his back and the fatigue from a summer heat. Up and down, he bent, soaking the dirty sponge into the murky water and on the car. Washing every stain, crease, and mark on the car as fast as he could, and there was nothing more he wanted than to stop. He willed his body to drop everything and just leave.

It didn't. He stayed put like a *good* boy.

Out of anywhere I could be in the world, he thought. *Why did it have to be here?* He spent each miserable second trying to imagine something to look forward to, a reward for putting up with all the tiring labor. Even the pay wasn't close to what he deserved. Every hour only made him $3.75—half the federal minimum wage. That was the most money anyone could make inside those cages. They were prisoners, after all. *Safety-First* ensured the citizens were separated in almost every way from the outside world, including financially.

It had taken Lukas three years to purchase his used busted truck from an illicit seller. The only way in and out of East Haddam was the swing bridge that connected the town to Haddam. There was no other way out. He was sure of it.

But Lukas didn't want to think about that now.

He closed his eyes, and there she was. Soft brown hair falling *perfectly* on her shoulders and a voice so soft he was sure it was made of silk. She was perfect.

Rebecca Waylow.

She was lucky to have him as her boyfriend because the day he has power, she'll be right there next to him—weaving their life together. He wondered where she might be right now, perhaps painting a landscape on her porch, unless she lied to him. Unless she was going behind his back. The thought flustered him, but he shook it off his mind. *No, she wouldn't.* She was loyal to *him,* and she wouldn't do that to him. *Right?*

Finally, it was done. Another car washed. Satisfied, Lukas approached the driver's side to collect payment, knocking on the window.

No response.

He knocked again, harder.

The engine turned on.

This time, he pounded with his fist. "Hey!" he called. The conveniently tinted windows didn't allow him to see who was inside.

In a flash of a second, the orange Hyundai sped off like he was nothing, the back wheel running over his foot.

Lukas yelped, gripping his foot. It pulsated with an unbearable pain. He collapsed to the floor, letting out a small cry, whimpering.

"Lukas!" Ian shouted from behind. "Goddamn it, Lukas! He got away! You lost our money! You useless idiot! Fuck!"

Every bark from Ian's mouth filled Lukas with rage. *Fuck you, Ian!*

Lukas trembled on the scorching road in pain before another car pulled up to him, honking for him to wash again.

The sound of evening traffic pierced through the thin walls of the East Haddam Social Services building, specifically the office of Madeline Harkins. A small, cramped room of filing cabinets lit by a single hanging bulb and a table in the middle where Lukas sat across from her.

Killing is bad.

At least that's what Lukas told himself. Whenever someone would interrupt him, walk over him, or lie to him, he had to remind himself. *Killing is bad.*

He wrote it down twice a day in the journal Madeline gave him. Once in the morning, and then again before his restless night. But he never believed it as much as he wrote it down, because there was something euphoric about hurting others. Most days, he fantasized about hurting his enemies. Lukas imagined them screaming as they pleaded for mercy. He even imagined what Ian's hoarse, wailing voice would sound like. Ian's screams then became a soothing relief that replayed in Lukas's mind before he tilted his head up at Madeline.

The silence between them both grew uncomfortable now as he now stared down at his aching foot. But that didn't matter anymore. His mind gripped at the idea of not knowing where Rebecca was. What she was doing? Who she was speaking to at the moment? If not by his side, she probably didn't want to be around him anymore, he thought. She's moved on to some other guy. He was sure of it.

"What happened to your foot?" Madeline finally asked, though her tone seemed like she might've already known the answer.

He had forgotten about the silence they sat in.

His eyes flicked up to meet hers as he recounted to her how the car had run over his foot and sped off. Then he paused, but only for a moment. "I'm gonna need more Oxy. For the pain."

"Lukas, I'm sorry that happened to you, but I'm not sure that's a good idea. The dose prescribed is already well enough. A higher dosage may lead to something more *lethal*," Madeline said.

Her velvet lips parted as if she were about to say something. Instead, Madeline let out a low sigh, her pimpled cheeks deflating.

"Let's talk about you and Rebecca again. Do you still feel those *strong* emotions?" Madeline finally asked.

Lukas's brow twitched. His mind blazed with theories of what Rebecca was doing. If only she'd be a good girl and update him throughout her day. *What're you doing, Rebecca? Huh? If I'm right, you should be taking a stroll down by the river because you say it clears your mind. Then you'll watch the seven o'clock news because it keeps you updated on the outside world. Then you'll have a random man spend the night with you, right? Because you find it amusing how I won't find out.*

"I just *need* to know where she is. Whenever I'm not with her, she has the power to do whatever she wants without me watching. I know she's sucking another man's dick right now. Of course, she would be," Lukas said.

And there it was again. Silence. Silence slowly burning his mind, waiting for Madeline to reply. She was fairly young, so he wondered why it was so difficult for her to empathize, to make all his pain go away. All it took was a prescription slip from her. That's all she had to do.

"Sometimes it might help to write these thoughts in a notebook to keep track of how you're feeling. I wanted to tell you, since our funding's being cut and given to the police, our sessions might become more scarce," Madeline said.

The throbbing in his foot returned, and the building rattled as the traffic roared by.

"Who am I supposed to talk to then? Why are you abandoning us?" he mumbled.

Madeline sighed, her eyes falling to Lukas, rubbing his foot. Maybe then she finally felt a glint of compassion.

"I'll get you another prescription of OxyContin, but only as a painkiller for your foot. OxyContin can only do so much," she said.

On the corner of Main and Norwich stood the New Horizon Apartments at the end of a line of red brick buildings. Not the type of place one would choose to live, but it was there or sleeping on the streets. Lukas barely made enough to afford the rent, an absurd amount to pay for such a small space. A tall lamp post illuminated the apartments now that it was dark, standing like a beacon for wandering travelers. Being outside at night was a sure way to meet trouble—where shadows lurked behind street corners and alleys. Shadows who mug, steal, and deal.

Lukas hurried inside the apartments with a small bag, limping. *Two tablets a day*, all for the pain, he cheerily thought. The inside was just as outdated and dreadful as the outside, lacking in color and life. Torn furniture sat in the lobby, with leaking ceilings and a small puddle in the corner. Though this was far better than where he lived most of his childhood, nothing could compare to that hell.

Walking up the wooden stairs, going floor-to-floor, he held onto the railing, leaning onto it. Of course, if there was an elevator, he would've taken it. But the cheapskate landlord, Dimitri Pauk, wouldn't ever purchase something as grand as that. With the OxyContin, the pain in his foot had lessened, the nerves calmed.

Lukas looked up at the stairwell of his floor. A little boy dangled his feet from the edges. A familiar childish face. Jake was his neighbor's son, and he frequently stayed outside his apartment more than he was in. Wrapping his brown hands around the rail, he watched Lukas walk up the stairway, greeting him with a small smile.

"Right according to schedule," the boy said, beaming. His cheeks smeared with dust, and his black hair matted.

Lukas wondered whether Jake had simply been waiting for his arrival, like a train arriving at a station before departing to its next destination.

"Out again, huh? Were you waiting for me?" Lukas chuckled.

Jake turned his head to his apartment. The echo of shouting parents and broken dreams bounced off the walls to their ears. It didn't take a word from him, but Lukas immediately understood because the voices sounded like his own parents all those years ago. In fact, he saw himself in the boy, always on the outside looking in.

"You always come at this time every night, just like an old woman visits Ms. Warren's at noon every Friday, and how Karina goes downstairs Tuesday nights to read her books in the lobby. I like to pay attention to you guys. It's fun. It's like a clock. Going around, then coming back around," Jake said cheerily. His innocent eyes twinkled at his own observation.

"Have you even eaten today, kid, or do you just sit here?"

He didn't respond. Jake's smile sagged into something more solemn before he turned his head down toward the descending stairs. Now, the arguing in the background seemed to grow even louder.

A child should never go hungry, he thought. *Not ever.* Not like he did.

Lukas pulled out his wallet and flipped through the folds, pulling out a five-dollar bill. Enough for a small meal. There wasn't enough food to go around the town. Some days, Lukas would go without any meals.

"Well, I ain't got much, but here's a five for you, kid. Don't spend it all in one place," he said, kneeling to give it to him.

The door behind them flew open. The sight did not please his mother, Vivian.

"What the hell are you doing, Lukas? Don't talk to my kid. Jake, get in here, now!"

Before Jake could grab the money, he turned and ran inside, past his mother's legs. Vivian scowled at Lukas with glaring eyes before slamming the door on him.

Bitch, he thought.

Defeated, he stood up, his iPhone buzzing in his pocket. He'd bought the counterfeit refurbished iPhone from a shadowy dealer one night—six months of savings down the drain for the small thing. But it was worth it because it gave him the ability to speak to his amazing girlfriend.

Lukas imagined knowing Rebecca's schedule perfectly, so he'd know where she was at any moment, like Jake did with the lost people who lived in the apartments. He slipped his hand into his pocket and took out his phone. As he held it in front of his face, his eyes widened. Rebecca had finally texted him, this time something unusual, and Lukas didn't like that. He read the text:

We need to talk.

Lukas

Many Years Ago

Scarlett, orange, and yellow. Lukas used all three markers to color the fire in his paper drawing.

He laid his stomach flat on the white tile of his room. It had been his room for the last few weeks, but it couldn't compare to his actual room back home.

Boston's Psychiatry for Children wasn't an actual home. It wasn't like a hotel either, where he'd always be excited to stay because he and his sister, Erica, could get away with staying up late. At the hospital, they told him when he'd have to sleep, when he could leave his room, or what he could wear. And Lukas couldn't think of a single hotel or home that made you take a weekly test asking weird questions like if he wanted to hurt anyone. In fact, the hospital felt like a long time out, but he wasn't sure when it'd finally end.

With a small black marker, he drew a messy figure of a man in the fire, but the man didn't seem too happy about it. Lukas drew his face. Now the man was screaming. His hand moved to the other side of the page, where he drew another figure, this time of a girl standing in front of the burning man. She smiled. The image was always the same: the one stuck in his mind and now the one right in front of him.

No matter how hard he tried to re-imagine the scene, it was always the same. And he wished it wasn't because then it wouldn't have been true.

A girl smiling.

The fire blazing.

His mother wailing.

The consuming white of his psychiatric bedroom seemed to fade into the background as he focused intently on the girl. His eyes narrowed, glaring at her misshaped smile, hating everything about her. Just her very existence in his drawing made him squeeze the marker in his hand until his knuckles flared white.

On the wall facing him, a single poster of a cheerful pale woman standing before an endless sunny plain looking down at him, a bubble of words coming out of her smiling mouth. Lukas read the words again:

SAFETY FIRST! I WANT YOU TO BE SAFE!

He didn't quite understand what she meant or why she cared so much for his safety, but she always watched him from the wall, smiling. But something caught his eye. There was something different. A brown blur—a speck. With the lights off in the room, he couldn't quite make out the shape. The lights made the overwhelming white sometimes too bright. Intrigued, he focused his eyes, trying to make out the shape.

A brown recluse, he thought.

He remembered its distinct color from a book of spiders his mother had gotten him for his eighth birthday. A brown recluse's venom was supposed to be lethal, he recalled from the book. The recluse had weaved a small web in the ceiling's corner and was stringing down onto the woman's face.

Lukas stared at the idle spider. How could something so small be so dangerous? He wondered. But then he looked back at the girl in his drawing.

A gentle knock echoed in the room before opening. A woman's long shadow cast over him and the drawing.

Lukas looked up at his disturber, a nurse who met his confused face with disappointment, like he'd made a mess. He thought he might've done something wrong, broken a rule because it was the same eyes his mother used to give him. He dropped the marker, forfeiting his picture.

The nurse squinted her puke-colored eyes like those of a jungle snake. The venomous kind. "This again, Lukas? We talked about this," she hissed.

Silently, he fixed his eyes on the ground, his face flushed.

The nurse kneeled down, holding the picture in front of him like he'd somehow forgotten what he colored.

"No, we didn't," he finally mumbled.

She sighed in frustration. It seemed like she always found something to get mad about in him or someone else. A long line stretched across her forehead as she furrowed her thin brows at him.

"*This*—This isn't real. It's just the nightmares that are leaking out again, remember? Our dreams can't hurt us because they're just that. Dreams. Say it to me so you don't forget again."

Lukas considered it for a moment, stealing one last glance at the picture.

"It isn't real," they said in unison.

At noon, a few hours later, all the kids in the hospital gathered around in a large living space where they could engage in different activities. Though there wasn't a wide assortment of choices, they found fun in the few because it was better than doing nothing at all. Some played board games on tables, others conversed in corners of the room, and some, like Lukas and Wes, his friend, colored on a small table.

Wes sat across from Lukas, coloring an image he had never seen before other than his television, and Lukas watched with his chin resting on the table. He wanted to color, too, but the nurses wouldn't let him because of what he had drawn that morning. He didn't understand why it upset them so much. His image *wasn't* made up.

The blue-colored pencil Wes used pressed deeper into his drawing, forcing the darkest shade of blue; it sent little chips flying into the air and across the table. Lukas scoffed, wiping them away from himself.

"Have you ever even been to California?" Lukas asked. A place so far, he was sure it wasn't real. A dream, like the nurse said.

Wes stopped coloring and looked up at him. His light blue eyes contrasted with the dark blue in his drawing. Lukas wondered if that's where all the blue skies had disappeared to. Wes had stolen them for himself, leaving Boston with bleak rain skies.

"Not yet, but Mom said that after I get out, we could take a trip down there to Disneyland and—"

"When?" Lukas asked, now sitting up.

"After they let us out—"

"No. *When* are they letting us out?"

"Probably soon...I think," Wes finished. He picked up the pencil again and resumed coloring, only this time much softer.

The unbearable silence grew between them, the itch of Wes's olive hand moving the pencil up and down the page moved with the seconds passing by. Lukas scanned the room, looking for something, some other distraction from his mind. A boy playing with a toy plane, a girl talking to a stuffed animal and—Erica, alone, burying her face in the pages of a book. Lukas glared. Her black hair brushed against the pages she read.

Of course she is, he thought. Maybe if she opened her mouth for once and talked, she'd have friends. And he was set on not being the one to talk to her, especially after what she did to him. In fact, the whole time they'd been there, neither of them spoke a word. The thought of talking to his sister made his knuckles flare white.

No matter, he didn't care, anyway. She did that to herself, and she deserved it, *all* of it, Lukas thought. Even though he was the oldest, now twelve, she needed to learn to adapt to survival just like everyone else.

"They were talking about you, Lukas. The nurses, I heard them," Wes said.

"About what?" he asked, though he was sure he already knew the answer.

Nothing seemed to escape Wes's eye; only a couple of years younger, he seemed to be aware of everything that happened around him. Lukas thought an older man lived inside that young boy's mind with how much he seemed to know about the world.

"They talk about what you keep drawing. They think you're going crazy—"

"I'm not crazy. I know what I saw that night," Lukas said, his face now flushed.

Wes dropped his pencil. "Between you and me, though, is it real? Or did you just make it up?"

And there it was again, the silence between them growing like a parasite. Defeated, Lukas buried his head between his arms, escaping to a black abyss of his own, where nothing existed but infinite black. He replayed the images of that night in his mind.

A girl smiling.

The fire blazing.

His mother wailing.

It was the same; it was always the same. And Lukas knew it was real. No matter how many times they told him it wasn't or how many times they made him deny it, he knew it was. But a small doubt lurked in his mind. Had he made it all up? Was it just a nightmare, like the nurse said?

No, he quickly thought. No one could make that up. That night was all too real in his mind. And why didn't Wes believe him? Lukas thought he was his friend, but now he thought Wes saw him as some liar who just wanted to make up a story.

He finally lifted his head from his arms to find Wes coloring again, his brown curls sitting neatly on his head, but his face had gone pink. Lukas thought he must've felt bad for asking.

"It *is* real." The words caught in his throat. He wanted to cry, wanted someone to believe him, wanted someone else to be there that night, but all he could do was stare down at the table, listening to the faint scribbles across.

There was a loud crash from behind. Both boys turned to see. An older boy had shoved another boy off his chair to the ground, seething.

"What the hell did you just say? I'll kill you, asshole!" he said, now jumping on top of the boy and thrashing his fists into him.

It all happened so fast, only a few seconds after Lukas whispered the words.

The older boy created an image of his own, and he didn't need colored pencils or markers. The boy's blood splattered on the white tile, a violent red picture.

Screams and cries filled the room.

"Security! Get him off!" one nurse cried.

Lukas held his breath.

Stretchers rolled into the room. The security guards pulled the older boy off, but both boys fought back, trying to free themselves from their firm grasps, trying to get one last punch. The boys screamed, trying to shake both nurses' and security's arms off as they were carried and strapped into the stretchers.

A sight one wouldn't have expected to see in a children's hospital. People are supposed to live, not die. There was already enough of that happening outside the walls around the country.

Lukas watched the screaming boys on the stretchers hurried out of the room and into the narrow hallways. Wes trembled, the pencil quivering in his hand. The other kids, especially the younger ones, seemed just as shocked, crying, waiting to be comforted by a hug.

But something was *off*. He took a few deep breaths. A feeling, like something or someone was watching him.

He turned his head, looking around the room, and there it was. A pair of black eyes, like an arrow, shot around Wes and into Lukas. Erica's cold black eyes narrowed on him.

She finally looked up from her book only when blood spilled. Lukas glared back. Her eyes made it seem what had occurred was a threat to him. And after what she *did* that night, that haunting idea seemed entirely possible to him.

3

LUKAS

MANY YEARS AGO

THE NEXT EVENING CAME quick. Every week, it happened the same, and it was now time again. The nurses led all the kids to a large room that looked much like a classroom. The same test they had to take every week, but it differed from any test he took in school. He wasn't sure if there was a right answer to the questions because every week, he answered the same, *every* time.

Inside, the nurses assigned Lukas and Wes different desks, with a small black tablet waiting for them. A woman with blue scrubs led him to his, where he waited for everyone else. The black glass of the tablet reflected his soft silhouette.

A few minutes later, everyone was at their desks, including the two boys who fought the other day, all bandaged now. They didn't dare make eye contact with each other. Lukas turned his head. Wes sat across his right, and, peering forward, he saw her, Erica, at the furthest row in the front. The sight made his jaw clench.

Conversations filled the room, which didn't surprise Lukas, as they had eaten dinner before, but the only thing he could think about was his drawing and how it could cause so much stir among the staff.

Idiots, he thought.

"Alright! Settle down now, boys and girls!" Father Harris said. The priest was the director of the hospital. His white beard crept right below his rough chin. "As you already know, these assessments allow us to care for you in the best way possible, so please answer as truthfully and the best you can," he said.

Father Harris explained the rules during their assessment, rules that Lukas knew too well: simple rules like not looking over your shoulder or speaking at all until everyone finished.

"All right, guys, you can begin," Father Harris finished.

Lukas held the tablet in his hands, the screen now shining white. A question faded on the screen, one he already knew how to answer.

IN THE COURSE OF THE PREVIOUS WEEK, HOW ARE YOU FEELING?

(1-10)

Lukas tapped the *8*, the same as last time and the time before.

The next question popped on his screen, and without reading it, he tapped the same number.

And he did the same for the next question, and the next, and the next until it came to one particular question. He paused for a moment to read the question again.

IN THE COURSE OF THE PREVIOUS WEEK, HAVE YOU FELT VIOLENT OR AGGRESSIVE TOWARD ANYONE? WANTING TO HURT TO THEM? (1-10)

He was glad he stopped his mindless pressing before he hit *8* again because, this time, he hesitated. Reading the question again, he felt his finger glide to a lower number.

Erica, he thought. The thought froze him. She deserved it, all of it. Everything that happened to her. Her name echoed in his mind, taunting him to press the bigger number, but he shook off the thought. No matter how much he wanted to, he couldn't. Play it safe, he concluded quietly, exhaling out his mouth.

He tapped the *2* on his screen.

An emoji of a smiling face popped on his screen, and he knew he had finished the test again this week. And one by one, the others finished too until, finally, everyone had.

It was taking them longer than usual to let them out of the room. Something had to be wrong. Lukas was sure of it. He watched a concerned nurse hurry over to Father Harris, holding a larger tablet in her hands, and together, they examined it. Looking around, he seemed to be the only one who took notice while everyone else conversed in whispers. Wes had fallen asleep on his desk.

Father Harris cleared his throat. "Blessed be this wonderful news. Will Jake Silverman and Matthew Gray please follow me while everyone else goes with the staff to get ready for bed?"

Following his command, the two boys who had attacked each other the previous day followed Father Harris out of the room, beaming with anticipation. Everyone else followed the staff into the hallways. Lukas stayed behind with Wes, watching Erica follow the congested crowd of children.

"Where do you think they went?" Lukas asked him.

Wes stood up, heading toward the door. "Where do you think? They're letting them out, like I told you! It's about time," he said with a smile.

Lukas watched Wes leave the room, thinking back to the poster in his room, the woman smiling. He replayed the moment of Father Harris taking the two violent boys out of the hospital.

But to *where?* He wondered. The woman's words flashed in his mind again.

Safety First.

4

LUKAS

JUNE 17

MOST PEOPLE, WHEN THEY try to run away from themselves, make a new life some place else. But in East Haddam, the furthest Rebecca could escape was deep in the forest outskirts of the town.

But it wasn't far enough.

As Lukas drove through the forest, maple and oak trees stood like pillars touching the sky, with windows down; a gentle breeze played with his hair. The edges of the grove, however, were polluted with lines of litter. After the unsympathetic glance to the side, he continued down the winding road deeper into the vast array of trees, wondering what Rebecca was doing right now, probably anticipating his arrival so she could finally kiss him, he guessed. The sweet thought made him grin.

How Rebecca had gone all her years without him leading her life pleased him because he had saved her miserable life from what it once was. But ever since she moved here, she seemed to regress to the woman she once was, the woman that Lukas didn't *understand*—and then the air smelled of fear. The distances that grew between them only seemed to expand. The road seemed to never end. It might've been half an hour now.

Finally, a decent-sized cabin appeared on the horizon, nestled between an umbrella of towering oak trees. A small stream wrapped around the side of the cabin that would eventually join with the Connecticut River. The cabin was old and rustic, with rotting logs and fogged windows peering from every wall. It was the type of place one would drive right by without taking notice.

Rebecca spent most of her days painting off her terrace, isolated from the rest of the town. A gift she seemed to explore more deeply since abandoning her life in the town. Lukas always knew she had a brilliant eye, but he wished she'd use it to look at him more.

Lukas drove up to the cabin, parking his car at the foot of the tree so the towering leaves would shade it from the beating heat. Stepping out, the air turned sweet, filled with the soft chirping of birds and leaves fluttering like butterflies in the breeze. The ground crunched beneath his feet, walking toward the steps to the wooden front door of the cabin. Taking a deep breath, he painted a smile on his face.

Knock, he knew the sound echoed within her home.

A few moments went by with no response.

This time, he pounded his fists against the door, calling her name, and as he did, every reason she wasn't opening the door flooded his mind. The door swung open, and there stood Rebecca, smiling uncomfortably.

"Thanks for coming," she said.

Lukas stepped inside the cabin, looking around. "What took you so long to open the door?"

She closed the door behind him and followed him. "Oh, you know, just working on a piece. It's a new project I thought of a few days ago."

Rebecca's eyes were like the maple foliage, a vibrant oak, and her auburn hair was pinned up with a pencil. With skin so soft, Lukas wondered how she could be so beautiful. He stared at her soft pink lips and leaned in to kiss them so he might remember what they felt like. As he did, she let out a small groan while they kissed, pulling away after a few moments. Lukas tried pulling her back.

She pressed him back. "Lukas—"

"Show me your new piece. Although I'm sure it couldn't be *perfecter* than you. Is that why you texted me?"

"Lukas."

"Show me," he said, brushing his hand against her cheek.

Rebecca pulled back, agreeing to show him, leading him deeper into her cabin.

"I wanted you to come over so you could get out of that town. I know how it makes you feel. And I would've driven down there, but—too many memories. And I like it here, and I think you would too," Rebecca said as she fluffed up a yellow cushion on her small sofa.

Lukas looked around in awe. How she had turned the cabin, once abandoned and secluded, into a beautiful piece itself.

"You know I can't do that," Lukas said, slightly irritated. "My job, my life, is in town—not out here in the woods painting pictures all day. Is that what you want? For me to abandon everything?"

Rebecca's head sagged towards the floor, shaking her head. "No—I'm sorry. Please don't get mad. It was a stupid comment," Rebecca said, now showing a sympathetic smile. Finishing fixing up her sofa, she waved him toward her. "Here, follow me."

The cabin was warm and inviting, and he understood why she loved it so much. A small fireplace illuminated the room. All the charm within the walls was made of smooth glossed logs and smelled of pine and earthy spice. Scattered around on floors and tables were different paints and brushes, and Lukas looked back to the stained denim overalls she wore. A place this cozy almost seemed like an illusion to him, especially when the exterior was rotting. With all the furniture and paint supplies Rebecca's parents gifted her, she could live a comfortable life.

He followed her into a wide hallway, looking up at the paintings on the walls. He had never seen such vibrant paintings before. They depicted beautiful landscapes and wildlife, and each one seemed to tell a story. He could tell that she poured her heart and soul into her art, and he deeply appreciated her talent.

"You're amazing," he said, still looking around. "I can see why you love it here."

Rebecca said nothing but gestured him toward a small room.

His heart racing, Lukas followed her inside, where he saw an easel set up in front of a large window. The floor was covered with large mats colored in splashes of different paints, and a large table stood against a wall with all her brushes and sketchbooks. A small, single-hanging light lit the room. On the easel was a canvas covered by a cloth. Rebecca walked over to the easel and slowly removed the cloth, revealing a painting that made Lukas's breath catch in his throat.

It was something he had seen nothing like before.

A painting of herself strung up and trapped on a large spider web, thin white lines wrapped around her throat, suffocating her. She couldn't move, she couldn't escape, Rebecca was stuck—trapped in a web she found herself in over a black abyss. It was something so different from what she usually painted; it shocked him the painting was hers.

"This is my latest work," Rebecca said, her voice tight. "I've been working on it for weeks, trying to capture how I feel. And I feel—I feel trapped. Especially here in East Haddam, we can't escape. We can't go anywhere in this shithole!" Her hands ran through her hair before they wrapped around her body like a hug. "Since moving down here last month, I've had a lot of time to—to surrender myself to the painting. It's all about letting the brush take control of each stroke instead of trying to force the picture. I hadn't realized it was my body I had strung up in the painting until it was finished. It's kinda funny, isn't it? It feels like everything we do is pre-destined to happen, like we don't have control over anything."

Rebecca stood before her painting like she'd seen it for the first time, and it caught her in a trance. But he couldn't blame her. It was such an unusual piece for her and had such intriguing prose that he could stare at it for hours and lose track of time.

Lukas looked at her in awe. "It's *beautiful*. I've never seen anything like it before. You're so talented, Rebecca."

Rebecca turned her head away from him and remained silent at his words.

"Lukas—I—We need to talk," she started.

He walked over to her, running his fingers through her hair and caressing her pale face.

"Shh," he whispered. "Let's not talk now."

She groaned as he softly kissed her neck, trailing down her body. *Perfect*, he thought. Everything about her was perfect.

"Lukas—stop!" She pushed him away. "We need to talk! We need to talk about us! Today!"

His heart pounded in his chest as he heard her words. He knew she was unhappy, and that she wanted to leave their relationship. But he couldn't let that happen. He wouldn't let her leave him, not after everything he had done to keep her by his side. Lukas's face tightened with frustration.

"What does *that* mean?" he asked, the words choking out of his mouth.

Rebecca took a step forward, clasping her quivering hands around his. Her pink lips curled innocently into a grin. "We just need to talk, babe. That's all. I'm sorry I shouted at you."

Lukas studied her pale complexion. She was so desperate to not upset him, he almost let slip a chuckle. But she wasn't as well at disguising her true intentions, which was to break up with him. He was sure of it.

No, I won't let her. Lukas needed to get her away from her cabin, somewhere he'd have control of her again. Somewhere where she wouldn't be able to escape him so easily.

Lukas leaned back, his obsidian eyes narrowing as he gazed at Rebecca. "Remember the times we used to paddle down the river? Those were some of our best moments, weren't they? Just you and me, away from everything and everyone else."

Rebecca hesitated, a flicker of discomfort crossing her face. "Yeah, I remember."

"And remember you promised we'd do it again, just like old times? I've been holding onto that, you know. Hoping we can reignite those special moments again," Lukas said, stepping closer.

Rebecca's eyes wandered anywhere except towards him. "Lukas, things have changed. You're scaring me, and I just need space."

The idea of Rebecca wedging more space between them made Lukas glower. And he lowered his voice, leaning in. "I'm trying to make things right, but you're shutting me out. You always do this every time I try to do something for you. I just want to take you canoeing down the river. Why are you making that so difficult? Are you really going to deny us more special moments together? Come on Rebecca, just for old times' sake?"

5

LUKAS

JUNE 17

THE WINDING STREAM THAT began at Rebecca's cabin stretched into the Connecticut River where Lukas and Rebecca were now at. The June sun shined in the sky, casting a warm glow over them as the canoe glided through the water. With each stroke, Rebecca sliced through the water, paddling them further into the river. However, she took care not to sail too far in, as boats were prohibited, since the police feared they'd sail out of the town.

Lukas turned his head, watching the small cabin in the distance shrink with the horizon. Flocks of birds chased above them, chirping.

His heart pounded against his chest, threatening to break out. His entire body tensed like he was ready to fall. Fall from Rebecca's love. Now, he wouldn't be able to run; he would be forced to listen to every word she said. Trickles of sweat ran down his back as neither of them had said anything. *Silence was the disease that killed people,* he thought.

Rebecca halted the boat. Placing the paddles down, she mournfully stared at the water like she'd received news of someone's death. Lukas's nails dug into his knees, waiting for her to speak, the boat rocking back and forth with the gentle waves.

"I think I know why you brought us here." Rebecca started with a small grin. "I see how calm the stillness of the water makes you. I remember when you first asked me to be your girlfriend out here. I was so happy that day." Her grin faded.

Lukas shifted forward. Rebecca was right. The gentle waves rocking them back and forth were comforting, like a newborn being cradled in their mother's arms.

He smiled. "Yeah, I remember. I thought you were the most beautiful woman I'd ever seen, and I wanted you to be mine. Mine only."

Rebecca paused, tilting her head down.

The creaking of the swaying boat filled his ears before Rebecca parted her silent lips.

"Lukas—this is really hard for me to say." Her voice trembled. "I need you to please understand. But that painting, I—I feel trapped not just by this town but, um—but also by you. You exploded at me for moving over here because you thought I was trying to get away from you, but the truth is—I *was*. Something about us just doesn't feel right anymore, and I've tried. I've really tried to bury these feelings, but I just can't anymore. It's too much," she said, with tears falling down her cheeks.

The words echoed in his mind. *Trapped by you.* It cut deep into him, making every happy memory they had together bleed. The beating of his heart rang in his ears. This wasn't the woman he loved. She was someone else. It had to be. Rebecca would never try to abandon him like this. His mind raced.

"*Trapped* by me?" The words came out in a quiet breath. "How can you say that? How can you say that after everything I've done for you? You're happier with me, and you know it!" Lukas said, now gasping for breath, sobbing.

The world was out of balance. Everything he knew crumbled before him into nothingness. His head continued to throb with pain, even though he had taken the OxyContin. A broken heart can't be medicated. Crying, his head spun everywhere, trying to make sense of her words, but no matter how hard he tried to decipher them, it still made little sense. He buried his red face in his hands.

"Lukas, please! Please try to understand!" Rebecca cried. "I'm not happy! I haven't been happy! And every time I'm with you, I feel like I'm walking on glass to keep *you* fucking happy! I feel your eyes on me all the time, and I'm scared. I'm honestly scared of you. It's for the best that we just stop. Stop trying to make *us* work. We have to let it rest now. We've—I've tried, and I just...can't anymore. I'm sorry, but really, I *really* need you to just try to listen to me."

They were both crying now. The string between them had finally ripped, and everything he once believed was burned and buried. No—no, it couldn't be. He wouldn't let it. She won't do this to him.

"So, that's it? After all the shit you made me put up with! After you got fired and got addicted to OxyContin, which I'm now on! *Thanks* for that, by the way. You're just throwing me away, just like that! No, don't lie to me. You've found some new guy, right?"

"What! No!"

"And now you're tired of me because *he's* so much better than me. Tell me the truth, you whore! Who are you fucking behind my back?!"

"God! You know what the problem is between us? It's you, Lukas! It's always been you! I didn't need your help! I could've handled myself, but you forced yourself into my life trying to play a godforsaken *knight in shining armor!* And you know what? I *don't* love you anymore. I've. Never. Fucking. Loved. You. You just happened to be there when I was at the lowest point of my life, and I needed a quick rush. My mom was right about you. You're pathetic," she spat.

Lukas's nails dug into the canoe seat. "You're a disgusting whore. You've only ever been a piece of ass to me, and that's all you've ever been good at. And you know, that night at the bar when I first talked to you, that's what I saw because I know how to recognize a desperate, miserable soul."

"Fuck you, Lukas." Rebecca curled her upper lip. "I finally realize why I could never truly love you. It's because you're unlovable. There's not a person on this planet who could ever love you. And I wasn't going to tell you this, but since we're telling each other the truth now, I'm still in love with my ex-boyfriend," Rebecca sighed heavily at the last word.

You fucking bitch, Lukas thought.

"God, he treated me better than you ever did. And he knew what I liked and how I liked to get fucked. I even think about him while we have sex so I can bear the feeling of you on top of me—"

At the last word, Lukas lunged at her. The boat roughly swaying as fury poured out of him. Rebecca gasped as Lukas wrapped his coarse hands around her neck.

She writhed in Lukas's tight choke. Pathetically, she even tried splashing water on his face with her flailing hands, but it was no use. She couldn't overpower him.

"You pathetic slut! You're not leaving me! Not you! Nobody!"

His fingers dug deeper into her neck as Rebecca choked on her pleading words, her face turning blue. No one was going to abandon him again. No one. And no one could have her if he couldn't.

Her frail hands futilely scratched his face as the boat continued rocking. "Lukas," she mouthed.

Lukas remained on her like paint on a canvas. She tried flailing her legs and pushing him off with her weak hands until, finally, her hands collapsed to the floor. Small tears fell one last time from her blood-soaked eyes down her discolored face.

Rebecca stopped struggling. She'd lost consciousness.

He did it, and it was real. There was no going back from this. Lukas, trembling, stared at her petrified eyes and parted lips, and held his quivering hands in front of his face.

"No—no—no, no..." he whimpered, cradling his hands around her face. "What have I done? Why did you make me do this, Rebecca?" he cried.

Howling in agony, he pulled her corpse to his body so that he might feel her one last time. Rebecca was finally his, and his alone.

He rested her stiff body back down, his hands throbbing with adrenaline.

Power. The word flashed through his mind like a neon light. *Is this what it is?* He didn't want it to, but killing her was exhilarating; the familiar drug rushed into his veins. It was something much stronger than OxyContin.

The bloodthirsty cravings that he buried for several years were now dripping out like a cracked pot. All the memories he had locked in a box in his mind were now seeping out. He could see it all again.

The Room.

And for the first time in forever, he felt a sense of control back. He changed the course of his life in his direction.

Lukas let out a small chuckle as he examined her unresponsive body. Rebecca's face was still frozen with fear.

Anything seemed possible. Even the thought of taking control back in his life seemed right within his grasp. He squeezed his fists as the boat rocked back and forth.

Now, he needed to show the world, show them he would not be a bug anymore. That he could weave a web of his own. And as he thought the words, Rebecca's painting flashed through his mind with the picture of her strung-up body. Lukas studied Rebecca's body, a twisted smile forming.

In East Haddam, no one could run away. Not even from him.

6

LUKAS

MANY YEARS AGO

THE WINDOW FOGGED WITH Lukas's gentle breath. *I'm always on the outside looking in*, he thought, staring out of his room. Boston was always an incredible sight, even if it was behind one-inch glass. Raindrops trickled down, and monstrous gray clouds filled the sky. It seemed like the city couldn't ever get a break from the relentless storms.

It had been a week since the two boys left the hospital, but some unnerving doubt lingered in his mind. Had they finally gone home? Of course they *did*. He shook the question off his mind—he believed it would only be a matter of time before the hospital also released him. But after they released him, *then what?* He hadn't thought that far ahead. And when he pictured the moment leaving, he squeezed himself tighter, and his face saddened. Not the image he hoped for. Surely, though, there had to be someone out there or something waiting for him. Something to make all of this suffering and isolation worth it. He dreamed of waking in the warm bed of his home again with the faint echo of foghorns from the morning ocean.

Just a dream, he thought. And just like the nurse said, dreams weren't real.

Lukas sat curled against the window, staring out at the world that was once his like a prisoner gazing behind bars, claps of thunder rattled his body. The hospital overlooked an enormous park surrounded by red brick buildings and orange maple trees.

The rain didn't seem to stop the families there from enjoying a brisk wetness in the air, and their different colored jackets were bright on the gray day. Mothers pushed their children on swing sets, and the exhilarating joy that painted across their children's faces cracked his heart one push at a time. He would've done anything to be there, in that child's place, being pushed by his mother.

Neither was possible. Not anymore.

Barefoot on the floor, Lukas's feet numbed from a burning chill. He glared at the warm familial sight of a mother hugging her little boy because he had now fallen off the monkey bars. Serves him right. He should've known they would be slippery—and Lukas hoped they'd catch his icy glare so they'd know they were being watched, envied. In fact, he even wished something *bad* would happen to them because it wasn't fair that they were there, happy, and he was stuck in a suffocating white room watching everyone else.

But he also found it a strange sight because just a couple of years ago, those faces used to be strangled with fear and dread. The parks and playgrounds were empty, and his mother was always too scared to go out into the dark by herself. It scared her to go anywhere by herself. His father would always be with her anywhere. Even when she didn't want him, he'd still be there. And she was sure to never upset him because when she did, bad things happened, things he never saw, but he knew they were bad.

But with all the weird changes happening in the world, everyone outside seemed happier. But he didn't quite understand why.

He had seen it on the news years ago. All the children of bad people had to be placed in these *hospitals*. If he were to step back out into the world, would other kids be scared of him? Would they all scatter from the playgrounds if he walked toward them?

His stomach grumbled. Hungry to know why and hungry for food.

The chiming bell for lunch made his head jerk awake, and all his previous thoughts sank into nothing, like water down the drain.

The hospital cafeteria was not much different from his school's, but it was well kept and tidy. Rows of metal tables were filed across the room, and there was a certain stench of sourness in the air, which made Lukas think that the food was expired. And just like school, everyone had their friend groups established—he was glad he wasn't on the outs and had Wes across him.

Lukas poked at his food with a grimy fork. Mashed potatoes and meatloaf would've sounded good had it not come from a can. The meat looked dry and had always been stale and chewy. Not exactly a home-cooked meal like they'd call it, but his stomach continued to growl. Gazing at his food, he had no appetite, so he wasn't sure why his stomach craved food. Eating felt like a chore, something he could just put off for later.

His mind still choked with the fiery image the nurses assured wasn't real. But if he knew one thing was real, it was this dreading *feeling*. He couldn't describe it, but it weighed on his shoulders. Something was off, and it was more than the dry food on his plate.

Everything was cleared off Wes's plate except for the green beans. He used those to create little faces—two for the eyes, one for the mouth.

Lukas raised his brow at him. "You're supposed to *eat* them, not play with them."

"Oh, yeah?" Wes said, smirking.

Without warning, he chucked a couple of green beans at Lukas's face.

Snarling, splashes of mashed potatoes flew back at Wes, who was now chuckling.

A few moments later, both boys' laughs echoed in the cafeteria, smeared in different colors of green and potato. Better used than eaten.

"Boys, settle down over there!" a nurse called.

They continued snickering in silence, wiping stains off their clothes with their fingers.

Lukas looked down at his still-full plate of food.

"You've barely eaten," Wes finally said.

Lukas picked up the fork, picking at the plate below again. His belly ached but not with hunger, like he sat at the top of a rollercoaster waiting to drop, waiting for *something*.

"I'm not hungry."

He focused on the different conversations happening around him. His ears rang like a radio, trying to pick up the right frequency for a station. Unfamiliar voices talking about what they would do in the activity room today. He even picked up Wes's low voice, excited to color again. And after a week of not being able to draw or color, Lukas thought he should've felt excited, too. Instead, he tried to focus on the surrounding noise, to find a familiar voice of a girl, to see what Erica might be talking about.

"Dad's not coming back," Wes said gloomily.

Lukas focused back on him, ignoring the frequencies around him once more.

"What do you mean?"

"Mommy told me he's moving to a small town in Texas because he killed that man. Dad's not a good person—I'm scared of him. And they're going to punish him for it." His voice trembled. Wes wiped his flushed eyes with his skinny arm, sniffling. "I just wanna go home—I just want my mom. I want things to go back to how they used to be, and we don't even know how much longer we'll be here. It feels like forever now." He choked on the last words.

The small cries across the table stabbed Lukas's chest into his heart. He tried to push the aching feeling out, but it sank deeper with every passing second. Trying to find the right thing to say, his body grew heavier until he rested his head against the table.

"Neither was mine," Lukas whispered.

He hoped his sympathetic look would make Wes feel better or would shed a little hope. But his eyes could do only what anyone else could about Wes's situation. Nothing. His father had done what he did, just like Lukas's father. And he couldn't bear seeing Wes suffer from that, too, because he knew the feeling all too well. But Lukas hadn't cried about it—he buried the memory so deep into his mind, only traces of that *night* leaked out, like drips from a broken clay pot. He wouldn't let the pot shatter. Not again.

"You've never told me how you got here," Wes said, his eyes glossy.

Lukas's eyes widened. The question sucked him back into his mind. He took a deep breath, trying to push back the memories that threatened to surface, but they were too strong.

Drip.

A girl smiling.

Drip.

The fire blazing.

Drip.

His mother wailing.

"I'll tell you some other time. I need to eat."

No more drips. No more. *Don't let it leak.*

Wes was right. They didn't know how much longer they'd be there, stuck like prisoners *forever.* As he focused back on the voices around him searching for Erica's, he reminded himself of the two fighting boys leaving. If they left, one day, so would he.

Lukas took a bite of his food. Dry and cold, just like he thought it would be, but he knew he had to eat. It wouldn't be right to starve.

A few moments went by, and Lukas still couldn't find her voice among the many girls speaking.

He looked up from his plate, spinning his head, trying to find her. His eyes jumped from table to table, wondering which one she might be at, if she had finally made any friends.

Why do I care so much? he thought.

"What're you looking for?" Wes asked, also turning his head.

"Nothing, I just—"

Finally, he spotted Erica's melancholic face resting against her cradling hand while the other slowly fed a spoonful of food to herself. On a table tucked in the cafeteria's corner, she sat alone, hidden. Her eyes sagged like she didn't care for a single thing in the world, and she stared into space, watching the world pass before her. Lukas thought how, just a few months ago, she was beaming with her small arms wrapped around his body, giggling. And now, it was as if he couldn't recognize her at all.

Lukas's stomach ached again. The many voices of other children and Wes's that echoed in his ears were undecipherable.

Approaching Erica's table were two older boys, laughing.

"Oh great, Alexander and Hunter are going over there. Hey—isn't that your sister? I didn't know she knew them."

They sat next to her, pressing their bodies against her, Alexander on one side and Hunter on the other. Lukas had never talked to them before, but in the short time he's seen them, they seemed to always find themselves in some mischief. But Erica didn't bat an eye at either of them. She remained still, unbothered—putting another spoon of food in her mouth.

He couldn't hear what they were saying, but they let out quick laughs, and their faces stretched with disgusting smiles. As he watched, Alexander leaned closer to her ear, whispering something while Hunter nudged her. Erica's face went pale, and she dropped the spoon on her plate. The boys laughed at her reaction, continuing to say things to her relentlessly.

Lukas's fists tightened by his sides.

Hunter must've been the last straw for her because, after he finished saying something, Erica slowly stood up and trudged away—the same emotionless expression hung on her face. And as she did, their laughs followed her, completely amused at whatever they'd said. She appeared so unbothered, but Lukas knew her, and he knew they must've said something. And no one was going to do that to her. No one.

Without thinking, he stood up with his heart racing. Rage flooded his veins. Teeth gritted, he marched over to Alexander, ignoring Wes's futile calls for him to stay put.

What he would do, he was unsure. But he knew one thing: they were going to *pay*.

The two boys still sat at her table, chuckling to themselves.

Lukas nudged Alexander. "What did you say to her?" he demanded.

"Who?" He turned back to Erica, who was now burying her face in her palms in the cafeteria's corner. "Oh! Your weird ass sister—"

"Don't call her that." Lukas' body began throbbing with fury as he clenched his fists. He wasn't going to let those two idiots get away with bullying his sister.

Both boys laughed.

Hunter shoved Lukas back. "Or *what*? You're gonna tell your *daddy*? Oh wait, you can't because he's *dead.*"

"Shut up."

"Ooh!" Hunter chuckled.

"We just think it's funny that you and your sister should get used to it here." Alexander bent at Lukas's seething face. "Because you don't have anywhere else to go. Your parents are dead."

Like a flash, Lukas launched his fist at Alexander's mouth. Blood splashed as he yelped in pain.

But it wasn't enough.

He threw himself onto Alexander, thrashing him with his fists on the tile floor.

"Get off me, you little shit!"

Red.

Red on the floor. Red on his clothes. And red on Alexander's face.

Lukas's ears rang with both their yells, ignoring the tears streaming down his own face. Both boys tried pushing him off, but he wouldn't budge. He remained anchored on top of him like a crayon on a page.

The echo of crying children and Wes screaming at him, muffled in the background. Everything distorted.

Was it a dream?

No, this had to be real. The blood was real.

Lukas continued clawing like a savage animal for what felt like an eternity before a heavy arm tore him off a crying, bloody Alexander. He tried fighting back, trying to free himself from the brute arms restraining him, but it was no use.

Someone or something stabbed him in the arm. Lukas let out a small cry. From the corner of his eye, a nurse had injected him with something.

Voices around him slurred as he spotted Alexander's red body fading away. With Lukas' head spinning, he caught a strange look in the cafeteria's corner. Erica had let a contorted grin slip on her face.

Everything went blurry. The haze one got after spinning for too long, and the world looked like it was rocking.

Finally, his world went black.

7

LUKAS

MANY YEARS AGO

FIVE HOURS. IT HAD escaped Lukas so quickly, just a blink of an eye.

When Lukas woke earlier, dazed, he thought it must've been the next day, but now he sat in the large test room, ready to take the weekly assessment. His head was light, and the world still seemed to sway. The pain from the injection still lingered in his left arm.

Lukas replayed the violent scene in his head again. In those few moments, the world around him seemed to have been blurred in a red lens, like he could only think about hurting Alexander. But he wondered why it lasted so long? Why was he able to punch Alexander for as long as he did? Perhaps the nurses and security guards had assumed it was just boyish banter. Until the agonizing wails filled the room. Lukas imagined them watching him beat Alexander with no regard, like they hadn't cared enough to stop the fight.

Yawning at his desk, he watched the other kids escorted to their seats. Some bringing their excited conversations with their friends, others were anxious, probably because no kid enjoyed taking any type of test—especially one so personal. Lukas wondered how honest the others were on their tests, if they were as truthful as he was.

A small hand patted against his back, Lukas turned around.

Wes strode by, trying to form a hopeful smile, but it seemed his eyes were still trapped with the atrocious thing Lukas had done. Rightfully so. Lukas watched him sit quietly across the room.

He didn't want to be seen as the monster. He thought he was the knight saving his sister from the flaming dragon, Alexander, and how could someone sympathize with a beast like Alexander? A monster can't be loved.

Finally, everyone was now ready with their black tablets waiting on the desks. Father Harris entered the room, greeting them, going over his usual lines and the rules they would follow during the assessment. Lukas drowned out his mundane voice. How could anyone be excited about this?

His hands trembled below his desk, and they wouldn't stop. It was almost like they begged to hit someone, just one more time.

I should've killed him—no. Stop it. I shouldn't have. I'm glad he's okay.

He took a deep breath, trying to slow the world around him, remembering the bloodthirsty thought was only the adrenalin still in his veins.

The tablet in front of him lit up, and it was now time.

Lukas held the tablet in front of him with a shaky breath. This time would be different.

He read the first question:

IN THE COURSE OF THE PREVIOUS WEEK, HOW ARE YOU FEELING?

(1-10)

Pressing *8* would be lying because Lukas knew this aggressive feeling he'd had hadn't been good. His hatred for Erica consumed his mind, and so did attacking Alexander because he'd angered Erica. It wasn't good.

So his finger slid to the *4* and pressed it.

He continued through the questions, scaling himself different numbers than he normally did; this minor act of rebelliousness made his heart race with uncertainty. At last, he reached the last question in the assessment—the one that always made him pause.

IN THE COURSE OF THE PREVIOUS WEEK, HAVE YOU FELT VIOLENT OR AGGRESSIVE TOWARD ANYONE WANTING TO HURT TO THEM? (1-10)

Lukas read the question repeatedly like the answer was hidden between the letters, his leg now quietly bouncing below him. Taking a long breath, he thought of the two violent boys and how they might've answered this. Whatever they put, it was *correct* because they were finally released from the hospital. But the pressure to choose the right number daunted him. His beating heart rang in his ears, and his back beat with heat.

Minutes went by, staring blankly at the screen. In his defocused surroundings, he saw the other kids already finished, and he could feel their impatient eyes waiting for him to finish as well.

Hurry!

Then, in the corner of his eyes, he spotted Alexander glaring at him, his face still bloodily scarred. His words began echoing in his head, making anger boil within him.

"Your parents are dead." The words looped in his mind. And the words became just another drip in his clay pot.

Lukas stared back at his screen, scanning the numbers before him. A flash of rage overtook him, and he slammed his finger toward the *10*.

After a few minutes of sitting silently staring at the black screen of his tablet, Father Harris re-entered the room. As he did, an anxious nurse hurried to him with a large tablet in her hands. They both examined it for a few minutes, and Lukas watched her whisper something to him.

Father Harris cleared his throat. "A great day today in our hospital! Will Lukas Retter and Erica Retter please follow me—oh, brother and sister? How nice. And then, can everyone else follow the staff for bed, please?"

This was it. Finally, they were going to be released. His whole body flooded with anticipation of walking out the doors and never looking back.

He stood up, walking toward Father Harris, and as he did, a pair of small arms wrapped around his torso. Turning his head, Wes clutched him, only letting go after a few seconds.

"You'll be fine, I promise," Lukas said.

Wes nodded in silence. He let out a sigh, then leaned into Lukas's ear. "Be careful," he whispered.

Lukas paused at the words, confused, but then quickly made his way to Father Harris, who had been calling his name. Erica stood next to Father Harris, her head turned away from Lukas, and together, they all left the room.

They traversed the hallways of the hospital through doors he'd never entered before and corridors he'd never seen. The white walls were illuminated with the reflection of the hanging light panels from the ceiling. Surely, any minute now, they'd reach their destination. They'd be out. Erica followed behind him like a ghost, silent with the same stoic expression nailed on her.

Father Harris led them down a winding stairwell, not saying a word since they'd left the test room. As they descended further into what seemed like a dark abyss, the walls dimmed, and the lights became few. Each metal step Lukas walked down sent an icy chill up his spine, and the sharp noise rattled his ears.

He wondered why they had to descend to a place so dark. This couldn't have been the way out. Maybe there was one final test they had to pass before they were released, or maybe his parents were waiting for him—no, they couldn't.

After going down many flights of stairs, they reached the bottom. A pair of doors waited for them, beckoning to be opened.

Lukas wrapped his shivering arms around himself. As the cold air rushed through him, the stench of gasoline filled his nose.

Lukas and Erica paused before getting too close.

"What is *this?*" Erica finally asked, a slight annoyance in her voice.

Father Harris didn't reply. He waved them toward the doors, where he stood ready to open them. Lukas considered it for a moment, then stepped toward the doors, still hearing Wes's warning play in his mind. His heart was ready to burst out of his chest.

Erica followed, and Father Harris finally opened the doors.

No more assessments, no more Alexander and Hunter, no more stale food and white rooms. No more Wes. No more *anything*.

Within a quick flash of the moment, large camo-dressed men swarmed them and restrained both Lukas and Erica.

Lukas screamed, trying to free himself, "Let me go!" But it was futile.

A sharp needle pierced his neck, and the world hazed around him. But before darkness swallowed his eyes, he heard Father Harris's last words echoing in the distance.

"*Congratulations.*"

8

LUKAS

JUNE 19

Breaking News

"The ongoing investigation for the murder of Rebecca Waylow still continues two days after her body was found in the St. Judas Cathedral in East Haddam. The town in question, in the past, has had its fair share of crime for being a correctional city, but the Haddam Police Department has seen nothing like this before. Officials say Rebecca Waylow's body was found brutally dismembered and strung up inside the cathedral—the same way she had painted herself just days before. Tonight, a statement from the Haddam Police Department."

The scene cut to a policewoman in front of a press conference, flashes of light hitting her face.

"I am Detective Amelia Mayman with the Haddam Police Department and Captain of the East Haddam Patrol. The death of Rebecca Waylow devastates us. It devastates our community and her family. Our thoughts and prayers are with them. While, as of tonight, I cannot disclose the details of the case, I encourage anyone with any information on what happened the night of June the seventeenth to contact either the Haddam Police Department or East Haddam Patrol immediately. My team and I will not rest until we find the monster behind this vile murder. Safety is our utmost priority. Thank you—we will not be answering questions at this time."

Still, crowds of journalists and news media bombarded her with questions. The scene cut back to the anchorwoman.

"Residents of Haddam are reporting their fears as news of Rebecca Waylow spreads through neighborhoods and homes in this community."

The scene changed to a reporter in front of a tall, pale man.

"Since Haddam is so close to a terrible place like East Haddam, I'm honestly scared for me and my family's safety. Could something like that happen here? When I heard what happened to that woman, I thought: does the killer think they're like a spider or something—"

The man's voice quickly distorted, and the television screen became a muffled static.

"Damn cheap TV," Ian said in annoyance.

Lukas stood silently behind the carwash counter, watching Ian shut the TV off. Hearing her name again sent an ache to his chest. Two days without her had been too long. But she had disappointed him for the last time, and for that, she needed to go so she wouldn't hurt anyone else the way she hurt him. A kind of wound you can't heal.

But then there was a stroke of fear. Would they discover it was he who did it? No, they shouldn't. Not at least for a while. He had taken extra precautions, removing any link to him.

"What was he saying, anyway—a killer who's like a spider? Spiders are reclusive, aren't they? What's this fucker have anyway, eight *legs,* too?" Ian laughed. "They said the chick that got herself murdered was Rebecca Waylow? I used to see her Sunday nights at The Red Head. It's a shame she died. I miss staring at her tits as she handed me a cold beer."

"Ian! Relax," his co-worker, Mateo, said from the corner of the room. "That was Lukas's girlfriend. Don't be such a dick right now."

Ian's cheeks flushed pink. He carried a stench of arrogance and beer as his brow twitched. The navy tee he wore imprinted with Captain America's shield was two sizes too small on his porky body. The sleeves must've been cutting off his circulation, and his belly poked seamlessly out from the hem. "It was a *joke.* There's no need to get so emotional. Besides, Lukas has barely said a word since she died. How am I supposed to know anything when people don't use their damn mouths! The bastard can tell me himself."

Ian picked up his bottle of beer and took a large gulp, wiping his mouth with his large arm. Though some brown drips still escaped his lips and fell on his shirt. He walked over to Lukas, leaning his face close to his. His rank breath clogged Lukas's nose with a bitter stench. The stench was so foul it reminded him of Rebecca's lifeless body when he chopped her into bits and strung her up in that cathedral a couple of nights ago.

"So Lukas, why so *blue?*"

Lukas held his breath, peering into Ian's diluted brown eyes. He held his tightened fists hidden by his sides, glaring at Ian. "I loved Rebecca," Lukas muttered. He bit his tongue before he accidentally hissed an insult.

Ian sneered at him, then pulled away, muttering to himself. His grating voice made Lukas want to lash at him, but he couldn't. He needed that job as terrible as it was.

"Well, I hope you're an early riser. You're gonna have to open the shop tomorrow," Ian said.

Lukas swallowed his rising fury, watching Ian smirk with unbearable arrogance. He wanted so badly to wipe that smile off his face.

The evening sun hit his face through the windows with a warm touch. There hadn't been a single car to wash in the last hour, probably because everyone was so focused on the Rebecca Waylow case, wondering how it could've happened to her. And if she were still alive, she would also be caught up in trying to unravel the murderous web. Those were the things that kept her up at night. Each unanswered question biting her mind away until solved.

Ian's pocket buzzed before he whipped out his iPhone. This time, a new face smeared across him—not one Lukas was familiar with. Shock, almost fear.

"I'm sorry about Rebecca, man," Mateo started. "I can't even imagine what that's like. If my girlfriend died, I wouldn't know *what* to do."

But Mateo's voice buzzed like a fly to him. The remark surprised him as he tried to focus close on Ian's expression. Lukas remained silent at the words. It was only until his hand gripped his shoulder in a type of hug that he remembered Mateo was still there.

"What—oh—yeah. Thanks. She was truly *everything* to me. I don't know what my life is now that she's gone," Lukas said.

"Find your power to keep pushing through. There's more to *this*. This place really *is* an illusion, but they won't call it how it actually is. Just a bigger prison. We can't leave. We're still being monitored like some fucked up lab rat experiment. And now, if there is some serial killer here now, they're just gonna let them take us out one-by-one until all of us rats are dead."

Power, the word, soothed him like a tea. Lukas glanced over at Mateo for a moment to catch Ian now frantically texting a message.

He looked back at Mateo. "Rebecca found a way out."

"What do you mean? That's not possible."

"Death," Lukas mumbled. A morbid ending to their conversation, but Lukas thought it was true. In a place with walls on every side, the only way out is to die. So maybe he was *her hero* to give her finally what she had always wanted: to be free from the chains of East Haddam. She might've not realized it then, but he knew if she were still alive, she'd thank him with a soft kiss.

"You two go home. We're closing early tonight," Ian said, tucking his phone back in his pocket. He didn't even glance back at the two of them before heading out the door, ready to lock up.

"But it's only seven o'clock?" Mateo asked.

A scowl crossed Ian's face as he clenched his phone tighter. "I said go home, Mateo. You too, Lukas, it might do you good to get drunk," he barked.

Lukas could still see the uneasy look on him. Whatever Ian had read on his phone, it took control of his mind. But what could do that?

9

LUKAS

JUNE 19

"WHEN I CLOSE MY eyes, I'm—I'm still *there*. I can feel them hurting me again. And then there are these doors—locked doors I can't open them. But behind them, that boy keeps screaming," Lukas said.

Madeline took a long breath, watching his bouncing leg, impatiently waiting for her reply. Lukas sat across from her on a small wooden chair. The small lamp on her desk did its best to light up her office. The open windows revealed a night sky where the stars wrapped around the city like an endless net.

She folded her arms. "And how often does this happen? These *flashbacks* to your past?"

Lukas hesitated. He wondered if he should tell her at all. *Memories are weapons. They torture your mind until you beg for death just so you can stop relieving them.* "I haven't thought about it in a while. But recently, it seems like it's all coming back to me in bits and pieces—like I'm following a breadcrumb trail of my childhood. I can't remember everything, though. I've spent so long burying those memories that it feels like I'm reliving them again for the first time," he said, now avoiding her eyes.

"When you talk about this happening *recently*, would this have anything to do with Rebecca's murder? That's something I also wanted to talk to you about. It must've been a terrible shock to hear. Well, for all of us, but especially *you*. How are you handling it?"

Lukas closed his eyes, replaying her question in his head. He wasn't sure for himself how he felt. Her death was bittersweet. The rush of killing her was exhilarating and made him feel powerful. But then again, Rebecca was dead. The only person who ever understood him, now gone. But maybe it was a small price to pay to regain control of his life.

"I was—*devastated* when she died. I don't know how I can live without her. The only thing that's been helping is the OxyContin," he said, forcing a choke into his voice.

Madeline examined him for a moment like she was staring at a puzzle, trying to fit different pieces together.

"In our last session, you had mentioned this *need* for control over her. If Rebecca were to try to...push back, or try to establish boundaries of her own, I should say, would you have had a *violent* outburst at her, maybe?" Madeline said, tightening a mug in her hand.

"What're you asking? Are you trying to say if *I* killed her? Out of all the fucked up people here, me?"

Madeline took a long, shaky breath at his comment.

A storm of anger clouded within him. How could she accuse him of such a thing? She knew nothing about anything—trying to pretend like she knew the man sitting in front of her. Maybe she should use her own brown *shit* eyes to analyze her own pathetic life, Lukas thought.

"I'm just saying maybe something could've happened that triggered some sort of reaction. You have a violent history—"

"*I'm* the only person who loved her. Not anyone else." Lukas clenched his jaw as he leaned forward. How dare she insinuate he would hurt his perfect Rebecca. It was clear Madeline didn't know anything. She was antagonizing him on purpose; he was sure of it.

Madeline tightened her maroon lips into a thin line, a flicker of fear crossing her eyes. "I see." She sighed in defeat. Her shoulders tensed before she placed the mug on a small table at her side.

Lukas's heart raced with rage, peering at her as she looked down at her desk. Seething, he wanted to jump across the table, bash her head in, and make her blood splatter. Maybe then she might finally learn to keep her mouth shut. But he couldn't. He had to be the good, *obedient* boy sitting in a chair until told otherwise, all for one thing. The thing that could make him feel better.

Breaking the silence, Lukas tried to calm his mind. "Can we talk about what I actually need now? My OxyContin prescription."

Madeline furrowed her brow. "Lukas, I'm afraid, from the looks of your current emotional and mental state, that wouldn't be a good idea. OxyContin is a powerful drug, and I think it'll just make things worse. I'm going to contact the pharmacy to nullify your medication this time."

Claps of thunderous rage roared within him again. "Are you serious? I ask for one thing. One simple *fucking* thing from you. And you can't even do that?"

"I'm sorry, but there's nothing I can do," she said, uncaring.

"No, you know what? Fuck you." He shot up from his chair. "You know I need that drug. Without it, I'm nothing! And you're just gonna take it away from me? Wow! What a cruel bitch you are, and you'll get what you *deserve*—"

"Get out. I have other people I need to see. Go." Madeline waved him toward the door like he was nothing.

Lukas stormed out of her office, muttering threats to her.

The hallway was narrow, with different offices on either side dimly lit with buzzing panel lights and different voices muffled within the walls. Right outside Madeline's office, an older man sat on a chair. Lukas noticed the man's lips parted, and his voice groaned like he was ready to tell Lukas something, but the man stopped himself as Lukas hurried by—searching for anything to numb his pain.

Lukas's fingers wrapped around the cold glass of counterfeit whiskey on the bar, enjoying the burning bitterness that had just slipped down his throat. A young woman sat next to him, burying her face in her iPhone, scrolling.

Numb with the pain, he thought. *Drink, drink, drink, to numb the pain.*

The Red Head was by far the most popular spot in town, even though they didn't sell *real* alcohol—it was all homemade and replicated. Some said they made it from antifreeze, or nail polish remover, or even paint stripper. He didn't believe either. The barflies who came usually had a more ulterior reason for being there rather than drinking homemade vodka soda, but The Red Head was special to Lukas as a familiar bartender from his past used to tend there.

Lukas knew what he wanted that night and the easiest place to find it was at that dive bar.

The glowing lights above him flickered as Lukas surveyed around him. A shadowy man in mangled clothing slid a younger, muttering woman a small plastic bag filled with a green herb. She scratched her skin excitedly before sliding him a few dollar bills. They quickly parted different ways after.

Lukas shifted his body to the side, the metallic stool he sat on creaking. A carefree, jubilant laughter filled the room, and there was something about the pink faces that smiled mindlessly behind him that made him think he wasn't in a prison anymore. *Wouldn't that be nice if it were true?* Maybe another shot or two. He might've just believed it.

"Two more shots," Lukas said to the bartender.

"One for me? You shouldn't have." The woman next to him chuckled.

A look of confusion struck him before he turned to see his solicitor. A young olive-skinned woman was tapping her nails rhythmically along the wooden bar. This must've been his lucky night. Lukas's eyes flitted across her green crop top and let a sly grin escape. "I wasn't. But I suppose I could share—for a price, that is."

The bartender poured the two drinks.

The woman raised her brow at him. "Oh? I don't really have any money. Medical student over in Haddam, but I come here for my job. Every cent I earn goes back to pay for this endless schooling," she said with words laced with loss, like she'd lost the winnings of a gamble. Her shoulders slumped lower now as she clutched the cold drink.

"Then how about your name?" His voice was hoarse.

The woman smiled. "Sophia."

Sophia looked like a college student, as she had said, her olive eyes gleaming with yearning knowledge—the same shade as her crop top. And her brown skin glimmered as the warm light of the bar showered it. And he knew from her gentle smile she was looking for *something* too.

"I'm Lukas." He held his faux whiskey shot in the air with Sophia ensuing. "To whiskey: for making life more *tolerable,*" he said, grinning.

They clinked their glasses, chuckling, then drank.

"Amen to that." Sophia licked her lips as she set the glass down.

The loud music rang in his ear, the bass beating his chest—or maybe it was heart racing with excitement from the way she looked at him.

"So, Sophia. What brings you to this dive bar on a Wednesday night?" Lukas leaned closer to her.

"Just needed a break from studying and work. And the cheap drinks don't hurt either, and I guess neither does the *chivalry* around here." Sophia laughed.

Lukas's heart raced as he looked into Sophia's sparkling brown eyes. The music and the alcohol flowed through his veins, giving him a reckless energy. He couldn't resist the temptation of Sophia's curves and smooth skin. He leaned in closer, the smell of her sweet perfume like a flower's pollen—the same as Rebecca's.

"You're a student?"

"At Yale. Clawed my way to the top of my class, flipping off the rich white girls who got their lives handed to them on a silver platter. But I'm interning for a doctor now, and I have a space where I crash when I have to stay or use for *other* things." She chuckled.

Lukas knew he was determined to make this night one he would never forget. Maybe Ian was right after all.

"Oh yeah? What kind of *things?*" he whispered with a soft breath.

Sophia grinned, a spark of mischief in her eyes. "Come with me, Lukas, and I'll show you."

They both rushed out of the bar, and Lukas could hardly contain himself.

Sophia's apartment door shut, and Lukas was pressing his lips on her neck. As he did, they both moaned in delightful ecstasy as they fell on her bed, their lips meeting in a heated embrace. And together, they spent the night lost in each other, forgetting about the world, East Haddam, and all of their troubles.

***

"Lukas! Lukas! Lukas, where are you?" a boy screamed amongst the flashing red sirens and scrambling bodies.

And Lukas noticed he was a boy again.

"Lukas!" the boy cried again. But Lukas couldn't see him. He spun, trying to find the boy, but he was nowhere to be found.

"Thomas! Where did you go!" Lukas screamed.

And then deafening bullets rampaged the red room, bodies falling like rain.

"Lukas! Lukas, wake up! Wake up!"

Lukas awoke with a gasp of breath in a dark bedroom. Sophia's bedroom. Cold sweat trickled down him, soaking his entire body. He sat on her bed quietly, panting, naked. Luckily, he had taken his clothes off earlier that night, and they hadn't gotten drenched. But his mind raced to move—to escape, to fight. He held his phone to his face, the bright blue light blinding him. 2:08 AM. *Jesus*, he thought.

Sophia slept softly next to him, her duvet wrapped around her bare back. Of course, she wasn't perfect like Rebecca, but Lukas thought maybe she could've been a close second to her. Only if she didn't misbehave like Rebecca had.

Lukas crept out of her bed, pulled his shirt over his head, and threw both his underwear and pants on when he noticed a gleam coming from a small table in the corner. A Red Sox keychain that hung from her leather purse, and it was open. Now it was asking to be looked through. He quietly rummaged through it, making double takes at Sophia, making sure she was still asleep.

After a few moments, he found something better than money or cheap makeup. Prescription notes. For a second, he wondered how she would've gained access to them but then quickly stuffed them in his pocket.

How fortunate he had found two things he was looking for that night: an escape and a substitution from Rebecca. And he didn't want to wait any longer for the drug he wanted. It had been too long since the last time. So Lukas slipped out of her apartment and into the web of night like the recluse he was.

10

LUKAS

MANY YEARS AGO

IT WASN'T A DREAM. It was a nightmare that Lukas couldn't wake from. Instead of waking in the white room of the hospital, Lukas awoke in a grimy darkness on a coarse bed, his head throbbing with pain.

Groaning, he lifted his head. At first wondered if he had died when they injected him with a needle, but heaven couldn't have looked this bad, and it couldn't have smelled like something rotting.

He squeezed his eyes and rubbed them with his small fists, hoping that he'd rub away this bad dream, but he couldn't. The pain that choked his body was real, and there was no escaping this time.

Lukas focused on the surrounding room. It was a small cube with only the sheetless mattress he laid on and a small table next to it. The room was dimly lit by a flickering, buzzing orange light—nothing like a star in the night sky. It brought him no comfort because he could see it for what it was.

On the table was a cracked, stained plate with what looked like moldy bread and, next to it, a cup of murky, gray water. But he noticed the biggest thing there was in the room: a giant black steel door. He wondered if he was in some type of prison, but he didn't think he had done anything illegal. He couldn't have been a criminal.

The image didn't feel real. He thought it was the type of dark scene one might see in a television scene or a scary book. But Lukas didn't like this picture. It wasn't colorful or happy, and he wanted out.

His mind raced faster than he could process each thing that popped into his mind, with questions flooding like hurricanes. This couldn't be real. This couldn't be where he really was. From one prison to another, it couldn't have been.

Lukas's heart pounded in his chest, and he knew he had to get out, escape. Sitting still was not an option for him. Leaping from his bed in panic, the cold stone floor made his feet freeze and numb within a matter of seconds, but he didn't care. He couldn't.

He pounded on the large black door with both his fists. "Help! Let me out! Somebody! Help!" he desperately cried. But no one came. No one made a sound except the metal echo of the steel.

But he didn't stop. Lukas relentlessly pounded his fists against the door, screaming until his hands were aching with pain, and still, no one came. A stream of tears fell down his face and onto his cold feet.

The sight of everything around him made him sob. The cramped, dark room, the hospital robes he still wore, and the ripped mattress in the corner. Out of everyone, why did it have to be him here? What did he ever do wrong? In his mind, he pleaded to be saved, but no matter how many times he prayed it, no one saved him.

His tears distorted the surrounding room, un-focusing it into a blur, but it was still there—he was still there.

Lukas examined the tall concrete walls that made the cell he was in, tracing the cold rock with his fingers, the sharp bumps prickling into them. With his breath shuddering and dry tears on his face, he touched every part of the wall, trying to understand it, and he wondered if there might be something he was missing. Like the answer would be right in front of him, and everything would be explained.

After a few minutes of his freezing hands traveling through the pitch-dark room, he found nothing. And at that moment, he knew there was no way out.

Lukas's hand pushed through a small hole. The small hair on his neck rose, and his eyes widened at his new discovery.

He pulled his hand out. It was tangled in a dusty web, but when he brushed it off, a small spider scurried up his arm. Lukas squealed as he smacked it off. There's nothing he hated more than school, but spiders were a close contender. Eight legs was not a natural thing to have, he thought.

He kneeled down, his heart racing, and poked his eye into the small hole in the wall. What Lukas saw sent another of what he thought was a spider prickling up his back. He couldn't believe it.

Erica sat on her bed, unmoving, perfectly still like a statue, and for a moment, he thought she was. The swarming darkness from the scarce light made it difficult to make out her figure, a shadowy silhouette of a girl. And he was sure it was her because of the blackness of her hair, also sucking the light away.

"Erica," he whispered through the hole.

She didn't reply or turn her head to see who might be trying to get her attention.

Lukas frowned at her silent reaction, whispering her name once again through the hole. His skin burned from the cold rush of air that filled his room—no, he wouldn't call it that. It was his *cell*.

"Erica!"

"Leave me alone," she said with a low groan, uncanny for a girl her age.

Her words stung him worse than the icy burn that crawled through his skin, and Lukas grew more frustrated. How could she not care about where they were or how they ended up there? He wondered. Finally, he came to the conclusion that she didn't care. Erica was selfish—something so clear that he could imagine her smug face through the wall.

"This is your fault. If it weren't for you, we wouldn't be here," Lukas said coldly.

Erica finally stood up from her bed and walked toward his voice. "*My fault? How is any of this my fault?*"

Lukas's heart pricked with anger. He wanted his words to sting her, to make her feel his pain, because everything was her fault. "You're the reason we ended up at that hospital in the first place and now here, which is probably worse."

"No, it's not. I didn't—" Erica said, her words choking.

"This is all because of what *you* did. You killed Dad—"

"No, I didn't—"

"Yes, you did, Erica! And after you did that, Mom was terrified of us!"

"You don't understand, Lukas! Mom told me—she trusted me. I was only doing what she asked me to do." Erica struggled to get the last words out as she sobbed quietly. The first tears she'd shed since the night it all happened.

Shut up! Shut up! Lukas felt tears fall to his bare feet as his body trembled with rage. He wouldn't believe anything Erica said. "You're lying! She wouldn't do that!"

"No, you have to believe me! You never saw what he did to her!" Erica pleaded with sobs.

"No! You're the monster! Not her!" Lukas said, wiping a tear from his cheek. His heart ached and pounded. Nothing made sense as he glared at her pink face.

He pulled away from the hole in the wall, quietly crying to himself. Erica was the monster. He kept telling himself that words could soothe him and that he might actually believe them if he told himself enough times.

But he heard his father's roaring voice in his head, his face red with violence and hatred, and he knew his father had always been the monster in the Retter household. Even then, he could still smell the sour stench that followed his father from the bottle he always kept in his hand. It made him wonder why he would poison himself like that.

The door behind him creaked and whined as it slowly opened. Lukas turned around expecting to see some hero there to save him, just like the ones he saw on TV with superpowers and shining capes. Except the man who stood by the doorway didn't look like any type of person who would try to save him. He wore a thick black uniform and carried a large rifle in his hands. This was no hero. He was a tall military man with annoyance spreading across his face.

Confused, Lukas stared blankly at him, his eyes trying to ask questions. But the man had no interest in explaining anything as he marched over and forcefully lifted Lukas—like he was nothing.

Lukas's face contorted with panic as his heart raced. *Is he going to kill me?*

Across the room, Erica yelped in pain as the sound of a heavy force striking her echoed both rooms, her body collapsing to the floor. Lukas glimpsed her unconscious small body through the door as he was carried past.

"What did you do! Stop! Don't hurt her!" But the large man dragged him past her cell through the corridor, ignoring his cries, refusing to show any sign of acknowledgment. Lukas was sure he might've been some sort of robot, not a human. What person would hurt a little girl like that?

With the military man's tight grasp around Lukas's wrist, they traveled down bleak, dimly lit corridors, cells on both sides of the walls.

"Where are we going!" he begged, but it was futile.

The facility they were in reminded Lukas of a corpse, rotting and dirty. It sucked away any hope of all those trapped inside, and it locked away any outside light, unable to sneak its way in. Traversing corridors and down a large stair pathway, Lukas thought they had traveled from heaven to hell in a matter of minutes. Not the type of thing he wanted to think of, but it felt true as his heart raced and his wrist throbbed with pain.

After a few minutes, they approached a tall pair of iron doors, a small block shining red next to it. Lukas found the picture all too familiar with how he ended up there in the first place, how Father Harris had tricked them, lied to them—it was all a sham. Nothing good ever waited behind doors, just a snake waiting to strike, just another trick.

Behind the door, different voices of other kids echoed, not with any type of joy in their tone, however. As the man dragged him closer to the door, the voices became cries, and their voices became drenched with fear. Lukas tried pulling back, but the man only pulled him harder toward the doors. The guard swiped the box with a small card. Lukas watched it flash green, and the door opened to another black abyss, a void of tormented children.

And without another moment passing, the guard hurled Lukas into the wailing room.

11

PERCY

JUNE 20

AT ONE HUNDRED AND seventy pounds, it'll take about three shots for me to get drunk, Percy thought as he downed his first shot of vodka.

That was one.

Safe to say what he was doing wasn't exactly legal either since he was only seventeen, but who needed drinking laws, anyway? In Europe, the drinking age was much lower, and Percy thought that's how it should be in America as well.

He slammed the shot glass back onto the bar counter. The raging music blasted from every corner of the club, with dance poles scattered throughout and half-naked men and women strip dancing. Colored lights like lasers beamed across the club, pointing in all directions. The scene was something straight out of a trap music video.

And it was only because of the fake IDs they'd paid a dealer for so that Percy, his girlfriend Tiffany, and his two friends, Sam and Adrian, could get in. It was one of the few underground clubs that the police weren't aware of.

The cops were always spoiling their jubilations.

We're all fucked anyway—inside or outside of East Haddam. At least this way, I can have some fun. He smiled at a woman seductively spinning around her pole. Crowds of both older men and raunchy women rained dollar bills on her, excited—still wanting more. He wanted more, too. Percy's heart raced as he examined every part of her body, imagining what her soft skin would feel like—

"Percy! Percy, did you hear what I just said?" Tiffany shouted over the loud music.

Tiffany's pale face shimmered like a disco ball from all her glittery make-up, though Percy thought she looked ridiculous. The pink highlights on her golden hair lit up like blazing fire amongst the different neon lights flashing in the club.

Percy stared at her blankly, trying to remember what she might've said.

"*Lavender Haze*! You know? The Taylor Swift song that's play-ing—never mind! How can you drink that without chasers, babe? It tastes like actual nail polish!" Tiffany's face twisted in disgust as she drank.

"I guess I just don't mind the burn!" But he lied. It felt like fire falling down his throat. But there were only two more to go.

Tiffany gave him an impressed grin like he'd conquered some unimag-inable feat.

A sweaty arm wrapped around Percy's shoulder as he turned to Adrian's jubilant red face, laughing. Adrian's black tank reeked and was drenched in his musk. Sweat dripped from his thick black hair and down his forehead. He fed off the laughs he got with his amusing antics, and Percy appreciated him for it. Smiles were never scarce around Adrian. He leaned in, trying to kiss Percy's cheek, aggravatingly smooching. Percy playfully shoved his face away.

Tiffany's eyes immediately flashed to Adrian, and she laughed at his hopeless romantic antics.

"Check out lover boy over there!" Adrian pointed into the distance.

Their friend Sam was lifted onto one of the pole stages, where a near-naked muscular man guided Sam's hand to his oiled chest for a few moments before returning him below. The stripper moving on to his next lucky funder.

Percy noticed how excited Sam appeared in those few moments, drunk on the excitement of touching a near-perfect man and let out a quick laugh. Sam had never been the type to be so daring, unlike Adrian.

Tiffany and Adrian cheered and laughed at Sam's few seconds of fame. "Looks like Sam's in his hoe-*era*!" Tiffany chuckled.

"Oh yeah, I bet you wish that was you were up there instead of Sam, huh!" Adrian laughed at her.

Tiffany playfully scoffed, rolling her eyes. "Why would I when I have *two* gorgeous men right here?"

Two?

That was weird, he thought.

Percy let out an awkward laugh, mostly at the fact he tripped over his own suspicious thought. "Come closer!"

Tiffany approached Percy, feeling his chest with her hands, swaying her hips to the deafening music. But before Percy could lean in and softly kiss her, Adrian nudged Tiffany and tilted his head toward the dancing crowd, a collection of different glamor and colors, each sparkling like treasured jewels.

She pulled away from Percy's body. "Right—I'll be right back, babe!" And then, without another glance behind, she followed Adrian into the crowd, her skin-tight pink dress blending in.

Strange, he thought. But what was stranger was that he wasn't drunk yet, barely even tipsy, so he concluded he should take another shot to loosen up, to shake his unwanted thoughts like—no, he wouldn't even imagine it.

Stop, Percy. They wouldn't do that.

Percy ordered his second shot of vodka. Grey Goose. It flowed like lava down his throat, an intense burn in his throat, then to his stomach. He couldn't help but sour his lips.

Shot two.

Slamming his glass down, he felt a rush of loneliness, like he hadn't really been at the club tonight. Just watching it from behind a screen and the confident mask he wore would eventually break. And they'd all see right through him, right to all his insecurities.

He watched Sam in the distance dance excitedly with other men, and Percy felt a slight jealousy. Like Sam, he craved to be desired, too.

He'd known Sam the longest out of anyone. They were both there for each other growing up in the town, having to deal with the consequences their parents made. And Percy was the first person Sam came out to, loving him regardless.

It wasn't fair they were stuck there. But there was nothing Percy could do about it. He was a small, powerless child.

And then there were Tiffany and Adrian. He tried spotting them in the crowd, but he couldn't find them. This worried him, a wave of questions flooding his mind, still trying to suppress a certain revolting image.

Percy made his way to the crowd, a wave of heat striking him even with just wearing a white tank top. The lights on the dance floor turned to a white strobe, and there were flashes of light and darkness. Pushing through different people, he searched for Tiffany and Adrian, but it almost felt like trying to find a needle in a haystack of sweat and BO.

He pushed through a couple of ecstatic dancers and finally found the two making out.

Adrian was pressing his body against hers, and she didn't pull away. She wanted him, unknowing that Percy was standing a couple of feet from them, watching, heartbroken. A growing anger rang in his ears. There was an ache in his stomach that felt like it was gonna blow. The music faded, and he could see the image in front of him, the one he suppressed for the last couple of months. He didn't want to believe it could be real.

It ached in his stomach until it finally blew in words. "What the fuck!"

Tiffany immediately pulled away with guilt, her face stunned at Percy's appearance.

Adrian turned to him. "Bro, it's not what it looks like!"

"Really? 'Cause it looks like you're kissing my fucking girlfriend! You asshole!" Anger stormed through his veins as his face sweltered. He hated

Adrian more than anyone. The fucking prick he was. How could he do that to him? Percy would never forgive him. Never.

"*She* kissed me!"

Hot tears spilled down Percy's cheeks. "Fuck you, Adrian! How could you do this to me?"

"Nah, fuck you, Percy! It's not my fault she likes me better than you, bro!" Adrian scowled. The red neon lights that fell on him villainized him greater.

Percy's heart thrashed against his chest. His fists craved to feel blood; Adrian's blood. *Fuck you, Adrian! Fuck you!* Everything about Adrian was disgusting.

Tiffany was now sobbing into her hands, refusing to look at either of them. Her victim complex was repulsive.

Adrian stepped forward, his hands in the air. "We didn't mean for you to find out this way—"

But Percy's fist had already launched at Adrian's face. Violence was never the solution he grew up hearing, but in this case, it was.

In a flash, Percy and Adrian were lurching at each other, trying to throw punches. Bloody tears splashed from Adrian's mouth. Then a heavy blow met Percy's stomach. But Percy remained on him like the red lights on Adrian's skin, trying to slam his fists on every part of him.

Both Adrian and Percy yelled.

The music stopped, and the surrounding crowd had a mixed reaction of panic and excitement at what was happening. Jeers and cheers filled the air, but didn't last more than a couple of minutes as the club staff pulled Percy and Adrian apart and dragged them to the exits.

"Hey! This kid over here is only seventeen!" a man shouted, pointing at Sam, who had presumably tried to hit on the man. Sam must've forgotten they checked for IDs before a lap dance.

The bouncers threw them all out of the underground club and onto the midnight streets.

Damn, Percy thought. *And with only two out of three shots taken.*

12

PERCY

JUNE 20

LOOKING AT HIS IPHONE, Percy read the time: *2:15 AM.*

The town streets they walked on were empty and dark, lit dimly by the buzzing lamp posts scattered along the cracked road. The brick row of homes that lined each side were asleep, unlike their dwellers lurking throughout the town. The best dealings always happened at night.

On the roof of one small dilapidated building, a shadowy figure was spraying paint on the wall of an adjacent building. Percy glanced as blue and red mist drifted around him as the figure continued spraying. It was always interesting to see what murals those silent artists were crafting. *It's always the quietest person with the most things to say.*

Percy made a double take at the buildings. They appeared like they had significantly aged since daytime, like they were wearing masks trying to fool those who passed by that they weren't cold confined cages.

It was still another half-hour walk back to Percy's shack house he'd occupied, and Sam kept closer behind him than Tiffany and Adrian, who lingered several feet behind. Since they left the club, no one had said a word. The veins in Percy's hands still pulsed with rage, wanting to punch the nearest thing.

A howl pierced the stark air from a nearby alleyway.

Percy's head revolved to the grunting across the street to see a pair of large men pinning another man against a brick will while they brutely punched him. The harsh blows against his bones reverberated against Percy's anger.

He felt strangely relieved watching the scene unfold. He imagined himself as the man, and of course, Adrian as the man getting assaulted.

"I'm sorry about you and Tiffany," Sam whispered, trying to sound sympathetic.

Percy didn't reply, but he appreciated the remark.

They walked toward a small cafe with different colored neon lights hanging from the windows, one of the few places still open after midnight. But it was a facade. It was more than just a cafe—a speakeasy hidden in the basement. It was one of the few places you could purchase *real* liquor, and it didn't come cheap, but Percy had been saving for a while now to have a fun night.

His parents, just like the rest of the outside world, didn't care what happened to him in East Haddam. They didn't care about what happened on the inside, as long as it was contained, just like shoving the worst of society into a box and throwing it into the ocean, never giving it a second thought.

Percy thinned his lips. He didn't want to think about that anymore. He just wanted to get drunk, drown his feelings about what happened that night, and move on. Standing outside the cafe with Sam, Tiffany and Adrian still hung further from them.

Percy reached into his pocket.

"Shit, we don't have the IDs anymore. They took them." He ran his hands through his dirty blond hair, annoyed. Everything was wrong.

Sam surveyed around. "We could just go back to our trailer. I found us some cloth that'll make some nice blankets."

Percy shook his head. He looked around, trying to find any sort of life that might've still crept the streets at these hours, preferably twenty-one or older, but it didn't seem likely. And he was not going to ask the angry men around the alley.

Then, a dark blur approached. Percy squinted his eyes, and the blur became a hurrying man coming down the same street as him.

Percy waved at him. "Hey, sir! Excuse me! Could you buy my friends and I some booze? We can pay you back."

"Sorry, not interested. Find someone else. I'm in a hurry," he said in a low voice.

Percy stepped closer. "Please?"

The man stared at him for a few seconds. His black, greasy hair fell just below his forehead, and he didn't look like he slept in days or possibly weeks from the dark circles under his eyes. His eyes were as black as the bleak night they were in but still piercing in an unsettling way. His skin was almost white, like chalk, though he still looked fairly young. But it didn't matter to Percy as long he could get what he wanted.

Then the man's eyes shifted to someone behind him, glaring. Percy turned around to find Tiffany leaning against the store window, her arms folded, staring back at him—confused, her eyes still red and puffy. He knew there was something strange about the way he looked at her, like he was searching for something in her. A few seconds too long.

"What the hell? Why not? Just tell me what you guys want," he said.

Percy handed the man some cash and explained where to go inside the cafe to purchase the booze. After a few minutes, he came back out of the store with a crate of different alcohol bottles, including an extra one, one Percy hadn't asked him for. A bottle of Pink Whitney. He placed the crate by Percy's feet.

"Pleasure doing business with you, man," Percy said a bit awkwardly. He was hoping the man would walk away and continue on, leaving them alone now. But he didn't.

He still lingered there for a few moments after Percy tried to excuse him politely. Burying his hands in his pockets and letting out a small chuckle to himself, he stared at Tiffany again.

"Why don't you ditch these guys and come with me? I have better stuff in my apartment anyway," he said, grinning at her.

Tiffany's eyes widened in disbelief. "What the fuck? No," she chuckled awkwardly.

Percy stood straight with his shoulders tensed. "Hey! Fuck off, man! That's my girlfriend you're talking to! I gave you your money. Now leave us alone."

"She's not going anywhere with you, you creep," Adrian spat.

The man turned his cold, bleak eyes toward Adrian. "Oh, are *you* dating her too? I guess that's why she's standing so close to you."

"You don't know what the hell you're talking about!" Percy shoved the man back, making him stumble to the floor. "Fuck off and leave!"

The man stood up, brushing his pants with his hands, cursing beneath his breath. He caught one last glance at them before hurrying down the road.

"Jesus Christ, what the hell was *he* on?" Sam said, picking up the crate.

Percy let out a heavy breath as his shoulders slumped. His eyes burned from exhaustion, and from all the tears he shed.

The cold glare from the man's black eyes still lingered on his mind. Like they were cages hiding, containing something dangerous, something *worse*. It sent a chill up his spine, and he couldn't shake the feeling.

Adrian began comforting Tiffany as she trembled in his thieving arms.

Revolted, Percy turned away from sight, back to the shadowy figure on the roof. They'd disappeared, but they'd left a large mural behind them. The painting was *loud*, and unlike anything he'd ever seen before.

An enormous boulder with the American flag was weighing down on a line of small black figures trying to carry it. They were all in chains and tethered together as they struggled to withstand the boulder's weight on them. Some figures had given up as they collapsed while others cried, trying to hold the boulder.

The mural on the wall seemed to jump toward Percy every moment as he gazed in a trance. It was him that was trying to carry the boulder, and it was him that collapsed under the weight of it. Just like every other inmate citizen inside East Haddam.

He turned back to Tiffany, who was behind, cradled by Adrian. Even though he was pissed at both of them, he still loved her and wanted to do everything to protect her, but he wasn't sure about Adrian.

Haunted by the look the man gave Tiffany, Percy wondered if it was eyes like those that stared at Cassandra Holland and Rebecca Waylow before disappearing.

13

LUKAS

JUNE 20

LUKAS STOOD IMPATIENTLY IN line at a small pharmacy. The fact he had to get up early and open the carwash that morning was already annoying him, and then there was also the *incident* late last night. How that little bastard shoved him to the ground. *Fucking kids. Why would that little shit's girlfriend rather be with him instead of me?* Someone as pretty as she deserved to be with a man like Lukas.

He clenched one of the prescription notes he'd stolen from Sophia, and now that he had those, Madeline was useless to him. And once he'd had his medicine, everything would feel better. All the pain would fog and blur into a haze. What's the point of keeping a memory if it wasn't happy? The flashbacks he'd been having of his past certainly were not. They kept creeping up into his mind unexpectedly. He wanted it to stop.

An old woman in front of him finally received her pills after haggling with the pharmacist for the last ten minutes about which medication was her husband's and which was hers.

The pharmacy was small, tucked in the back of a cramped convenience store. There were leaking holes that dripped an orange liquid into buckets scattered around the store, and it made the store smell like bitter piss. The carpet was torn and outdated, a style that had somehow lasted since the eighties and all the industrialization that happened when East Haddam transformed into a correctional city.

Lukas approached the counter, sliding the note onto it. The old pharmacist stared at it for an uncomfortably long moment, then looked at him.

"Fifteen milligrams of OxyContin? This is an unusually high prescription from Dr. Harkins," he said with concern.

"She's increasing my dosage. It's supposed to help."

The Pharmacist crossed his arms and raised his thick white brow. The wrinkles etched on his face seemed to twitch with skepticism. "Is it now?"

"Yes," Lukas said. His head pounded with fear and sweat as he narrowed his gaze at the old man. He needed this medicine, no matter who he had to lie to.

He looked at the note again and disappeared into the different rows of medication and pills. A few minutes later, he came back out holding a small capsule bottle and placed it in a small white bag.

The man approached the counter again and placed the bag down. "What did you say your name was again?"

"Lukas Retter."

"Well, before I give you this, I want to call Dr. Harkins and just verify the dosage she recommended."

Lukas clenched his jaw and glared at him while the pharmacist turned to dial Madeline on the phone. The second he turned his back, distracted by the ringing of the phone, Lukas quietly leaned over the counter and snatched the bag.

Running to the exit with his heart racing, the man shouted at him to come back.

He didn't.

And no one tried to stop him.

———————

Chronic headaches were a bitch to deal with. It seemed like every second. His head was pounding, wanting to burst open, and some days, Lukas wished it would, so it would all end.

He put the small pill in his mouth and swallowed it with water. The pill caught in his throat for a moment but then flooded down. Soon enough, it'd kill the pain or at least make it more bearable in the meantime.

His apartment was still. Sometimes, the silence became too loud, like a violent ring in his ear. It was small, outdated, and had nothing more than the bare essentials. But it was like living in a coffin. The cracked and stained tile in his kitchen would stick to his foot when he walked over it.

A yellow lamp sat by a pile of old photos that had collected dust over the months. The photos had once lived in a storage box tucked in his closet, but he thought seeing Rebecca's face would bring him some familiar comfort.

Lukas poured himself a glass of Pink Whitney. He had gained a new fondness for the drink. It burned, but in a passionate likeness he'd never tasted before. It was pink, just like the strands of that *one girl's* hair.

Placing the cup on the counter, he picked up the pile of photos, unsure of what he might find. It seemed appropriate to re-conjure the memories he and Rebecca had once captured on her camera. He brushed the dust off with his sleeve for a few seconds, then peered down at them.

The first photo had been taken the first night they fucked in his apartment bedroom. He had never told her he had lost his virginity to her. Rebecca smiled blissfully at the lens holding the bedsheets over her breasts, her bare skin paper white from the light of the flash, while Lukas forced a thin smile.

"Just smile!" she said.

"Why? Don't you wanna keep going?"

"I just don't wanna forget this. How happy you make me."

The memory made him smile. Why did she have to think his love was more confining than a prison? Or maybe that's just what love was—a continuous tightening noose around your neck, squeezing every best moment of your life until it's dried, he thought.

He moved to the next photo. Rebecca had taken a photo of herself wearing a yellow summer dress with stitched sunflowers wrapping around, a smudge of green paint smeared across her cheek. She had been laughing at the fact she felt like she was a summer painting herself. And then he saw himself in the background staring at her from her couch, unhappy. Not smiling, a glint of contempt in his eyes.

"Is something wrong?" she had asked.

"No, nothing. Why do you have to take a picture of *everything?*"

"Is there something wrong with that? I just like capturing the moment."

"Then capture this," he said sarcastically.

But Rebecca rolled her eyes, storming out of her living from her old apartment in town and into the bedroom.

"Don't walk away from me!" Lukas shouted. But he didn't want to hurt her then. If he did, she would've left him long ago. So he had to make sure never to cross the line where she'd try to run away from him but also creep his foot just barely through so she'd know Lukas had the power. And that kept her close to him for as long as he could.

Lukas frowned at the photo, pulling a small lighter from a drawer. Unhappy memories should burn, just like the one from his childhood. The night Erica ruined everything, but he quickly pulled his mind back. He flicked the small lighter on and lit the corner of the photo, watching their faces blacken and crumple until they were completely burned.

There was a loud knock at this door, followed by a moment of silence. Lukas dropped the photo.

The door banged again. "Lukas! Lukas, I know you're in there. I saw your truck outside!"

"Hold on!"

Dimitri wasn't one to wait patiently, a stubborn, pushy man used to getting what he wanted. Being the landlord of the apartments seemed to put him in a power high. Lukas dropped the blackened photo in his trashcan and rushed to the door, opening it.

Dimitri was a tall, well-built, hairy man. His curly black hair, though looked like he hadn't showered in a few days. Every part of his body had hair, especially his face. It was hard to remember there was a mouth under his thick beard. He hurried into Lukas's apartment the second he had a chance to enter.

Lukas closed the door behind him, squinting with confusion. "Dimitri, you can't just come into my apartment."

"I need a favor."

"I'm not really *available* for favors," he said with a strain of annoyance.

The two most important things to him, memories of Rebecca and *Pink Whitney,* already occupied his mind. At least, that's what he called the seductive young woman who clung around that annoying boy since he didn't know her name. But he knew she needed to be saved from that boy, saved like he saved Rebecca.

"I think you'll want to do this. Especially after I helped you when you were thrown into this place with nowhere to go. You were squirming around like a helpless spider waiting to be crushed."

Dimitri pulled out a large glass jar from the bag filled with white powder.

"What is that?" Lukas pointed at the jar.

Dimitri gave him a black expression. "Cocaine," he said, as if expecting Lukas to already know.

"Jesus. Where did you get so much from?" He took the jar from Dimitri's hand and examined it.

"Haven't you heard of The Raven?"

Lukas perked his head. "Raven?"

"They're the biggest kingpin on the East Coast, and the police are doing everything they can to break the network and find out who's in charge. The last couple of days, the cops have been watching me closer. Any day now, they're going to search my home. They think I might be involved, but I'm not. I just buy," Dimitri said in a low voice.

There was a moment of silence. It surprised him he'd never heard of any sort of narco-trafficking happening.

Lukas placed the jar on the counter. "So, what do you want me to do?"

"Hide it here. Keep it safe until they stop investigating me."

"I don't know, man," Lukas sighed. "What if they find it here, and then we both get caught with drug possession? Can't you ask your daughter to do this?"

"No. Karina doesn't know, and that's how I intend to keep it. But listen—we will not get caught. Just don't do anything stupid. And anyway, you owe after all I've done for you."

Lukas considered it for a moment, taking a deep breath. Dimitri was, unfortunately, right. If it weren't for Dimitri, he wouldn't have had that apartment or even a job, even though it was a shitty job. But the whole notion upset him. That Dimitri had the upper hand, and Lukas was indebted to repay his generosity. It made him feel powerless. And after murdering Rebecca, that was a feeling he killed with her. He just had to play the part longer.

Killing Dimitri would just make things worse.

"I'll do it." He paused for a second. "How is she, by the way? Karina."

Maybe the wrong questions to ask as Dimitri shot a glare at him. "She hasn't been the same ever since my wife, Isabelle, died last year. And the whole thing with Cassandra Holland has just made things worse. I wish I knew why." Dimitri gave him one last contempt look before leaving the apartment in silence.

And the silence swarmed the apartment, and he wondered if that's what death was like. Just another type of prison, but one where there was—nothing. Just eternal silence. Maybe that's where Rebecca was, in some black void, and still, she would try to capture the moment with a picture.

But then Lukas realized, why hadn't the OxyContin subdued the pain yet? Not his headache, but the emotional ache of thinking about Rebecca.

He knew he needed something stronger than his dose of OxyContin, and the answer sat clear in front of him, whispering his name.

The glass jar on the counter.

Quickly unscrewing the lid, Lukas laid a small clump of it on the counter. His mind itched, wanting to experience some sort of rush again. It craved to be lost in ecstasy, to forget about all his problems and pains. It would feel so good.

But before he could cut the cocaine, shouting from his neighbors echoed in his apartment, and the rumbling of their knocked-over furniture made his walls rumble.

Enough of this.

It had been the fourth time that week they'd done this. And he had finally had enough.

Lukas groaned and stormed out his apartment door.

Jake sat by the stairwell, covering his ears with his hands. He shot Lukas a solemn stare—right on schedule. A familiar feeling.

Lukas pounded his fist on their door, seething. And he continued until a red-faced, angry man threw the door open, glaring at Lukas.

"What do you want?" the man said in a low, annoyed tone.

"I am so sick and tired of hearing you guys fucking argue all night! We have thin walls—"

There was a heavy blow to Lukas's face from the man's fist. For a few seconds, everything went black. His eyes slowly opened, and he realized he was on the floor, his face sharply throbbing. A drip of blood trailed down his nose as he touched it.

Lukas slowly stood up, groaning in pain. He caught Jake's face in the corner of his eye, who was now quietly sobbing.

They argued even louder now. Rage pulsed through his veins, and without thinking, both his fists were pounding on the door again. "Hey! Open the door! HEY! Open this fucking door!"

But no one answered.

14

LUKAS

MANY YEARS AGO

CHAOS—COMPLETE DISORDER AND CONFUSION. That was the best way Lukas could describe now being in the room of wailing children. His head spun as he tried to make sense of what was happening around him. The air was musty and damp, and the cold, bitter touch of the concrete floor stung his feet. Lukas looked around, taking in the dimly lit space. It was a large room with concrete walls and floors. The only light came from a few flickering fluorescent bulbs overhead.

He saw other children huddled in corners, their faces etched with fear and confusion. Some were crying, others were silent and staring blankly into space. A surge of panic rose in his chest. He still didn't know where he was or why he was there.

Lukas called across the room, "What's going on? Where are we?"

"We don't know," a girl whimpered. "But somewhere bad."

"Hell," another boy said.

Then Hell is cold, he thought. "Are they planning to kill us?"

Erica flashed his mind how they beat her senseless, with no remorse. And she hadn't brought in the room yet. Did that mean she was—no. He wouldn't think about it.

"They need us for *something*, or they would've killed us when they took us from the hospitals," a girl said.

A lump grew in Lukas's throat. "They lied to us."

"Who hasn't?" a boy muttered from a corner, his words as cold as the prison they found themselves in.

Lukas didn't blame him. If he hadn't been caught in the overwhelming trance of his new environment, he would have been angry, too. Instead, there was a heavy guilt on his shoulders, like it'd somehow been his fault he was there. It seemed as if they had taken his childhood from him, stolen right out of his grasp. And there was nothing he could do.

A door at the far end of the room opened, and a group of men wearing black uniforms and carrying rifles entered. They didn't speak, but their expressions were cold and unfeeling. Lukas thought they could've been some sort of robot. But there was someone with them, a little girl, caught behind their bodies. And then he glimpsed her face.

It was Erica. They tossed her to the ground like she was nothing.

She grunted in pain.

A tall, shadowy man stepped forward and examined them for a few seconds. "Upstairs, let's stay *quieter.*" He pointed at Erica's beaten body, whose face was stained with dry blood. "I don't want to hear children screaming. You all are better than that." The words were like a snake's hiss, and it sent a chill up Lukas's spine. The man appeared too calm, and there was something unsettling about it because that meant he'd be worse if he was angry.

Erica trudged over to Lukas, tears streaming down her chin, trying to keep an unbothered expression, but he saw right through her. Seeing her in pain sent a fury against him that made him want to leap onto the man and kill him for what he did, but he couldn't. He knew he was too weak to do anything. He clasped Erica's small, scratched hand and held it, pulling her tighter into him. And as he did, Lukas felt the eyes of the other children watching them with horror, terrified at what the men did to his sister—a small girl.

"Now then. I expect you're all wondering why you're here. There is no need to be afraid." His voice was cold and emotionless. "You are all here because you have been *chosen.* And we will train you to become lethal, to be a soldier. To fight for a cause that is greater than yourselves. You may not understand it now, but trust me, one day you will."

Chosen?

The man examined all the children with a twisted gaze. He licked his dry lips with a devilish pleasure as he stood like a burly wall. "But I'm getting too far ahead of myself. I'm Director Miller, and while you're in here—you will do as I say. Obey—and survive, or disobey and face the consequences. Now, let's begin with today's lesson," he said, lifting his hand gently.

The armed men in black suddenly began herding Lukas and the other children toward the middle of the room until they stood body-to-body against each other. Lukas's mind raced with confusion and panic as he held Erica close to him. The room filled with the small cries and panic between them, and he thought of a new word to describe the room. Hopeless. No way out, nowhere to go, no way to fight back. It was suffocating. And there was no way for the sun to squirm its way out and save them. And the thought made his eyes water.

Director Miller continued, "In combat, it's not about brute strength or firepower. It's about pushing your enemy to their breaking point. Breaking their spirit, their will to fight. And the key to doing that is getting control. Control of the battlefield, control of their emotions, control of their actions. To make your enemy bend to your will. And that's what you're going to learn here."

He gestured toward a pair of girls standing in front of the group. They were sisters at the Boston Psychiatry and left a few weeks ago, but now he knew they'd been here the entire time. "These two will go first. They will fight against each other brutally and without mercy, and they will do it because I say so. Because I control them." The armed men pulled two of the girls forward into an open space at the front. They tried pulling back, grunting, but it was no use.

One appeared a few years older than the other, and it was clear to see they were sisters with the same brown eyes and the same arched nose. The only difference was height.

"No, this is crazy! I'm not fighting my younger sister! She's like two years younger than me! This is bullshit!" With her fists by her side, she stomped toward Director Miller. The older sister's face flushed with stubborn rage.

Director Miller scoffed, waving his hand again. This time, one guard beside him walked toward the older sister, pulled her forward with brute force, and held out her hand.

"Hey! What're you—"

They all watched the man pull out a pocketknife from his vest.

Lukas's face went pale with dread.

The girl screamed, trying to loosen her hand from his grip, "Stop! Let me go!"

The guard squeezed out a finger, and with a quick slash of the knife—

Her pinky finger fell to the floor with a bloody splash.

The girl's screaming stopped.

She stood frozen, staring at her bloody finger on the floor. The man released his grip on her hand, but she remained there in the middle of the room—looking down at it. The echoes of her shuddering breath made Lukas's skin crawl.

"You see, kids? I have control. But don't worry, nine fingers are still good enough to make a fist. I am in no mood for games, and I will not ask again. Now fight."

Lukas stared, petrified. He wanted to look away, but his eyes wouldn't budge.

Erica's body trembled next to his.

They watched the two sisters quietly cry as they raised their fists weakly, Director Miller screaming in their faces.

"Hit her!" he continuously shouted. Tears streamed down both girls' faces.

The younger sister flailed her fists at her, sobbing. But her sister wouldn't move. She took every punch, every hit—unwavering from her place. Lukas couldn't tell if she froze with love for her sister or *fear*.

There was a flash of movement, and suddenly, Director Miller had the younger sister in a chokehold with a knife held against her throat.

"Olivia! No!" the older sister screamed.

"I will slash her throat right now. Don't test me. I control you," he said as Olivia whimpered in his grasp. "Hit her, or I'll fucking kill her!"

The scene blurred as tears now flooded Lukas's eyes. And as he wiped them with his arm, the quick rush of her steps, followed by a blow, echoed throughout the room.

Olivia was on the floor. Her sister had just punched her face. She then let out a piercing, anguished scream, her face pumped with rage.

Director Miller nodded.

Groaning in pain, Olivia stood up, limping toward her sister. A stream of blood trailing down her nose.

The older sister shoved her Olivia to the floor. Olivia yelped, wincing in pain. But it wasn't over yet.

Her sister launched her foot at her chest. Olivia now begged her to stop, pleading for her sister's mercy. But her sister drowned at her screams with her own, and she continued until Director Miller finally spoke.

"Good. Now kill her."

The room fell silent again.

"What? No! No, I can't kill her! She's my sister!"

Director Miller waved his hand, and the armed men lifted their rifles, pointing at both of them. "Kill her! Or I'll kill you!"

The older sister went pale. She looked back at her finger on her floor and stared down at her bloody hand, whimpering. Olivia was muttering cries and pleads beneath her sister's feet.

Erica squeezed Lukas's hand so tight he thought she'd cut the circulation off.

The sister kneeled on her sister's small chest, pinning her arms down with her knees and wrapping her hands around Olivia's neck.

"Alicia! Alicia stop! Alicia!" Olivia screamed, trying to kick and shove her sister off, but her strength wasn't comparable to Alicia's.

Alicia wailed as she squeezed her sister's neck, and her screams deafened Olivia's cries for mercy.

Lukas watched, petrified with horror. He couldn't ever do this to someone—especially Erica. Would the director force him to do the same to her? No, he'd never.

Olivia began choking on her own gasps for breath; her struggling became weaker.

"Alright. That's enough now. Get off her."

Alicia immediately let go of her neck, sobbing.

Now panting for air, Olivia weakly stood up.

"You were so willing to kill your own sister because I told you to? Both of you, get back in line." He turned back to face Lukas and the others. "*That* is control. Anyone else feeling dramatic, or can we carry on without the crying?"

He examined them for a moment, scanning each of their eyes. And to Lukas's horror, Director Miller's eyes locked on his. An instant chill ran up his spine as he immediately looked away, his heart racing with panic.

He squeezed Erica's hand.

"You two," Director Miller said.

Lukas looked up and saw the director's finger pointed at him and Erica.

Erica immediately burst into tears, wailing. Lukas stood frozen, his face struck with fear.

"Come up here, now!" And Lukas knew the next time he asked wouldn't be as *polite.*

But he couldn't move, like his legs were cemented into the floor. They wouldn't obey. His heart rang in his ear, beating like an endless drum of despair.

"I can't," he finally mumbled.

"Can't? Or won't!"

Lukas paused for a moment to decide his next words carefully. Erica was his sister, and even after she did to him, he could never fight her the way Alicia and Olivia just did. He was no killer.

"I can't..." he said under his breath.

Director Miller glared at him with eyes so sharp, Lukas thought they killed him. His black eyes could suck the hope and life from anyone he stared at, and there was no escaping their reach.

After a few long moments, Director Miller raised his hand, and the armed men swarmed around Lukas, the other children herding away from him.

"Let this be an example of what will happen if you disobey me."

And before Lukas realized what was happening, someone knocked him to the ground with the end of a gun. His head throbbing with pain—but it didn't stop there. They continued beating him, thrashing him with as much force as they could.

Lukas yelped in anguish. Every part of him was being whacked, punched, and kicked. The noise of it rattled his ears, and he felt a warm stream dripping down his head and down his back.

Blood.

His head was ready to burst with pain as they ignored his endless sobs and pleads to stop. Then, finally, Lukas's head burst, but not with pain—with a pitch darkness.

15

LUKAS

JULY 1

REBECCA'S CLOSED CASKET WAS mere feet away from him. Sunday evening had been painfully somber, even though a couple of weeks had passed since Lukas had murdered her.

His eyes were red and swollen from sobbing during the service. It was a beautiful, endearing tribute to her life. A large array of her favorite flowers surrounded the casket. Her mother and father shared stories of her life and memories, but Lukas took offense when they didn't ask him to share his own words about her. He was her boyfriend, after all. Who could've loved her more than he did?

Rebecca would love what I'd say, he thought. *I would kneel at the casket and weep until they believed how much I loved her. And as everyone would gather to comfort me, I'd wail confessions of love to her.*

He stood next in line to pay his respects, as if he had somehow owed her his *respect*. His benevolent presence was already paying that after she tried to leave him.

Rebecca's weeping mother, Margaret, stood by the casket, receiving sympathy as hugs and condolences from those who passed by. Not one person had done the same for Lukas, which flustered him. Didn't anyone care he loved her, too? He thought Margaret was a terrible mother, anyway. Lukas cared more for her daughter than she ever did.

It was Margaret who killed her daughter first, not him—Rebecca had already been dead. Margaret leeched the life of her daughter until she was bled dry. She was always asking for money and favors to fuel her own addiction until Rebecca had nothing left to give her. When Rebecca was younger and her mother had been caught stashing opioids beneath their home's floorboards, Margaret threw the blame on Rebecca. They arrested Rebecca the next day.

It wasn't love, just business.

Lukas shifted his flushed eyes to her father and found it strange he was present. He'd been absent through most of her life, sifting through failed careers across the country. According to Rebecca, her father had taken a strong disliking for her pursuit of the arts instead of focusing on something he called more practical.

The man in front of Lukas finally stepped aside, and as Lukas approached, he saw the closed casket. It was a simple wooden box adorned with a golden plaque bearing Rebecca's name.

As he stood there, Lukas wondered whether he should look away from the closed casket. He wasn't sure if he'd be able to look at it, to be so close to her body after what he did to her. But after deliberating for a moment, he cocked his head to the casket, even though it remained closed.

Rebecca was sleeping, or at least that's how he imagined her inside, and the image was so peaceful. *A beautiful casket for a beautiful woman*, Lukas thought as he examined the closed casket. The wood was smooth, and he couldn't see her lifeless form within, but he imagined all the many dismembered parts of her yearning for his touch again. Her memory was preserved in that box, and Lukas couldn't help but think he had killed a part of himself with her.

A small tear streamed down his cheek. For a moment, he felt a flash of guilt, like what he had done to her was wrong. But before it could grow into a parasite, he killed it with affirmations that he'd done the right thing. He was right. He always was. When he couldn't control her anymore, he was to dispose of her, just like he was *taught*.

Lukas turned to find Margaret scowling at him. Her lips tightened into a sour, wrinkled line.

Taking a step toward her, he held out a condoling hand. "I'm sorry about your daughter. I loved her just as much as you did. We both lost someone special to us."

She glared at his hand for a few moments, her breathing becoming heavy. "You ruined her," she spat.

Lukas frowned at her. *You ruined her, you old bitch.*

He pulled his hand back. "I was the greatest thing that ever happened to her. And I think she would've agreed," he hissed back at her.

"No. I know what you did. How you treated my daughter, I will never forgive you for that. Never."

"I treated her better than you ever did." He glared at her. And as he walked away, he could feel her cold eyes following with contempt, but there was nothing she could do about it. Margaret's quiet sobs echoed behind him, and the sound made him grin.

Lukas looked around and noticed the other mourners had been sneering at him after his brief conversation with Rebecca's mother. Though they would say nothing to his face. If looks could kill, they would've publicly executed him in that moment.

Frustration overcame him as he caught more looks glaring at him, his face flushed.

Lukas knew it was time to leave.

As he made his way out of the funeral home, pushing through groups of mourners by the door, he noticed a group of people gathering outside. A crowd of outside journalists and news outlets from Haddam swarmed. Curious, Lukas pushed his way through the mourners and reporters and noticed they gathered in front of a tall woman in a police uniform. There was a familiar look about her, like he'd seen her before.

Then he remembered her from Ian's television inside SuperShine. Detective Amelia Mayman, the lead investigator in Rebecca's murder. *A waste of time*, he thought. She wouldn't be able to catch him. If she did, Lukas imagined his face plastered all over the news around the world, his name echoing in the ears of the country. They'd all know him—his story.

Amelia was speaking into a microphone, and the surrounding cameras were flashing as she delivered a statement on the ongoing investigation. The detective held up a photo of Rebecca and appeared somber as she spoke about the case. He imagined it disappointed the detective from chasing trails that led to nowhere, lost in a maze with no exit, dead end after dead end. Enough to drive anyone crazy.

Lukas stood at the back of the crowd, listening intently to what Amelia was saying. He couldn't help but feel nervous, knowing that the investigation was still ongoing and that he could be a person of interest.

Impossible.

As he listened, he felt a sense of unease settle in the pit of his stomach.

"Ladies and gentlemen, thank you for coming today. As you all know, Rebecca's death has left a deep impact on her family, friends, and community. Today, we celebrate and mourn her life. Our deepest sympathy goes toward Rebecca's family. I am here to assure you we are doing everything in our power to get to the bottom of this case and bring the responsible party to justice."

She paused for a moment and shot a quick glance at Lukas.

Detective Mayman cleared her throat and continued, "We have been working tirelessly to gather evidence and interview potential witnesses, and I am confident that we will find the answers we are looking for to build a proper case. While I cannot give specific details about the investigation, I can assure you that we are making progress. I ask for your patience and cooperation as we continue to work on this case. Thank you."

As Amelia finished her statement, a reporter immediately shouted out, "Detective, can you tell us if you have any suspects in the case? Or if this is related to *The Raven?*"

"Like I previously mentioned, I cannot disclose specific details about the investigation, but I can tell you we are following multiple leads and considering all suspects," Detective Mayman replied. Her gaze narrowed on the media swarming around her like vultures on a carcass. Amelia's shoulders tensed slightly as her lips tightened.

"Is East Haddam still safe, Detective? Or should its citizens be concerned for their safety?" another reporter shouted, pressing a microphone closer toward Amelia.

Amelia parted her lips blankly. She seemed to struggle to find the words as her gaze sifted through the audience. "Well...for the last five years, East Haddam and the Haddam Police Department have been under my supervision, and this is the first time we've ever seen anything like on this level. The inmate citizens here have never shown any major aggression, and I will stand by that reformation is the goal of the system. However, I advise caution to all at this time."

A new flood of questions bombarded her. But Lukas couldn't shake the feeling of the look she threw at him. It could've just been a coincidence, right? The more Lukas pondered, the more it made sense—he was the boyfriend, after all. The obvious prime suspect. He almost got lost in the void of his own consuming mind, but was saved when a reporter shouted a familiar name.

"Is the murder of Rebecca Waylow related to the disappearance of Cassandra Holland?" a reporter asked.

Amelia paused and shot another quick glance at Lukas. An unsettling sense of panic hit him.

"That's all the questions I'm answering today. Thank you."

Reporters still continued to shout questions at her even as she stepped away. Finally, after a few minutes of being ignored, they dispersed, packing their cameras and microphones to go search for the new news spectacle for American eyes.

Lukas remained behind, his mind still etched with how Amelia looked at him. The clouds above him seemed to have darkened within the last hour. A storm was coming. There was an unsettling chill to the air as it rushed through his hair, and it wouldn't be much longer before it poured down on the town.

Before he could turn to leave, he heard a woman calling for him.

He turned his head to find Detective Amelia Mayman approaching him. "Mr. Retter, I'm glad I caught you before you left. I was hoping I could have a few minutes of your time to ask you a few *questions* regarding the murder of Rebecca Waylow. Normally, I'd ask you to come down to the station, but this won't take long," she said in a stern tone.

His mouth went dry. "I think I should get back inside—"

"It wasn't a question. I need to speak to you about the murder of your girlfriend and anything you may know."

The tone in her voice suggested that she had already suspected him. A chill crawled up his back like a spider. He hadn't considered the possibility that she would consider him a suspect in the case, at least not yet. Lukas knew the only way out was to play calm—play smart. Play the game, however long it may be.

"I really know nothing. She really wasn't all together there at the end. She had taken a fascination with some dark subjects, but I've missed her every day. Every single day," he said, the last words choking in his throat.

Amelia stared at him for a few moments, studying him. "Were there any times in your relationship where things became *physical?* Or might've gotten out of hand?"

Lukas stepped back, his brows furrowing. His irritation crackled as his nose twitched. "What? No, never. I'd never hit her. What're you saying?"

She raised his brow at him. "I'm only trying to understand your and Ms. Waylow's relationship. Mr. Retter, can you tell me where you were the night of Friday, June seventeenth, the night she was found murdered?"

He took a deep breath. "At the bar, having a drink. I usually go after work."

"Is there anyone that could verify your alibi?"

Lukas thought for a moment, and he pondered the question delicately. He was careful with his words, knowing that anything he said would be used against him. Beads of sweat formed on his forehead.

"My friend Mateo. We work together," Lukas said.

Amelia seemed to force a grin, trying to appear warm, but her eyes were cold. They probed every part of him as she kept her hands on her waist, close to her gun. "Did anything happen between you and Rebecca prior to her murder?"

"No, we were fine. What're you asking me? If I killed her? I was her boyfriend, for fuck's sake! I loved her, and I would've never laid a finger on her. But instead of searching for the actual murderer, you're here questioning me. I have nothing to hide, detective," he said.

Amelia nodded, keeping her hands on her waist. "Alright, Mr. Retter, that's all I wanted to ask you. But I'd appreciate that if you remember anything or know anything else, you phone me down at the station or citizen patrol. You have a good night and seek shelter before the storm."

"Of course," Lukas said, forcing a smile as he watched her leave.

Lukas felt a cold sweat break out on his forehead. He had been so careful to keep all his tracks covered, but what if the police had already found something to link to him? He knew he needed to be quick. There wasn't much time.

But what else was there to do? Then it became clear. The image flashed through his mind, and his eyes widened with fear.

Rebecca's canoe. It was still out there, right where he'd left it.

There was no time to be wasted. He'd have to go look for it that night and destroy it—bury it, make sure no one ever found it. It could be the biggest thing that linked him to Rebecca, and he had to find it before Amelia and the police found it. He had to protect himself, no matter the cost.

A raindrop fell on his nose and down his face.

I will not get caught on my web.

16

PERCY

JULY 1

THE COLD WATER CREPT up on Percy's bare feet by the shore. A brisk wind rushed through his hair, although he thought the messier hair looked better, anyway. The swollen clouds above them cast a gray overcast. A storm was surely coming.

It hadn't exactly been ideal for Percy and his friends to swim in the river bank, but they weren't *ideal* either. Neither was how the man looked at Tiffany a couple of weeks ago—Percy hadn't been able to shake those cold eyes from his mind. Definitely not ideal for a grown man preying on a teenage girl.

Fucking perverts.

Uncomfortable, Percy sat on the shore, hugging his muddy knees as the water pushed and pulled him, beckoning him to come in. But he wouldn't. He'd never. Not again. The Connecticut River stretched miles through the forest, an empire of great lush pines that stood like pillars overlooking all who had stepped within.

And as he watched Tiffany, Adrian, and Sam playing in the river, splashing water at each other, a rush of envy grew in him. The last couple of weeks had been nothing short of awkward tension between him and both Adrian and Tiffany, with their paltry affair. The very thought of it made him sick. He never wanted to look at either of their faces again, but he had no other friends besides them, and there was nowhere else to go, so their infidelity trapped him.

Sam had been accepting of it too quickly, he thought. But Sam was always the middleman, never the fighter. Sometimes, a weakness and strength, and in Percy's case, he thought it was a weakness.

The water pushed and pulled again. Though the air was chilly, his back sweat as he anxiously stared at the water. The nightmarish scene that coursed through his mind paled his skin. He couldn't forget how he'd almost drowned in the river when he was younger. As he watched the water brushing his toes, he could almost feel the water surging through his lungs, suffocating him. His heart raced at the perilous thought.

Water suddenly splashed on him, over his hair, bare skin, and black trunks. Tiffany, in her Malibu pink bikini, giggled at his soaked sight. She always looked like a Californian model in everything she wore.

Percy rubbed his eyes. "Fuck off, Tiffany."

She playfully scoffed. "Don't be so lame, Percy. Get off your ass and get in with us."

"He's scared!" Adrian called.

Percy's face flushed pink. He contemplated picking up a small rock to launch it toward Adrian's head. His words were daggers slicing their thinning friendship. "I'm not! Just piss off Adrian."

"Whatever," she spat, kicking another splash of water before wading back.

Percy shot up, ready to chase after her, but his feet wouldn't budge. They remained still, like they were cemented into the shore. Finally, he clenched his jaw and forced his legs to move one step into the water and then another—and another.

He stood ankles deep in the water, but already the fear had suffocated him.

Percy gazed at his cavorting reflection in the murky water, moving with the gentle waves. Examining closer—his heart leaped. For a split second, his reflection looked like someone he once knew. The memory of a boy screaming his name rang in his ears like a shrill. Percy's head throbbed with unbearable agony. The water was crawling up his legs to drown him, he was sure of it. He couldn't handle the awful wet feeling any longer.

Percy leaped off the water, panting with panic. He hurried into the forest, ignoring Sam's concerned call for him.

"Percy!" Sam kept shouting in the distance. "Where are you going?"

But Percy kept walking—and walking further in, trying to get anywhere other than where he was.

The cold mud squished beneath his feet as he followed a trail into a foggy thicket. The path was along the river, and as he kept going, he hoped he'd walk out of East Haddam and into the *real* world outside the town. Or anywhere instead of with his friends. *Friend is just another word for enemy,* he thought.

But Percy knew he could never leave East Haddam. Not after his sentencing. How cruel it was for the country to exile as him as a child for stealing food to survive. This country would label everyone a criminal for stealing resources from the rich if they could, he thought.

I just want to disappear.

The misty air was bitter and almost tasted acidic, and as he continued upstream, the sound of splashing water from a nearby waterfall grew, and the air became uncomfortably cooler. He hadn't realized his arms were covered in goosebumps until he glanced at them. No matter how far he walked, though, he still couldn't escape the boy that haunted him. He was always there—screaming for help, only for no one to save him.

Finally, Percy found himself at a small shore at the bottom of the waterfall. Mist flew in all directions, sprinkling his face with a soothing touch. Lush moss and pine trees that stretched far into the sky surrounded the waterfall and towered over him. On a nearby hill sat an archaic, decrepit cabin. Its appearance was as dead as the dark logs it was built from. Somehow it looked hollow, like there'd never been life inside. Or maybe something drained the cabin's life, he thought as police lingered around the cabin taping its wooded perimeter.

He surmised it was probably best to keep away from whatever they were investigating.

Percy spotted a large rock sitting by the edge of the river and sat, letting out a deep sigh. He thought his thoughts might've been louder than the falling water nearby. It splashed louder anyway, like a typhoon. Closing his eyes, he tried to wash out the painful memory that plagued his head. But memories never leave. He knew you could try to bury and throw them away, but memories would still always find a way back—creeping up again at the worst moments.

And this time, it was too strong.

Percy buried his face in his hands. It was a never-ending movie, repeating itself in his mind. He could see it all. That horrifying day. He remembered it all too well: the water, himself as a little boy, his screams, and making an enemy with that son of a bitch: Water. And this was Water's way of taunting Percy. Making a mockery, a game, out of his fear.

If only he hadn't—

There was a loud creak nearby. Percy immediately looked up.

Somehow, it had been his saving grace before jumping too far into his memory. He listened closely, and a few moments later, it creaked again. This time, he shot up, looking around for what had been making the peculiar noise. For a second, he wondered if it had even been real, but then he heard it again, this time louder, like something trying to break free.

Percy walked down around the edge of the river and saw something unusual. A beautiful antique canoe washed on the shore, covered in moss and branches. He wouldn't have noticed it was there if he hadn't heard it creaking against the water.

He hurried towards the rocking canoe. Examining it closer, he slowly picked off the branches and glided his hand down the edge, feeling its smooth wood.

A loud rush of voices trampled through the thicket behind him, and, one by one, Percy's friends appeared at the shore, confused and tired.

"Percy! Where are you?" Sam cried.

He heard Tiffany obnoxiously groan. "Dude, he clearly doesn't want to be around us. Let's just go—"

"I'm over here, assholes!"

Percy watched them rush around the riverbed to the shore, where he and the canoe stood abandoned.

Sam wrapped his arm around Percy's shoulder. "Jesus, Percy, why'd you go so far?"

"Holy shit, is that a canoe? Get off me, Adrian!" Tiffany shoved Adrian's arm off her shoulder and ran to the old canoe. The small waves tried pulling it into the water, but the old thing was too heavy. "I've only ever seen canoes like this in my dad's old photos when he lived in Maine. It's unbelievable that East Haddam doesn't let people here own boats anymore. I wonder how there's one here?" she asked.

Percy had been thinking. Why would anyone abandon a beautiful canoe like this? They examined it in silence for a few moments. Tiffany let her fingertips slide against the edges of the wood and Adrian grabbed the edges, looking at it from different angles, which Percy found quite bizarre.

"We should take it out for a ride." Tiffany beamed.

"Yeah, let's risk getting seen by the patrol just so you can live out *Daddy's* dream," Adrian spat.

Tiffany and Adrian painfully argued over who was right and what they should do with the canoe, which made Percy roll his eyes. Sam approached the canoe and leaned over to check every facet of the boat for himself, from the growing moss to the engravings on the glossed wood and the murky water drifting inside.

"Wait, what's that?" Sam picked up a small object from inside the canoe.

Percy curiously jerked his head up, still ignoring the arguing behind him. "What'd you find?"

"It's a wallet. Whoever this belonged to probably accidentally left it here. Kind of irresponsible, if you ask me."

"Let me see it." Percy carefully grabbed the small brown wallet from Sam's hand.

The leather was wet and cracked, a small flimsy thing. He opened it and, as he spotted the Connecticut driver's license, his brows raised in confusion. A small wave of fear made his heart rush. He stared at the name for a few long moments, making sure his eyes weren't fooling him. Another trick from his brain.

"Guys. The wallet. It was *hers*. It was Rebecca Waylow's," Percy muttered with a shaky voice.

Finally, Adrian and Tiffany had ceased their petty arguing and blankly stared at him.

"Rebecca Waylow? Isn't she that one chick that was found dead a couple of weeks ago?" Adrian said with widened eyes.

"*Murdered*," Tiffany bleakly corrected him.

"If her wallet was in there, you mean this canoe was *hers*?" Sam said uncomfortably. Percy knew they all knew the answer to that question, except he wasn't brave enough to answer it because then it would've been real. "And we just got all our fingerprints all over her stuff."

The wallet trembled in Percy's hands as he stared down at it. *What happened to Rebecca? Is this where she died? Why is her wallet here?* He wondered. She must've had her back turned when someone attacked her, and then her killer tried to hide the evidence by hiding the canoe. Percy wished he'd kept walking, ignoring the creaking sound of the canoe. He could've lived his whole life without stumbling over what they'd found. It was all his fault—everything was his fault.

They all remained silent.

Percy's breaths became heavy as he continued fixating on the wallet. This must've been Death mocking him for avoiding his death as a child. Death would follow him anywhere he went, and Death would be patiently waiting for him. The mere thought made his heart beat heavier, like a drum.

Sam kneeled down in front of him. "Percy—what is it? Are you good?"

"I mean, how could he be? None of us are okay!" Adrian threw his hands in the air. "We just found some dead lady's shit, for Christ's sake!" He turned to Tiffany, whose face was pale with fear. "You still wanna take it out for a spin, huh, Tiff? Maybe we'll hear the echoes of Rebecca screaming when she was murdered—"

"Shut up, Adrian! God! You're not helping!" Tiffany cried.

A clap of thunder roared in the distance.

It wasn't Rebecca's canoe or Adrian's words that bothered Percy. It was the fact that it all came creeping back to him. The suffocating floods of water crashing through his body. He'd felt it more since he saw that shadowy man. And no matter how hard he tried, he still couldn't rid the childhood memory of near-drowning from his mind. If it wasn't for an older woman swimming in the lake the day, he would've died.

Water—what a terrible evil fucking thing it is, he somberly thought.

"I'm fine," Percy mumbled.

"See, he's fine!" Adrian spat.

Sam stood up, looking up at the gray clouds darkening by the minute. "We should go. The storm's coming."

"Are you sure, Sam? Tiffany *really* wants to ride a dead lady's boat," Adrian said.

Boat? Water? Stop talking. Stop talking already. I can't focus.

Tiffany stepped forward. "Can you shut the fuck up already? And that's actually super insensitive to dead people, so if you could just not Adrian, that would be great. I *try* to respect the dead," she snarled, shoving him away.

A louder clap of thunder rumbled the air.

"Guys, stop already!" Percy shot up. "We need to figure out what we're going to do. Now that we know it's here, we can't just leave it."

Sam studied the canoe for a moment and turned back to them, smirking. "What if we use this canoe to sail into Hartford? It's small enough to not get noticed by the patrol—especially if we go at night.

Sailing? Through—water? Oh, no.

"Yeah, that's good, Sam. This should be able to fit all four of us," Tiffany said, her glittered face radiating.

Adrian ran his hands through his hair. "No, wait, guys. Shouldn't we just turn it in to the police to help with their investigation? I mean, we could get into serious trouble if they catch us?"

Percy narrowed his trembling eyes at a random tree in front of him. He tried counting the amount of fluttering leaves to distract himself as his mind continued storming. *Stop. Stop it, Percy. Don't think about it.*

"Seriously?" Tiffany scoffed. "And give up our one-way ticket out of here? Oh my god, I need to go explore the world. I can't stand being in this place any longer—I saw a TikTok that said it's unhealthy to limit your horizons! At least with Rebecca's murder, we get something out of it. So yeah, I think we should do it."

Percy's breaths became more labored as his heart raced. A cold, sticky sweat dripped down his back. *Stop it, everything's going to be okay! No—wait, what if Adrian's right? What if we got caught? Which is worse: having to sail through water or get caught by the police? Fuck—I don't know!*

"I agree," Sam said.

"Fine. Whatever," Adrian sighed.

Sam approached Percy again. "What do you think, Percy? You've barely said a word."

Percy parted his dry lips, but the hoarse barks of nearby dogs interrupted him. They were getting closer.

"Hey, one of the dogs picked up a scent!" A man yelled.

Percy's heart fell to his stomach. A chilling silence infected them.

Tiffany's eyes widened with horror. "Shit, what do we do now? It must be a cop from that cabin over there," she pointed in the distance.

Percy let a cold rush of air exhale through his nose. "Let's take the canoe."

17

PERCY

JULY 1

THE STORM HAD FULLY arrived now. Dark heather clouds were like monsters in the sky. Thunder roared, and the chilly wind rushed through them, with rain now pouring down as Percy and the rest carried Rebecca's canoe through the muddy forest.

A few minutes passed of the group wandering through the storm, trying to escape the police and their dogs. Percy's lips curled in disgust as sappy rain drenched him, but he swallowed his frustration. They needed to find a shore quickly to sail out of so they could finally leave East Haddam once and for all.

They trudged through small a creek, up small hills and different thickets around the forest and still nothing. Percy and the others hadn't said a word since admitting his brother's death. The tension between them seemed more violent than the raging storm.

Lingering behind them, Percy watched Sam and Adrian spinning their heads, trying to find a new direction to explore, but it was difficult with the rain blowing into their faces. Tiffany wrapped her arms around her body, trying to stay warm. Her pink bikini was now smudged with mud, and her golden hair was now messy.

Tiffany groaned. "Guys, this isn't working! We've been walking around in the rain for an hour now, and I'm getting cold! I'm wearing a bikini, for fuck's sake—"

"Wait, do you guys see that?" Sam said.

"Oh, my god! You're literally silencing me, Samuel," she hissed.

Sam pointed to a nearby grove. "Look, Tiffany!"

Flashlights waved in the distance, illuminating the surrounding trees. Percy's ears rang with the mixture of drumming thunder and barking dogs. *No, no, no. How are they following us?*

"It's the cops," Adrian muttered. "But how are they so close behind us?"

Sam shook his head, strands of wet, brown hair falling over his eyes. "No idea."

Glimpses of bright white lights scattered over them.

Percy pushed the canoe forward, forcing the others to move. His body trembled from the chilly rain, but he bit his lip with determination. They were going to make it out. We will make it out, he thought. "Don't stop. We have to keep going, guys."

They took a few steps forward, Percy's feet sinking into the mud.

Adrian yelped, and the canoe collapsed to the ground. Rest of them collapsing with it, groaning. Percy fell face-first into the mud, staining his trunks and bare skin a cold brown.

"My ankle, I twisted!" Adrian howled.

Tiffany quickly kneeled down by him, covering his mouth. "Babe, you have to be quiet."

Percy sneered at them. A flash of anger stirred within him as Tiffany called Adrian what she used to call Percy. Adrian deserved it, all the pain. Rain blew in his face as he remembered the cops looming closer.

The barking dogs grew louder, just a few feet away, and the flashlights scattered brighter on them.

"Oh no," Percy said. "They caught us." He caught his breath as a few police officers were just a thicket away. Percy sat frozen in the mud, petrified. A few steps more and they'd staring at the police with guilty eyes. *No—this can't be happening!*

"Listen," Tiffany ordered. "I'll create a distraction and try to steer them away from us. Don't you guys dare make a sound."

Whatever Tiffany was planning was a terrible idea—Percy was sure of it. But before anyone could protest, Tiffany sprinted toward the officers in the thicket, screaming at the top of her lungs.

Three piercing bright lights fell on her, as the large German Shepard dogs circled around her, sniffing every part of her.

She is chaos, Percy thought.

"Hey! What're you doing out here?" An officer started.

"Help me, officers! Oh, my god!" She pretended to sob. "I can't find my friend anywhere, and it's been an hour, and I don't know what to do! Please, help me! I've looked everywhere, and now I'm just really fucking cold and tired!"

Percy stared blankly at the chaotic sight with a slight amusement. Even though he was still furious with her, he still couldn't help but admire the dedication she put into herself. He crawled backward trying to get out police's line of sight. His palm slid back, snapping a twig. Percy's heart leaped. Panic swarmed through his head. He messed up, and it was completely his fault.

Shit! Shit! Shit!

"Hey, what was that?" Another officer said, aiming his flashlight toward Percy.

Percy caught Adrian's and Sam's petrified looks. They were going to get caught. Then they'd be punished for stealing Rebecca's canoe, and worse, they'd never be able to escape East Haddam.

Tiffany grabbed one of the police officer's arms. "THE BEAR! I think it got to her! There's a wild fucking bear out there, and I think it probably ate her! Oh, officer, please tell me it's not true! She's too beautiful to be covered in blood!"

A wave of relief overcame Percy as he sighed. Tiffany had saved him, again.

"Okay, just calm down, miss." The officer said.

Tiffany stomped her foot. "I AM CALM!"

The officer groaned. "Ok, where's the bear? We'll try to immobilize it."

It was clear the police officers were getting impatient with Tiffany now, trying to dismiss her away. Good thing Tiffany's stubborn, Percy thought.

"It's—uh—West! That way!" She pointed the opposite direction of where they'd been.

"We'll check it out, but please go back to town. I don't want to catch you out here again," the officer said. The trees whipped back and forth around them.

Tiffany nodded as the police officers led the dogs away from her and the rest of them. After a few moments, the flashlights dimmed into darkness.

For the first time, the rain that spilled on Percy's skin felt clean as it washed away his worries. He stood up and caught Tiffany beaming at them, and as soon as she saw their success, she jumped on top of the limp Adrian, wrapping her arms around him, kissing him, and giggling. Adrian smiled, congratulating her for her excellent performance.

Percy furrowed his brow. A barrage of thunder roared in the sky as the violent wind stung him. Or maybe it was seeing Tiffany kiss Adrian that stung, Percy wasn't entirely sure.

Sam helped Adrian up, wrapping his muscular, muddy arm around Adrian's for support. Adrian couldn't walk, not with his twisted ankle. He groaned in pain as Sam helped him limp forward.

Adrian scratched his black, coarse hair. "What now?"

Percy squinted as he spun around, thick rain blowing in his face from all directions. He was sure there'd be more police surveying in the area, and the closest shore still had to be more south. Shivers of realization ran up his spine as his feet sunk into the mud.

"We can still sail out of here, but we should split up. Sam can help Adrian get down to the shore and distract any officers along the way while Tiffany and I carry the canoe to the south shore," Percy said.

There was no time to object to the new plan, or at least they were too exhausted and cold to object. It was risky, but Percy was ready to finally leave East Haddam forever and never turn back, even if it meant sailing on his greatest fear. *Anything is worth to never look back at this town.*

Sam nodded and helped Adrian limp further into the forest, agreeing they'd all meet at the shore.

Together, Percy and Tiffany grunted as they lifted Rebecca's canoe and started hurrying deeper into the depths of the forest.

The turbulent night illuminated from cracks of lightning. Percy and Tiffany scattered past sharp branches with heavy rain blasting in their faces. Percy gritted his teeth with exhaustion as he carried the canoe from behind. His red, numb fingers ached as they hurried, and each second he begged his body to stop and rest.

The forest was thick with tall, shadowy pines with their branches reaching towards the violent storm above. Percy's bare feet crunched thick layers of muddy foliage, making their path difficult to navigate. Every few steps, Percy or Tiffany would slip before catching their balance again.

Neither of them dared to look back. All they could do was keep running as branches, wind, and rain lashed them. The sharp pines scraped and cut through Percy's skin as he pushed past them, almost slipping while trying to keep up with Tiffany. She groaned in pain as the thick branches around her slashed her bare skin. Blood dripped down both their arms and legs, but she kept trudging forward as she quietly cried.

Percy pushed her to keep running and not stop, despite how tired they were. Flashlights shined like spotlights in the distance and the rough barks of the dogs echoed from afar. *Oh no, did they find Adrian and Sam?*

Tiffany and the canoe collapsed into the mud, her foot tripped over a large root. She whimpered in pain as she sobbed on the ground.

Percy's heart drummed against his chest from fatigue. He wanted to fall down with her. But he was sure they had to be close any minute now. He reached for her arm and pulled her up. "We have to keep going," he begged her.

Tiffany nodded as she sniffled. They lifted the canoe and continued once more.

Both panting from exhaustion, they fought past the thick mud and sharp branches. He knew he could keep running for a while longer, but he wasn't sure how much longer Tiffany could last. Still, he wouldn't let anything happen to her—but for a moment, he thought maybe he should. She broke his heart, after all. A small whisper in his mind considered abandoning her, and then she'd get caught while he and the others escaped. But he quickly shook the idea out of his head. He could never do that.

Percy's eyes wandered as his breaths sharpened. He couldn't see the beaming flashlights anymore. Maybe they'd lost them. *No, what if they were hiding behind the trees, waiting to catch us?* He wondered. *Or what if they caught Sam and Adrian?* His heart leaped at the thought.

Despite the thunderous rain, it was too silent. The fact Percy had seen no sign of the officers was unsettling to him. He hoped they'd at least a make a sound so he could know where they were. But they didn't. He needed to stay on edge because the second he'd let his guard down, they'd find him.

Finally breaking free out of the forest and into a small plain of foliage, Tiffany sighed and collapsed to her knees in exhaustion.

Percy set the canoe down. A quick break wouldn't hurt. He caught her labored breaths. It was probably the most running she'd ever done.

Tiffany gripped her arm, a long trail of blood and mud running down. Her face tightened as she held it. "Shit. Those branches cut my arms."

Until he held his arms out, Percy hadn't realized how much blood and pine needles mottled his skin. He hadn't even felt it. His mind had been so focused on running away from the police. "Same," he said.

Maroon blood dripped like tears from his legs, cheeks, and bare chest.

"Percy—I have to take a break. I don't think I can carry this all the way there," Tiffany said, laying on the ground.

Percy's eyes widened. "But we have to keep going. They'll find us if we stay here."

"I know—I'm just so tired and so cold. I'm out of energy." She let out a small chuckle. "I should've brought my fucking kombucha."

Percy let a small grin slip. He knew Tiffany could be a lot for others to handle, but never for him. Her comments were always appreciated. He always thought her voice was like a small flicker of a candle in the depths of darkness. And if he followed it, he'd find her again, find himself again.

He sat on a small patch of foliage, hugging his knees, watching as the wind blasted through a grove of slender aspen. As the rain showered him, he found it rather amusing how it cleansed him. A new confidence coursed through his veins that assured him he could conquer any challenge set before him.

"You know I'm sorry, right?" Tiffany muttered.

Percy looked over at her, a brow raising. Wiping his hair away from his eyes, he laid down next to her.

Tiffany's eyes twinkled like a midnight sky, and they glowed like a cosmos. The raging tempest filled her navy eyes, and Percy was sure it had been the universe that swam within them. It was amazing; he thought.

"What for?"

"Lying to you. I didn't mean to hurt you. And I should've told you sooner about me and Adrian, but I just felt so bad about it. I didn't want to admit it to you or myself." Tiffany turned her face up, the rain splashing on her face and down her hair.

Percy sat up, his face shrinking into a frown. He'd almost forgotten about the pain of catching her with Adrian until she cruelly reminded him. "I don't want to talk about that right now."

Tiffany stood. "But we're going to have to talk about it at some point, Percy. You can't keep pretending like nothing's wrong. I know you," she replied.

"Do we though? I don't know if there's anything else to talk about." Percy could feel the weeks of pain he'd buried within him growing again, beckoning to escape.

"Yes, we do. We can't just pretend like what happened never happened and ignore it forever."

"I'm not pretending like it never happened. I just don't want to talk about it right now," Percy said, a slight annoyance in his tone.

Tiffany scoffed, "Well, when are you gonna want to talk about *us* then? Do I just have to wait until *you* feel like talking?"

There was a quiet rustle coming from somewhere in the trees, but Percy ignored it as he stood up. "I don't know, okay? But right now, I just want to focus on getting this canoe and us out of here."

"God, you're still so selfish. You only care about yourself and what you want. This is why I wanted to end things with you," she spat.

"That's not true, and you know it," Percy said, feeling his own anger growing.

"Oh really? Because it seems like you're still holding a grudge about something that happened weeks ago and you're refusing to even talk about it. You're honestly gaslighting me, because now I feel like I'm the selfish one for wanting to be honest."

"Well, maybe if you had been *honest* with me from the beginning, we wouldn't be in this mess. And you did this for what? Fucking Adrian? My best friend out of all people," he shot back.

Tiffany finally stood up and pressed her flushed face close to his. "I already said I was sorry. Is that not enough for you? What more do you want from me, Percy?"

"I want you to help me get this stupid boat out of here so we can finally leave this town. *That's* what I want. We can talk about all of this after we get out of here."

"Unbelievable," Tiffany shook her head as she walked away from him. "I'll see you at the shore. You can pull the canoe yourself." And just like that, Tiffany abandoned him by the plain of foliage.

Percy watched her disappear into the forest. *Goddamn it!* He kicked the boat. He needed something to blame, and it was easier than arguing with her. There was no winning with her.

Staring at the canoe with rain dripping down his bare back and his hands aching, he knew it would take a lot longer to move it without Tiffany. And he was not excited. If only she hadn't brought up the stupid topic in the first place, they could've been halfway to Hartford by now.

He heard the rustle again coming from the thicket. Percy's heart leaped at the eerie sound, his head jerking towards it. *Shit, is it the police? No, maybe it's Adrian and Sam?* He wondered. They'd wasted all that time arguing when they should've been moving—a careless mistake thinking it was safe to rest.

Paralyzed in fear, Percy narrowed his petrified gaze at the aspen trees where the rustle came from. And he didn't dare look away. After a few silent moments, he rationalized it must've been a rabbit or other animal lurking around for food. Taking a deep breath, he took a few steps towards the boat and lifted it up, preparing to drag it across the forest, his heart still racing from the unexpected noise.

Percy had barely dragged the canoe up the shore when it jumped out behind him. It was too late before he saw who it was. There was a heavy blow at the back of his bead, a stab of pain.

Percy's eyes exploded in a blur as he collapsed.

18

LUKAS

MANY YEARS AGO

"VIOLENCE IS NEVER OKAY," Lukas's mother had always urged. But he thought there was one exception to that rule: spiders. They were the worst kind of creepy crawlies in the night. Nothing should have eight legs, and he thought nothing was scarier than a spider crawling up your skin when you weren't looking.

The mere thought of it made him shiver in the summer heat.

Sunday afternoons were a haze. The day always felt like a dream to him—the kind of day you'd soon forget. But this Sunday had been like a bad dream, which he thought was odd considering how bright and blue the day had been. Then he remembered that the inside of his house felt cold, almost as if it were still caught in a winter storm. It was hard to be smiley and playful inside a place like that.

Because he wanted to play, Lukas's mother kicked him out of the house. "Daddy's in a bad mood. Let's not bother him right now," she'd said. But Daddy was always in a bad mood.

In fact, he couldn't remember the last time his father had let a genuine smile slip on his face. He'd buried it beneath his temper, behind his tired dark eyes that always sagged, and his scruffy skin that he never shaved.

He always kept his bottle close, closer than he did with Lukas or his sister Erica, but he seemed to keep his mother closer. His father kept a sharp eye on her, and it scared him when she'd leave the house without him. Lukas couldn't understand why.

She'd be nervous when his father walked into the room. His father would say to her, "Lipstick makes you look like a slut. Take it off," or, "Are you hiding my bottle, Eleanor? If you did, I will beat your ass." His voice was rough, like cogs grinding against each other. The very sound of it sometimes made Lukas nervous, too, as if he'd do all the things he'd swear he would.

But his mother always assured him and Erica, "He'd never hurt us. Daddy loves us. He's just tired." Lukas tried to believe her. He didn't see a reason not to. His mother would never lie to him.

But he thought back to the spiders.

Now, there he was, his knees on the dirt, peering below the foundation of the house. A small boulder in his hand, he scanned the dark black pitches beneath, looking for anything that would move—that would crawl. Because if something did, he'd be ready, ready to strike. He wouldn't take any more chances at having another spider secretly crawl up his shirt until it was right there next to his face again, the most horrifying sight. He would have to kill any spider near his house or under his house in this case.

Lukas wiped the swampy sweat from his forehead with his free hand, still keeping a close eye on the dirt abyss under his house. The traffic in the distance echoed in the air. Boston was a sleepless city; people always had places to be, even in the dead of night. His father always had somewhere to be when he wasn't being a frightening dad.

Then, in the corner of his eye, something black scurried across the ground. Lukas quickly slammed his boulder on it before it came closer. And when he lifted it, a dismembered black spider smeared across the rock and ground, his face squirming at the sight. Spotting another spider scattering across the dirt, he slammed the rock again on it, pushing it as deep as possible into the ground. He had to make sure it stayed dead.

A small grin smeared on his face. He didn't feel any guilt or remorse for what he'd done because, to him, it wasn't bad. They were just disgusting spiders, after all. No one really cared if they were gone. He was doing his family a favor by ridding his house of them.

Lukas spotted a suspicious rock sitting on a patch of black dirt, and as he lifted it up, his heart stopped for a moment. A swarm of spiders came scurrying from the rock in all directions. With his heart racing, he threw the rock at the scattering blackness, though it didn't have the deadly effect he hoped it would have. Ss some of the small spiders scurried toward him like a wave. He fell back on his head, yelping in pain.

The bright world around him blurred for a few seconds as he cradled his head. He lay on the grass, staring up into the sky, his skull throbbing with pain. At any second, his brain felt like it might explode, but he noticed something peculiar as he looked up.

One window was latched open, and a small muffle of whispers came from within. Lukas's father had said the windows may never be open—one of their many rules. But it had been a blazing day with heat waves rippling in the distance, so he assumed someone had cracked it open to cool down the house.

"A/C is expensive, so you better not touch the damn thermostat, Lukas. Go outside if you're hot," his father said. And he'd never dare disobey him.

Lukas stood up, rubbing his hand on the back of his head. He peered inside the window to be met with a soft breeze. Erica's room was just as hot and sweaty as outside, except it was empty. The door in her room was open, a trail of light shining inside, almost touching the window. If it had, Lukas would have been noticed, and he was relieved that it didn't. Right outside Erica's open door, his mother had been whispering something to Erica, but he couldn't quite understand what they were saying.

Lukas pressed his head deeper inside the room, listening carefully.

"You love Mommy, don't you, Erica?"

"Yes," Erica replied softly.

"Then you understand how important it is that you do what I'm asking you. And it's very important you do *exactly* as I say. Daddy's sickness is getting worse, and I need to care for you and your brother, no matter what. Do you understand, baby?"

"Yes."

"Good—good girl, now listen carefully. This must happen tonight. We can't wait any longer. And then after, we'll never have to think about it again. Everything will be just how it used to be."

"Can I tell Lukas?"

"No, no, Erica," his mother quickly muttered. "This is our little secret. That means we can't tell anyone, and only you and I can know. Remember, Mommy knows what's best."

Lukas suddenly noticed something soft prickling up his leg. He looked down, and as he did, he wished he hadn't. A small spider was crawling up his skinny leg. Lukas let out a small scream, stumbling to the floor, trying to flick it off with his hand.

To his horror, beside the creepy crawly on him, a rush of steps came hurrying to the window. Lukas's mother peered outside the window, her face smeared with disappointment. He thought it was because he'd been so easily defeated by something so small and weak—but not harmless. His mother's black curls fell down her head like oily coils. Her eyes pierced at him and seemed to waver with a glint of worry.

Lukas thought he might've gotten caught listening to their conversation as sweat dripped down his forehead. What were they hiding that he couldn't know? He wondered.

"What are you doing down there, Lukas? Get back inside, child, before your father sees!"

Lukas nodded, standing up like a defeated soldier from a lost battle. And as he watched his mother close the window in front of him, he didn't know which was scarier: the spiders or his father.

19

LUKAS

MANY YEARS AGO

THAT NIGHT WAS QUIET, too quiet for Lukas's comfort. The streets and city outside finally seemed to settle down, but that was almost unsettling to him. He wondered where all the people outside had gone as he lay still in his bed with the sheets hugging his body. He wasn't sure how to handle the lack of noise. It was an unfamiliar feeling. If nothing was happening, the world might've been out of balance. In fact, it was so quiet he could hear the gentle breath of Erica in the other bed.

Lukas and Erica shared a small room upstairs, and it was almost always perfectly tidy. The wood floors never knew dirt or laundry. It had to be that way. Lukas didn't want his father to find it in any other condition—not since what he did last time.

He had come home from work late that night and went straight to drink from his bottle, his only friend, and when he went upstairs to find a pair of jeans and scattered t-shirts on the floor, he shouted furiously at Lukas.

"That's the way you wanna treat your clothes then, huh? Then you don't deserve them at all!" His father picked up the clothes from the floor and marched straight down to their basement, where the old blazing incinerator roared.

Lukas followed him down, begging and pleading for him not to. But he wouldn't listen. He tossed them straight into the fire, making Lukas watch.

"You deserve nothing, Lukas! You work for it! Do you understand me?"

Now that the memory had crept itself back into his head, he couldn't sleep. He rolled from one side to the other, groaning. *Sleep!* But it was easier said than done. It must've been well past midnight by now.

The pale moonlight crept through their window like an intruder of the night. Lukas thought something that bright didn't fit in the Retter household. His father would snuff the light from the moon, too.

As he lay silent in his bed, cradling his knees, he couldn't stop thinking about the conversation Erica and his mother had had earlier that day. What couldn't he know? He kept thinking, his face furrowing into a frown.

Erica's bed creaked gently for a moment. The sudden noise paralyzed him as he lay still under the sheets, listening sharply around him. But all he could hear was his heavy breath. He let out a small sigh of relief.

Her bed creaked again, louder. Without facing her bed, Lukas knew there had been some sort of motion over there. Perhaps Erica couldn't sleep either and was fumbling between her bedsheets, too. But then he heard the gentle sound of her feet touching the floor. It was clear she didn't want to wake him, so he lay quietly in his bed, not wanting to surprise her with his sleepless self.

Erica took a sharp breath as Lukas heard her gently approach his bed. He noticed she tried to keep her steps silent so that she could creep behind like some sort of ghost. But ghosts weren't real—only Erica. But that might've been the same thing. Lukas shut his eyes tightly, clutching the inside of his bedsheets, listening to quiet breathing get closer and closer toward his face. So close he could feel the smoggy warmness of it.

"Lukas," she whispered, "are you awake?"

He lay silent, not making a sound.

Finally, she pulled away from his face, and her steps became heavier because now she thought he was asleep. But still, he listened closely, trying to uncover what she might be up to.

The door whined behind him as it opened and gently closed. Lukas wondered if she was trying to escape, run away from the soulless house and find a new life some place else, but she was too young to come up with an elaborate plan; she wouldn't make it far. Erica couldn't even figure out the train system in Boston yet.

Lukas dipped his feet out of his bed, then his arms, and finally his whole body, careful not to make a sound. Whatever she was up to, he was going to find out.

The moon from their window dimly lit the room, and in the corner, he saw Erica's empty bed with neatly tucked sheets, as if no one had laid on the bed at all. Creeping across the room, the floor was oddly warm to his bare feet. He thought it was because the summer heat had crept inside his home. The air was muggy, and it made him constantly sweat.

He gently opened the door, which let out a small whine as he did. A chill ran up his spine, and his heart rushed. With his breath trembling, he continued to pull open the door until it was finally open.

Lukas slithered outside his room into the dark, winding hallway. His head spun, looking for any sign of his sister and where she may have gone, but he couldn't see anything. What could she be doing this late at night? He wondered.

As he stepped further into the pitch-blackness of the hallway, he carefully listened for any sounds. The old floorboards creaked under his weight. His heart stopped for a moment, hoping that no one had heard, but all he could hear now was the pounding of his heart against his chest. Taking a deep breath, Lukas crept, his eyes now adjusting to the darkness. As they did, he saw a glint of pale light shimmering from his parent's room at the end of the hallway. Someone had creaked the door open. A faint clutter echoed from the room.

Erica was in there, he was sure of it, and the thought horrified him. If she woke their father, he'd be furious, and there'd be no way to control his temper, especially this late at night.

Lukas slowly followed the faint sound to his parent's bedroom, and when he finally arrived, he gave the door a gentle push so that he might get a better view of what she was doing without being seen. The door opened slightly wider but enough to press his eyes inside, and what he saw was haunting. The kind of thing he never would've imagined seeing outside of a bad dream—a nightmare.

Cold sweat trickled down his back as he watched Erica pull a small bottle from under their bed. He wasn't sure what it was exactly, but he'd seen it occasionally around his mother's painting supplies. Erica carefully opened the lid before creeping up on their father's side, where he slept. His arms wrapped around their mother, holding her tightly as if he was afraid she might try to escape his grasp.

Like sneaking by a sleeping lion, he thought. Erica was playing a dangerous game, whatever it was.

What she did next made Lukas's lips part with silent horror. Now he knew he wasn't dreaming.

Erica poured the clear liquid all over their father. The room reeked of a sour, bitter odor. Lukas held his breath, trying to cover his nose with his sleeve. It was foul, and it made his eyes water, but he fought back the acrid smell, trying to keep watching her.

Reaching inside her pajama pocket, she pulled out a small matchstick and struck it against the box. Erica's face glowed from the small flame. It illuminated a twisted grin on her face that sent a foul chill up Lukas's spine. She knew what she was doing.

Lukas wanted to stop whatever she was about to do, but he couldn't. He couldn't move. His legs wouldn't respond. He was trapped in the prison of his own body, forced to watch but not intervene. He couldn't cry. His face froze at what she was about to do.

Erica dropped the matchstick on her father, and he immediately combusted into flames. A ball of fire.

His father screamed in pain as he burned and rolled off the bed. His body twisted and writhed in agony as his skin blackened and peeled away. The burning, sour stench made Lukas hold his breath.

A few moments later, his mother rolled out of the now combusting bed, screaming in terror at the sight.

Lukas could feel the heat of the fire on his face, warming his skin and making him feel as if someone had trapped him in an oven. As he glanced at Erica, she stood staggered away from the burning bed. She watched the flames dance, a look of twisted pleasure on her face as if she was enjoying the destruction she had caused—the murder she had just committed.

The room rang with the deafening shrills of their wailing, burned mother, who shot toward Erica and pulled her from the fiery scene.

The growing heat continued blasting him as Erica and their mother fled the room, leaving his father's blistering body flaming.

"WHAT DID YOU DO!" their mother wailed. "Erica! What did you do!"

Lukas looked down and noticed the bottle was against his foot. He bent down and picked it up, his eyes widening with horror as he read the bottle.

Paint thinner.

Erica's face was mottled with a mix of horror tears. Her bleak eyes were scarred by the fiery sight she'd caused. "I did what you asked me to do!" Erica sobbed. "You told me!"

"What the hell are you talking about? You stupid girl, I never asked you to do anything for me! Lukas! Stop standing there and hurry up! The house is going to burn down!"

"You told me! You told me!" Erica kept pleading as she was dragged down the hallway, sobbing.

Lukas staggered back, watching the fire stain the walls of the dead house, now with a dead father inside. It was a cursed home, after all.

The world around him seemed to haze as the room filled with thick black smoke.

He's a spider, he's a spider, he's a spider.

20

PERCY

?

THE GROUND WAS COLD. That was the first thing Percy felt. But, shortly after, his head throbbed with pain. He thought it must've been cracked open because it was exploding with a sharp pulse.

His eyes slowly opened, and it was dark and blurry, but he could make out a blurred figure in the grim room's corner. A shadow, maybe a ghost, but then he saw the shadow move closer toward him.

Percy tried moving his hands to touch the back of his head, but they were bound with silver tape. And he quickly noticed, so were his legs and mouth.

"Looks like I got you pretty good, huh? I bet your head feels like it's about to explode—sorry, I know how that feels. There was quite a bit of blood leaking from your head. I thought I almost killed you," a man said with a low, husky voice. An ugly grinding voice. One that sounded horrifyingly familiar. He let out a small chuckle. "But we'll get to that later."

The words sent a sharp chill up his spine. They were like needles poking at his skin. And the man, still blurry, took a few steps closer to him. The cold room was dimly lit by a small flickering bulb on the ceiling. It was clear they were in a basement somewhere. And when the man stepped under the light, Percy's heart beat faster than ever.

The same creepy man from a few weeks ago stood there grinning at him on the floor. Those same cold eyes peered at him as Percy stared at them.

His face was rough and scratchy, his black hair was greasy, and black bags surrounded his eyes. He looked like Death himself.

Percy tried shifting his body, hoping he could break the tape and escape, but it was no use.

"Don't bother," the man said, amused. "You aren't getting out anytime soon. You're caught in my web like a little bug."

Percy felt tears falling down his cheeks. His body was trembling with fear. Every second, he begged what was happening to be a nightmare he was having. He pinched his eyes shut, hoping to wake up next to friends who'd tell him they found him unconscious in the woods. But he didn't wake up. It was real. The fear that rushed in his heart was real.

He watched the man pull a chair close to him and sit in front of Percy. There was a small black bag sitting at the man's feet, and Percy didn't want to imagine what could be inside.

"It seems like we were both after the same thing. Rebecca's canoe. You see, she was someone very special to me. Just like how that girl is to you. And that canoe is also important to me, and it looks like you knew it was, too. Someone must've told you where it was and that it was Rebecca's."

Percy trembled on the floor. His mind raced because no one told him where the boat was.

"I'm going to take the tape off your mouth, and you're going to tell me who told you, understand?"

Percy didn't move, but his eyes shifted with terror that must've come across as a *yes* to the man. The man reached down to his mouth and peeled the tape off.

"No one told me," Percy cried. "Please, I just found it while I was with my friends—I didn't know it was hers!"

"Oh, Percy." The man chuckled. "Why are you lying to me? Are we really going to start like this?" The man reached into the bag and pulled out a large kitchen knife. "Now, I hope I don't have to use this yet, so I'm gonna give you one more chance, okay? Think very carefully." His tone mocked a concerned parent.

"No—no—no! I swear, please, I swear!" Percy said, now sobbing. "I promise no one told me! I found her wallet in the boat, and it said it belonged to her! Please don't kill me! You can let me go—and I promise I won't tell anyone!"

"Wrong, again, Percy," the man grimaced, shaking his head.

"No! I promise—" But the man placed the tape over the mouth again.

"I really didn't wanna do this, Percy, but you made me. You're making me do this to you."

Percy watched in horror as the man drew the knife to his leg and started slowly cutting in. Percy's screams were muffled as he shrieked in unfathomable pain. His leg throbbed in unbearable anguish as the knife cut deeper in. He shrilled and tried shaking his leg away, but the man kneeled on it. He could feel the warm blood dripping down his leg. Tears were streaming down Percy's face and onto the ground.

"I know, I know it hurts, doesn't it?" He lifted the knife, which now dripped in blood. "Now I can keep going, or you can tell me the truth. It's up to you."

The man peeled the tape off Percy's mouth again.

Percy was sobbing uncontrollably. The man tried relaxing him by gently rubbing his head and trying to have him take deep breaths, like he was some sort of parent. It was disgusting, a mockery.

"No one told me!" Percy sobbed. "Please stop! Please—I swear—I didn't mean to find it! It was an accident!"

The dark creases on his pallid face tightened. "It always is, isn't it?" the man said.

This time, he stared at Percy for a short while, thinking. But Percy could hardly focus, as his leg throbbed from being sliced.

"Okay, maybe I believe you. Maybe nobody told you about the boat. But unfortunately, I can't let you go. But I promise your death will be painless since I trust you're telling me the truth. And I'll stage your body *beautifully,* I promise, Percy."

Percy's heart sank. "No—no! You don't have to do this! I promise I won't tell—" But the man placed the tape on his mouth again.

The man grabbed a clear plastic bag from his black bag and walked behind Percy.

Percy tried everything in his power to escape, to break the tape, but he was too weak. He squirmed, trying to move away, but the man held him still.

"Take a deep breath," the man muttered.

The bag wrapped around his face, and everything went blurry again. His breaths became sharp and labored. He was running out of air. *I don't want to die,* Percy pleaded in his mind.

"Shh, it's okay. It'll be over soon."

And he was right. The basement went blurry, Percy's tears stopped, and finally—so did his breath.

21

LUKAS

JULY 2

KILLING IS EASY. IT'S living with the consequences that's hard. But that was a price Lukas was willing to pay.

Lukas stood with his hands bloody while thick, acrid smoke blew in his face. Dawn shined on the East Haddam forest after the long, murderous night. He hadn't intended to murder Percy, but he wasn't upset with the unexpected encounter.

Power was a fickle thing. It didn't come from his victims but from the fear of him from the living. And hearing the kid beg and plead for his life was like an addicting high, he thought. He wished he could've recorded it so he could watch again how Percy whimpered and squirmed like a little bitch. And how Percy had no choice but to take the pain of Lukas cutting into his leg because he was at the mercy of him.

It reminded him he had power, and no one would take that away from him. No one would make him feel small again. And he was sure once *they* found Percy, they'd know, too.

And in the end, Lukas got what he wanted. The canoe.

It writhed and cracked at his feet; the fire swallowing it into a charred blackness. He had dumped an entire canister of gasoline over it to make sure it combusted and disintegrated. The wood blackened and collapsed on the ground until it was ashes. And now, with the canoe destroyed, it'd be near impossible for that intrusive detective to link him to Rebecca.

It's not enough.

Amelia must've known something he didn't with that smug grin on her twisted face, like she was toying with him—a game she was not expecting him to win. And whatever she knew still haunted him. *But don't panic,* he thought. *That's what she wants.* She wanted to get in his head so he'd let his guard down and get arrested. *She doesn't really know anything,* he concluded. It was just a lie to scare him, to keep him on edge.

But it worked.

It didn't help how much smoke was blowing into his face and drifting into the air. It was relentless. He watched the fire send acrid clouds of smoke into the sky like signals. *Like signals,* he thought as he stared into the sky. The smoke was visible from miles away. Anyone could see smoke coming from the forest if they looked. Even the patrol and Haddam Police.

Lukas gulped. He'd gotten comfortable admiring the fire burning the last piece of Rebecca. He'd forgotten the dangers of being so visible during the day. His heart raced as the fire destroyed Rebecca's canoe. There wasn't much time.

There was a loud crunch of branches in the distance and hurrying footsteps.

"This way! The smoke's coming from over here!" a man called from the distance.

Lukas bit his lip. There was no time to put out the fire. He had to leave now. No matter how he tried to repaint the scene in his mind, he still looked guilty to the city patrol. A man with blood on his hands standing next to a fire. That didn't look good to anyone who might see him.

Without a second to lose, Lukas slipped out of the scene into the thicket, trying to keep his steps light. He hoped if he made a sound, they'd suspect it was some sort of animal lost in the woods or looking for food. That must've been what Percy thought when Lukas watched him through the bushes. Being a predator was easier than being a prey.

But now that's what Lukas was as he pushed through the endless sharp branches, a hunted prey. And he hated it. The branches scratched and cut his arms, and he ran past them. His jaw clenched in pain. *Damn things!* But he wouldn't stop. The pain of being cut by branches was no comparison to the pain he felt at Rebecca's death.

Finally, the hurrying footsteps drifted further and further into the distance until there was silence.

Keeping his head down with his hands buried in his pockets, Lukas hurried toward the apartment complex. Luckily, the early morning had few people already out on the streets. The town was still waking up, opening shops, people getting their morning coffee, and not paying attention to someone hurrying down the street. Someone who had murder on their hands. Keeping your head low was just enough to not get noticed.

Lukas finally reached the building with the cracking sign *on* New Horizon Apartments. Not exactly the place one looks forward to calling their home. Slipping inside the building, he hurried past the small lobby and headed up the winding staircase. He kept his steps light so he could move like a ghost in the building. He already felt like one. No one really knew him.

"You're early today," a light voice said.

Lukas looked up at the stairwell. It was Jake. He knows me, Lukas thought. That little boy who always played by the staircase knew everyone too well in the building. But this time, Lukas couldn't stay around to talk to him and lighten his day with loose change or jokes. He needed to go straight to his room and wash up before anyone else noticed.

"Yeah," Lukas said. He brushed past him, trying not to make eye contact with Jake because he knew if he did, it would spark a never-ending conversation between them both.

"You smell like camping. Were you camping?"

Lukas paused for a moment, then turned to the boy with a small smile. "I was. And I saw a gigantic bear and fought him, but that's a story for another time."

Jake's mouth fell open with awe, amazed at the returning hero that stood before him. At least he was a hero to someone, even if it wasn't Rebecca. Lukas quickly unlocked his door and slid inside.

It was dark. All the lights had been turned off. No one had been waiting for him to come home, not anymore. But he always had one friend: his bottle in the cabinet, and the thought of him having a drink sent a wave of relief to him. He was in the clear; he was safe.

Relieved, he flicked the light on in his small kitchen but noticed a small folded paper beneath his shoe. Lukas bent down and picked it up, confused about what it could've been. He'd never seen it before, so it couldn't have been his. And as he unfolded it, his eyes widened with fear, and the blood drained from his face.

It couldn't be, he thought.

Lukas stared mindlessly at what he was reading, paralyzed. The words seemed to jump from the paper and stab him in the face. He carefully read the words again.

I KNOW WHAT YOU DID.

22

LUKAS

ONE THING THAT NEVER changed in East Haddam was the mundanity of SuperShine. It was always the same. Nothing ever changed.

But now fear spread through the air—fear of the Recluse Killer. There were exchanges of whispers about it between Lukas, Ian, Mateo, and the owners of the cars they washed. "First Cassandra, now Rebecca. Who's it gonna be next?" one customer had said.

All the talk of who was behind the attacks seemed to make Ian more on edge than usual. "It's all a bunch of bullshit. I ain't scared of whoever it is," he reminded anyone who brought up the topic.

Hearing the alias spread like wildfire around East Haddam gave Lukas a spark of pride. They feared him, and they didn't even know *who* he was. But then he thought back to the threatening note on his floor. *Except one person*, he thought. He stared mindlessly into a corner of the shop, lost in the haunting words on the paper.

A wet rag splashed against his back. Lukas jerked forward in shock, and as he turned around, he caught Ian's cold glare from across the room. It hadn't been the first time he'd thrown a rag at them like they were animals. Ian must've seen himself as some sort of warden for Lukas and Mateo. And no matter how much Lukas wanted to slam Ian's head against the wall, he needed that job.

"Stop standing and go clean something, Lukas! Jesus, you lazy shit. No one wants to work anymore. Everyone just wants to get paid to stand around and piss."

Irritated, Lukas bent over and grabbed the rag. "I was about to, Ian" he spat.

Mateo gawked with disbelief from the corner of the shop, mopping the gray tile floor.

Lukas's body tensed, he shouldn't have replied so sternly. He should've known better, Ian's porky body couldn't contain his temper.

Ian march straight toward him, his face swelling with anger. "Are you giving me attitude? If you don't like this job, you can leave, but don't expect to find another job out there. You're lucky you even have this one, you ungrateful shit." His face pressed closer to Lukas, who took a step back.

Lukas was sure Ian hadn't showered in a few days. A bitter combination of sweat and alcohol made him hold his breath.

Lukas sneered at the fact Ian was right. He needed that job, but he wanted to tell Ian to go fuck himself, and any other curse he could procure. Instead, he bit his tongue, letting his flared fists hang by his side. *Watching a pig squeal until its death must be satisfying. I wonder what this hog would look like impaled.*

Lukas grit his teeth. "I'm sorry. It won't happen again."

Ian's scruffy lips stretched into a repulsive grin. It was derogative. Completely and unremarkably disgusting.

Fury welled up in Lukas's chest. Just one strike into his oily chubby face was all he wanted.

But before Lukas let his rage overpower his self-control, a small bell chimed, announcing someone's car had arrived.

Lukas sneered one more time at him before brushing past him with a rag and bucket in his hands. *Be a good boy, Lukas, you need this job.*

A small, rusted truck waited outside, which Lukas found somewhat amusing. No matter how hard he cleaned that truck, it would not look any cleaner. But he held his sponge, rag, and bucket ready to clean as he approached it.

The summer heat was like an oven he couldn't escape, and it reminded him of the throbbing pain in his head that still hadn't gone away. He'd gone through the OxyContin he stole from the pharmacy weeks ago, and he doubted they'd give him more, no matter how he told the story. For a moment, Lukas planned to call Sophia and perhaps persuade her to supply him with some but was defeated when he remembered he didn't have her number.

Lukas dipped the sponge in the bucket and started by the driver's side. The sponge glided across the car door but made really no difference. Killing is more fun than car washing, he thought. There had to be something more for him. He couldn't bear the thought of doing this any longer. Being on your knees, getting dirty just to service other people like somebody's servant and going home every day stained with grease and grime.

What a dreadful way to live. He was nothing—no one. Just a face doing his job. *They say the quiet ones are the most dangerous, and I'm living proof of that*, he thought.

Nevertheless, it was better than being back *there* in that terrible place when he was a boy.

As Lukas continued washing the car door, he noticed the window rolling down above him. An older, pale man poked his head out with a small grin. His face was stubby, some of his ginger whiskers had turned white with age, and he was balding.

"I knew it was you," the man said with an amused, husky voice.

Lukas stared blankly at him. "Me?"

"Yeah, you who stormed out of Dr. Harkins's office. What a shame. I heard what she was saying to you. How they're cutting off your medication. These pigs just want us to die."

It finally struck Lukas's head. He remembered that familiar face from the hallway after leaving Madeline's office because he looked like he was debating whether to say something. But he found it odd that the man was speaking to him now.

"I know. My headaches haven't stopped since she cut me off. And now I have nowhere to go to get more OxyContin."

"What if I told you that wasn't true, that there's a way you could get your medicine back," the man said.

"How? Who are you?"

"Just a friend who wants to help a desperate soul. I saw you stand up to that crooked lady at social services. I feel terrible that they took what you need away, so I want to help. The name's Bill. Bill Meyer. I live up there in the woods, and if you drive down later, I can get you what you need."

Lukas paused for a moment, puzzled. Still, the possibility of getting his OxyContin back intrigued him. He'd do anything to make his head stop pounding like a drum already. Lukas let a small smirk slip. "I appreciate the offer, but how're you going to do that?"

Bill stared at him, amused, as if the answer were obvious. "Have you heard of The Raven before?"

Lukas thought about the familiar name. He knew Dimitri had gotten the cocaine that Lukas was hiding for him from The Raven, and also, at the news press at Rebecca's funeral, they'd mentioned them, too.

"Kind of," Lukas concluded. "Are you saying you know *them?*"

Bill turned his head, looking around. "I can't say anything out here, but come by later, and I'll explain everything."

Lukas considered for it a moment. Bill called him his friend, which was enticing to Lukas, since he hadn't heard that word in a long time. If what he was saying was true, this was an offer he couldn't refuse. He wanted to know who The Raven was that everyone kept speaking about. And Bill clearly knew something about it that nobody else did.

23

LUKAS

MANY YEARS AGO

THE SECONDS WERE ENDLESS. Lukas studied the small hand on the clock revolving over and over again. It was the only thing he could focus on. Everything else in the room seemed to spin and jump at him.

Just focus on the clock, he thought. He hadn't noticed his leg had been bouncing for the last several minutes or that he was nibbling on his small fingernails. In fact, he lost track of how much time he spent waiting in that small office.

Watching the clock, he tried not to close his eyes. Because he knew if he did, he'd see the whole nightmare again in the split seconds of blackness when he blinked. His father's burning body and his sister smiling at what she'd just done. It had only been a few hours since it happened, but Lukas could still feel the ringing in his ear from both Erica's and his mother's screams.

The nightmare didn't end there.

After that night, he couldn't recognize any of his family anymore. Not even himself.

Then time itself froze because everything after his father's death was still. Not a word, not a single sound but of his own shaky breath, but even that didn't seem real in the moment. He wasn't sure how long time froze. It was only when they fled the house and police officers took him and Erica away that he knew time had resumed.

Now he was waiting. And waiting. As the seconds passed, his heart beat faster. *What's taking so long?* As he sat on the small sofa chair, Lukas felt the weight of the night pressing down on him, suffocating him with each passing second. Daylight couldn't come soon enough.

Finally, the door opened.

His eyes jumped from the clock to the tall, middle-aged woman who entered the room with a sympathetic grin and clipboard. Lukas studied her as she walked across the old carpet with her heels to her desk. Her dirty blonde hair was tied neatly in a bun, her orange sweater had no rips or stains. Everything about her was neat. Still, whoever she was, Lukas knew she couldn't fix his family.

As she took a seat in front of him, the woman gave him an honest smile. "And you must be Lukas. I'm Dr. Elizabeth Ainsley, but you can call me Liz if you'd like. I'm a doctor here at the hospital, and I just wanna ask you a couple questions, if that's okay," she said.

Lukas stared at her in silence.

"Do you know why you're here? Has anyone told you anything?"

He knew why, but he couldn't form the words to say it like he'd forgotten how to speak. Because if he said it, he'd have to relive those terrible moments again. So he simply stared at the doctor with his eyes trembling.

Elizabeth's smile faded into a look of concern. "It's okay. I know this must be really hard for you. I just want you to know that this is a safe space for you, Lukas, and you can tell me anything." She stood up, walking over to a small cabinet. "I forgot. I have these for you if you'd like to play or color while we talk." Elizabeth placed a small plastic box on the table between them and opened the lid.

Lukas kneeled down in front of the table and peeked inside. There were different toys, fidgets, crayons and markers. After considering the different colorful treasures inside, he took out the crayons and a piece of blank paper.

There was a silence lurking in the room again as he colored, and he could hear the horrifying clock ticking again.

"My sister, Erica, killed our dad," he said.

Elizabeth was silent for a moment. "And how does any of this make you feel? I imagine this all feels kind of scary."

But Lukas ignored her and kept coloring. With a black crayon, he drew a figure, then picked the red and orange and colored wild flames around the stick-man. Even in rough scribbles and marks, he could feel the scorching heat from the paper.

"Who's this?" Elizabeth pointed to the drawing.

"Dad. I can still see it. He's still burning in my head. It won't stop."

Elizabeth kneeled down in front of him, smiling sympathetically. "Lukas. What you're going through is very tough for a little boy. But I'm wondering if perhaps there's more going on here than just what happened with your sister and father. Can you remember any time you've had hallucinations or saw things that weren't there?"

Lukas placed the crayon down and stared at her in confusion. "What do you mean? I saw it happen. I'm not making anything up."

Elizabeth made a few notes on her clipboard. "Sometimes, when people go through traumatic events like this, it can cause them to experience things that aren't real. Like seeing things or hearing voices that aren't really there. Do you ever feel like that?"

His heart raced faster this time, and a lump grew in Lukas's throat as he spoke. "I'm not making it up, I promise, Liz. Are you saying it was all in my imagination? But I saw it," he said.

Elizabeth immediately shook her head. "No, Lukas, I'm not saying that at all." Her tone was more stern this time. "But sometimes our brains can play tricks on us, especially when we're under a lot of stress. It's possible that what you think happened tonight might not be exactly what *actually* happened. Do you understand, honey?"

Lukas felt a cold sweat break around his body. The room spun. Nothing made sense. It made little sense. *Why would she say all this?* He wondered. Lukas knew what he saw, and he wasn't making it up. But he sat, refusing to look at her, his breaths growing heavy with frustration. Through the stillness of the room, he replayed that haunting moment—it couldn't have been made up.

"I know what I saw. It wasn't a trick. Just ask my mom. She was there!"

"It's not your fault, Lukas. The things that your father had said and done over the years would take a toll on any child. Your mother said it was a terrible accident what happened tonight, that you and your sister didn't mean to do what you did. Someone can accidentally ignite fires through different household items—"

Lukas shot up. "What *I* did? I did nothing to Dad. It was all Erica!"

Elizabeth made some notes on her clipboard. "It's all right, Lukas. Let's take a deep breath. All that pressure and negativity you felt in your home that's supposed to be a safe space for you sometimes can't be contained anymore, and it's perfectly understandable you'd feel this way. But sometimes those bad feelings can turn into bad actions, and I know you didn't mean to start the fire in your home tonight, but it happened."

Lukas stared at her, petrified with confusion, his face flushed. Nothing she was saying made sense. She wasn't the kind of doctor he expected. She was a whisper of chaos, like a storm throwing different voices inside his head, and he wasn't sure which to believe.

Tears streamed down Lukas's face. "I didn't do anything, I swear." He paused for a moment and looked around the room. It looked different from before, more cramped and lifeless, like the colors had drained off the walls and toys into a dull neutrality. "What is this place?"

"It's okay. There's no need to be scared. This is a hospital for boys and girls—just like you."

He looked back at her smile. *Just like me?*

"How long do I have to stay here?" Lukas's eyes fell back to the drawing on the table.

Elizabeth grinned. "Just until you and your sister feel better."

"How long is that?"

But this time, Elizabeth's smile faded into something more somber.

Lukas's ears rang with something more violent. It pulled him away from the office in his memory. For a few moments, he hadn't realized his eyes were open because he'd forgotten the pitch blackness that swallowed the room. Still, that ear-deafening shrill pierced through the stone walls that caged him and reverberated around him. The blood-curdling sound made Lukas press his hands deep into his ears as he lay on the cold floor, but it made no difference.

It must've been the boy across from him, he concluded. And then the haunting thought flooded his mind. What were they doing to him?

Lukas was still wrapping his mind about where he was. The last thing he remembered was being beaten by all those men and everything going black. Now his body ached and throbbed with pain.

After a few minutes of the being screaming and begging to be let go, his cries faded deeper and deeper into silence as he was taken away. And finally, there was stillness again—the sweet loudness of nothing.

As Lukas sat up on the cold floor, he was immediately struck with an unfathomable pain in his stomach. It was empty. He couldn't remember the last time he'd eaten, and he wasn't excited about having to eat the dirty scraps they gave them. Anything was better than that bitter mush they fed them. But it was better than starving, and he could feel his energy depleting.

Lukas crawled over to the dog bowl in the corner, and as he dug his hand inside, there was nothing. They'd given him no food. Desperately, he felt around the bowl to see if they might've missed, but there was nothing as his stomach continued to grumble. This must've been some sick, twisted form of punishment for not fighting Erica, but he was glad to endure it if that meant she'd survive.

There was a faint whisper that brushed his ear like a gentle breeze, and at first, he thought it was just that. It must've been another trick from his head, because there was nobody else in the room. But then he heard it again whisper his name.

"Lukas," the soft voice whispered. He turned his head around the room and followed the gentle voice to the small hole in the wall where the spider's nest was. And as he poked his eye inside, he saw Erica on the other side, her face tainted with tears streaming down her face.

"I thought they killed you," she said, choking on the last word.

Lukas shook his head. "How long was I unconscious?"

"I don't know. Maybe hours. Days. Weeks? It's hard to keep track of time in here. It all feels like a dream. Sometimes, I can't remember if you're real or if I've made you up in my head to keep me company. You *are* my brother, right?" Erica said, with tears streaming down her face.

Erica's cracking voice struck Lukas's heart with a sharp ache. Lukas couldn't let her forget about their bond, not when it was the only thing keeping him from drowning. "Yeah—yeah, I am. And you're my sister." He paused for a moment as his stomach grumbled louder this time. "I'm so hungry. They won't feed me."

"Here." Erica crawled away for a few minutes, then returned with a handful of mush dripping down her hand. "You need it more than I do," she said.

"No, you eat it. It's yours. I'll be fine. They're going to have to feed me at some point. They clearly want us for something. Did you hear that boy screaming? Where do you think they took him?"

"I don't know," Erica started. "But it probably can't be good. That's the second one I've heard now. The first was a girl. We have to figure out what's going on here, Lukas. I'm getting lost. I don't know how much longer I'll be able to remember myself before I'm gone too—"

"You won't lose yourself because I'll remind you who you are."

But as he said the words, a haunting image flashed through his mind. Erica grinned as she struck the match before lighting their dad on fire. Was that who she was? He hated himself for thinking of that first, because he knew her better. And Lukas sat there by the wall. He noticed something strange. The room was no longer cold. There was a low hum of heat coming from a vent.

And for a second, Lukas's heart stopped because he swore it almost sounded like the boy's scream humming from the vent. But he concluded he must've heard his stomach grumbling or the wind howling through the vents.

It had to be that, he thought. *Right?*

24

Elizabeth

July 2

ANOTHER WITHERED ROSE PETAL fell from the white ceramic pot, and it floated down onto the edge of the chipped wooden porch. The once blooming lust rose had become a grotesque thing of dull reds and black. It reminded her of her house, which was once coated in a delicate white, but now the paint cracked and chipped off the walls.

And, of course, Elizabeth knew that beauty faded with age.

It was a brisk morning on the outskirts of East Haddam. Two towering willow trees enveloped a small, forgotten cottage. It was a complete change of scenery from the London smog and Boston skylines. But then again, she had also changed over the last several years. That's what East Haddam did to people.

As she swayed back and forth on her rocking chair, her focus was pulled from the gentle song of morning birds to the withering roses on her porch. Elizabeth squinted her eyes at the sight.

That's the fifth one now. She frowned as her wooden chair stopped rocking. The many wrinkles on her pale face popped with an angst pride as she squeezed her silk pants, her knuckles swelling white.

She turned her head toward the open front door. "Sophia! Sophia—the roses are wilting!"

Moments later came the hurrying footsteps down the hall and to the porch. Sophia took a long breath as she approached the doctor.

Elizabeth had first noticed her while giving a guest lecture at a university. She'd never seen such an inflamed passion toward the medical field, so it had made sense to fan the flame. She did the responsible thing and took Sophia under her educational wing while sponsoring her tuition at Yale's School of Medicine. Which Elizabeth quickly found to cost a pretty penny. But to have Sophia *close* to her made the shackles of hefty tuition worth it.

Sophia pinned her brunette hair in a bun and wore a red scrub over her olive-tanned skin. Elizabeth stared blankly at her for a few moments. Sophia's skin seemed to glow under the sun. Elizabeth couldn't help but feel mesmerized by her beauty. Sophia would never wilt. Never.

Elizabeth quickly remembered the withering roses as she pointed her pale, wrinkled hand at them. "The roses, why are they dying? I thought we watered them yesterday, for goodness's sake. And the bloody sun's out. By all means, they should be lively! I knew you shouldn't have bought them from those *charlatans* at the gardening shop."

Sophia let out a soft chuckle as she approached the roses, inspecting them. After a few moments, she turned to Elizabeth with a confused smile. "I don't know why the roses are dying. I'm not a gardener. I'm a nurse, Dr. Ainsley. But if my botany class taught me anything, it's checking for aphids. And this pot is full of those little bugs."

"Oh—enough of the formalities, Sophia. You don't need to call me Doctor Ainsley. This isn't an interview. It's just 'Liz.' Is that understood? Now, you'll need to go back to that circus of a plant sanctuary and get some pesticides first thing tomorrow morning. Or lest this home be confused for a cemetery. Go on inside and finish reading what I gave you. I'll be there in a minute," she sighed.

Sophia stood silently for a moment. "Right," she said, hurrying back inside the home.

As she did, Elizabeth turned back to the rotting porch. The sweet melody of the birds had stopped, and she could only hear the harsh creaks of her wooden home. She looked around and spotted cracks in the panels and cobwebs growing on the walls. It was no Boston penthouse.

How did I get here?

Just years before, she had been leading the country, fighting for her revolutionary saving grace for criminal theory. She thought she saved the country with the Safety First Act, but she gave them a weapon. One they didn't fully comprehend. *And now,* she thought, *it's come back to bite me on the butt.* Maybe this was her punishment for everything she did in her past. For destroying everyone close to her and the only ones she's ever loved. But nothing would compare to the pain she felt for the worst thing she'd ever done. Not even self-induced memory repression techniques could make it go away. Sometimes, in her dreams, her mind would force her to relive it—just to taunt her.

Elizabeth rubbed her finger against the dusty armchair. "I hate this house," she muttered. It was empty. Even though she'd occupied its intimate walls, there was something hollow about the house, like it was a husk of something once livelier. Now she feared she was a ghost living in the house's memory.

Elizabeth sagged into her rocking chair. She was empty. There was nothing left for her. The once vibrant and bustling life she had in Boston now seemed like a distant memory. But that Elizabeth was someone else—a caring, smart woman and one of the most distinguished psychologists and psychiatrists of her decade. But now she lost everything: her reputation, her career, and her beloved family. And she was trapped in a cage of her own creation.

Sophia needed to be more than her. Elizabeth was determined to have her carry on her legacy.

Elizabeth's eyes flitted to a spider crawling on its web in the corner. No, she hadn't lost everything yet. She still had her ambition—her work.

As she let out a sigh, the familiar sound of her cell phone chimed in her pocket. Disgruntled at the interruption, she reached into her pocket, pulled out the phone, and noticed the missed voicemail. Elizabeth immediately noticed it was from that same number that'd been calling her repeatedly for the past month. She furrowed her brow in annoyance as she played the voicemail.

"Hello, Dr. Ainsley. This is Detective Amelia Mayman from the Haddam Police Department, reaching out *again* to see if you've hopefully changed your mind. I know you're probably tired of getting these calls, and I won't drive down to your residence because, well, you refused to open the door last time. I would really appreciate your help in furthering our investigation into your ex-fiancé, Frank Sallow. We believe he is responsible for a series of narco-trafficking acts happening across the East Coast. I'm sure you're familiar with it. It's hard to not hear the name *Raven* on the streets these days. Please call me back as soon as you can so we can discuss this matter further. Take care, Doctor."

Elizabeth glared at the screen. *Frank Sallow*, the name echoed in her mind. It made her squeeze the phone in her hand with rage. Whatever happened to him, she didn't care. *And if the police are trailing behind him,* Elizabeth thought, *that's fortunate for me.* A few seconds later, she deleted the voicemail from her phone. Enough was enough of Amelia's futile attempts at cooperation. All that she needed to know was that Frank was a liability, and Elizabeth wouldn't risk being with him any longer.

She sighed as she stood up from her chair, sliding her phone back into her pocket. She'd almost forgotten about Sophia inside. Taking one last look at the withering roses, she stepped inside the dusty cottage. Inside, she hurried past the cluttered foyer and into the spacious living room. A large sofa where Sophia was reading pressed against a large window overlooking the forest. Elizabeth thought she looked too comfortable lying there. A large, heavy rug of a beautiful mandala stretched across the hardwood floors. Scattered around the floors of the living room were piles of folders and old medical charts from when she was still in the field.

Sophia lifted her head from the sofa. "I was just finishing up."

"Never mind that right now, Sophia. Guess who just rang my phone again—it seems my attempts to ignore her aren't being well understood."

Sophia sat up, this time surprised. "That detective called you again? Amelia? What did you say to her this time?"

"Nothing, of course. I might have to destroy my phone if this persists. Let's see how she tries to contact me then." Elizabeth paused for a moment. "Anyway, let us continue our earlier discussion." Elizabeth bent over and picked up a pile of readings filled with different colored annotations and bookmarks sticking up. It was a collection of essays on medical ethics she had previously written in her earlier years.

As she stared at them, she shot a quick glance at Sophia, who sat flipping through a copy of its pages. Elizabeth pondered for a moment as she watched her. *I wonder,* she thought, peering at her with an intrigued eye.

"Um—right." She started skimming through her notes. "Suppose you face a patient who discloses using illicit drugs, and you must decide how to proceed with that information. What would you do?"

Sophia quickly scattered through the endless piles of notes, her hands grabbing any paper she saw and skimming through it. She tried to form an answer, except nothing she said made sense to Elizabeth among the quick breaths and mutters.

"I can't find this prompt in our notes. I'm looking everywhere. Are you sure we've gone over this, Doctor—"

"Liz. How many times must I repeat myself? And this is simply a test of your morality and ethics."

"Right." She paused for a moment, taking a deep breath. "Well, if a patient disclosed to me they were using illegal drugs, I would have to weigh the potential of the doctor-patient privilege against my obligation to report illegal activity to the police. But I'd still treat them just like another patient." Sophia's eyes flickered with uncertainty.

Within an instant, Elizabeth could tell she was unsure about her own answer. And the thought of Sophia being unsure or not knowing the answer made her frown slip on her face. Because she knew, the moment you don't believe yourself, everyone knows you're lying. "But what if you found out that one of your patients was a drug dealer or involved in something *dangerous?* Would you still treat them the same way, or does your moral scale weigh to reporting the police?"

Sophia stared at her with a confused and almost offended expression. "What're you asking me, Elizabeth? What's made you want to talk about this suddenly?"

But right as Elizabeth was going to answer, a familiar black car pulled up outside her window. And immediately, she lost track of all previous thoughts. *The damned car,* she thought.

Rage pulsed through her body. Her bony hands flared white as she squeezed them.

Elizabeth's ex-fiancé stood outside. *Frank Sallow.*

25

ELIZABETH

JULY 2

ELIZABETH SHOT A DETESTING glare at Frank as he stepped out of his car with a cigarette between his hairy fingers. "Oh—absolutely not!"

"What is it? Should I come with you?" Sophia turned her head with concern.

"No, don't bother yourself, dear. I'll take care of this *bastard* myself." She stomped outside toward him, her tightened fists rocking by her side, glaring at Frank, his black curled hair sat on his palpable face. The face of a coward who ran from his military services during the Vietnam War and who abandoned their relationship. He had made it clear their love was a hoax all their years together.And as he came closer into view, she felt her regrettable heartache once again. Something she promised herself would never happen again.

He would never hurt her again.

"You imbecile! How dare you come back here!" She grabbed a handful of dry leaves and twigs on her lawn and chucked it at him, hoping his new expensive blue coat would feel half the pain she did.

Frank quickly dodged her attack, amused. "Listen to me. Just—listen to me! I didn't come here to argue, Liz. I don't wanna fight."

"Don't you dare call me that." She trembled with rage. "Leave. Leave right now! Did you know that bloody policewoman has been blasting my ear, begging me to help arrest you? What's to say I don't call her back right now to tell her I've found her prize, and we can end this once and for all."

"Ainsley, come on! You know why I had to do it. This is all one big game. The police are playing it like a chessboard. They had me cornered, and the only way I could slip out was to—"

"Sacrifice your queen," she finished, swallowing her frustration.

Frank took a deep breath. "Look. I really am sorry I had thrown your name under the bus like that last time. But listen, I want to *change* the game so that way the police would suspect neither of us of anything."

"I nearly got arrested because of your selfish idiocy! The police almost caught on to everything you and I have been up to in this godforsaken town."

Frank pressed the cigarette to his lips for a few moments before exhaling a cloud of smoke. "I know Ainsley. But this time, *it's* big." He leaned closer to her ear. "It's two hundred fifty thousand dollars just for setting up a new network through Hartford."

She pressed him away as she smoldered at him with resentment. She admitted it was an enormous opportunity to make money, but the last thing she ever wanted was to spend another second with him. "Why, in God's name, do you think I would want to work with you anymore? You've done nothing but screw me over time after time. I should never have let you into my *business.* You were better off not knowing anything. I should have had you killed after I found out about your impetuous affair, Frank."

He sneered at her. "Is that a threat? You need this money, and you know it."

"I need nothing from you, and I want no part in your new dealings. Be lucky I don't hand you straight over to the police."

Frank immediately pressed his face closer to hers. Unfortunately, he had aged finer than she had, something she'd secretly envied. But she kept her eyes glaring at him so he could know she reveled in her own hatred toward him.

"No," he started. "Be grateful. *I* don't hand you to the police. Let's not forget who's the great mastermind in all of this. They're not looking for an accomplice as much as they're looking for The Raven."

Elizabeth stared at him for a few moments at his sharp face. He always knew the words to light her on fire. And they did. Rage beat at her heart like a storming fire. And she wanted to unleash it on him so that it might consume him and swallow them both together. But she didn't.

"Go," she spat. It was the only word that she could conjure.

Frank rolled his eyes for the last time as he cursed her under his breath. "You'll need me eventually, bitch."

She watched him snuff the cigarette on the ground with his foot, get in his car, and drive off. And as she watched him, she hoped that in some tragic event, he'd get distracted while driving and crash into a tree. Mother Nature was the best killer, she thought.

Even after he left, her heart still raced. She couldn't believe he had the nerve to appear unannounced after everything that had happened. But it had only made one thing clear—that she needed a drink.

As she made her back, her phone rang in her pocket once again. Once again annoyed, Elizabeth grabbed the ringing phone and held it toward her ear.

Petrified in silence, she listened carefully to her caller.

"So, this is what it's come down to then. I see," Elizabeth started. "Do what you have to do, then." Elizabeth slid the phone back into her pocket, her face flushed. The greatest successes require the toughest sacrifices, and she made the most difficult one yet. But she couldn't think about anyone else in East Haddam. Survivability was for the smartest.

Elizabeth made her back into her home, where the clutter of medical essays and charts waited for her. But then she noticed Sophia, who was now dressed in her usual jeans and sweater, and she was packing her bag, preparing to leave. But it was too early. She usually stayed a few more hours.

But before she could inquire further, Sophia had already spoken.

Sophia looked up while she gathered her papers neatly. "What did he want?"

"Sex, of course. He's a lonely man. What more was there to expect?"

Sophia crossed her arms, her upper lip curling with disdain. "Jesus, what a pervert. I hope he knows there are underground clubs for that. You're so much better off without him, Doctor—I mean, Liz."

"Oh, I quite know that Sophia, my dear. No one will be impressed with the extra-small penis of that charlatan," she said, both chuckling at the remark. "Where are you off to in such a hurry? It's only noon."

"I just got off the phone with my mom. She needs to go visit her in town while I'm here. She says it's urgent. But then again, I've known her long enough to know sometimes she says that just to get me away from all this."

Elizabeth stared blankly at her for a few moments. "Well—how touching of her. You're free to leave right now. We can finish our discussion next time. Don't let a regretful old woman like me stop you from seeing her."

Sophia chuckled for a moment. "You're too hard on yourself. Also, I don't mean to nag you like this, but the university just emailed me again about the late tuition payment. It's past due now. Are you paying for it soon?"

She let a small smile slip on her face, but it strained with disappointment. "Oh! Thank you for reminding me. I will do that immediately. Well, when you're old like me, you notice all the cracks in the mirror that you've never seen before."

As Sophia finished packing her back, she gave Elizabeth a small hug and left the cottage. And as she did, the smile quickly faded from Elizabeth's face.

How dare she smile in front of Sophia after what she'd just done. All these lies to her face. She didn't exactly have the money to make the payments to the university anymore. But she could never tell Sophia. It would break her heart, and then she'd leave her for someone else.

Elizabeth's mind was on fire. But she didn't want to think about it, she couldn't. After everything that had happened so far today, she couldn't take one more haunting regret inflaming her. She hurried to her kitchen, where she threw open different cabinets and drawers. The entire room seemed to spin around her. Finally, she grabbed a bottle of vodka and quickly poured it into a glass. But she couldn't hold it still as she spilled it onto the counter and floor, trying to steady it into her glass.

She held the glass to her lips, smelling its bitter odor, and downed it. And as she did, she collapsed to the floor in tears, but she couldn't stop drinking because if she did, the picture would be more vivid in her head.

Elizabeth hid her wet eyes with her hand.

"I'm so sorry, Sophia," she cried. "I'm so sorry for what I've done to you."

26

LUKAS

JULY 2

LUKAS FOLLOWED THE FORK in the road and drove up a winding gravel road. A road was so well hidden that Lukas had driven past it countless times without noticing when he used to drive to Rebecca's cabin. The thick canopy of pine trees obscured the view, and only the faintest hint of a dirt path was visible from the main road. He never imagined it would lead to Bill's ranch.

As he drove through, the towering trees of the East Haddam forest loomed overhead, their branches reaching out like gnarled fingers trying to scratch his car. The dense foliage cast long shadows across the road, and the only sound was the crunching of gravel as he drove down the path.

He found it odd that he lived so far away from town. Bill must've liked to stay hidden as well. People think they're safe behind locked doors and hiding in the woods. But they forget, I was once just like them, Lukas thought. Percy and Rebecca thought they were safe.

The glaring sun blazed through his car windshield and blinded Lukas's eyes as he continued down the road, his car shaking from the rough path. With his hand blocking out the blinding light over his eyes, he could make out the silhouette of a small house nearing in the distance. It was small, almost like a shack with fences wrapping around it.

After a few seconds, the sight became clear as he approached the house and parked at the entrance. There sat a one-story ranch home, which appeared almost abandoned. Its windows were cracked with missing panes, and a few shingles were loose or missing. Fences, made of aged wood and rusted wire, wrapped around the small house and enclosed a small front yard. The front yard was sparse, with patches of dirt and weeds spreading around like a parasite. As Lukas parked his car, he couldn't help but notice the rusted mailbox by the road, which read *Bill Meyer* in faded red letters. Lukas thought for a moment he must've been at the wrong house until he saw a familiar man sitting on a haystack.

Bill had been focusing closely, holding something in his hands. But Lukas couldn't make out what it was from inside his car. As he stepped out, Bill looked up and threw him a welcoming smirk. Whatever it was he knew about The Raven, Lukas had to know.

As he approached Bill, the sound of cracking twigs and crunch of rocks filled the air. "What's that you got there in your hand?"

Bill placed a rag down, which had spots of red and brown stains, and held a small hunting knife up. "Just cleaning the blood off. It has to be done, or the blade will rust."

"You kill?"

"I hunt," Bill corrected. "It's not the same. Killing is for savages, hunting is for survivors. And you know in here, you have to survive."

Lukas watched him carefully rub the teeth of the knife with the rag until it shined new again. He couldn't even tell that it had cut through the flesh of an animal, but maybe that wasn't such a bad thing.

"That's a nice knife you have. How'd you get it? The town's not allowed to sell us weapons."

Bill paused for a moment and looked up, amused, his face shining from oil and sweat. "There's always a crack in the system. It's just a matter of finding them and exploiting them. Let me show you," he said as he stood up.

Setting the hunting knife on the haystack, Bill waved Lukas over as he showed him toward a large shed behind his house. As he did with the heat beating down his back, something caught Lukas's eye in the distance. A large rotting wooden barn that sat abandoned near the edge of the forest was a sore sight compared to the greenery behind it. The type of place that could hide the darkest of deeds.

Lukas stopped. "What's that over there?"

"Oh, it's part of the property. It's just an old barn, but I don't use it much except for storage," Bill said.

"What kind of storage?"

"Grain." Lukas felt Bill's hand on his back as he nudged him forward. "But over here, my friend, I think you'll like a lot more."

Bill led him to the shed, almost like a tiny house that someone could live in. But Lukas quickly noticed the padlock hanging from the door of the shed. Whatever was inside clearly must've been valuable as he watched Bill hurry to the door, spinning the dial to unlock it.

"Are you scared of someone breaking in?" Lukas asked.

He turned his head toward Bill and noticed that Bill's face had become serious, almost as if he felt threatened by the question. "There are valuables in here. I can't let them get out. Now, come inside quickly."

Lukas hesitated for a moment but followed him inside the shed after reminding himself that Bill was his friend and just wanted to help him. Stepping inside the room of shadows, it stank of a dampness that filled the shed, and it was much warmer than it had been outside. Almost like stepping into an oven. Bill brushed past his body toward the center of the pitch blackness, and after a few moments, there was a loud flicker when the room illuminated in light.

Lukas stood, amazed at the sight. He'd seen nothing like it before and couldn't believe such a thing existed in some place like East Haddam. There before him stood a vast array of shelves filled with different weapons. Bill had it all: guns, knives, traps, bows, axes, along with many tools for hunting. They were specifically designed to kill animals, but Lukas thought a person was no different from an animal. It's hunting, after all. And he watched Bill place the large hunting knife he had been cleaning back on the shelf next to the others like a trophy he was displaying.

"Now I bet you're looking around my fancy collection and wondering where I got all this shit." Bill paused for a moment. "Tell me, Lukas, do you know the name Elizabeth Ainsley?"

Lukas flashed his eyes toward Bill at the sound of the familiar name.

It couldn't be, he thought. *Elizabeth.*

The name was like a lighter to his past, and once it flickered, it all caught on fire. In his mind, he was there again, reliving it again. Lukas could feel the hot smoke blowing in his face the night his father died, and as he looked at his hands, they were drenched in thick, scorching blood. And when he turned his head, he saw Elizabeth in the corner of the fiery room whispering with a patronizing smile, "I know you didn't mean to do it."

But he quickly thought about Bill's questions again, pulling himself out of that night and into the now. He hadn't realized his mouth was open, about to breathe the answer, Bill patiently waiting for his response.

"No." Lukas's shoulders hunched.

"Well, she was one of the most prestigious psychiatrists on the East Coast. It was her research that created these messed-up *correctional cities,* or whatever they're calling cages these days, but it came back to bite her on the ass." He chuckled for a moment. "Because now she's locked in her own creation, too."

Lukas's heart raced. "Where?"

"East Haddam Correctional City. And that's not even the best part about all of this. She's set up one of the biggest drug networks here. That's how I could get all this." Bill turned to his proud collection behind him. "It's all from secret dealings paid with the commissions. The government thinks they own this town, but they're wrong. It's her. She's The Raven of East Haddam. No doubt she's behind the murder of that girl, Rebecca."

Lukas watched Bill's eyes as he finished and thought maybe he was trying to bait him into admitting he had murdered Rebecca. Maybe Bill already knew—no, he wouldn't. And if he did, he'd be naïve to bring Lukas into a shed full of weapons. Within a second, Lukas could leap forward, grab the nearest sharp or heavy object, and smash Bill's face in until it was nothing but spilled brains and thick blood—no longer a person, just an animal. The image made a smirk slip on his face, but he watched Bill turn to a small cabinet in the corner and pull a dusty object out.

"What about the Recluse Killer? I thought *they* murdered Rebecca."

"Eh—it's all a load of bullshit. I mean, really, now there's someone else we have to worry about here? No, my money's still on that crazy psycho bitch Elizabeth. That girl must've messed up real bad to get killed like that. But here." Bill held out his hand. It was a small pistol, and it must've been as old as Bill was because the design was outdated, with its long, narrow barrel and metal finishes. Despite that, it was a gun, and Bill was handing it right to him. "Just in case that murderer tries to come after you, you can blow their head off with this. Just aim and shoot."

Lukas stared blankly at him for a few moments. "Why are you doing this? You don't know me well enough to trust me with a gun."

"You have that look in your eyes. I saw it when I first saw you storming out of that office. Time and time again, people have screwed you over. You've been beaten into a corner with nowhere to go. And if that monster comes after you, you'll be killed because you've never protected yourself." He paused for a moment. "I know how to recognize a desperate soul."

They stared at each other in silence, the gun hanging by Lukas's side. "Desperate souls," he repeated beneath his breath. And as he did, Rebecca's face faded into his mind. Lukas's fingers wrapped tighter around the cold pistol. He imagined himself raising the gun and pointing it directly between Bill's eyes, and they would widen with the realization of what Bill had just done. But before he could say anything, Lukas would pull the trigger and watch Bill's head blow up and taint his hunting collection with his blood.

But the fantasy was quickly interrupted when Bill cleared his throat. "Let me give you what you came here for: your medication. I have a crate here filled with small bags of OxyContin. I'm supposed to sell them—for the doctor, of course. But this one's on the house for you, my friend," he said.

Lukas watched Bill pull a blue tarp off a large wooden crate in the corner. "Right—thank you."

Propping open the crate, Bill pulled out a small bag filled with white powder. Lukas's heart raced with anticipation. He hadn't felt its sweet relief in weeks. His head throbbed with pain more than ever as Bill handed him the bag.

And his head pounded like a drum as he held it and pounded—the room was pounding.

It wasn't his head.

The shed was pounding with a low hum from somewhere in the room. Lukas's head spun, trying to find where it was coming from. But then he felt Bill's hand on his shoulder.

"It's the animals. I kept some chickens that came with the property. They're great for eggs and obviously meat," he said.

But as Bill continued to explain how unruly and wild his chickens were, Lukas's mind wandered. Bill's voice drowned into a small buzz like he wasn't even there anymore. He couldn't throw his mind off the fact Elizabeth Ainsley had been living in East Haddam the entire time. It reignited a burning desire for revenge inside him.

There he was again in the room, face-to-face with that woman who ruined his life. And now, standing in this shed filled with weapons, Lukas couldn't help but entertain the idea of returning the pain to her—making her feel his pain.

As the pounding sound persisted in the background, Lukas's grip on the bag of OxyContin tightened. He could feel the rush of anger and determination coursing through his veins, overpowering any sense of rational thought in his mind. The need to hurt Dr. Ainsley, to make her pay for the suffering he had endured, consumed him.

And finally he realized Elizabeth was the animal, and Lukas was the hunter.

27

LUKAS

JULY 2

LUKAS LEFT BILL'S SHED, his mind consumed with the sick satisfaction that would come from making the doctor suffer. The weight of the bag of OxyContin and pistol clutched tightly in his hand. He decided it would be best to stash it in the jockey box of his car until he needed it; Bill was more useful than he thought.

As he made his way back to Dimitri's dismal apartments, the evening quickly approached, the air becoming heavier. Lukas had lost track of time with Bill. With the window down, the car engine pounded in his ears, each second leading him back home. But the air turned bitter as he approached the street, and when he turned the last corner and caught sight of the New Horizon Apartments, his heart stopped.

The tall building was burning down.

Flames burst from every window in the building like a fiery monster consuming every brick and person inside. The chaotic scene cast an eerie orange glow in the sky, panic swarming around the area. Ambulances, firetrucks, and police cars were all stationed around the building. Lukas rushed from his car to the nightmarish scene.

And as he pressed through swarms of crowds, a woman roughly bumped into him before squeezing past him. Lukas turned to see her and was taken aback by the sight of Dimitri's daughter, Karina. They stared blankly at each other for a few moments. Her face was pale with horror, her eyes trembling as she saw him. But before he could say anything, she continued rushing through the crowd.

The air burned his skin as he pushed through toward the building, and the screaming of different voices and sirens rang in his ears and made his head violently pound. The acrid smoke that filled the skies made his eyes water and suffocated his lungs.

Now trying to cover his mouth with his arm, he watched firefighters from Haddam finally swarm the area, their hoses spraying water from every direction, trying to quench the monstrous flames. But the smoke continued to rise into the sky, casting a blackened red shadow over East Haddam, and it seemed destined that the acrid smoke and ash would suffocate the entire town.

If it did, the rest of the country would say, "Rightfully so."

"We have a body!" a fireman shouted.

The ambulance paramedics immediately hurried to the building, rolling a stretcher while the Haddam Police Department tried to clear everyone back, but Lukas needed to see. Who was it? The question caught his mind on fire. He pushed through other people toward the front, trying to get a better view of who had died. And as he finally did, he saw the blistered body on the stretcher rolling toward the ambulance.

It was a woman, a neighbor he had rarely spoken to who lived on the same floor he did, and she always seemed to have visitors, which he sometimes found odd because she never left her apartment.

But then another woman leaped from the crowd, screaming in agony at the sight of the dead woman. She sprinted toward the stretcher crying, trying to cradle the woman's face while the paramedics tried to pull her away.

And when the screaming woman turned her face for the fire to cast its glow on her, Lukas's face widened with shock, and his heart dropped.

It was Sophia. And she was screaming and crying like a newborn at the sight of the dead woman. Her smiling face at the bar flashed through Lukas's mind. And how they fucked that night before he slipped out of her sheets, disappearing into the night. But now, her violent shrills filled the air.

It took the firefighters about twenty minutes to quench the devouring flames, but the thick smoke still hung in the sky like a shadow. By then, the crowds had settled, and the ambulances rushed back to the hospital. But the police cars and officers had remained investigating the scene.

Sitting on the street curb, Lukas had nowhere to go now. It was all gone. He reeked of smoke, and his skin stained with ash and grime. He turned his head back to the New Horizon Apartments, where he saw the upper half of the building burnt down or charred. A memory of what once was a haven for people like him, for people who had nowhere else to go. A place to survive.

Bill was right. The world beat him into a corner with nowhere to go. Fire seemed to burn down everything in life. Or maybe he was the conductor. Fire burned because of him; everything burned at his touch. Either way, he hated himself because of it—if his life was on fire, there was no way to put out the flames.

I know what you did. The words seethed in his mind.

Did they *start the fire?* he thought. *Was it meant to kill me?*

Lukas held his breath at the thought. Maybe this was their way of sending a threat because they knew something about him that no one else did. Something that would ruin him. Or maybe it was a warning for something that was coming. The unshakeable thought of both gnawed at him.

But then he looked up and caught the somber eyes of a familiar face.

Dimitri was across the street next to a police car, his clothes and skin stained with ash, his eyes red. They stared at each other for a few moments before Dimitri began making his way over to him. For some inexplicable reason, Lukas felt an unfamiliar comfort in seeing him in the aftermath.

And at the moment their eyes met, Lukas felt an unspoken connection. It was a shared understanding of the darkness that consumed them both. And there was truth in his eyes, words that could not be uttered of their timely friendship. Dimitri had been there for him first when Lukas got thrown into East Haddam, and he knew the best spots for a drink. The kind memory made Lukas grin.

But before Dimitri could make it to him, a police car pulled up on the side of Lukas.

He watched two officers step out and approach him: a tall, pale man with a brown mustache and a shorter woman who looked disgruntled to see him. "Are you Lukas Retter?" the man asked.

Lukas hesitated for a moment, daring not to respond. Either way, he'd have to grapple with the consequences of his response. "What is this?" he replied.

"Mr. Retter, we're with the Haddam Police Department. We're taking you in to answer some questions about the events leading up to tonight. It's time you talk."

28

LUKAS

MANY YEARS AGO

YEARS SLIPPED LIKE DUST down an hourglass. Lukas's life was now spent in The Room; no longer a boy, but not a man either. What were once innocent children were now war machines, killers, and every training and day spent in the facility hidden from the world made them into savages.

As the days turned into weeks and weeks into years, Lukas couldn't recognize the others anymore. Over half of them were now gone or killed by each other. Though their faces matured, their minds sharpened into something deadly. Almost everyone had.

Everyone except Lukas.

He wasn't a killer. Not even a little, not even at all. Out of everyone, he struggled to do what was asked of him by Director Miller because they were terrible, evil things.

Lukas had once been asked to burn a boy's skin with a lighter who was being punished for disrespecting the director. He tied the boy down and made everyone take turns and burn his skin until it seared into his bone. And they had all done it without question, including Erica, who had a sick satisfaction at seeing the boy shrilling in pain.

But Lukas wouldn't. As they waited in silence, waiting for Lukas to burn the boy too, he stood frozen. His hands trembled with the lighter, refusing to obey the commands that echoed in silence. And as the others watched, bored, their eyes gleamed with an insatiable hunger, their thirst for blood unquenchable.

Director Miller waved his hand from the shrouded corner of the room, where no light would touch. He was unamused by Lukas's rebelliousness and saw only one thing fit to do to him. He untied the tortured boy and ordered him to burn Lukas until he bled so that he would remember to always be a good boy.

And Lukas thought he was a *good* boy. Just not the type of good the director meant. He still stood by his mother's words, "Violence is never okay." But still, after all those years, he found one exception to that rule: spiders. Spiders were the only creatures that should be killed. And that boy wasn't a spider.

But there was still one thing that troubled his mind. While he lay on his bed rubbing his finger up and down the bumps of his ribcage, he felt the hot air humming from the vent in the corner of his cell. It was the same cycle: the guards would take someone from their cell, and then, a few minutes later, the heat would start. He had an unpleasant idea about why the hot air was blowing, but that would make the nightmare worse.

Then again, maybe it wasn't such a terrible thing. At least if they were dead, they wouldn't have to endure another day hidden from the world. If it was better to be dead or to be a prisoner, he wasn't sure.

But it was now day one-thousand-something, and it was the day Lukas had been dreading, but he wasn't sure how long. Tracking time was like trying to catch smoke in your hands. But the weight of the day and the impending dread consumed his mind.

Shortly after, a guard led from his cell Lukas down the caving hallways that seemed to suffocate them. The air was always thin and bitter, like walking through a cemetery. He followed the man through the eerie dark corridor, the rough cuts of cold stone scratching Lukas's feet as he anxiously followed until they reached The Room.

And like last time, they shoved Lukas into the room with no warning, like he was being fed to a monstrous beast for a live spectacle.

The dim light of The Room flickered as Lukas stood frozen inside, the light casting an eerie shadow across the walls where Director Miller emerged from the shrouded corner. Lukas's heart skipped a beat at the sight of his cold, scratchy face, and it haunted him knowing the director held their fate in his hands. There was no escape from the clutches of this barbaric facility, this prison, and Lukas knew if he dared to disobey, he would be met with a steep price.

His head spun around, looking for his sister, Erica, and he glimpsed her at the opposite end of the room. Even as she had grown older, her hair remained matted, and her black eyes continued to pierce him like no other. He wondered if there was still a girl behind those black impenetrable orbs or if she'd been lost to her newfound bloodlust.

Erica was the most feared now. She'd killed more of their peers than anyone else had, and each time, she did it without regret, without showing a glint of mercy. Lukas remembered she had crushed the nails of a girl without hesitation, with a smile. It was that same sick satisfaction Erica had killing their father.

Lukas stared longingly at her, trying to convince himself that she wasn't his sister, just a different version of her.

But she wasn't. She was a spider.

Finally, a command dripped from Director Miller's lips, his voice cold and devoid of mercy. "Lukas, Erica. Brother and sister. You will fight with each other today. And only one of you will live on today. No weapons will be allowed except for your hands." His eyes gleamed with a twisted delight, savoring the thought of pitting the two kids against each other.

And Lukas hated it. His eyes shifted back to Erica, who was twisted by the darkness that enveloped their cells and the others because, in this hell, there was no more room for friendship—only survival.

"Erica," he mouthed.

Erica launched forward without a second thought, like a predator.

Lukas trembled as he stood paralyzed.

He was met with a heavy blow in his stomach that knocked him to the floor. Blow after blow was slammed onto his chest, stomach, and head. Lukas wasn't quick enough to defend each barraging strike.

Erica was on top of him. Somehow, she was heavier than she appeared for a frail girl.

Lukas tried throwing her off, but it was no use. Her knees were pinning Lukas's arms to the floor. She'd made up her mind. Lukas was the one who would be killed.

His body reverberated with agonizing pain. There wasn't a glint of remorse from Erica.

Blood dripped down his nose and mouth as her fists continued to smash them. She ignored his shrieks of pain. With his arms pinned down, there was only one thing he could think of to escape.

Erica punched his mouth. But he trapped her hand with his mouth and bit down to the bone. She tried pulling her hand away, beating his head until he let go, but he wouldn't. His teeth sank deeper into her hand as she squealed in anguish.

The metallic tang of blood filled his mouth as he crunched onto her hand. Pain continued to radiate throughout his body, but he refused to let go. He refused to be killed without a fight.

As his teeth dug deeper into Erica's flesh, she wailed in pain, her cries echoing in the room. She had no choice but to fall back away from him, which freed his arms and legs.

And the second she was vulnerable, Lukas threw himself on her, knocking them both to the cold floor. This time, Lukas was on top of her. She groaned in pain, trying to kick him off, but Lukas was older and bigger than her, and there was only one thing pounding in his mind.

To kill her.

Erica had ruined his life. She was better off dead.

The suppressed hate flooded through his veins and made him lose control of himself. Without thinking, Lukas gripped Erica's head with both hands and began slamming her head against the floor. She wasn't his sister anymore, just a stranger, a killer.

She shrilled in agony as he continued slamming her head. "Lukas, stop!" she begged. But she was already dead to him.

His heart raced faster than ever, feeling her head rattle in his hands. Just a few more, and she would be dead. But before he could, a guard pulled Lukas away from her. He tried freeing himself to finish the job. The guard's arms were too heavy.

"Enough," Director Miller started. "I think you've made your point, Lukas. Take her away," he said.

Lukas glared furiously at the director, his arms still throbbing with adrenalin. "You said one of us had to die! And now you're saving her?"

"Have I not done the same for you? That's why you're still here. Do not disappoint me again, or you *will* regret it," he spat.

Later that night, darkness enveloped their cells once more, the dim buzzing orange light casting a feeble light. Lukas continued to lie in bed, thinking about nothing. He lay like a corpse with no life left within him. He continued to replay the moment of smashing Erica's head against the floor because it had felt so great to see her suffer. So she could have felt an ounce of pain he had felt in his life. It was a terrible thought, he knew, but he wished he could've finished the job as the director instructed him to. It was what she deserved because she wasn't his sister anymore. Just a shadow of who she once was.

And as he lay still on his bed, he heard the faint groans through the wall from Erica. The soft noise painted a sick smile on his face, knowing she was suffering.

But then his stomach ravaged again, like it had been for the past few days. There hadn't been food in the dog bowl for a few days now, and the only thing keeping him alive was the repugnant water in the toilet bowl. Anytime he drank out of it, his face with squirm in disgust, and he'd gag before sometimes throwing up. But he did what he had to survive—just like everyone else. Because that's what a prisoner is, a survivor.

Crawling to the dog bowl, looking for scraps, he heard steps in the distance growing louder. He pressed his ear against the wall, trying to listen, and wondered if they might take someone else. His skin tingled at the thought of the hot air from the vent touching him. Sometimes, the humming would be like a voice, a child's voice. And the haunting sound always kept him up at night.

The steps seemed to stop in front of his door, and Lukas's heart sank. They'd finally come for him, and they were going to burn him just like they did the others. He sat on the floor, paralyzed, staring at the door, waiting for it to open and take him away. And as he waited, his skin crawled like he was being pricked repeatedly, his breaths heavy. At his horror, the door opened, and Lukas felt a tear drip down his face as he accepted his fate.

But it wasn't his door that opened.

It was Erica's.

Lukas's face widened with shock as he hurried to the small hole in the wall. The buzzing white light from the narrow corridor crept into her room and cast two long shadows over her sleeping body. Lukas watched the two guards creep into her room.

"She's asleep," the guard said to the other.

"It doesn't matter. He said she's ready for *Phase Three*," the other said.

Confused about what they were talking about, he watched a guard creep up to her and carefully lift Erica out of her bed. She didn't wake. She was still unconscious in their arms. Lukas's heart beat faster than ever. He was sure this was the last time he would ever get to glance at her, but he saw something he hadn't seen before. The back of her scalp was still tainted with dry, dark blood, and his heart sank with guilt at what he had done to her. He didn't mean to hurt her. But then the guards carried Erica out of the cell and hopefully up from hell. And what was the guard talking about? He wondered. *Phase Three? What's Phase Three?* he thought.

And what's Phase One and Two...?

But the door remained open as they left. Thoughts of somehow breaking down the wall and running out excitedly swarmed his mind, but the impossible thought was quickly shut down. Another guard was carrying an unconscious boy in his arms as he entered the room and laid him on Erica's bed.

A new boy. This was strange. There had been no one new before.

Lukas watched the guard leave the room and shut the door, locking the boy in his new nightmare. And there was something else strange tonight: the vents didn't hum, there was no heat. So Lukas wondered, what was *Phase Three*?

29

LUKAS

JULY 2

ONE MORE TIME, LUKAS went through the events in his mind.

On the day she was murdered, he went to Rebecca's cabin after work. She said she was on edge lately talking about someone stalking her. He left her cabin a few hours later, went to the Red Head pub, and met up with Mateo for a drink. Later that night, he discovered someone murdered her on the corner TV in the bar. He was distraught at the news because he did not know who would do that to her. To his beautiful Rebecca. His innocent Rebecca. His perfect Rebecca.

Lukas's eyes fixed on his reflection on the glass pane in front of him, rubbing his hands together on the metallic table, trying to subdue the sweat on them. The bitter taste of ash still lingered on his tongue in the aftermath of the vehement fire that had happened just hours ago. But the fact he hadn't properly been charged with any formal charges meant the police didn't have any concrete evidence against him.

Yet.

Maybe they found something. Maybe Rebecca rose from the dead and confessed the truth. But Lukas didn't see killing as a crime more than a passion or a hobby, and the euphoric feeling was an addictive high that he was now constantly craving. The warm rush of blood spewing from skin and the cries of pain that followed made his skin crawl with excitement. Even just sitting there, waiting in the interrogation room, the thought made his heart race with bloodlust in anticipation.

It must've been the effect of East Haddam. When the outside world started treating them like animals, Lukas started believing it, too—that they were unruly savages. But it wasn't until the police car drove him through Haddam on the way to the station that confirmed his suspicions.

The sun seemed to shine brighter in Haddam than it did its counterpart, and the residents walked the streets without fearing for their safety. As they drove past a park with a playground, there was a boy who watched them drive by, but there was something familiar about the pale boy. It was a haze to him, but he could tell from the stark connection they momentarily had that the boy had the same plagued childhood and that the boy also enjoyed killing spiders until, one day, he'd murder his Rebecca.

The door in the interrogation room swung open as Detective Amelia Mayman entered. Her eyes shot directly at him, glinting with snide. Her buttoned-down striped shirt was ironed impeccably, with not a wrinkle in sight, and the file she placed on the table was organized and had thorough annotations. And as she explained to him his rights, Lukas focused closer on her lips and how they curled with each spoken word and had such a force to them, almost as if they were trying to badger him for a confession.

But for what confession? he thought. He was innocent; he had done nothing wrong.

"Do you understand, Mr. Retter?"

The detective's question caught him off guard.

Lukas stared blankly at her for a few moments. She had been talking about something with attorneys and the jurisdiction of which something happened. He wasn't really sure, nor did he care. But he nodded in agreement.

There was only one thing he knew: tell as little as possible.

Amelia sat across from him. "It's a terrible thing what happened tonight, so my team and I are really trying to understand what caused the fire. You were one of the tenants, correct?"

Lukas studied Amelia's face. Her irritated jaw jutted forward as her patience shortened, and her thin brows pinched together.

Amelia was right. It was a terrible thing that happened that night. It was terrible she kept stalking him like a shadow, waiting for him to be at the wrong place at the wrong time. She was raining any sort of accusations on him, he was sure of it. "Yes. But why am I the only one here?"

"You're the only one that's also a person of interest in an open murder investigation."

"I did not murder Rebecca," Lukas spat.

Amelia stared at him for a few moments. "I didn't bring you in here tonight to talk about *that*. I'm only interested in what happened with the fire because right now, you could be looking at first-degree arson unless you tell us what happened. So, let's start from the beginning. Recount to me where you were today."

The last twenty-four hours had been surreal to him.

That morning, Lukas burned Rebecca's canoe in the forest before almost getting caught by the police. But someone in the apartments: Jake saw him. Then there was the note. Somebody knew what he had done. After work, he met Bill at his ranch, where he finally discovered the whereabouts of that narcissistic bitch Elizabeth. Then there was the fire and seeing Sophia shrill as she clutched at the clothed dead body. Seeing her in that dreadful state made him wish he leaped out from the crowd and held her tight in his arms to be her hero.

But of course, he couldn't say any of that.

Amelia's eye twitched as she waited for him to answer, and she must've known he was planning some answer, some lie. He opened his mouth, hesitating to hear what words might slip out and possibly be used against him.

"I was at work during the day, SuperShine," Lukas began, his voice calm. "After work, I went to grab a drink at a bar. And on my way back to my apartment, that's when I saw the fire. I was shocked," he said.

He watched her jot some notes on a clipboard, but for all he knew, she could be writing *guilty, guilty, guilty,* over and over again.

Lukas tried studying her expression for any hints of doubt or suspicion in his story. He couldn't afford to give away too much information, especially regarding his own involvement in Rebecca Waylow and Percy. He knew he had to keep those dark desires and secrets hidden, no matter how tempting it was to reveal them.

He thought about confessing and reveling in the glory of how easy it had been to murder and how incompetent Amelia and her entire department had been. But the game had barely just begun, and Lukas wasn't ready to stop the cat-and-mouse yet. No, he needed to show them how big of a threat he actually was—to defame the good name of the HPD and make a mockery of it.

Amelia continued asking him questions while she kept her stone personality with no emotion. She was impossible to read.

She asked Lukas about any potential vendettas someone would have against Dimitri, if there were any known gas or oil leaks in the building, if there had been any suspicious activity in the building. All of which he shook his head with the same calm expression. He was innocent, but the moment he stopped believing he was, she would sense his guilt with her piercing brown eyes.

But if Amelia were to question Jake, he might spill everything about everyone in that building. Lukas wasn't opposed to hurting a child as young as Jake, especially if he was going to say something he shouldn't.

Lukas watched Amelia turn a file toward him and open it, revealing a pile of photos of Rebecca's cabin, both inside and out. He scanned the bizarre photos in front of him, trying to interpret what Amelia was trying to show him.

She slid one photo toward him. It was a picture of Rebecca's canoe shed. Both canoes that used to hang from the ceiling were missing. Rebecca was proud of both of them. They were handcrafted and passed down from her father. Sometimes, she would swear she could hear her father whispering his love to her while she sailed down the river.

Lukas examined the photos closer. He knew what happened to one of them—it was now nothing but ashes of a distant memory. But the other canoe—he did not know what could've happened to it. Perhaps someone was getting closer than he thought to this case, and that was dangerous.

"Someone broke into Rebecca's shed the other night and stole a green maple canoe. Now, both are missing. Any idea on how that could've happened, Mr. Retter?" Amelia's brow twitched as she finished.

The walls in the room seemed to squeeze closer together as Lukas held his breath. He stared down at the photo for another moment, trying to catch some detail they missed that might explain the missing canoe, but he concluded it was no use.

He once again met Amelia's cold, impatient eyes, flickering with animosity. "No idea. I haven't been near that place since she died."

Lukas could feel the pouting annoyance Amelia was trying to hide with a forced grin. She wasn't getting anything from him. Once again, Amelia slid two more photos toward him, one of which made his heart leap. If Amelia had seen his eyes, she would've known of his guilt because they widened, but only for one vulnerable moment.

"What about them? Know anything about them?"

It was a picture of Percy, still healthy and alive. His athletic build and innocent smile must've made it easy to charm others, something Lukas envied. But that raging envy made it more satisfying at the fact he murdered Percy.

The other was a picture of a middle-aged woman. It was his neighbor, the dead woman from the fire. He'd always seen her skulking around the second floor of the apartments, muttering to herself. But the more he stared at her contemplating stoic expression, the familiar likeness grew. She looked like Sophia if she was much older and emotionally worn from the years—always tired and sad. They had the same olive skin, and their eyes were carved in the same shape, with their noses slim. It was Sophia's mother, no doubt about it.

"We have made Percy Romano a missing person." She pointed to his picture. "And Natalie Warren was killed in the fire just a couple of hours ago. Have you ever met either of them before?"

Lukas paused. It all made sense—the game Amelia was trying to play with him. *This was all for a confession.*

But she'd lost. She had nothing on him to prove anything.

Lukas examined her for a few moments, matching his expression with the frustrated disdain in her eyes. "I've never met either before," he lied.

30

LUKAS

JULY 12

THE FAUX BOURBON BURNED Lukas's throat as he drank. But mostly, it burned his pain. All those flammable memories of the last month caught on fire and withered away in his mind. Rebecca, Percy, the note-sender, the fire, it all burned to ashes.

For the last week and a half, he kept his head low since meeting with Amelia and leaving her frustrated with no leads. The police haven't made Percy's murder public yet, except for a futile missing person's advertisement. Maybe because the HPD thought Percy would one day turn up saying he was lost in the woods, or the police had been confused and that he wasn't missing at all. Lukas imagined it scared the police to publicly declare Percy another homicide case, as that would confirm their worst suspicions.

That there was a crawling nightmare in East Haddam—a serial killer. The so-called 'Recluse Killer.' It was a fitting name. After all, they were both deadly in the dark.

Lukas finally left his truck for the first time in several hours that day. He'd been sleeping in his truck while reconstruction and repairs were happening at the apartments. At first, the ripped driver's seat was uncomfortable to sleep in, but he quickly found how peaceful it was when he didn't have to listen to his neighbors argue or fuck through the walls anymore. The warm summer nights wrapped around him like an airy blanket as he lay on the seat.

But Lukas couldn't sleep. He hadn't for the last several nights. His mind could still feel Amelia's daunting eyes closing in on him.

Defeated by the worry of getting caught, he drove to the only place he felt safe.

So now there Lukas was in the only dive bar in East Haddam he knew: The Red Head, and it welcomed him like a familiar friend ready to numb his pain. With each shot he drank, he could feel the bitter air in the bar hugging him—whispering to keep drinking. And he did so. But he choked on the rancid air—a combination of tobacco, drugs, and alcohol.

It was well past midnight, too, but the soulful joy of R&B still filled the bar from all directions, and the drunk dancers took center stage, flailing their unsober arms, which appeared to be attempts at dancing. Still, their jubilance was infectious, and Lukas ached to be part of that blissful cloud so that he wouldn't have to worry about anything any longer than he had to.

Lukas watched some men attempt to pull a woman closer toward them, only to be shoved away. And there was a pair of women making out in the middle of the dance floor while other guys jeered at them. But they were lost in love, which made Lukas squeeze the glass in his hand tighter with envy.

He took another shot, and as he did, two words appeared in his mind. *Fuck Amelia.*

Lukas made his way to the center of the room, feeling the bass of the music vibrate his body, the strobing lights shining from all corners of the ceiling. He drifted like a cloud through the floor, his body airy. Sweaty bodies pressed against him as they lured him to dance with him, and he wasn't refusing to be part of the crowd—to finally be on the inside.

As the night slipped further in, Lukas continued dancing on the floor with a euphoric high. He attempted to dance with other women by pressing his body against theirs or rubbing their shoulders—all of which got him shoved away and jeered at. His face flushed, and his lips soured at the many rejections he faced, and he wanted to make them pay for making him feel outcast, to make them hurt.

If only Rebecca had been at this bar, Lukas and she would've danced until dawn like they used to. Their hands would cling to each other and stay drunk on the feeling of each other.

But as he spun around in the middle of the bar looking for an exit, he caught a familiar face drinking by herself at a table. Maybe that night hadn't been a complete failure yet. Without thinking, he floated toward Sophia, who had just poured herself another glass of vodka, and the sight of her made his heart race faster than ever.

Lukas brushed his fingers along the seat opposite her, mustering the courage to speak. "Is this seat taken?" he asked, though his mind was already made up, ready to sit regardless of her response.

Sophia's gaze lifted slowly, her dark eyes heavy and distant, and her once vibrant olive skin seemed paler. Almost as pale as the white blouse she wore. It must've been the death of her mother that made her slowly disappear. There was no doubt about it. But Lukas couldn't deny the guilt that washed over him.

"I didn't think we'd see each other again, considering the fact you left me in the middle of the night without saying a word," Sophia started, her tone laced with anger and hurt. "You jackass."

Lukas sat down, his face flushing with remorse and fear of her rejection. "I'm sorry about that. I guess I was just scared. And I did the only thing I knew how to do—run."

Her eyes softened, her sage eyes glimmering from the hanging lights. "Why're you here, anyway? Did you come back to take more prescription notes?"

Lukas hesitated at the bitter words, his breath catching in his throat. He stood up, ready to scurry back to his truck. What a stupid idea this was, he thought. "Sorry to bother you. I'll just leave."

But before he could leave, Sophia's hand shot across the table, gripping his arm. "Wait, no—stay. Please," she pleaded, her voice tinted with desperation.

He sighed as he sank back into the seat, his eyes meeting hers. "I'm trying to get drunk. This last week has been a shitshow," he admitted to her.

A wry smile tugged at Sophia's lips, and her face showed the reflection of her dry tears. "You're telling me." She slid the bottle of vodka and glass over to him. "Here, drink."

Lukas did so as the dim lighting continued hanging above them, with the music vibrating the wooden floors of the bar. They clanked drinks before drinking away their unrelenting pain and sorrow. And as the glasses slammed the table, he watched Sophia wipe her wet eyes with her arm. He wondered if he should try comforting her, but the word *comfort* was as unfamiliar to him as it was expressing it.

So, instead, he solemnly watched her pour herself another glass.

"I saw you the night of the fire—hugging the dead body," Lukas said. But as soon as he did, he wondered if that was the right thing to say, because more tears seemed to stream down Sophia's face.

He felt guilty for thinking about it, but he couldn't stop imagining touching her and thrusting inside her once again. Her body was slim like Rebecca's, and she moaned just like her, too.

"It was my mom." She choked on the last word. Sophia rubbed her eyes with her hands. "She'd been living in those apartments for the last several years ever since she got booked in this town, but I know she got involved in some awful shit—she just never told me what it was. And now, the only person who's been keeping me from offing myself has been my boss. It sounds depressing—I know," she said, burying her face in her palms.

"Your boss?"

Sophia poured her sixth glass a few more, and she could dance on tables or completely black out. "She's more like a friend, but she's a doctor here." She hesitated for a moment. "Elizabeth Ainsley is definitely a *one-of-a-kind* person. She almost reminds me of my mother—as awful as that sounds."

Lukas's brow twitched at the name. It made sense now. Sophia was on the way in. He could hear the doctor's screams in his mind as he imagined torturing her, the bloodlust thought smearing a wide smile on his face. Not because of Sophia's self-deprecating joke.

He watched Sophia try to pour herself another glass, only to find the bottle empty. She must've been trying to find the answer to her problems at the bottom, just like him. But also, like Lukas, she found nothing.

Sophia cursed under her breath as she waved down a bartender with an empty bottle of homemade vodka.

Lukas turned to the bar behind him. "She'll have water," he called behind him.

Sophia's soft cheeks beamed to a rosy pink as her dry lips pursed with anger. She clenched the bottle tighter. "Why'd you say that? I think I'm old enough to decide when I stop drinking."

"I want to make sure you're still sober when I do this."

Sophia stared blankly at him. "Do what—"

Without thinking, Lukas leaned across the table and pressed his lips against hers. The soft taste of her lips only lasted for a second, though, before she pulled back. At first, her eyes were cold as she scowled at him for making such an intrusion, but after a few seconds of silence, they softened.

"You're right. Water's fine," she said with a soft breath.

How adorable. They continued kissing in the bar, and the feeling was insatiable. Lukas couldn't get enough of the taste of her. He was addicted to her skin, her lips, her hair. He wanted all of her to himself. Maybe Rebecca wasn't the only perfect girl in his world. Sophia was indeed perfect.

Everything about Sophia was perfect.

Lukas's hands explored her thighs and traced them up her loose blue skirt until her breaths became heavy. He decided now was time to leave the hectic scene. He clasped her hand and led her out of the bar toward his rusting truck parked under a willow tree.

It scared Lukas that Sophia would be disappointed by the car he drove. Maybe she was expecting to be fucked by a successful businessman who drove a Mercedes or BMW, or maybe just fucked by someone who was living a successful life. There was nothing more unsuccessful than being trapped in some sort of cage his entire life, and Sophia would see right through it.

But as he laid on top of her in the backseat of the car, caressing her neck and face with his lips, he wanted nothing more than to please her. To make her feel love no other man had done in her life until now. If he could make her trust him enough, maybe she would take him to Elizabeth, where they *both* could murder her together.

Sophia's soft hands found their way under his navy tee, feeling to his chest. She pulled the shirt off over his head. Lukas moaned in ecstasy as she did. More than Rebecca ever made him.

Lukas began kissing her breasts. They were rounder than Rebecca's. His fingers slid up her thighs, reaching to pull off her panties—he felt the soft silk of them, which sent a rush in his heart.

"Wait—" Sophia grabbed his hand. "I can't do *this*. I know I'm going to regret it in the morning."

Regret it?

The words stabbed and sliced his heart like a knife as he watched her sit up, fixing her blouse and skirt. Lukas sighed. "Tell me where you want me to take you. You're not to be trusted behind the wheel after how much you've drunk tonight."

She quickly laughed at the comment, but it was forced. "You can just drive me to Elizabeth's house. I'll tell you how to get there."

The rest of the car ride was in silence, and it was well into 2:00 A.M. now. Sophia was making all efforts to avoid looking at him, running her hands through her hair, glancing at her phone every few seconds, and pretending to send a text when tapping mindlessly on the home screen.

Lukas's fingers squeezed the wheel as he drove until they were bone white. What did he do that upset her? He couldn't figure it out. He was the best thing for her. Sophia just didn't know that yet. But maybe it was also a test to see how good Lukas could treat her before *rewarding* him.

Sophia guided him through the forest, past Bill's ranch and the obscure cabin on the hill that once belonged to Rebecca, to a small overlook near the edge of town where a small cottage sat. Two cars were parked outside, and the moonlight made their gloss finishes shimmer. It was a bizarre location to live as the city limit tall wire fences were just a couple miles ahead, containing everything inside.

As Lukas approached the front lawn, he noticed Sophia had already cracked her door open. Leaning closer to kiss her goodbye, Sophia thanked him for the ride, hurried out of the truck, and slammed the door behind her without a second thought.

Lukas sat in silence.

His head pounded once again like a hammer was nailing him into the driver's seat. He needed to take his OxyContin.

Sophia's rejection made his buried rage seep within. Flashes of strangling Rebecca found their way back to his mind, and his hands wanted to lunge at Sophia's throat to make him experience those buried feelings once more.

Reject. Outcast. Unlovable. The words taunted him in his mind and made his eyes twitch with fury.

Even if Sophia didn't want him, he didn't need her anymore. If this was Elizabeth's house, he now knew where she lived, and he could do with that information as he pleased. But he couldn't decide who he hated more in that moment: The Raven of East Haddam or Sophia.

Lukas wondered who he'd enjoy watching beg for his mercy more as his breaths became heavier. Drunk at the thought of hearing someone scream.

And the answer became obvious.

31

ELIZABETH

JULY 12

BLOOD SPEWED FROM THE boy's mouth.

The horrific sight made Elizabeth's tears spill down her face and trail to her bloody hands. She was almost out of time. The boy's skin was growing bluer by the second as he suffocated in his own blood.

His face was masked with thick scarlet stains that made him unrecognizable. Choking, his bloody arms flailed by his side as more blood spilled from his mouth onto the metal table.

Elizabeth couldn't get him to breathe. Nothing was working.

She spun around sobbing, looking for any surgical tools in the blurry room—but there was nothing.

There was nothing.

They were sealed in a doorless room, illuminated by a single hanging light over the boy. Her pleading wails reverberated off the walls and echoed into an endless chamber of suffering.

She spun back to the dying boy, who was now looking more like a ghost fading into a memory. His youthful blood was dripping down the table onto the floor as she clasped her hand over her screaming mouth.

Without a second to lose, Elizabeth placed her bloody hands on his convoluting chest. Cardiac arrest was imminent. But as her trembling eyes fell down to her hands in front of her, she noticed a small, long metal object was tucked in her hand. How could she have forgotten what she was holding?

She held the long, hollow needle in front of her.

Elizabeth gasped in relief and, without a second thought, thrust the needle into his cricothyroid membrane just below his thyroid. The cricothyrotomy had to work. The puncture would allow his airway to continue through the needle, and every ounce of her being prayed that he would breathe. He had to. He just had to.

A few long seconds later, the boy fell silent as his arms collapsed and dangled off the table.

The blood stopped bursting from his mouth.

She cradled his head in her hands. "Breathe, baby!"

The room fell silent as she listened carefully for the faintest catch of his breath. But he didn't.

He was just as lifeless as the ghosts that followed her.

"Breathe!"

But this time, her eyes sprung open to the darkness of her bedroom, panting.

That damn night, she thought.

Taking a deep breath, Elizabeth's hands found the lamp on her nightstand and flicked the small light on. She let a sigh of relief out as the room she was sleeping in was still her own, not the one from her nightmare. Her bedroom was small and warm light, with a French window at her side peering into the creeping night and a large closet opposite her bed.

The closet was mostly filled with stacks of boxes of old medical files and research papers that led to criminal rehabilitation across America. Her entire life's work sealed into a box. Her worst enemy, just behind a closet door.

She buried her face in her hands, reminding herself her dream wasn't real, that she was safe. *Memories can't hurt me,* she repeated to herself. Some holistic cognitive behavioral foolishness. It never worked with her. The mind was the untamable animal, the king of beasts, and Elizabeth found it easier to let it run wild rather than contain it. Elizabeth's thoughts were free, and she would speak them without a filter. It was better for her to accept there was no amount of therapy or mental exercises to make her feel better about what she'd done and the lives she'd cost.

Especially when the evidence that made her the devil was the surrounding cage in thirty-foot concrete walls around the town.

Her fingers traced up her wrinkled face and brushed the tears dripping from her eyes. The tears were real. Even after all the years, the memory gnawed at her like a hoard of flies to a carcass.

It's Sophia. It has to be, she concluded. Her very presence was a reminder of what she didn't have, of what she'd lost. It brought up all the buried memories.

Elizabeth uncovered her white sheets and slipped her feet into a pair of slippers. The silk blue nightgown she wore draped down her sides and slid across the floor as she made her way to the window. She reached behind a small hanging portrait of herself and her first husband, James. Her fingers brushed the small hidden box of her Marlboro cigarettes as she pulled it from behind the portrait.

The box trembled in her hand. She'd sworn off her last cigarette two years ago when she first got thrown into East Haddam. The hatred and guilt she'd built within was like a pit ready to be kindled. Once it burned, it'd all go away.

Except it didn't. The fire always burned everything next to her, her hopes, her fears, until everything was ash. But the box of cigarettes in her hand whispered her name with a faint crack of fire.

Burn it down.

Elizabeth unlatched the window as she pulled out a single cigarette from the box, stashing the rest behind the portrait. Her heart raced as she spun around, thinking of where she might find a lighter. As she hurried to her kitchen drawer, her mouth watered, yearning for the hot smoke in her mouth. Elizabeth grabbed the electric lighter and made her back to the window, where she lit the cigarette in her hand.

Burn it down.

She pressed the white cigarette to her pale lips as she inhaled the bitter smoke. It swarmed her mouth until she breathed it all out into a thin cloud drifting into midnight, breathing out all her anxiety, the dream, it was all drifting away. It was all burning down.

As she leaned over her window smoking, a rush of wind struck the room, and a pile of papers flew off her nightstand. Elizabeth let out a groan as she placed the cigarette on the windowsill and walked over to the scattered papers. The different colored papers lay by her feet before she held them up to the warm light of the lamp. The pile of papers felt heavier as she stared down at the black-lettered words. Scanning through them, she remembered why she'd left them untouched.

Invoices from Yale's Financial Department and notices for unmade payments. All the schooling she was supposed to be funding Sophia was so far barely paid for, but she could never tell Sophia the truth. It would devastate her.

Elizabeth had mostly taken out loans to sponsor her tuition, but now she owed the school $150,000. Disappointment consumed her as she realized she'd never be able to get that money before the coming semester in the fall. Surely, they'd kick Sophia out for not being able to pay. The last bit of money she'd made from the narcotic network had gone to buying the cottage. Sophia would find out Elizabeth barely had a dollar to her name, and she'd resent her for the rest of her life.

Even the cigarette couldn't burn *that* down.

No, that couldn't happen.

That won't happen, Elizabeth thought.

She ran her fingers through her silver-blonde hair as her eyes wandered around the room, as if the money she needed would magically appear in a pot of gold. And she was sure this wasn't a fairytale where the answer to all her problems would be a wave away.

Until it was. Her eyes fell on her phone lying on the bed.

One phone call was all she needed to solve her problems.

32

ELIZABETH

JULY 12

MIDNIGHT BY THE SOUTHSIDE sweltered. Abnormally sultry, but then again, it was now July.

Elizabeth waited by the Connecticut River shore, her brown trench coat draping down her waist. She tasted the humid air with her quick breaths as she waited. Frank, to no surprise to her, was falling behind schedule as he'd made her wait half an hour now. Again, he'd left her alone with nothing but the echo of the river crashing upon its rocky shore. Just like the night he left her.

Wrapping her arms around herself, she spun, looking for any sign of a person. Looking for the incompetent man known as Frank Sallow. A roaring helicopter above made Elizabeth's heart race as its searchlight fell in different directions of the night. What they were searching for, she didn't care, but she had no intention of staying out long enough to find out.

What she was doing was a risk. Anything with Frank was. The golden watch on her frail wrist faintly ticked every second going by.

She groaned at the sound. But more at the fact that Frank couldn't do something as simple as meet her on time. He couldn't do anything right. She was sure of it.

Taking a step forward, Elizabeth shot a glance across the vast river to Haddam. The world she once belonged to, where she now watched from the outside.

But something more pressing infiltrated her mind: she was *alone* on the south side of East Haddam. Hopefully, if anyone was watching, they wouldn't mistake her lonely presence as an illicit affair. But to the wrong eyes, it would be deemed so. The Southside was known for its inconspicuous location to commit actions you didn't want others to see.

And that's what she was doing. Something she didn't want others to see. Especially Sophia.

Pebbles crunching echoed from the distance.

Her eyes shot back to the sound behind her.

Approaching in the midst, the silhouette of a tall figure formed. Hands in his pocket and keeping his head low, Elizabeth suspected maybe it was a ghost. But as he came closer, it was clear who was approaching her. Frank Sallow, unfortunately still alive and breathing. Her wish of him dying hadn't come true. But it had been a ghost, just not the kind she thought.

Elizabeth rolled her eyes and buried her hands in her coat pocket as he approached her. "Your car. Where is it?"

Frank's eyes flitted up and down her body. "I left it a mile up north and walked the rest. Unconventional, I know, but I didn't want to risk being followed here." Frank paused for a moment and scratched the back of his head. A look of puzzlement crossed his face. "So, you changed your mind, after all. I knew eventually you'd come around. Not even *you* can resist a quarter-million job."

He was irritatingly right. It was a perfect opportunity that landed right on her front lawn, but she couldn't let him think that. The thought of succumbing herself to his taunts repulsed her. "I'm not here for you. I'm doing it for *her*," Elizabeth snarled.

"The girl—Sophia?" Frank chuckled for a moment. "You know she's not your daughter, right, Ainsley?"

Elizabeth's body tensed as her face shrunk. Even though, Sophia may not have been her daughter by blood, Elizabeth planned to do anything she could to protect her. *It's what a good mother does,* she thought. "She may as well be. I'm the only one looking out for her."

Frank shot a disdainful glance at the last word. His cheekbones clenched as he squinted at her. The disgruntled look made Elizabeth wonder what she had said to upset him. Not that she cared about his feelings, just curious about what she had done.

Their eyes met in the longest silence she'd ever known. In an instant, she relived the memories between them. All her smiles, laughs, and tears seemed to replay just behind his black eyes. Who was once a boxer in Boston and one of Elizabeth's patients, now harmed her more than any other man had. The way he left her like she was nothing. Abandoning her at her worst to find a younger woman, a better woman. How cruel that fate would bring them together again in the cage of East Haddam. Elizabeth for trying to destroy what she had created. Frank for deserting his position in the military like a coward.

And she hated to admit it to herself, but Frank looked good. Even in his middle age, it was clear he still took good care of his physical appearance. He always was an active man who enjoyed long hikes in the mountains. It was there in Middlesex where he proposed to her during their hike. It was a beautiful ring, a simple diamond, but she didn't care about the material value.

And he didn't care about her either. His proclamations of love were lies used to get what he wanted until he bled her dry. Her research, her name, and her presence meant more to him if it brought in money. It was always about the money for him—and it was never enough. Never enough.

Elizabeth let out a sigh. "What do you need from me?"

A conniving grin curled Frank's lips as he began explaining the plan to expand a new narco network to Hartford. He talked about gradually sending small shipments through carriers up north, where then small transactions would be made until they set a steady network into place. Frank was more interested than Elizabeth was, luckily.

While he continued rambling, Elizabeth slithered her hand down her brown coat pocket. Her hand wrapped tight around the cold metal object, and her eyes latched onto his, making sure he wouldn't suspect a thing. Her lips tightened as she staggered back swiftly, drawing out a pistol and pointing it directly at him.

Frank's eyes widened. "What the hell!"

"And *why* should I trust you now, you lying bastard?"

Frank scoffed, rolling his eyes. But still, he kept his hands raised in the air. "Come on, Ainsley, we both know you don't have the guts to pull that trigger," his thick voice shivered.

Unfortunately, he was right as her finger trembled over the trigger. "Oh yeah? You don't think, after everything you put me through, I'll hesitate to kill you right now? How could you do it, Frank? How could you lie to me? You promised me you loved me. You *promised* me. Did none of that mean anything to you? After lawmakers and politicians took an interest in my work, and I stood at the mercy of the public eye, you executed me, too."

Frank's eyes filled more with terror. Now, he believed she would shoot him.

Rage pulsed through her veins. It tempted her to pull the trigger and tie another loose end. A simple pull of her finger. That's all it would take to be rid of him once and for all. She just had to burn it down. She held the gun steady and pointed between his eyes.

But she would never pull the trigger, as much as it would satisfy her. She needed him for Sophia.

"You left me to be criticized by the country," Elizabeth continued with tears streaming down her face. "You say it's not my fault, but it is! I built the system! And just when I believed you, I found out you were having an affair. But it looks like that didn't work out for you either, seeing as she left you, too, after she found out how much of a coward you are. I need you to promise me, Frank, that you won't throw me under the bus like you did our last operation. I don't want them to think I'm associated with you anymore. That's the only way this works. The police are growing more desperate every day to find The Raven of East Haddam, and I'll be damned before I go down with you," she spat.

There was a moment of silence before Frank smirked. His cockiness was loathsome to her.

"God, I miss that passion. Now, could you put that damn gun away? You could hurt someone." Frank took a step forward, dropping his hands. "Follow me. We're supposed to meet one of the carriers on the other side of the shore."

Just one strike. That's all she wanted to wipe his smug face off. Think of the money, she thought. *Think of Sophia.*

She dropped the pistol back into her pocket, defeated. "Let's just hurry and be done with this, Frank," she sighed, her heart still racing.

Elizabeth followed Frank along the edge of the shore and ventured into the abysmal forest of the night. A pleasant aroma of damp moss and leaves drifted in the air, with an incessant chirp of crickets echoing. Dark maple trees towered over the two as they walked together, trampling over the foliage without speaking a word to each other. She felt torn between her hate and need for Frank. She despised the feeling of power he still had over her. So long as he didn't speak, they could do their job and get their money.

For a while, the walk was peaceful. Until Elizabeth's eyes shifted a quick glance over to him, where she caught him staring at her already. A chill ran down her spine as she glanced back at the dim path ahead. His eyes were smoldering coals to the pale light of the moon. She was caught like a child misbehaving where she'd be chastised. What made it worse was the silence that lingered between them, making her heart race faster. She couldn't discern the meaning behind the intensity of his stare.

What's he thinking? What does he know? She couldn't figure him out, but then again, she never once did.

"Does Sophia know?" Frank finally spoke.

Elizabeth's heart leaped as her jaw tensed. She'd forgotten how to breathe as she turned her pale face, utterly horrified. She knew exactly what Frank was talking about, but she'd play the fool instead. "*Know* what?"

"So she doesn't. That's good. You wouldn't want her finding out you started the fire that killed her mother. I saw the whole thing on the news the other night. At first, I didn't want to believe it was you, but you always loved lighting things on fire. That's the work of Elizabeth Ainsley if I know her, I said. But tell me I'm wrong, Ainsley. Please tell me you didn't ruin the kid's life." His voice strained at the last word.

Elizabeth held her breath as her nails dug into her palm. A lump grew in her throat as she tried to justify her heinous action, and it tempted the acid in her stomach to burst from her mouth. Sophia wouldn't understand why she did what she did, but one day she would. Frank knew her too well that it'd be futile to keep the truth from him forever. But it wouldn't hurt to try. Maybe he was still daft.

"I didn't," she muttered.

"But you had someone do it?"

Elizabeth shot a cold glare at him. "No."

They stared at each other for a moment that lasted forever. She wasn't sure if Frank believed her. Though by the shifting of eyes, Elizabeth had instilled a sliver of doubt in him and that was all she needed.

Elizabeth let an exhausting sigh out before trudging past him. *Too much vulnerability for one night.*

They didn't speak for the rest of the walk as tension clouded the space between them. Her hand remained burrowed in her pocket, gripping the pistol. She wanted to shoot something, someone, anything. *Release the pain*, she thought. But she shook her head, trying to calm herself. The whole confrontation had made a wave of fury torment her. Frank for pointing his large crooked nose in her business and for herself for being so messy with how she dealt with her problems. The possibility of Sophia discovering the truth made her heart ache like never before.

It was Frank's fault. Somehow, it always was.

The charcoal clouds thickened, and the restless wind threw chills at Elizabeth. Claps of thunder roared around them before small droplets fell onto both Elizabeth and Frank.

She shot glances at Frank, who, this time, kept his sight straight to the path of the forest. *The Northside is just past here.*

Together, they pushed through a small thicket of wet trees that led to another path toward the Northside shore. As Elizabeth pushed past the branches following Frank, the air turned bitter, and an overwhelming acrid smell filled her nose. Beyond, the thicket was almost pitch black, with branches spiraling from every side of her view, covering the light of the moon. Elizabeth tried continuing down the path of towering trees and rain, but the putrid smell became blinding. She wiped her eyes as they watered as if they had intruded into an onion field.

Frank let out a series of disgruntled coughs. "What's that awful smell?"

"Quiet down, Frank. Let me see." Elizabeth grabbed her phone from her pocket and tapped on the flashlight icon on the screen. She shined it in every direction before the light illuminated something terrifying.

The horrific sight froze them both. Blood drained from her face. Fear imprisoned her body. She couldn't budge a muscle. She couldn't blink at the horrendous display intertwined with the branches of the trees. Her eyes widened, quivering.

There was a boy.

Dead.

33

Elizabeth

July 12

Elizabeth stared, horrified, at the dead boy in front of them.

But he was more than dead. The boy was dismembered and strung up. Multiple ropes and wires ran through his bloody severed limbs, making a web. A bloody head hung from the top, looking down at them. His eyes were open and petrified at the last sight he caught. A small silver piece of tape concealed his mouth, blazed with blackened letters.

Bug

The aroma was vile and rotten. Thick maroon blood stained the white ropes and wires entangling his limbs. An act of pure evil that sent a harsh chill up her spine.

This—this isn't real.

But she couldn't bring herself to blink. To make it disappear. The horrific sight was oddly alluring, entrancing. She couldn't look away. She didn't dare.

"What the fuck?" Frank whispered in a shaking voice.

Elizabeth noticed small bugs were eating away at his gray flesh. His body was decomposing, and it appeared the body had been for a while now. Maybe a week.

"Oh my God," she mouthed. But she couldn't bring herself to say the words. Or anything.

No doubt about it. This was the work of the *Recluse Killer*. First, that missing girl, Cassandra Holland, then Rebecca Waylow, and now this poor boy.

"What the fuck! What do we do!" He shot an urging glance toward her. She was the doctor, after all.

She ignored him for a second, paralyzed in place. Trickles of sweat and rain dripped down her neck. *Do I—should I?* She gulped as she examined the dismembered body in front of her. What she was about to do would break many laws. If she were to get caught, it would mean the end for sure. But it wasn't a long debate. She made up her mind. Elizabeth turned to Frank, who was retching on the floor and wiping his mouth with his hairy arm.

She threw a sharp glare at him. "Let's get him down."

"Are you insane! You've lost it! You've actually fucking lost it! I'm not touching that bloody—"

"Listen to me, Frank!" she cried to him, cradling his face. "I need you to trust me on this. We need to get him down."

Frank's eyes bulged with a crazed look, his hands twitching spastically. "But why! Listen—listen—listen to me, Ainsley. We could leave the body, walk away, act like this never happened, and wait for the actual authorities to find him."

"Mud! Our shoe prints!" She lifted her foot. "If we wait for *authorities* to find this boy, they're going to see our shoe prints scattered in the mud. You and I are already in deep with the police. We do not need to give them a reason to suspect we're behind this!"

Frank's now-soaked hair fell over his forehead. His jaw clenched as he gazed at the murderous sight.

Elizabeth held her breath as the rotting fumes grew stronger. Gagging, she took a few steps toward the dismembered, bloody boy.

"We'll loosen the limbs from the rope—" The sour smell made her retch into her sleeve. "And get the head last," she finished.

Frank whimpered as he approached the wet corpse. He pinched what seemed to be part of a leg and tore it from the rope. It splurged blood as it hit the muddy ground. The sound sent shivers up Elizabeth's spine and made Frank vomit once again.

"I can't do this! Please, let's just go! My guy is waiting, is still waiting for us," Frank panted.

"Do it, Frank!"

Elizabeth tore a hand off the web. In her mind, she tried to envision herself anywhere other than where she was. Perhaps, picking berries instead of human parts from bushes in her garden. But the cheerful sight she envisioned didn't last long. Still, she remained hopeful that she'd wake up and that this entire night had been a nightmare. But unfortunately, she knew everything was all too real.

Her hair and coat were now soaked from the sultry rain. It soaked into her skin. She wanted to die at the discomfort of what she was doing, but no matter what, she had to push through.

One by one, they tore the limbs from the web. They ripped fingers, parts of legs, ears, arms, from the ropes and wires.

Then, it was just the head. A single bloody rope from a branch held the crown of the web. They both examined the severed head, dreading to hold it. Frank turned to Elizabeth with a pleading look.

I'll do it. Just like everything else, you coward.

Frank tossed her his pocketknife as she examined the ropes around the head. She pressed the small button, springing the knife out, ready to cut.

But to her horror, another group of voices and rustling echoed from the distance. Seconds passed as the rustling of foliage grew closer, and the voices grew louder.

They both stood paralyzed in fear. Elizabeth's breaths shortened as she realized how she appeared. A knife in hand, a dismembered body. Blood everywhere. Compulsively unwelcoming. Blood drained from her face as her body went pale. This was the end. They were about to be caught. Small beams of light illuminated from behind the thicket.

"Sam, are you sure we were over here?" a girl asked.

"Yes, Tiffany! The waterfall's just up ahead," a boy presumed to be Sam said.

"We've been walking around here for hours, Sam. Let's just call it at night already. He's not here," another boy said.

The obscured beams of light shined directly at Elizabeth through the thicket. Her heart dropped as she choked on her breath.

"We're not leaving without Percy! He's *my* friend. Besides, we don't even have the canoe anymore. We lost it. Let's try further south. Wait—what's that smell?"

"It smells like shit over here," the other boy said.

"We're probably in the wrong area, that's why! Let's keep going," the girl, Tiffany, said.

Without warning, the dead boy's head fell and splashed in the mud. Elizabeth's heart leaped. The rain must've loosened the rope.

"Did you guys hear that?" Sam said.

"I didn't hear anything. Adrian's probably just dicking around..." The voice faded away.

Elizabeth turned to Frank, relieved.

Frank was struck with a look of amusement. "The Mystery Gang almost caught us. Those meddling kids," he said.

She didn't reply as she stared down at the boy's limbs and head scattered around the ground. This was someone's son and someone's brother. Whoever he was mattered to someone, and they didn't know he was dead. He didn't deserve that brutal fate.

Elizabeth carefully examined the severed limbs with a careful eye before she caught Frank's disgruntled look. There was only one way to do this.

"We need a car. Your car, Frank," she said.

"I am not putting some kid's body parts in my car. I'm drawing the line there."

A car engine roared among the thunder and rain from the nearby road. Elizabeth gazed in the distance at the sound.

"Follow my lead," Elizabeth muttered before hurrying toward the other end of the thicket. She pushed through the thick branches and onto the winding road through the forest.

"Wait, what—I don't know the plan! We didn't discuss—Ainsley!" Frank called from behind.

Elizabeth scurried across the wet road, waving down the speeding car. Frank followed and threw his hands into the air, manically waving them. They didn't give the driver a choice to not stop, as they were directly in his lane. Unless the driver wanted to be charged with two counts of manslaughter. The headlights beamed directly on their faces. She held her breath as she glared at the car.

The car slowed until it came to a stop, the engine still growling. Elizabeth could feel the annoyance of the driver at the inconvenience. Maybe the driver would become so infuriated that they would run them over. She took a deep breath, clasped Frank's hand, and pulled him toward the driver's window.

Elizabeth watched the annoyed driver roll his window down. "Sorry to bother you, but my husband's car's battery died, and we need a jumper—"

"Can't help. Now get out of the outta the street, you crazy bitch," the man spat. Without a second look, he rolled up his windows and sped off into the distance.

"Eat shit!" Frank shouted.

She trembled with rage, peering at the car. *I hope he crashes.* But to their luck, another car sped from the distance. She curled a smile at the sound. Once more, they frantically waved the car down. And once again, the car slowed and stopped in front of them.

They both approached the car as Elizabeth squeezed her eyes, trying to force buried tears from the edges, hoping it'd appear more pleading. She didn't care anymore about exploiting sympathy.

The man rolled down his window.

"Sorry to bother you, man, but my wife and I are stranded. My car battery died, and we need jumper cables—"

"Look, I'm in a hurry, sorry—" the man started.

A wave of fury crashed through her.

Enough of this!

Without thinking, Elizabeth grabbed the man's head and slammed it against his wheel. He fell back in his chair, his nose bloody and crooked.

"What the hell was that? I thought the point was to not draw attention to ourselves!"

"We don't have time to wait for a bloody Samaritan, Frank! We need to get these body parts in the trunk now! I know where we can go," she said.

Her blood rushed, and her head pulsed at what she had just done. She needed to remind herself why she was doing all of this. Why she was going through all this trouble? To fix what she couldn't before. Her biggest regret.

Closure, yes, this is closure for Thomas.

My little boy.

34

LUKAS

MANY YEARS AGO

DESTROY YOUR INNOCENCE. THAT was the order Director Miller commanded that day.

He lined up everyone in The Room and shouted in their faces, "Look at the blood on your hands! You are not innocent!"

The director was right. They weren't innocent. After all the things he'd made Lukas and the others do, there wasn't a shroud of innocence within a mile. Lukas's eyes were unwavering as he met Director Miller's sunken, black eyes, and Lukas was sure to not show any expression toward him. Because if he did, the director would take it as a sign of aggravation or, worse, intimidation.

After, it was time for the next part of their lesson. Lukas didn't know what to expect. Each day in The Room was something crueler they had to do, and each day, there were one or two fewer kids than in the last lesson. Those nights, the vents would hum with a shrieking heat.

The guards brought a large crate into the room, and they handed each of them a small hunting knife. Lukas wondered if he'd have to torture another boy or girl for that lesson. Hurting someone didn't bother him as much anymore. He hated to admit it, but there was something almost exhilarating about the infliction of pain on another human being. It made him feel good knowing *he* was in control of someone. Whether they'd get to live or die was completely up to him to decide. The ripping of skin, the tortured shrieking, the shrouding silence after death. It was all music to Lukas's ears.

As he looked down at the knife, an excitedness rushed through his body, anticipating what they'd get to do today. Who he'd get to *hurt* today.

Lukas quickly shook his mind off the subject. *Stop thinking like that. I'm not like them. I'm not like Erica.*

Director Miller ordered the crate to be opened, and the guards followed his command as they marched toward it, pulling a small latch. As they did, a hoard of different colored bunnies scurried from within the crate.

Lukas stared blankly at the innocent sight. Confused with the others, he watched as a few of them ran past his feet and scattered around the room, lost in their new environment. It cast an eerie reminder of when he was first thrown in The Room, wandering with questions with no answers. Normally, the sight of bunnies would have put a smile on Lukas's face as the soft, plush animals ran around him. But in time, it painted his face with a look of dread.

Lukas looked down at the trembling hunting knife in his hand. He didn't want his presumption to be true. He would've been fine hurting someone in that room, but not an animal. Especially not a white bunny. *How could anyone kill an adorable bunny?* he wondered. The answer creeped into his mind like a spider on his back. His father would've.

He wondered if Erica would be so compliant as to kill her favorite animal. But knowing her now, she would've. Her face would've grimaced as she'd prowl like a predator behind the fuzzy creature. And without a second thought, she would've murdered it with no remorse. She'd hold its innocent white head like a trophy for her allies, and use it to suffocate her enemies. That must be why she was moved to *Phase Three,* whatever that was.

All these questions he's had, and still no answers. What made it even more strange was the new boy in her cell. Lukas wondered why the guards didn't bring him to today's lesson.

But Director Miller's hoarse voice interrupted his thought. "Everyone, grab one! And hold it by its neck," he said.

The guards circled them, making sure everyone followed orders. Lukas watched as others slammed their foot on a bunny, or sprang onto one. Alicia chuckled as she choked hers on the floor. The barbaric sight sent a stiff chill prickling across his skin.

Hurry! Lukas looked down at his numb blue feet. To Lukas's inevitable fear, he snatched a scurrying bunny by its neck and held it in the air. His heart raced as he looked at its quivering black eyes. The small creature trembled in the grasp of his fingers. It stared mindlessly at him. He wondered if the bunny could understand what was happening and how it had found itself in the most perilous situation.

If what he presumed was true about what the director would make them do, he wouldn't do it. He couldn't do it. Lukas only hoped that the others would think the same about hurting such a small thing. It wasn't fair—they were innocent.

The room filled with a dreadful echo of meek squeaks as the bunnies writhed in each of their grasps. Lukas's ears pulsated with an excruciating pain that made him want to slice his own ears off just so wouldn't have to listen anymore.

But as he looked up, he caught a twisted smile widening on the director's face.

"Slice its head," Director Miller demanded.

Lukas spun around, watching the other kids follow the director's order. In a swift motion of the knife, the bunnies' bloody bodies fell to the ground while they held the head in their hand. Puddles of bright red blood formed along the floor. Lukas stood paralyzed in horror, the knife still trembling by his side. For a second, his eyes scattered to the multitude of decapitated bunnies along the floor, then quickly looked back to the bunny he held.

He didn't mean for it to happen, but the inhumane sight made a tear stream down his pale face, and his breaths became laborious until it was the only sound in the room. His shaky breaths reverberated through the prickling silence.

It was quiet, too quiet, he thought.

Lukas bit his lower lip as he caught every eye falling on him. A look of contempt smeared on their barbaric faces. Their peering eyes sharpened his breath until Lukas's face widened with panic.

"Why are you hesitating, Lukas? Slice its head." Direction Miller sneered.

Lukas's eyes fell back on the whimpering bunny in his grasp. *I can't do it.* Lukas shook his head as another tear fell down his face. How the others could do it without a sliver of hesitation, he couldn't understand. Everyone in this room was an animal.

Lukas's heart pounded in his chest, the thumping reverberating through his entire body. His hands trembled, causing the bunny to squirm even more in his grip. The weight of the knife in his other hand suddenly felt unbearable, as if it would kill not only the bunny but also his own fallen innocence.

"Slice its head," the other kids began chanting.

Lukas spun in terror at seeing their wicked grins. A chill ran up his spine as they continued.

"Slide its head! Slice its head! Slice its head!" they continued.

"I can't do it! I can't do it!" Lukas dropped both the small knife and the bunny.

The sound of the sharp metal crashing on the floor echoed throughout the room as they all watched Lukas with silent amusement. After a few long seconds, he watched the director approach him. The others laughed and snickered as Lukas held his breath. Terror stiffened him, cementing his feet to the cold floor.

Oh no, he's going to kill me right now! I'm dead—what do I do? I can't fight back! I can't move my body! Why won't my body move! Help!

Director Miller grasped the dropped bunny from the floor, picked up the knife, and sliced its head while peering into Lukas's horrified eyes. His sharp breaths rang in his throbbing ears as the director bent to his height and snarled.

"Don't expect any meals for a week," he spat.

35

LUKAS

MANY YEARS AGO

LUKAS GROUND THE PIECE of stone in his hand against the metal spoon, sharpening it with each swift motion. He ignored the persistent grumbling of his stomach as he curled against the frigid concrete wall. A day had passed since he last ate, not that he would've enjoyed eating the bland mush anyway, but at least it was something. Now, he was regretting disobeying the director. Maybe he should've just killed the stupid thing.

With every slide of his arm, the metal spoon's tip sharpened. It had taken months to get it to the point of maybe penetrating something soft like skin. But one day, Lukas thought, it'll be worth it. He set his mind on the idea of escaping this hell, and he refused to turn back from the notion.

There were just a couple of issues with his plan. He didn't know how to escape. The facility he was in had many dark, narrow corridors and locked rooms he had never explored, and he knew he couldn't overpower all the guards at once, or even one. They had guns; he didn't.

Lukas often wondered if the outside world still existed—if Boston was still real. Some days, the memories of the outside were like a dream that had never happened. The blue skies and towering skylines were just something of his imagination. He often believed that he was born inside the facility. It made sense. It's the only place he's ever known now.

A soft groan echoed in Lukas's room.

Lukas paused, placing the stone and spoon down. His ears perked, listening to the swollen silence that blistered around him. He waited for the noise to happen again, but it didn't.

Picking up the stone and spoon, he began sharpening the spoon once more, unbothered. He concluded his hunger must've made him hallucinate the noise just like he hallucinated Erica lighting their father on fire. At least, that's what that doctor told him long ago. It didn't matter what was real or not anymore, he just knew he needed to escape this place.

"Hello?" a soft voice groaned from the walls.

Lukas dropped the stone and the spoon once more, holding his breath. Was it a ghost? He certainly hoped it wasn't. But he crawled toward the stone wall that once separated Erica and him, gripping the small shank. His skin, as his knees touched the floor, froze from its cold. Like kneeling on ice.

His ear pressed against the wall as he called back to the voice, "Hello?"

There was a long silence.

"Over here, quickly," a boy said. His voice echoed through the small hole in the hall. Now it made sense. Of course, it wasn't a ghost, it was the new boy the guards placed after they took Erica.

Lukas hurried to the hole, where he peered inside. A younger boy was on the other side. He was pale, with streaks of blond hair sitting neatly on his head and his face smudged with grime and scratches. His cerulean blue eyes were red and puffy. No doubt he had been crying. Lukas didn't understand why. There was no reason to cry when no one could listen.

"Are you real?" the mysterious boy said.

"Of course I am. Why wouldn't I be?" Lukas snarled.

The boy stared at him for a second, probably debating whether Lukas was or wasn't a ghost.

"Where am I?" he asked.

"Home. This is home." Lukas didn't know how else to describe it. After the many years he had been here, he still didn't know exactly where it was they were. But *home* suited nicely. It had everything a home had.

"No, it's not."

"Yes, it is."

"No, it's not!"

Lukas stared blankly at him for a moment. "Well, now it's your home."

A look of despair now crashed over the boy as his eyes saddened. Lukas thought he might've been harsh with him, considering he was just as innocent as the bunnies the director made them kill.

"What's your name? I'm Lukas," he said.

"My name's Thomas. But there's been some kind of mistake. I shouldn't be here. I was just at the hospital the other day and—"

"You passed their test."

Thomas held his breath for a moment. "The test? You mean the weekly evaluation?"

"They tricked us," Lukas sighed. "They always meant to bring us here, but I figured they needed us to be violent first."

"Violent for what?" Thomas widened his eyes.

Lukas's stomach grumbled louder this time.

"Are you hungry? Here." Thomas disappeared for a moment before returning with a handful of mush. The sight of it made Lukas's stomach ache, but not with hunger this time, with disgust. He would've rather starved than eat more of the sour sliminess the guards fed them in their dog bowls.

Lukas watched Thomas's hand pierce through the small hole in the wall, attempting to deliver a handful of his food.

"No, Thomas. It's your food. You eat it. I'm alright." He lied, of course. He was far from being alright. All the questions he still had about *Phase Three* ate at him more than the fiery acid consuming his stomach. All he wanted to know was where the guards had taken his sister. What did she have that no one else had?

Still, Lukas knew he needed food and knew he needed it quickly, as his body became restless at the unsettling hunger. His eyes fell back on Thomas, pulling his hand out of the wall and retching from the vile odor of the mush in his hand. Eating that food was punishment enough, he thought.

A prickling touch landed on Lukas's hand. He looked down to find a small hairy spider resting. His heart leaped at the sight. Naturally, Lukas would've flung the malicious creature and shrieked, but he studied the perilous thing. His stomach growled at the small sight.

It was food, after all.

Lukas pinched its fuzzy body off his hand, holding it in the air. His heart fluttered at the touch. He gulped as he watched the pathetic thing squirm in his small, rough fingers.

"What're you doing, Lukas?" Thomas meddled.

But Lukas ignored him. He probably would've objected if he knew what Lukas was going to do.

The spider's tiny hairs pricked into his fingers like pins. Its black orbed eyes glared at him. He wondered if the spider knew what was imminent, how it had no control over what would happen to it, how Lukas was in control of its life.

Its life was lesser than his, and Lukas had to survive. Even if it meant eating a putrid *thing*.

Lukas's mouth watered, and a chill crept up his spine as he raised the spider above his mouth. His fist flared by his side as he tightened his eyes. The room now echoed with the sound of his grumbling stomach. He cringed as the spider moved its legs above him.

Survive, Lukas. Eat to survive.

Eat it.

He dropped the twitching hairy spider into his mouth.

"No, don't!" Thomas called from behind the wall.

It was the worst feeling Lukas had ever known. The spider squirmed in his mouth, prickling his tongue and gums, fearing for its life. The slimy sourness of its body drooled down his throat as he began chewing.

The spider's black orbed eyes exploded on his tongue. Now it blindly scurried. His teeth snapped its legs one by one. The crunch of its body sent a chill up his spine. Every second, Lukas wanted to spit it out as the vile tasted splattered around, but the aching pain in his stomach only grew.

Thankfully, the dismembered spider had finally died. As it did, he gulped every leg, every eye, and every hair until every part drowned in the restless acid of his stomach.

But as he finished, a series of loud steps echoed from outside Lukas's cell. *A guard*, he thought.

His ears filled with the pounding of his heart. Lukas could feel the scorching heat of the furnace the guard would drag him to.

No, he refused. He wouldn't willingly go to his demise.

Lukas scrambled to the shank lying by the wall, his breaths becoming heavy.

"Lukas, what's going on? What're you doing?"

"Shut up, Thomas, and don't make a sound," Lukas said, as he slithered next to the great metal door.

The director had intended for Lukas to die tonight; he was sure of it. Maybe that's what they did with Erica as well.

The door rattled as the guard unlocked it. Lukas stood like a shadow where the door would conceal him when opened. He squeezed the metal shank in his, ready.

A few moments passed, and the vast door swung open, casting a box of light into Lukas's cell. The guard entered the room clutching his rifle with both arms, surveying the dark, grimy room.

"Where's the boy?" the guard said.

"Look around. He couldn't have escaped," another said from the corridor.

Lukas's heart threatened to break out as it hammered against his chest, making his whole body heavy. The guard staggered further into the room and scanned around until his body faced where Lukas hid.

Without a moment's loss, Lukas shot toward the guard and leaped onto him. The guard howled as he collapsed to the floor with Lukas on top of him. But any second now, Lukas was about to be overpowered by his colossal stature. There was only one thing to do.

Lukas drove his shank through the guard's mask directly into his left eye.

The wailing guard threw Lukas off with a mighty force as he aimed his rifle and blindly fired. Lukas yelped as the gunshot filled the room and fired into the stone wall.

"No! Don't shoot! We're not supposed to kill him!" the other guard shouted.

Lukas lay on the floor, defeated without his shank. His hands felt wet from the blood that dripped from that guard's face.

"Little fucker!" the guard said as he stumbled out of Lukas's cell before it closed once more.

Now, the darkness of his cell swallowed him, where the light would never find him. A relieved smile spread across his face as he lay panting, his body throbbing with adrenaline.

"Lukas! What did you do!" Thomas called from Erica's cell.

Lukas sat up, facing the hole in the wall, a twisted grin widening on his face. "I did what Director Miller asked me to do. I destroyed my innocence."

36

ELIZABETH

JULY 12

THE TIRES OF THE stolen car scorched the pavement of Elizabeth's driveway. The night had been creeping into 2:00 AM now.

But before they arrived at her home, Elizabeth had driven them to a convenience store in town to purchase large black garbage bags and latex gloves. She refused to carry the boy's discolored limbs one by one into her home. With the bags, it'd make the grotesque action somehow more bearable. Not that there was a way to make moving a dismembered body pleasant, but she had no choice.

Until now, Frank had used every spare second of their drive trying to change her mind, but she refused. Elizabeth was unyielding—like a fortress impenetrable.

Elizabeth stepped out of the car, wiping her bloody hands on her favorite trench coat. Her lips curled in disgust as she did. But she'd rather have a dirty coat than blood on her hands. The warm air rushed through her as she took it off.

Frank had already made his way to the trunk with the black bags, and as he propped it open, he gagged at the mutilated sight. He had been halfway toward grabbing a severed arm when Elizabeth interjected, "Stop, Frank! The gloves. You need to wear the latex gloves, or your fingerprints will be all over that boy."

Frank gulped as she finished. He made his way to the passenger seat and returned a few moments later, wearing a pair of blue latex gloves.

Elizabeth took a step nearer to the trunk, and as she did, she was blasted with a vile, bitter aroma. Her nose buried into her sleeve as she watched Frank load the bags with the many parts of the dead boy. It reminded her of collecting parts to assemble some sort of toy or a doll. *Build-A-Boy, what a cheery doll that would be.*

As Frank continued loading the bags, a look of bitterness grew on him as he shot a sharp glance at her. "Aren't you going to help!" he spat.

"I'm perfectly fine letting you do the dirty work this time, Frank," she said.

Frank snarled at her as he continued putting limbs one by one in the bags until, finally, they were all removed from the trunk. They had separated it into two bags: one for the upper body, the other for the lower. The gloves Frank wore were now just as contaminated with the stench of death, a fitting follower for him.

Together, Elizabeth and Frank carried the heavy bags up the driveway and to Elizabeth's home. As Elizabeth carried one of the body bags up the porch, the bag snagged on the edge of the stairs. It must've been a poking nail. She tugged the bag with a forceful pull, and it ripped from the stair. Opening the front door, Elizabeth staggered inside the darkness of her home before flipping the lights on, the bag of limbs swaying at her side as if she were returning from grocery shopping.

She led Frank to the living where they dropped both bags on the mandala carpet. Elizabeth's bag rolled over to where a rather large hole was exposed. *That damn stair*, she thought.

"Oh, Jesus Christ," Frank said as one of the boy's arms poked out from the bag.

Elizabeth held her breath at the sight, disgusted. Now, she felt like a murderer. It appeared her hands weren't as clean as she thought.

But before Elizabeth could order Frank to fix the arm, the front door rattled. The sound pricked her spine as sweat dripped from her brow. The creaking steps of the floorboards grew closer as Elizabeth's heart pounded. *A robber, a killer—who could it be?*

It was worse. The intruder was Sophia.

Sophia had been wiping her tearing eyes when she walked into the murderous scene wearing her white blouse and blue skirt. The scene they had created paralyzed Elizabeth upon Sophia's unexpected arrival. A pair of ex-lovers standing by a bag with an arm sticking out. How terribly convenient.

Sophia looked up at Elizabeth for a moment. "Oh hey, I didn't know you'd be here—" But her eyes must've fallen to the arm because Sophia let out a piercing shrill at the sight. Her hands clasped over her mouth as she continued screaming in terror. "You monsters!" Sophia staggered back and rushed away from the scene. Rightfully so.

"Sophia—wait! No! It's not what it looks like! Please, come back!" Elizabeth chased her out of the living room to the entrance. She had to stop her before Sophia did anything irrational about what she had just seen. Of course, she'd never go to the police, but there was no way to be sure. She clasped Sophia's arm before she could open the front door and run.

Sophia jerked her arm away from Elizabeth's grasp. "Let go of me! You guys are murderers!"

The accusation made Elizabeth bite her lip. She wasn't entirely wrong. But about the boy, she was. "No—you're wrong! Dear, please, it's not what it looks like! Please let me explain! Please, Sophia!"

Sophia's blood drained face squirmed with fury. "Get the hell away from me or I'm calling the police!"

"I've been called a lot of things, but *murderer* is new," Frank said from behind, an irritating amusement in his tone.

Sophia paused, caught in a moment of perplexity, her hand on the knob of the front door. "Why is *he* here?" She pointed at Frank.

Frank scowled. "I'm helping. Why the hell are you here? Don't you have some college party to be roofied at right now?"

"Frank!" Elizabeth roared.

Sophia's face flushed. "Someone tell me who the fuck that is in the living room right now!"

Elizabeth threw her hands in the air. "We don't know! Frank and I were taking a walk when we came across—something horrible. It was a boy, but he was mutilated, completely torn apart. I couldn't just leave him like that, Sophia! I just couldn't. Please, Sophia, you need to believe me."

Sophia's eyes widened with terror. "So, you tampered with evidence? Elizabeth, you could have just reported it to the authorities!"

Elizabeth held her tongue. It would've been a terrible idea if she had reported the gruesome scene to the police, but Sophia could never know why that was. "I'm a doctor, Sophia. I took an oath. And one day, you will, too. Please—I want to do what's right," she said.

Sophia lifted her hands and squeezed them into fists, her flushed face shrinking with disdain. "The *right* thing to do, Elizabeth, would've been to not steal a mutilated corpse. I mean, what the hell were you thinking? Are you some kind of idiot? You don't think that detective woman won't figure what you've done?"

Elizabeth stepped forward. "I know. I apologize, Sophia. It was irrational to me, but I had to do something. I had to save his body, even if he was no longer living," she said.

There was a moment of silence between them as Sophia's eyes softened. Elizabeth felt a shroud of guilt over misusing her talent for persuading others, but she had no choice. Sophia was now part of this investigation, whether or not she liked it.

Sophia took a deep breath, rubbing her eyes. She seemed to swallow her frustrations. "Okay. Fine," she said. "What do we do?"

A soft smile slipped on Elizabeth's face as she led her and Frank back to the living room. Now that she'd convinced Sophia of their innocence, they could get back to understanding what happened to the boy. But first, she needed to move the bags somewhere other than her carpet as the stench of rotting flesh filled the room. Elizabeth buried her nose in her arm as she approached the two bags.

"We're not just gonna leave him there, right?" Sophia said, clasping her hands over her nose.

"I think it fits your house nicely. Don't you think, Ainsley?" Frank said.

Elizabeth shot an icy glare at him. "Of course not. But I know where we can put him." There was only one place she could think of storing the bags, and it was somewhere she hadn't visited in years. The thought of revisiting churned her stomach like never before as she began pulling furniture off the carpet.

"Now c'mon, Ainsley, what're you doing?" Frank said, leaning against the wall. His greasy black coat was sure to stain it.

But she ignored him as she continued. Finally, with a heavy breath, she lifted the mandala carpet, revealing a small trapdoor in the dusted floorboards.

Sophia gasped at the sight, and Elizabeth expected this. She would've reacted the same upon discovering her own secrets for the first time. And upon opening that trapdoor, she knew she would release the worst of herself back into the world. *Like opening Pandora's Box,* she thought.

Elizabeth gritted her teeth and steeled her eyes toward the trapdoor as she made her toward it. Sophia and Frank gathered by her as she lifted the trapdoor. An archaic chill shot through her body. A rickety stairway descended to the black abyss that engulfed her past. She held her breath as she kneeled at the foot of the trapdoor. "We can keep him down there for now," she said.

"What's down there?" Sophia choked on the last word.

Elizabeth stood up. "Help me take him down."

Together, they carefully carried the two body bags from the living room and down the trapdoor. Sophia whimpered behind Elizabeth as they did, and Frank's face had struck with fury as they reached the bottom—as expected. He always had something to be irritated at which consequently made Elizabeth irritated at his moodiness. But perhaps carrying bags of limbs could make his anger justifiable. No, it served him right. And there was something satisfying to Elizabeth about Frank's silent torment.

They laid the bags on the cold ground, the boy's limp arm brushing against Elizabeth's wool sweater as they did. She shivered from the soulless, icy touch. Like being grazed by the finger of death.

Elizabeth found the light switch on a tall panel of wood before she flipped it. Two brilliant bulbs hanging from the ceiling illuminated the basement and cast their glow within the somber, rustic walls. A project she had once started but never completed. Only half of the basement floor was filled with concrete, while the other was soil, but she would never finish filling the floor. Not since what rested in the soil now.

Her arms wrapped around her shoulders as the unnerving chill in this forgotten crypt froze her skin. Elizabeth took a step forward. She drifted toward the other side of the basement, entranced by the haunting memory of the Crucifix sticking out of the soil. Her ears filled with the bloody cries of that night. *Blood—blood—blood. I never want to see it again. Blood stains everything it touches.*

"Ainsley," Frank called from behind. There was a slight strain of fear in his voice. "Ainsley! Who is that?"

Elizabeth remained stagnant at the last bit of concrete floor. Her eyes glimmered with the life she buried years ago. The remarkable woman she once was now buried six feet underground. She turned to look at Frank's furrowed face, and with a single breath, she whispered, "My son. Thomas."

37

ELIZABETH

JULY 12

THERE WAS A PIERCING silence that lingered in Elizabeth's basement. Fortunately, the buzzing of Frank's phone in his pocket interrupted Sophia and Frank's immediate perplexity. A look of relief overcame him as he pulled it from his pocket. Elizabeth swore she glimpsed a swooning grin, but it must've been the intense lighting of the basement that made it seem that way.

Frank gulped. "Sorry—I need to take this." He hurried up the basement steps and up to the main house, his tail between his legs. Normally, she would've tried to stop him from leaving the scene, but she had no words this time. Elizabeth's memories were suppressing her voice.

Sophia had been gawking in disbelief. It must've been a grueling night for her, too. But no matter, they needed to figure out who this boy was and what happened to him, with or without Frank.

"This must've been the Recluse Killer." Elizabeth pointed at the bag. "The vile way he was strung up on some man-made web was the same manner in which that woman, Rebecca, was found."

Sophia perked her head, and her eyes widened. Her lips pressed into a thin line as she examined the bags sitting by her foot. "Open the bags. I want to see his face," Sophia demanded.

Elizabeth hesitated, her mind racing. She couldn't let Sophia witness the gruesome extent of this boy's mutilation. Such a barbaric image could scar her young mind permanently, and she refused to let Sophia be hurt anymore. She took a step forward, determination in her voice. "I'm sorry, but that's not something you need to see, Sophia. I won't allow it."

Sophia ran her fingers through her hair. "I'm not some little kid, Elizabeth! I can handle it. Please, show me." She nodded to the bags.

Elizabeth sighed in defeat as she met Sophia's unwavering eyes. It pained her to admit that Frank was right. Sophia *wasn't* her daughter, and she needed to stop seeing her like she was.

With trembling steps, Elizabeth approached the two black bags lying by Sophia's side. Her breaths became sharp as she undid the plastic knot of the bag filled with the boy's dismembered upper body. The rancid stench of him clogged her nose. She opened the plastic bag filled with bloody pieces of an arm, fingers, a torn torso, an ear, and his maroon-stained head. It wasn't so much a body as it was pieces of an animal scavenging for the best piece of meat.

Staggering back, Elizabeth held her sweater sleeve over her nose as Sophia clenched her jaw and scanned the many limbs inside the bag. It was only a matter of seconds before Sophia gagged at the contents within. She pulled away from the bag, retching.

"I was right." She coughed. "It's that boy. The one from the newspaper."

Elizabeth's eyes widened, and her brow raised. "What are you talking about, Sophia? What newspaper?"

But Sophia didn't answer as she was burying her nose in her arm. The vile odor of death spread around the basement like a disease, and it needed to be stopped. Elizabeth hurried to the open bag and tied any knot she could think of until she shut the plastic bag. The rotting stench lingered, but it was tolerable now, like leaving spoiled milk out too long.

"It's him. It's Percy Romano," Sophia cried.

The name stumped Elizabeth. She'd never heard of him before, but from the agony in Sophia's voice, Elizabeth had a grim premonition of who he might be. "What—who are you talking about?"

Tears dripped from Sophia's eyes. "The boy from the newspaper! He's a missing person! Oh, my god—I can't believe it's really him." Sophia collapsed to her knees, retching into her sleeve.

Elizabeth stopped breathing. Her heart ached at the cruel revelation. The boy's face was frozen in her mind and she couldn't rid the picture. Her mind wouldn't purge the thought. *Think of something else! Anything!* At her terrible wish, Percy's face morphed into her son's. Her mouth fell open in a silent scream.

No more of this. Elizabeth clasped Sophia's hand from the ground and lifted her without saying a word. This was why she hid in the basement; emotions always swarmed like bugs, and they needed to be purged, locked away. She led Sophia up the basement stairs and onto the sofa couch in the living room.

Together, they fell onto the plush red cushions as Sophia whimpered. Somehow, the living room seemed more still than the basement. The warm lights from the lamps cast a glow on their frozen faces.

Taking a deep breath, Elizabeth placed a gentle hand on Sophia's trembling body. "Are you absolutely sure it was him?"

Sophia turned her pale face, her eyes staring at Elizabeth in horror. "It was Percy. The Recluse Killer killed him," she muttered. "And I think the killer murdered my mother, too. The fire in the building, I think it was them that started it." Tears formed as she said the words.

Elizabeth's heart stopped. How could she have forgotten about the atrocity she committed? Sophia gazed longingly at her as if she were awaiting an explanation. Was she waiting for an explanation? *Does she know? No—of course she doesn't. Don't be ridiculous.* But all Elizabeth could do was pull Sophia near her and wrap her arms around her restless body.

In that moment, she envied Percy. Not because of his murderous fate, but because he was dead. Perhaps it would've been a great favor to everyone for her just to be dead, too. If Sophia ever found out the truth about her mother, she'd put a bullet in Elizabeth's head without hesitation. Pulling the trigger is easy when there's hate loaded in the barrel.

Sophia's breaths softened, which made Elizabeth grin. How lucky she was to have found such a diligent student to mentor. It would destroy her when it came time to let Sophia go. The very thought of it tore her mind.

But there was something else that tormented Elizabeth's mind. With a deep breath, she released Sophia and grasped her shoulders. "You were crying when you arrived. Why?"

Sophia parted her chapped lips, holding her breath. Her eyes darted elsewhere momentarily. "There's this man. At first, it was fun, but as soon as we were about to have sex again," Sophia paused, "I couldn't stop thinking about my dad. The way he touches me reminds me too much of what my father used to do. It feels so possessive, like I'm just letting him do what he wants to me, while my conscious just watches. I didn't feel like myself. I could see it happening somewhere else. I saw the way this man touched me. It was so—demeaning, like I'm just something for him to conquer. I think there's something wrong with me, Elizabeth. I can't seem to let go of my abusive past." Sophia sighed, clutching the skin on her arm.

Elizabeth had known of her troubled past and her unforgivable history of her father, but it was always rarely discussed. It was a terrible thing that happened, and she'd never allow it to happen again.

Elizabeth bit her lip. "My first husband was a terrible man. A CIA chauvinist. And every day with him was a battle for control in our marriage—he couldn't fathom the idea of me holding more governmental influence than him. Until one day, I divorced him and took our newborn son. My life has deteriorated ever since. He conspired against my life and lied to get me into this town, then he kidnapped my son for himself." She cradled Sophia's cheek with her wrinkled palm. "You are not to blame for what your father did. He was a disgusting man. And you're right to be careful with men. They're dogs who only want sexual pleasure from us, and they'll leave the moment they get it. But there is nothing wrong with you, dear. Absolutely nothing," she said.

Elizabeth brushed Sophia's loose, dark hair with her fingers and tucked it behind her ear, forming a sympathetic smile.

A rush of guilt surged through Elizabeth's veins as she pulled her arm back. That was a motherly action. But she wasn't a mother anymore, and she certainly was not Sophia's mother. And she was no daughter thief. Still, it felt as if she'd kidnapped someone's daughter and was convincing Sophia to love her rather than her own mother. At least, that's what Natalie Warren thought. The fragile memory made her heart pound against her chest.

Natalie Warren.

Sophia perked her head. "Elizabeth, what are we going to do with Percy?"

"Sophia, listen to me. I want to return his body back to his parents rather than the police. It's the proper thing to do. Do you understand?" Elizabeth sat up.

"I guess so," Sophia sighed.

There was a pause between them, as if Sophia was waiting to hear what they'd have to do next. *Reassemble him? Of course not.* For now, the cold air in the basement would preserve the body well.

Sophia spun around. "Hey—is Frank still on the phone?"

Elizabeth's forehead wrinkled in surprise. Frank had indeed taken a while on whatever business he attending too. Perhaps a phone whore, she thought. It wouldn't have surprised her.

"Perhaps. But I'm sure he'll return soon," she said

If he was ignorant enough to go to the police, he'd be turning himself in. That's why it was important to make sure Frank touched the body. So his fingerprints would be painted all over like a child's painting. It was a step important for her own security.

A low buzzing chime interrupted her thought. It must've been her phone. She reached into her pocket to grab but as her fingers brushed it, her phone wasn't vibrating. Elizabeth glanced over at Sophia. "Is that your phone, dear?"

"No, I thought it was yours." Sophia shrugged. A look of confusion struck her face.

They sat in silence as the low buzzing chime continued. But it quickly became clear as a chill prickled up Elizabeth's spine. Her lips pinched together as she shot up from the couch and hurried down the basement steps, Sophia calling behind her.

The intermediate buzzing grew louder. Elizabeth's eyes widened as she stared down at the black bag filled with Percy's lower body. A phone chimed from within. Without a second to lose, she tore the plastic with her clawing hands.

"Oh my god," Sophia breathed from behind.

Panting in fear, Elizabeth ripped a hole wide enough to reach her hand through. She didn't care about the repugnant stench anymore; she needed that phone. The bag full of severed pieces of leg made her hold her breath as she dug around with her hand. The feeling was vile, as Percy's cold skin squished against her hand. Elizabeth pursed her lips as she pressed her arm deeper into the bag until she finally grasped the phone.

Pulling it out, she held the shaking, whistling object to her face and read the caller.

It was *Her.* No other explanation but *Her.*

Sophia peered from behind. "Who is *Her?*"

It was such an obscure name to call someone. Clearly, Percy didn't want others knowing of her identity. But as the phone stopped buzzing, the screen faded to the wallpaper.

It was a photo of Percy, shirtless, beaming as a pale blonde girl in a bikini kissed him on his cheek.

38

LUKAS

JULY 13

"PULL MY TRIGGER," THE pistol in his hands whispered. Its cold metal touch sent a shiver down Lukas's spine.

It was the ultimate instrument of fear. When you pointed a gun between someone's eyes to see them quiver in horror, not a word spoken, but their eyes pleading for mercy. The bloodthirsty sight was as tasteful to Lukas as a carcass was to a murder of crows. A twisted smile curled on his face before he stashed Bill's gun back into his truck's glove compartment. Hopefully, no one saw it through the windows.

Lukas perked his head from the driver's seat, glaring at the apartment complex across the street. The re-opening of the New Horizon apartments should've been a jubilant celebration for him, but it wasn't. It was the re-opening of a zoo, waiting to put the savage animals back in their cages on display for the entire world to see. *"Look at that one!"* a curious child would say. *"He's here because his childhood was burned to the fucking ground!"*

He chuckled at the thought as his nails dug into the rubber of the wheel. Perhaps it would've been better if the fire consumed the entire building, but it had only destroyed the top floor, and within a week and a half, they reconstructed it without a trace of ash. That's what happened when an entire group of construction workers focused on one project, like ants for a colony.

Different tenants walked in and out of the building: a tatted woman struggling to light a cigar, a frowning old man pushing down the sidewalk with his earbuds, and Karina carrying a small stack of books inside. Her black locks bounced as she walked in her jeans and red top. She was a soft-spoken girl. It seemed she had been that way since the death of her mother. Fleeing into the fantasies of her books must've been an escape for her, just like killing was for him. Both were yearning fantasies.

But Lukas's heart hammered in his chest as he gazed at the building with dread. He hadn't seen Dimitri since the night of the fire. What a terrible coincidence the police took Lukas in for questioning while Dimitri stood across the street. He must've thought Lukas caused the fire and despised him now. He was sure of it. It's always easy to blame the first suspect in a crime rather than the perpetrator.

And he was no criminal.

He was an artist, an activist. Yes, that's what he was.

Lukas stepped out of his truck and walked across the deserted street to the apartments. Swaying trees lined the pavement and created pockets of shade along the road. He imagined Dimitri's eyes peering down his neck and weighing on him until he sank to the ground. Each step closer grew heavier on the ground as the sun beat down his back, a humid haze.

The tall lamppost on the corner continued to display the face of Cassandra Holland. It'd been almost three months now since the posters first hung and still not any information on her whereabouts. *That's good.* It gave the Haddam Police Department more of a reason to fear this city, to make them finally realize these cages they built weren't as safe as they naively thought. And it was easier to be feared than to be respected.

Lukas made a double take at the lamppost. There was something unusual this time as he stopped at the towering sight. He studied the glued posters until he caught a familiar face in black and white. His brows shot up in surprise at the pixelated graph of Percy Romano. He'd been declared an official missing person as of a few days ago. Amelia, naturally, hadn't found him yet because of her incompetence. A crooked smile widened on his face. At their slow pace, he could continue with his passion for murdering, creating new puzzles, shifting the game board until Amelia would throw in the towel. Until he'd make a mockery of her entire department. In fact, he'd already thrown her off his spotless trail during that whole interrogation.

Lukas brushed his head away from the lamppost and approached the vast double glass doors of the apartment building. Its faux elegance always made for an alluring appearance. His fingers grazed the handle before both doors burst open. Staggering back, Karina trudged past him with a harsh scowl, muttering under her breath. He caught a whiff of her perfume. Bitter, like the tart of an apple.

"Karina, you nearly hit me," Lukas said.

She turned back to face him, smoldering with resentment. Strange, he'd never seen her with knuckles flared by her side. "I don't care," Karina spat. She stomped on without giving him another thought.

Jesus, what a bitch.

He stepped inside the lobby of New Horizon. Flickering fluorescent lights illuminated worn-out carpeting and faded forestry wallpaper that seemed to have lost its charm decades ago. The air was heavy with the stench of neglect, like an abandoned child, and the lobby seemed to carry the weight of countless forgotten stories. Dilapidated furniture lined the walls, and plastic tables were set up in the lounge, their once-vibrant colors now muted and dull.

A battered reception desk stood in the corner, its surface marred by scratches and soda stains. An antique grandfather clock in the corner ticked away the seconds, the chimes echoing through the still space. The distant hum of traffic and the occasional creak of worn floorboards broke the lobby's silence.

Lukas's footsteps echoed as he moved farther into the lobby. Dimitri should've been at the desk. He was the landlord, after all. But he caught glimpses of a small figure giggling underneath one table.

Jake poked his small head from under the table, beaming. "Hi! Do you wanna play with me? I'm making my Power Rangers and Barbies fight."

"That sounds awesome." Lukas chuckled. "But my friend, Dimitri. Have you seen him?"

Jake pointed at the door behind the reception desk. "He's in his office. He went in there after Katrina and him got in a fight," he said in oblivious bliss.

"A fight?" Lukas's brow raised. "About what?"

"Well, I'm not sure if they were fighting, but they were whispering really angrily."

Lukas stared blankly at Jake, a perplexed expression tugging at his face. "Well, I'll go knock on his door. Thanks, Jake."

"By the way," Jake started, a mischievous grin spreading across his face. "I don't think you started the fire," he said, grinning.

Lukas spun around sharply, his heart racing. *What the fuck did he just say?* Did others besides Amelia suspect he started the fire? It didn't make any sense.

But all he could mutter was a pathetic "What?" as his breath caught in his throat.

"It couldn't have been you, Lukas. You're my friend," Jake finished, his voice filled with earnestness, before creeping back under the table.

Lukas's mouth gaped, his mind a whirlwind of confusion and shock, uncertain whether to breathe or ask more questions. His eyes continued staring at where Jake was, waiting for him to come back. Uncertainty swirled around him as he did. Jake was this wasting town's last bit of innocence, so maybe it was better not to take the things he said seriously.

"Lukas!" a hoarse voice called from the desk. Dimitri's voice.

Just the man he's trying to avoid. It must've been he who was spreading the rumor that Lukas caused the fire, and he hated the fact it wasn't an unreasonable assumption to make. It was Dimitri who saw Lukas get taken by the police that night.

Dimitri's hairy arms stretched across the desk as his jaw clenched sharply. His blue Yankees tee was one size too small. It must've been suffocating to wear.

Lukas attempted to meet his eyes, but Dimitri shifted his abruptly away, staring at anything in the lobby except him. The betrayal made his stomach contract, threatening to vomit. He buried his hands in his black jeans and pinched at the material as he faced Dimitri.

"Hey," Lukas mumbled.

Dimitri pursed his lips as he let out a long breath. "That jar of *snow* I gave you a while ago. I can take it back now," he whispered.

"Is that all?" Lukas said with a strain of annoyance. He crossed his arms as he peered at Dimitri, scratching the back of his curly hair.

Dimitri was holding back, unlike his bulging stomach. What wasn't he saying? The silence between them only grew as Dimitri gazed at the floor and walls until, finally, he gave Lukas a sharp frown.

"Well, I guess I'll just say it," Dimitri stammered. "A lot of the people who live here complain that they don't feel *safe* around you. You know, with the fire and everything, and with you being Rebecca's boyfriend—"

Rage shot through him. "That wasn't me!"

"Well, you know, *I* don't think it was you. But the homeowner's association here doesn't want you living here anymore."

Lukas stopped breathing. His ears filled with the hammering of his heart. "You're evicting me? Dimitri, c'mon, we're friends! Right?"

Dimitri remained silent, shifting his eyes back to the carpet floor beneath them.

"Right?" Lukas mumbled, a lump growing in his throat.

"I'll let you gather your things, but you need to be gone by tonight."

Lukas trembled with rage as he strutted in front of Dimitri. How could he have done that to him? He was speechless, like someone had drained his voice from his throat. Nothing made sense around him as the lobby blurred.

The gun.

If only he had that damn gun, he'd shoot Dimitri right in the fucking head for throwing him away like a piece of trash. But he couldn't do anything except gawk at Dimitri's disappointment. Dimitri wouldn't even acknowledge his presence anymore as he wandered behind the reception desk, pretending to look for something missing.

You fat fuck, Dimitri! Lukas's jaw clenched as his fists trembled at his side.

"Jake, honey! It's time to go! God, I can't handle another twelve-hour shift!" Vivian called from behind. That high-pitched whine was like the nasally cry of a dog.

Lukas spun around, his eyes narrowing on her callous expression. She had just come down the stairs. It didn't surprise him. She was only wearing a white bra and sweats, with obscene tattoos trailing down her skin. A snide grin stretched on her grotesque face as their eyes met. Fury rippled through him as she clasped Jake's hand, continuing to sneer at him.

Lukas could taste Vivian's blood as his teeth ground. "Vivian! You did this, Vivian! You pathetic cunt!"

Vivian crossed her arms tightly, snarling like a rabid dog. "What did you just call me?"

He shot a finger toward Jake. "I'll kill him! I'll fucking kill him and make you watch!"

Jake shrieked. He burst into tears, sprinting towards Vivian.

Lukas didn't care. That little shit was just her infuriating spawn, anyway.

"Enough—Lukas!" Dimitri intervened.

Vivian pulled a now frightened Jake away and led him up the stairs.

His rage felt good as he took a step forward, watching them leave. "I'll kill him!"

39

Lukas

July 13

Lukas had gathered his things from his apartment before he found himself at SuperShine. He collected the essentials, of course, such as clothes, toiletries, Rebecca's photos, and Dimitri's cocaine.

Dimitri was furious when Lukas said he'd lost it, but he had to lie. The cocaine was a type of safety insurance to make sure Dimitri wouldn't try anything stupid, such as talking to anyone he wasn't supposed to. And if he did, all Lukas had to do was *slip* it to the police.

After what happened with Vivian and Dimitri, the last thing Lukas wanted to do was now deal with Ian and work at the tiresome carwash. He had bitten his tongue when Ian chastised him for his slight tardiness for his shift.

Be a good boy now, Lukas, he'd told himself.

He needed the money now more than ever, especially now that he had nowhere to live. Even his friend Mateo profusely refused to let Lukas move in with him after he explained what had happened at New Horizons, largely because Mateo's girlfriend had moved in with him.

Lukas plunged a rag into the soapy bucket of water, a line of sweat dripping from his forehead. His charcoal shirt was glued to his skin as the blazing heat beat down his crooked back.

Lukas cleaned the shimmering black sedan from all stains and marks. It was a luxury car. Incredible that something of that value hadn't been hot-wired and stolen, as luxury was the rarest resource to come by in East Haddam. The windows were tinted, so he couldn't see the driver. His nose scrunched at the perverse sight. It mocked him how he couldn't see inside the car, but the driver could watch him.

He moved on to the side mirrors with a stroke of the rag, bubbles foamed as he did. The car engine of the sedan revved next to him—another impatient driver. For how cheap the service was, they had no right to complain about the time it took, especially since there was a stubborn grease stain on the mirror. Lukas pressed his arm deeper, scrubbing his reflection from the mirror. His black stubble had grown thicker since he last shaved, and the bags beneath his eyes had deepened from all the late nights awake.

He continued scrubbing. If only he were more attractive, Rebecca wouldn't have tried to leave him.

His arm pressed deeper. If only he knew who slipped the note under his door.

Lukas scowled. If only he knew what Amelia was thinking, what she was planning.

The rag tightened in his hand. If only Sophia had fucked him.

The side mirror cracked and crashed onto the asphalt ground.

Lukas's face paled. *Dammit!* The shattering of the side mirror echoed through the carwash, an unexpected moment of chaos amidst the monotony of the job. He froze, rag in hand, gawking at the broken glass on the ground, his heart hammering at what he'd just done.

From the black sedan, the driver's door opened, and a middle-aged man stepped out, his face contorted in a mix of anger and disbelief. "What the hell did you just do to my car?" he shouted, his voice cutting through the air like a knife.

Lukas's stomach churned. He hadn't meant for this to happen. It was a mistake, a stupid accident born from the frustration he'd been boiling up. "I—I'm sorry, sir," he stammered, the words catching in his throat. "I really didn't mean to break it. It slipped from my hand."

But his apology was no use. The man's face reddened, his fists clenching at his sides. "*I—I—I'm sorry,*" he mocked. "You fucking idiot! This car costs more than you'll ever make in your miserable life! God, this is why I never visit East Haddam, because it's full of brainless people like you!

Rage rushed through him as his jaw clenched. *Be a good boy, Lukas.* At any moment, he was ready to explode in a fury. "I'm sorry," Lukas spat.

The man threw his hands in the air. "*Sorry* is not going to fix my damn car, you idiot! How incompetent are you? You have one job in your life, and that's cleaning cars! Look at what you did!"

Lukas wouldn't turn his head. Rage tormented within him. It suffocated him as he remained still, his eyes twitching sharply. *Fuck your stupid car.*

The man stomped toward him and gripped the back of Lukas's neck before dragging him to the broken side mirror. "I said look at you did!"

Lukas's anger sprang to life and onto the man.

He launched a heavy fist into the man's face. Blood splattered from the man's mouth and onto Lukas's hand. The man howled in pain as he staggered back to his car. His hands cradled his face, touching the blood dripping from his mouth.

But Lukas didn't care. He trembled in rage as his breaths grew heavy. His skin prickled with satisfaction. Power, it felt great. A small grin slipped on his face. His nostrils filled with the savory tang of blood. This man had no idea what kind of nightmare he had tipped into.

Lukas grabbed the side mirror with his wet scarlet hand and chucked it directly at the man's face.

The man yelled as his red face shattered the same the side mirror had. His nose had twisted to the left side of his face, and his mouth had been carved in difference directions. Sprinkles of glass shrouded his opulent face. Now, he looked just like everyone else in East Haddam.

Lukas's eyes stretched with exhilaration. The sight was more pleasurable than anything he'd seen, and there was something delicious about hearing the man relentlessly yell.

But Lukas's enjoyment was short-lived as Ian stormed from the small building in front of them. Ian's face was swollen with fury, as it always was.

"You motherfucker!" The man shoved Lukas away with a heavy force and turned to Ian. "You better pray to God I don't report this to the police if you don't pay to fix my car and now my hospital bill!" He swung open his car door and stepped inside, seething.

"Of course, sir! We will gladly compensate you. I am terribly sorry on behalf of SuperShine, how you were treated today," Ian said with a pleading voice. But before he could finish, the black sedan had already sped off.

Lukas remained on the floor, his fists throbbing and red. That man deserved it, and he refused to feel sorry for maiming him. But the glower on Ian's face told him he was about to regret what he did.

"Lukas. You're fired," Ian grumbled. "Get out! Get the hell out of here, now!"

40

LUKAS

JULY 13

LUKAS RANG THE CRACKED doorbell of Bill's house. The evening glow had illuminated his rustic ranch on the prairie, making the bronze wooden boards radiate with the sun's gold. This was the only place left. Lukas thought he could seek refuge. After all, Bill had called him his friend and now it came time to see if he stood by his word.

He looked down at the prickling mat below his worn sneakers. *"Welcome! Hope you like hunting!"* it said in bold black letters. He thought of himself as a hunter, just not the kind that killed *animals*.

The front door whined as it opened. For a moment, he had hoped Bill wouldn't have to spare him the embarrassment of asking to stay with him. *What if he says no?* Lukas was sure Bill would laugh right in his face before slamming the door, rightfully so. Perhaps it would be too much of a burden to ask for shelter from a near stranger. They'd barely known each other after all.

But now he'd have no choice but to plead as he burrowed his hands in his pockets and forced a nervous smile at Bill. His wide frame filled the doorway as the shiny black butcher's apron he wore draped to the floor. It was stained. Not by blood, but something white, almost clear.

Bill stared blankly at him as if he was waiting for him to make the first greeting.

So he did. "Hey Bill," Lukas murmured. He explained what happened at New Horizons, how his landlord had evicted him, how his despicable neighbors were conspiring against him, and, of course, he mentioned Vivian, the mastermind of it all. But he left out the detail of Amelia and how she had suspected him of the fire and Rebecca's murder.

Bill's face grew more sympathetic as Lukas explained what a cruel boss Ian was, and what happened at SuperShine. How he accidentally broke a customer's side mirror, only for the customer and Ian to belittle and mock him for it until he was fired. He'd lost everything that day. Everything except Bill's sympathy. He wore it as a welcoming smile stretching on his wrinkled, pallid cheeks.

He waved Lukas inside his home. "Of course you can stay here, brother," Bill said.

Lukas stepped into Bill's rustic house. The evening sun cast long, distorted shadows that seemed to stretch like grasping fingers across the dusty room. The air inside felt heavy, as if weighed down by the memories that had long since become ghosts. For a moment, he wondered if he'd stumbled inside his childhood home as the dim lighting from flickering lamps did little to dispel the eerie atmosphere that clung to the entrance. A stark contrast to Rebecca's cabin.

He followed Bill further in. The living room exuded a strange and unsettling charm, as though the walls held secrets that were best left undisturbed. Bill had styled the walls with mounted deer and elk heads, their glassy eyes staring out from lifeless sockets as if frozen in a perpetual state of haunting. And the photographs that hung off the plaster walls seemed to capture black-and-white moments during Bill's hunting career. A group of hunters and Bill smirking as a dead bear lay at their feet, and another larger portrait, one that peculiarly reminded him of Rebecca and him.

A younger Bill stood by a pallid woman with long strands of black hair in front of a farm much larger than his current ranch. Lukas examined their expressions, taking a step closer. Bill was smiling with his broad arm around the woman's dainty shoulder. The woman's black dress and somber expression, however, made him think the photo was captured at a funeral because wherever they were, made her melancholic. It was clear she was trying to pull away. Lukas imagined Bill was trying to get her to stay put during the photo, as he should. There was always some dramatics with women and their photos. Especially with Rebecca.

"Her name is Helen," Bill said from behind, his brow twitching.

Lukas turned his head. By the looks of Bill, he'd been watching him examine the photo for a minute now. But too long where it now seemed invasive.

Bill signaled him to a couch. "Come, you can sleep here," he said.

The large, worn leather couch stood in the living room, but it seemed out of place as if it had been the silent witness to events that had unfolded in this cluttered room. Its brown surface bore faint gray marks that suggested its abandonment, or perhaps it was simply the result of time's cruel touch. Opposite the couch, a fireplace crackled, casting eerie shadows that danced on the walls like specters from the past. A gun rack stood nearby, which displayed a meticulously maintained rifle.

An unsettling chill brushed Lukas's neck as he sank into the cushioned seat of the couch, like he'd intruded on someone's reserved seat. The ornate armchair in which Bill settled seemed like a throne, where he gazed at Lukas with a sharp eye, ready to govern him.

As Lukas sat in silence, he couldn't help but feel as though the walls were listening, absorbing his words like some dark ritual. He shot a quick glance at Bill, whose hands sat neatly in his butcher-aproned lap.

Again, he wondered why Bill wore that. He should've asked, but he said, "Helen. Did—did she die?"

Bill took a deep breath as his head turned to face the photo. Lukas thought maybe he shouldn't have asked. Maybe it was too personal of a question. But as he sat on the couch, he could feel Helen glaring at him, and he imagined Helen crawling out of the photograph, yelling at him for intruding inside their home. But of course, she didn't.

"Yes, she died," Bill finally spoke with a low voice. "Helen didn't like when others were concerned about her, or when *I* was concerned about her. She kept her ovarian cancer hidden from me for about a year after she found it. Hospitals were a nightmare to get into since their funding was cut and moved to make these *towns,* and shortly after, she passed away." He choked on the last words.

There was a moment of silence as he finished. Lukas was unsure how to respond to such a terrible passing. He wondered if he should apologize or say nothing at all. Maybe the best thing to say was nothing. But Bill had his eyes fixed on him, flickering with anticipation, waiting for Lukas to reply with condolences.

And so he did. "I'm sorry, man. That's terrible."

"I know Rebecca was your girlfriend, Lukas. I heard about what happened in the news when the *Recluse Killer* murdered her. Is that why you're asking?"

The fireplace cracked next to them as Lukas forced a relieved smile. "Yeah—I guess it's nice to know that I'm not the only one who's lost someone. Rebecca, she also liked to keep secrets from me."

Bill's eyes sharpened. "Women and their secrets. They love them more than they love us. But what else can you expect from beings who run on their own selfishness disguised as independence? They'd be nothing without us. A man knows how to handle a temperamental woman, and that's the way it's always been. He must know how to discipline her disobedience. The media doesn't want to admit it, but I will stand by the idea that the Recluse Killer is a woman. And what woman would be cruel enough to murder Rebecca? Elizabeth Ainsley. Her soul is the darkest here."

Lukas's brow twitched at the vile name as he agreed with Bill.

Elizabeth Ainsley. Lukas had almost forgotten about her, but the name sparked a fury inside him. Maybe Bill was right. She needed to be *disciplined* for her disobedience. The thought of it smeared a grin on his face, and the symphony of screams he'd make Elizabeth unleash was sure to be addicting.

And the fact Bill hadn't suspected Lukas capable of anything violent was relieving, Lukas was getting better at playing the sinless part better. The innocent act. The victim. *I am innocent. Tell yourself every day, and one day, you might believe it.*

There was truth in every word Bill spoke. Lukas was the hero to Rebecca. He saved her from her pitiful life, and he was going to save Sophia from Elizabeth. She didn't know it yet, but Sophia needed him. And how lucky she would be to have him.

Bill stood up, wiping his hands on the apron.

Lukas pointed. "What's with the apron?"

"It's for the animals in the shed. Sometimes they're *unruly,*" he said, chuckling. "There's a blanket in a basket just behind you. I'll come check on you in the morning. Just don't go poking around outside by the ranch, or you might wake the chickens."

But before Bill left him alone in the living room, Lukas cleared his throat. "Bill."

Bill turned his head with a puzzled expression.

"Do you think I'm a terrible person?" Lukas's heart hammered in his chest. All those terrible things that happened to him today that couldn't have been his fault. He did nothing wrong.

Bill grinned. "No, Lukas. You're a good person who's found himself in a terrible place."

41

LUKAS

JULY 14

THE MIDNIGHT AIR WAS uncomfortably hot. It sweltered around Lukas like a blazing blanket. Restless, he tossed and turned throughout the night, his mind consumed with the thought of Elizabeth, and he needed something to soothe his bloodlust mind.

The thought of masturbating to Rebecca, Sophia, or Pink Whitney crossed his mind but was quickly defeated as his eyes drifted to the sight of Helen on the wall. Her dreadful picture killed any possibility of sexual relief.

Lukas stared at the still dark ceiling, his fingers tingling at his side. A cold sweat trickled down his back and soaked into the couch. His bloodthirsty cravings needed to be quenched. It had been too long now since he smelled the sweet scent of fear and tasted the metal tang of blood. Even the memory of murdering Percy was no longer enough. He licked his lips. They tasted sour. His lips needed to be coated with the sweetness of control.

He sat up, his heart rushing with excitement. Tonight, he'd eat a *bug*.

Creeping out of the couch, he slithered into his clothes, careful not to be loud. Bill might've been asleep, and the last thing Lukas wanted was to wake him as he snuck toward the front door.

The floorboards of the house creaked beneath his heavy step. Lukas held his breath, listening to any rustling from the bedroom next door. There was silence for a few moments before Lukas sighed.

He carefully opened the front door and crept outside to the soon to be perilous night.

The night enveloped him in a stark embrace. The ranch expanded into the horizon, casting a shadowy silhouette along the darkness of the forest. A chilly breeze brushed against Lukas's skin and through the tall grass in the winding fields.

He made his way to his rusting truck, his feet grinding the gravel road.

There was a loud crash in the distance. Lukas froze as his ears twitched. It must've been the animals nearby. Bill said they were restless. Sighing, he took another step forward, but another crash echoed from the distance.

Lukas flinched.

His body spun toward the sound. He fixed his eyes on Bill's hunting shed; someone had creaked the door open, casting a warm glow in the distance.

Bill warned Lukas not to poke around the shed, but Lukas was intrigued like a moth to a light. He needed to know what crashed inside. Maybe Bill collapsed and was scrambling on the floor, or maybe a burglar had found out about the weapons and was smuggling them. Either way, Lukas wanted to be a good friend like Bill had been to him, and he couldn't wait to see the thankful expression on Bill's face when he helped him.

He made his way to the shed, where his eyes fell on the padlock hanging on the door. It had been unlatched. Bill must've been inside. Lukas pressed the wooden door open as he stepped within. A warm glow shined on him and Bill's weapon collection from the hanging bulb.

But something was different. A tall shelf filled with different tools was propped open, a hidden flight of stairs. Lukas's lips twitched as his head throbbed with tension. Another loud crash echoed from the hidden passage. It came from below the shed.

A low, indiscernible voice shouted from within. Lukas crept closer, his stomach contorting. He was ready for something to spring out at him, but the only thing that jumped was a low whimper from below.

Lukas stared down the wooden flight of stairs. The trail of planks led to a basement illuminated by a flickering orange glow. It must've been a wild animal that snuck its way inside, he was sure of it.

His shoulders hunched as he took a step down the rickety stairway and he was careful to step light.

The hay-floored basement filled again with a small whimpering.

Lukas held his breath as he continued his descent. A large wooden panel along the stairway concealed whatever was making the peculiar noise.

There was a loud rustle, followed by a series of exasperated breaths from the other side. Lukas's eyes widened with alarm as his heart raced. *Someone's down here. Did they break in?* Whoever it was, Lukas was ready to confront them for his friend Bill. He'd gladly kill for his friend.

Lukas tightened his lips with determination as he stuck his head around the corner.

It was not the sight Lukas expected.

His breath caught in his throat, wincing. The air became stiff and cold as Lukas recognized what was happening.

It was her. The woman they'd all been looking for. She'd been here the entire time.

Cassandra Holland.

Lukas could barely make out her exhausted face as she was strapped to the table in a shadowy corner of the basement. Bill stood right behind her, a perverse grin spreading on his wrinkled cheeks. Luckily, Bill didn't see him.

The grotesque sight made Lukas pull his head back from the corner. His mind drawing to a blank at what he'd witnessed.

"Shut up, Cassandra! Take it!" Bill shouted.

Cassandra squealed, but it was muffled. Lukas held his breath as he creeped up the stairs, his heart thrashing against his chest. *Cassandra? Why is Cassandra down here? Why is Bill with Cassandra?*

"Oh yeah? You like that, you slut? You better get used to it because you aren't getting out of here anytime soon," Bill groaned. The shed filled with the echo of his moans, and flesh thumping against each other.

Lukas staggered out of the basement and outside the shed, his face stricken with disbelief. For a moment, he wondered if he should've intervened, but he concluded that would've been the action of a bad friend. *I'm a good person, and a good person doesn't tell their friend what to do.* He flushed the noises he heard out of his mind. They reminded him too much of Rebecca. Maybe he misunderstood the context of it all.

However, there was a slight relief to finding out about Cassandra. It meant Amelia couldn't pin her disappearance on Lukas anymore, not if he introduced Bill into the picture.

But Lukas didn't want to think about that right now. He didn't want to think about anything else except spilling blood and drinking the screams of Elizabeth as he made his way back to his truck.

The thought of unwinding his web on Elizabeth and ripping apart her body connived made his skin tingle with exhilaration. And thanks to Sophia, his soon-to-be girlfriend, he knew where Elizabeth lived. Fortunately, near to Bill. Lukas's truck howled as he left Bill's ranch and churned past the corner onto the road to Elizabeth's home.

It was a quick ride as his fingers tightened on the wheel. After he'd shoot her inside her home, he'd need to make a stop at the store to purchase more rope and wire. That bitch-boy Percy used all of it when Lukas webbed him up in the trees, creating a beautiful spectacle. Slicing him up felt good, like creating a collage of limbs. Rebecca would've loved it, he was sure of it.

The headlights illuminated Elizabeth's cottage. He could almost feel the rush of murder surging through his veins as he propped open the jockey box. First, he grasped the gun, then a rag soaked with chloroform. Even the cold metal instrument in his hand smelled like blood—a sweet tang.

With a deep breath, he stepped out of the truck and crept toward the front door. His steps were light and calculated like a predator hunting its prey. The house was antique, just like how Elizabeth must've been all these years later. White paint chips cracked and had fallen to the ground, revealing its true, grotesque nature.

His fingers twitched with a mix of anxiety and excitement as he reached for the cold silver doorknob. But when he tried to turn it, the door didn't budge.

It was locked.

Dammit!

A frown creased his forehead as he turned his head toward the parking lot. Not a car in sight. And by the darkness through the windows, no one was home. This wasn't part of the plan. He hadn't considered the possibility that Elizabeth might've not been home. His mind raced, considering his options. He couldn't just give up now, not when he was so close to finally quenching his bloodthirsty fantasies.

But a smirk slipped on his face. There was still Ian, Sophia, or Dimitri. Which one of his little bugs did he want to eat tonight? He had reason to loathe each one of them. And the answer was clear: he knew which one he'd most savor during their torture.

Sneaking back into his truck, he sped down the winding road in the forest. All he wanted was to murder something, someone—anything. The murderous withdrawal had suffocated him over the weeks, not even the OxyContin could remedy that. But as he sped down the abysmal forest, a blur flickered in the corner of his eye.

A figure shot across the road in the distance, waving their hands in the air like a lunatic. Lukas's eyes widened in alarm as his foot slammed on the brakes until the truck screeched to a harsh stop.

He examined the figure who forced his stop. It was an older woman, and she stood like a deer in front of his headlights, her pale wrinkles popping in shock. She must've been running from something as she panted in front him, a look of relief washing over her face.

But as she did, there was something familiar in the way her eyes softened. And there was something furiously familiar about the neat orange sweater she wore. What dumb luck it had been that she'd walked right into his web.

The doctor. Elizabeth Ainsley.

42

LUKAS

MANY YEARS AGO

THE STEAMING WATER WASHED the guard's blood off Lukas's hands and face. Streams of scarlet water trickled down his naked body and down the drain. Shortly after he impaled the guard's eye, they hoarded all the boys into the showers like cattle—not the cleanest of places. Thick grime stained the cracked tile on the walls, and the boiling water that rained on him was a heavy contrast to the frozen concrete floor that chilled his bare feet. The boys next to him laughed and roughed around, splashing water on each other like some game.

The showers were holidays for them. After all, they only happened a few times a year. But Lukas didn't care about celebrating his new cleanliness, his mind still tormented with unanswered questions about *Phase Three*. And he was determined to discover the truth about it all.

As Lukas rubbed the bar of soap over his filthy body, his eyes shifted to his right. Thomas fixated his eyes on the tile wall in front of him, his arms crossed tightly around his chest. His face flushed as he stood frozen, not flinching a muscle.

Why is he so tense? Lukas rolled his eyes as he continued scrubbing. Even though they'd barely met, Thomas seemed like a boy who came from money, and now he was struggling to survive without his comfortable luxuries. How dramatic. It's a wonder he hadn't killed himself yet.

He turned to his left. An older muscular boy had a lankier one in a choke hold while the surrounding boys jeered and laughed. Lukas tried to ignore the raucous noise, but it was difficult when so many voices yelled.

"You should have seen the look on that fat pig's face when I grated his skin yesterday. *Please don't hurt me!*" An older boy snickered. "Director Miller told me if I can kill that cunt Alicia tomorrow, I'll be moving into *Phase Three*," he finished.

Lukas's brow shot up at the words as he squinted into the corner of his eye. The hot water streamed down his hair and face. *Phase Three, what does it mean?*

"Hey, new kid!" an older boy called.

Lukas jerked his head. The boy appeared to be a couple of years older than him. His wide frame and great arms were just a sliver of his lethality in The Room. There was never a shroud of hesitation for him hurting someone, an unquenchable beast. And he was pointing his heavy finger in Lukas's direction. At Lukas.

Lukas gulped. No, wait—he was pointing at Thomas.

"Are you staring at my cock?" He smirked. "Hey! Who let this *faggot* in?" The smug boy trudged toward Thomas while the others chuckled in the background.

Lukas's heart hammered in his chest, his lips thinning as the boy's jaw clenched. He glared into Thomas's trembling eyes. Thomas's face was paler than ever as he stood petrified like a wounded animal.

"I wa-wasn't," Thomas stammered.

Lukas's throat dropped to his stomach. Thomas was a terrible liar.

"*I wa-wa-wasn't,*" the boy mocked. "You're pathetic." He shoved Thomas against the wall. "Maybe we should all take *turns* on you until you die." His face contorted into a twisted smirk.

Lukas squinted at him, his fists flaring by his side. Enough was enough. "Leave him alone," Lukas groaned.

"Watch out, guys, it's Lukas. The boy who couldn't even kill a rabbit." The room echoed with laughter. "What're you, his fucking boyfriend? Mind your business, or I'll kill you right here."

Without warning, the boy turned around and slammed his enormous fist into Thomas's stomach. Thomas howled as his eyes watered. But it wasn't over. The boy launched his fist into Thomas's face.

They all snickered as Thomas whimpered on the floor, his face stained with blood and tears. Lukas swallowed his frustration. He knew it was a losing battle. He was weak compared to the rest of them, and surely they'd gang up on him.

Thomas tried to stand, but collapsed to the floor. He had no chance of surviving. Just a bag for them to torture. As he lay on the floor retching blood, the boy slammed his foot into Thomas's chest, delightfully grunting with every kick.

Lukas brimmed with rage at the sight, his face mottled with red.

Without thinking, he shot toward the boy, knocking him off his feet. Lukas grunted like an enraged animal. A savage.

The next moment had been a blur. The sound of his ribs drowned the yelping of the boy cracking from the weight of Lukas's foot. But it wasn't enough. Lukas wanted to make him suffer. To conjure pain he'd never experienced before.

Lukas pinned the howling boy's arms with his knees and scratched his face with his nails. He clawed at his eyes and mouth until his nail beds filled with blood until it was enough. Until he was satisfied. He didn't want to stop. The barbaric feeling was addicting. And no one dared to stop him.

He'd never left The Room because the world was *The Room.*

The steaming water morphed into a maroon as the boy's face became unrecognizable with deep red scars. The boy stopped fighting back. Low groans filled the shower room as his ligaments ripped and bones cracked.

Satisfied, Lukas stood up, grunting. His red fists still trembled at his sight, his wet hair fell over his eyes, shading the mess he'd made. Silence filled the room as he took a step forward. He shot a disdainful glance at Thomas, who was now tainted in droplets of blood and petrified from the scene.

Lukas looked down at the boy at his feet, his lips twitching with power. He spat in his face.

"Idiot," Lukas mumbled. He reached for a towel and wrapped the dry thing around his waist.

"What a shame. I had high hopes for the boy you killed: Amon. You've impressed me, Lukas. Perhaps you aren't what I thought. You've proven yourself. Between this *incident* in the shower and my guard, I'll let you live another day. For now," Director Miller's coarse voice echoed throughout The Room. A satisfied smile spread across his wrinkled face, and his silver stubble glimmered under the fluorescent lights.

Lukas didn't reply. He frowned at the idea of impressing the director, like somehow he'd known the entire time Lukas would do those things. Lukas and the others watched a guard drag the boy's mutilated body from the director's feet and out of the room. The feeling of eyes watching weighed on him. Maybe now they'd finally respect him. The cold air stung him as he stood in line with the other kids, Thomas by his side, still wearing a long, dirty hospital gown. How Thomas would survive the cruelty, he was unsure.

Director Miller continued with their lesson that day without flicking a glance at Thomas. Strange, not even an explanation.

"To torture someone is to break their will. To make them submit by any means necessary," the director's order enveloped Lukas's mind. But as he marched in front of them, the director's black orbs fell on him and squinted narrowly.

Lukas broke into a cold sweat at his gaze. Not a speck of light was found in the director's eyes. They were an endless abyss of despair.

"Let's see if our new *champion*, Lukas, is up for today's task," the director said with a wicked smirk. With a wave of his hand, he signaled the guards against the walls. Lukas's lips parted in silence. Whatever twisted game he had planned, Lukas wasn't sure if he could do it.

The guards came from behind when it happened. They snatched Thomas from the line with brute force as the guards dragged him toward a chair in the middle of the room. Lukas held his breath at the sight, his face draining of color.

"What are you doing to me!" Thomas choked as the guards tied him to the chair. His breaths became sharp as his face swelled with terror.

An overwhelming dread crossed Lukas as he imagined every gruesome scenario this would lead to. Would he have to kill Thomas? No—he'd refuse to. Lukas gulped as his ears filled with the drumming of his own heart.

The room filled with the stench of sweat as Lukas stepped forward; the director waving him closer with a foreboding hand. Thomas whimpered in the wooden chair as his hands and legs were bound on rests with thick rope. Even his forehead was wrapped with a large black band to keep his head still. Lukas met Thomas's watering eyes with uncertainty and dread.

The director held out a small scalpel. "Carve his fingernails out," he demanded.

Lukas's trembling eyes widened as his mouth dried. There was no option to reject his order. If he did, Lukas was sure to be dragged down to the furnace.

"No—Don't do it, Lukas!" Thomas cried in front of him. A guard gagged his mouth with rope, but he continued to squirm in his chair. Helpless.

The scalpel in the director's hand shimmered as he nudged it toward him.

Lukas looked up. "Why? Why *him*?" His words were laced with anger. This must've amused the director, as a twisted smirk curled on his face.

He nudged the scalpel closer for a third time.

Lukas gulped. Wrapping his fingers around the cold, sharp thing, he approached Thomas with slow steps. He had to do it to survive. Thomas's muffled cries filled the room as his hands clenched into fists. The sound was unbearable as Lukas tried to drown out the blood-curdling muffles.

The scalpel trembled between his fingers as he felt the eyes of everyone, anticipating with cruel excitement. As his lips thinned into a firm line, he gripped Thomas's bound wrist on the wooden armchair. *Do it, Lukas!* His breaths sharpened with dread.

Clawing at one of Thomas's resisting fingers, he pierced the nail bed with the scalpel. Thomas twitched with agonizing pain in his chair, tears streaming down his face and down his gown. Blood leaked from his finger as Lukas continued carving his nail, a tear falling down his own face as he did. He hated every moment of what he was doing. The vile tang of blood filled his nose. He'd never smelled it so closely before. It was sour, like rusting metal. He never wanted to smell it again.

"I'm sorry, Thomas," Lukas mumbled. "I'll try to be quick."

His body prickled with a new rush he'd never felt before as he continued carving and carving. It couldn't have been a good feeling. It shouldn't have been a good feeling. Blood trailed down Thomas's hands as he writhed in the chair, crying.

"Stop!" Thomas's cries were almost indiscernible through the gag.

The mixture of quiet snickering and mocking echoed from the other kids behind him. They took pleasure in Thomas's torment, but their savagery was contagious.

A crooked smile widened across Director Miller's face in the corner of Lukas's eyes. For a moment, Lukas thought he heard the faint wail of a woman.

A mix of excitement and guilt washed over Lukas. A cold sweat. He didn't want to stop. The same rush that overcame him when he attacked that guard and Amon. Hurting Thomas felt good, as much as he hated to admit.

Lukas tightened his grasp on the scalpel, piercing deeper into Thomas's nail bed. He'd gotten four nails so far, six left to go. The bloody nails fell like gruesome trophies on the ground.

"Lukas!" Thomas wailed. His fists quivered, trying to shake Lukas's grip off.

And that was the worst torture, Lukas thought. Enjoying it.

43

LUKAS

MANY YEARS AGO

THE COARSE SHEETS FROM his bed scratched Lukas's throbbing body like sandpaper. His chest drummed from his heart as he gawked at the stark ceiling. The thought of what he'd just done to Thomas felt like a blurred haze. Even the mere memory of it seemed mottled with uncanniness that made it seem like a dream. He curled against the brick wall, waiting for Thomas to reply. The muffled echo of Thomas's whimpering from behind the wall made Lukas's stomach churn with guilt.

You're a terrible person, Lukas. Violence is never okay. He could've stopped himself from carving all Thomas's nails, but he didn't.

A line of sweat dripped down his forehead. Thomas's painful torment was a twisted rush for Lukas, like a drug. And like all drugs, he convinced himself that he could stop anytime he wanted. It wasn't an addiction. He wouldn't become the killer Director Miller wanted him to become in this game.

"I really didn't mean to do it, Thomas," Lukas said again, his fingers twiddling. "You knew I had to, or else they'd kill me."

A sniffle resounded from the hole in the wall. "I kn-know," Thomas stammered. "But it still hurt." The words quivered out of his mouth.

"We need to escape. And we need to do it soon. Every day, The Room grows crueler, and the walls become stained with more blood. I can't do it anymore. And if you can't keep up with the others, the director will kill you," Lukas urged.

"In the showers, I overheard something. That boy, Amon, he mentioned something about *Phase Three*. What is that?"

The words sent a crashing wave of fury through Lukas's veins. His jaw clenched with frustration at not knowing what that was. "I don't know," Lukas mumbled in frustration. "But I know it has something to do when they take us from our cells. They took my sister, but they didn't kill her—the guards took her someplace else, I'm sure of it."

"Take us from our cells?"

Lukas wrapped his arms around his knees. "I think if we don't meet Director Miller's expectations, he orders the guards to kill us. I can hear it from behind the door and through the vents. They carry us away, and then a few minutes later, heat blasts from the vents," Lukas said. He didn't bother to sugarcoat the reality they were in. There was no point. Thomas needed to know.

There was a silence for a few moments.

"The answer's simple, Lukas," Thomas spoke.

Lukas's eyes squinted with perplexity. Still, he was curious what he meant as he crawled into the hole in the wall. The air seemed heavier in Thomas's cell than his own as the darkness enveloped him. His streaks of blond hair seemed dirtier than before and no longer waved.

Thomas stared down at his bloody hands before peering through the small hole once more. "You traverse the vents, of course."

Lukas nudged his head closer. What a stupid idea Thomas had. "The vents? How am I supposed to do that when they're bolted shut? It could take weeks to break open."

Before Thomas could reply, a door whined from the corridor. Lukas jerked his head toward the sound.

"Let go of me—Stop!" The girl's shrill reverberated through the walls. Oh no, it was happening again. His muscles tensed sharply as he overheard the struggle behind his cell. Surely, he recognized the high-pitched wail of Olivia, a once sweet, innocent girl forced to fight her sister when they first arrived. Now, innocent was the last word he'd use to describe her. Ruthless was better.

"Now's your time, Lukas." He was unsure if it was Thomas's voice who called this or his mind.

Thomas pressed his face closer to the hole. "You can follow her crying through the vents. Hurry!"

Lukas spun around in the darkness, the cold concrete floor sending chills up his spine. "But I don't know how. I have nothing to—" he paused. The answer was obvious, just as he was about to ask. He had to use the shank. The tip end of it could be sharp enough to unscrew the bolts.

The girl's screaming became distant. He was running out of time. Lukas's hands fell on every inch of the floor, trying to feel for the shank. *Where is it? Damn it!*

A sharp pain stabbed his palm as he slapped the floor. Cold metal. Lukas howled, souring his lips, but there was no time to mourn his pain. He bit his tongue, ignoring the blood leaking from his palm, and grasped the frigid spoon. Warm wetness dripped down his hand as he crawled to the rectangular vent on the floor, his skin tingling.

"Lukas—are you okay?" Thomas's voice echoed.

Lukas narrowed his eyes at the four screws in each corner. "I'm fine. We're gonna figure out what the hell is going on in this place."

He jammed the shank in the screw, a perfect fit. The air in his cell never felt lighter as he sighed. Every nightmare and cruelty he endured led to this moment of trembling anticipation as his freezing hands rapidly twisted the shank driver.

One by one, the screws collapsed to the floor. A hum of heat blew against his face as he tore the metal register and tossed it aside. It clattered on the concrete floor and rattled by his foot. His mouth went dry at the sight. A tunnel of darkness lay before him that most certainly wouldn't lead to Wonderland.

His breaths labored as he gazed at the winding abyss. Worse, the girl's screaming was now faint, simply a whine that reverberated through the air duct. But it was now or never.

"Lukas, you're coming back, right?" Thomas cried.

There was a moment of silence as Lukas hesitated. "I'll be right back," he said with false confidence.

Lukas dropped to his fours and began crawling into the narrow metal air duct with only one thought in his mind.

Phase Three.

The air duct was warm as he descended deeper into the darkness. He couldn't see more than a few inches in front of him. A stench of gasoline plugged his nose and made his eyes water. His sweaty palms stuck to the warming metal as he crawled. The air duct seemed infinite, like traversing through a labyrinth. The fear of getting lost in the vents gnawed at him. No, he wouldn't. He promised Thomas he'd return.

Olivia's faint shrill reverberated through the caving metal walls around him. Focusing on the direction of the sound, Lukas held his breath and clenched his eyes.

Right, he thought.

Lukas turned right into another passage. As he delved further in, the metal pressed against his palms stung. Hot. The air duct walls around him rumbled. The thundering rattle of the vent deafened Olivia's cries, and he lost her in the chaos of noise. But worse, Lukas couldn't turn back. He couldn't remember the path out. The only way was forward. Gulping, he crawled toward the sizzle of gasoline and heat.

Lukas didn't know what he'd find on the side of the darkness. The answer he'd been seeking was just out of his grasp. Just another inch, just another vent away.

Lukas's hammering heart filled his ears louder than the beating of the walls. The air flexed and thinned. The burning heat seared his skin. He was running out of time. More vents appeared on his left and right, and he was unsure where to go. Lukas panted as he turned left, his breaths sharp. There was no way to know if he'd gone in the right direction.

As he crawled further, he was blasted with a wave of hot air, burning his skin. Lukas choked on the odorous gasoline. The taste was vile. He gagged on its fumes. He needed to find a way out now.

The scorching heat flooded the narrow duct he was trapped in. The air suffocated him as he gasped, sweating. His searing skin crawled as his palms fell on the blazing metal. Lukas howled in pain as his head spun distortedly.

A dim light blurred at the end of a vent. Panting, he crawled toward the bright light with every ounce of energy he had left. The sizzling of his skin intensified as he reached a corridor. But the metal grille was sealed in front of the exit.

He was trapped.

Lukas's vision blurred as he tried to push the grille off with every bit of strength within. It didn't budge. Lukas panted, a mix of sweat and tears trailing down his face. Both his hands and knees scorched like the touch of fire.

C'mon, Lukas!

Gritting his teeth, Lukas used both his arms to push against the grille with all his might. He howled as his arms pressed further and further against the grille. There was a slight creak, and finally, it blew from the vent.

Whimpering in relief, he crawled out from the vent to the bright, narrow corridor.

Lukas's body ached in the frigid tile. The narrow hallway was brighter than any he'd been in before, as fluorescent fixtures trailed all the way down. The air was much cooler here, a sweet relief. A series of disgruntled coughs echoed as he retched from the taste of gasoline. Laying still for a few moments, Lukas sighed. He'd never been so happy to be cold in his life.

It didn't matter that he'd lost Olivia's voice anymore. It wasn't worth the pain. He held up his palms. The skin was seared and ripped apart, throbbing red. They glowed tomato red.

Lukas perked his head up. It was a light on a white, glazed glass door that cast a red glow. He studied the bold blue letters on the door.

Authorized Personnel Only

His brow furrowed at the words as he stood up. What had he found? Was he still in the facility? The neat white streaking down walls and floor made him believe he was back in the hospital from all those years ago. But it couldn't have been. It's not possible.

Lukas took a step closer, a small wave of heat brushing against his skin as he did. Heat was blasting from inside. *Is this where they took Olivia?* His lips twitched at the sight. Great, another door standing between him and the truth. There was always a door blocking him from an answer.

The door buzzed open, almost as if it were waiting for it to be opened as his hands brushed the glass. A piercing scream filled corridors from the other side. Lukas flinched in terror, his eyes widening with disbelief.

Olivia.

Blood drained from Lukas's face. He'd found the right place, after all. The door strobed with blurry red lights as a cold child touched his spine. *I need to know.* But when he reached to open it, there was no handle. Next to the door was a small black box with a streak of red glowing on top. It must've needed a key card. The ones that the guards carried with them.

With his scorched fists falling at his side, Lukas made up his mind.

He was going to steal a keycard the next day and finally discover the truth about everything.

44

ELIZABETH

JULY 13

THE HUMAN MIND IS designed to kill. But *why* would the Recluse Killer kill? Elizabeth wondered. The wrinkles on her face twitched as she pictured Percy's mutilated body on the web. It's said that murder can be categorized into four motivations.

First was lust.

The parasite seemed to poison every man in this world.

Percy's phone on her ornate mahogany coffee table buzzed. *Please text me when you see this. I'm sorry.* The anonymous girl, *Her*, texted. It had been her tenth text in the last hour, which followed an *Are you mad at me?* And, *This isn't fucking funny, Percy.*

Over the last couple of days, Percy's phone had accumulated almost a hundred messages, mostly from *Her*. Whoever she was must've been an insufferable girl, like a mosquito to blood.

Sophia crept into the living room in a woven white cardigan, holding two steaming white mugs.

Second, love.

Killing who you love to spare them future ailment.

Sophia placed the two hot mugs beside the phone. Earl Gray for Elizabeth and green for Sophia—just how they liked it. Elizabeth thanked Sophia before grasping the warm mug. There was no soothing balm for the soul, like tea. It washed away all of one's problems, problems such as Natalie Warren.

"Has she called yet?" Sophia asked.

Elizabeth shook her head. If only they knew Percy's passcode, they could learn more about him.

"That's weird. People have only been texting him, but no one's calling. It makes you wonder if people even care that he's—you know." Sophia stopped herself before drinking her tea.

Shooting a glance at Sophia, Elizabeth sipped the mug as the hot, lemony citrus trickled down her throat. She let out a gentle sigh as she finished, a comforting grin slipping her creased face. The air always seemed lighter with Sophia around. But the heavy steps of Frank quickly interrupted the tranquility stomping up the basement.

Third was loot.

Money killed societies more than war. And Elizabeth was sure if Frank had the chance before, he'd have murdered her for financial gain. Elizabeth squinted her beady ivy eyes at him.

But she would've done the same for Sophia.

Frank groaned, drying his wet hands on his black button-down. "That's the last bag of ice. It should be cold as the damn arctic down there now."

"Good," she lied. Things were far from okay. Frank had been disappearing every few hours to make a phone call, and he wouldn't say another detail about it other than that his mother was in the hospital. The more Elizabeth thought about his reason, the more it seemed rational as she swallowed her suspicions. Frank may have been selfish, but his love for his mother was true.

She had put him in charge of finding the whereabouts of Percy's family to return the body, and for the last couple of days, he'd procured not one lead. It must've irritated him being ordered around like a servant, but he had no other choice. Elizabeth refused to resume their narcotic network operation until they returned Percy's body back to his family. That was her one condition.

The loud chime of the doorbell echoed throughout the room.

All heads turned toward the door as Elizabeth stood up and made her way toward it. Her mouth dried as her fingers brushed the brass doorknob. Who could be intruding on them? Whoever it was had no business on her porch, and she'd be sure to chastise her solicitor. Taking a deep breath, she parted the door just barely to see who it was, a soft whine creaking as she did.

Elizabeth scowled, biting her tongue.

The last motivation to kill was hate.

When a familiar meddling detective stood on her porch, trespassing with a cunning smile. This time, Detective Amelia Mayman crossed her line. Her speckless blue police coat fell just below her waist as her dark skin glowed warmly from the sun.

"Dr. Ainsley, it's a pleasure to see you again," Amelia said with a brimming smile. A fake nicety. "You haven't been answering my calls, so I came by to talk with you. Can I come in?"

Elizabeth swallowed her throbbing frustration, forcing a smile. If Amelia were to invade her home, she'd surely discover Percy's body, and of course, Frank inside her home was already treacherous. Two conspirators involved a drug network with a mutilated body in her basement. A detective in her home was the last thing she needed that day.

With a narrow sneer, Elizabeth snapped, "No, you may not."

Amelia's grin quickly faded into a glower. It must've been a new word for her to hear.

As Elizabeth began shutting the door, she glanced down to find Amelia's foot had already intruded in the doorway. Her face pressed nearer Elizabeth's as her face flushed with disdain.

"You'll want to hear what I have to say," she groaned. It didn't sound like a suggestion more than an order.

Elizabeth studied her for a moment. The way her eyes sharpened made it clear she wouldn't take no for an answer. For the last several months, Amelia had been hunting down the identity of The Raven of East Haddam. If only she knew she'd been staring at her. But Elizabeth didn't trust the police. She hadn't for a long time. The only community the police served was themselves, climbing the ranks off the chains they'd shackled the city with.

"Outside," Elizabeth said. She swiftly stepped outside and shut the door behind her before Amelia could peek inside.

A grin strained on Amelia's face as she waved Elizabeth off her porch. "Let's take a walk."

Elizabeth buried her hands in her pockets, but not her suspicions as she agreed. Amelia followed her off the porch, and together, they strolled by the side of the narrow road, the fluorescent forest on the other side. The green leaves rattled on the trees from the brisk air rushing through. A mixture of bird calls and cicadas called from within. Such a lush wonderland was sure to hold secrets within.

Secrets like what happened to Percy Romano.

The orange knit sweater Elizabeth wore hugged warmly against her skin as the wet grass on the meadow they walked on brushed against her ankles. Somehow, the detective's appearance made the summer day feel cold. Their sights strained forward along the path, not making a single glance at each other. Perhaps Amelia was the killer, and she was luring them into a wasteland for Elizabeth's demise.

"The District Attorney's office is prepared to offer you a deal," Amelia's voice broke the silence. "I was able to obtain a copy through a friend in their office before they contacted you, so you could have a few extra days before you decide."

Elizabeth turned and stared blankly at her. "A deal?"

"The DA is willing to grant you immunity from any drug trafficking charges." She sighed. "As well as the order for your immediate release from East Haddam Correctional City."

Elizabeth's heart leaped. It sounded too good to be true. "In exchange for what?"

"Give over any information you're not telling us about Frank so they can build a prosecutable case against him for drug trafficking and money laundering. You will also agree to testify against Frank in a court of law. Your ex-fiancé is not a good man, doctor. I know you know that, too. You're a smart woman—I won't deny that," Amelia said.

"Why are you telling me all of this? Why help me?"

She paused for a moment. "Because I'm on your side. You don't have to go down with him, and trust me, the DA will find some way to tie you with Frank if you refuse this deal."

Elizabeth stepped back, catching her breath. Could it be as easy as framing Frank for everything she'd done and walking free? She could plead that Frank had coerced her into helping him traffic narcotics. It was her word against his, after all. She could even pin Percy's mutilated body on Frank. He led her to him in the forest that night. It couldn't have been a coincidence they stumbled upon him. All she had to do was fabricate some story, and she'd never have to lay eyes on him again.

Elizabeth pursed her lips. She wouldn't ever see him again. But worse of all, she'd have to give up the network. The money.

No, she couldn't frame Frank. The thought of his name fluttered her aging heart, and she hated how it did. She wondered how she could care for someone she hated. But she could never truly hate Frank, not when the memory of their happiest days glimmered in her eyes and when she needed him more than ever. Unless he messes up again.

"Well, I must say, I am surprised," Elizabeth started, clasping her hands together. "That you would think I would help you investigate my ex-fiancé. The DA doesn't have any evidence other than circumstantial, seeing as both the Haddam Police Department and the State are seeking my cooperation."

The detective's lips thinned into a narrow line.

"I must admit, Amelia, you've made me feel corralled in my *long* sentence here. The only manner I shall accept this deal is when your lousy department can conjure anything more palpable than fairytales and theories of Frank and I indulging in narcotics trafficking," Elizabeth finished with a small grin.

The stench of animosity grew between them.

Amelia continued, frowning, "I see. Be careful, Dr. Ainsley. Your love for Frank will only be your downfall."

45

ELIZABETH

JULY 13

FRANK STOOD ON THE porch, leaning over the white Chelsea railing. His slicked black hair shined as he pressed a cigar against his pasty lips. The sweet vanilla fume of clover brushed against Elizabeth's nose as she approached. Djarum Brown—his favorite.

Elizabeth watched him breathe a cloud of smoke as she and Amelia returned to the cottage—not a word spoken, but they exchanged silent glares. In that moment, she envied Frank, specifically the cigar tucked between his fingers. She never wanted a smoke more than now, even though she'd sworn those damned things out of her life. But what's a promise if not broken?

Amelia paused at the foot of the porch as she shot a quick glance at Frank. It seemed she didn't trust him, either. "Take care, Elizabeth. Call me if you change your mind."

Elizabeth nodded as she watched Amelia return to her police car and drive off. One less problem to worry about.

Sighing, she walked up the steps and stood next to Frank. It was only noon, and already Percy, the phone, and Amelia had worn her out. Elizabeth leaned over the rail, the howling wind blowing through the vast forest in front of them. Summer always felt still, like a moment, frozen in time. The days hazed until they strung into a line of eternal similarity. Nothing ever changed.

Frank pulled the cigar from his mouth and nudged it toward her. She hesitated for a moment, but decided one more wouldn't hurt. The warm thing comforted her fingers before she pressed the sweet cigar against her lips and inhaled. Hot smoke filled her lungs before she breathed out the vanilla cloud. She licked the sweet tang off her lips as she handed the cigar back to Frank.

"We're running out of time, Frank." Elizabeth crossed her arms on the rail.

Frank turned to her. "What did she want?"

"She wants me to conspire against you, to testify. They're becoming desperate to shut these networks down. I'm worried, Frank, that they're catching on to us. Once a new line is set up through Hartford, we can use the money to bribe our way out of here. An officer should be easy to persuade with money."

Frank said nothing, but inhaled more of the cigar. A few seconds later, he blew a small cloud, looking out into the distance.

"Are you going to do it? They're obviously offering you something for turning against me—I wouldn't blame you if you did. I haven't exactly been the best man to you," he said with the soft grind of his voice.

Elizabeth sighed. "No, of course not. I don't trust them. They expect me to trust the same government that betrayed me and threw me in this town." She turned to him and placed her frail hand on his shoulder. "I need you, Frank. I can't run *our* network by myself."

His sulky face lightened into a small grin. Pulling her hand off him, Elizabeth felt repulsed she had comforted Frank.

"I found Percy's parents after going through some public records. They've been here the entire time. Not too far from here, maybe a few miles," Frank said, turning his head toward the field of trees.

Finally, some good news. All the many parts of Percy's body were haunting her house. "Strange. I wonder why they aren't making a fuss over his disappearance."

"Maybe a bad relationship? But it shouldn't matter. I did what you asked."

"We can head there tonight, then. I'll let Sophia know," she said, walking toward the front door.

But before she could twist the brass knob, Frank's irritating, bitter voice filled her ears. "You should've told her the truth, Ainsley."

Elizabeth paused for a moment, turning back at him with a face of perplexity. *Was that a threat?* But she ignored him as she walked inside, shaking her head. Frank was always trying to get under her skin.

Elizabeth's home welcomed her with an unfamiliar coldness, like she'd invaded her own home. There was a dismembered boy in her basement. Perhaps that was it.

Walking down the narrow entryway, she called Sophia's name.

But there was no response.

She called again, louder this time. A cold sweat forming on her neck.

Silence responded.

Elizabeth's breaths became rapid as her mind spiraled with many possibilities of Sophia's whereabouts. Was she abducted, murdered, or worse, did the killer find her? Rushing into the living room, Elizabeth halted midway step at the sight.

Sophia slumped against the sofa cushions, her olive face mottled with tears and red. The room reverberated with a still tense air as Elizabeth's brow shot up, wondering what had happened.

"You—um—missed a call, Dr. Ainsley," Sophia groaned. Her eyes narrowed at the wall opposite of her instead of Elizabeth. "They left you a voicemail."

Elizabeth's voice caught in her throat as she stood frozen in place. *What phone call is she talking about?* But she said nothing as Sophia leaned over the coffee table and taped a button on her cellphone. Elizabeth's wrinkles twitched as the disembodied husky voice spoke from the phone.

"You were right, Dr. Ainsley. Natalie Warren was still at the New Horizon Apartments, which made things easier. Good timing, too, huh? She could've become a big problem if we didn't take her out now. We used a

Molotov cocktail, but things got messy, if you know what I mean." The familiar voice chuckled. *"You'll probably see it on the news if you haven't already. One other thing, the daughter was there at the scene. If you think she could become a liability, it might be good for me to take her out, too, but it's your call. It always is. Let me know if you need anything else."*

Elizabeth's heart rang in her chest, and the surrounding room spun. For the first time in many years, she had nothing to say. Her mouth fell open, but she didn't speak, only exchanging a long silence. There was no point in denying what she had done. Marco, her hitman, had already confessed to her. *No—No. How could I let this happen? Where's my voice? I think I've killed that too.*

Sophia wouldn't understand why she did what she did, so there was no point in explaining.

And if given the choice of whether she'd do it again, Elizabeth would've as much it destroyed Sophia. Because Elizabeth *loved* her.

Strands of Sophia's walnut hair fell in front of her flushed face, concealing her teary eyes. "I trusted you," she mumbled.

Words escaped Elizabeth before she could grasp them as she stared at the hardwood floor. They'd never looked so brittle before.

"How could you do this to her? I don't understand, Elizabeth. I came to you for support when she was struggling here. I even loved you like my second mother," Sophia cried, her voice cracking like the surrounding drywalls.

Second mother. Never the first.

The room filled with a mixture of Elizabeth's pounding heart and Sophia's cries. Elizabeth didn't dare meet her eyes. She couldn't bear to see the anguish she caused. A hot flash of sweat formed above her brow. "You—you don't understand, Sophia. I didn't mean for...this to happen," Elizabeth stammered under her breath.

Sophia shot up. Her heavy steps quaked the floorboards. "What do you mean you didn't mean for this to happen?" This time, Sophia's sour words were coated with spite. "I think you did, though. That fire at New Horizon. You wanted that to happen, right? It was your idea just like that man said on the phone, right Doctor Ainsley?"

Elizabeth said nothing. Her frail hands trembled with guilt at her sides. She couldn't bear to look at Sophia and meet her with disappointment, so she narrowed her shameful eyes at Sophia's shoes. Black loafers, modest.

"Look at me," Sophia muttered in a raspy voice.

The piercing sound made Elizabeth flinch as her trembling eyes flitted up. Elizabeth hadn't realized she'd been crying as her own tears blurred Sophia's figure. Sophia's blur stood like a shadowy figure, seething. It was easier to not see the full picture.

Wiping her eyes on her sweater sleeve, Elizabeth stood uncomfortably still, at the mercy of Sophia's judgment.

Sophia's glassy eyes trembled. "Look me in the eye and tell me why you did it—please just tell me," she whimpered.

Elizabeth said nothing.

"Tell me!" She sobbed.

Sophia's screams drowned in her mind. The woman in front of Elizabeth was a stranger, One she'd never met before. Elizabeth's mind floated outside of her body, watching the scene unfold through the eyes of an invisible ghost.

Sophia's face swelled with tears and bitterness as she continued sobbing, pleading for an answer.

Elizabeth saw herself standing like a statue with an undiscernible face. A person with nothing left to say was a ghost, almost as if Sophia were screaming into the empty air, with no one listening.

Sophia trudged toward her, pressing her bitter, teary face against hers. "You're a coward, Dr. Ainsley. And that empty void in your heart is only going to keep growing until it consumes you because you're an evil woman who can't feel anything for anyone."

Elizabeth's lips twitched as tears seared into her wrinkled skin like lava. Her elderly heart pounded in her chest, holding her breath.

Sophia's running nose sniffled as her face crumpled to the timorous girl she once was. "I don't know who are you Doctor Ainsley, just like my mother. You're both dead to me," Sophia whispered with quivering words.

There was a long exchange in their eyes. Elizabeth saw herself in the glimmer reflection of Sophia's sage eyes. Love, betrayal, loneliness, and ingenuity. It was all there, and Sophia was all gone.

She walked past Elizabeth, who remained frozen, her sight narrowed straight. Sobs trailed behind Elizabeth until the front door slammed behind her, and Sophia was gone.

Elizabeth collapsed to the ground, wailing. She curled into a ball, sobbing like a newborn. And like a newborn, she cried herself to exhaustion until she slept. The words, "I'm sorry," reverberating off the soulless walls that spun around her. Her sharp breaths soon becoming labored as she passed out inside the cage of her creation.

46

ELIZABETH

JULY 14

ELIZABETH SOMBERLY WAITED INSIDE Frank's Ford truck as she leaned against the passenger window. The soft silver reflection of the midnight moon illuminated the corner of her eye. She kept her phone tucked in her lap in case Sophia called. Even a text would've comforted her. But the possibility seemed to be hopeless as she sighed, her shoulders sagging against the torn seat.

Frank and she had barely spoken a word since he found her asleep on the living room floor. Elizabeth cried into his arms for nearly half an hour, cursing her self-existence before she stood up and focused on the task at hand: returning Percy's body. It was the one thing that took her mind off Sophia.

Focus on the money. Everything would be better after she'd finished Percy and resumed her work with Frank, and with the money, she would buy an escape out of East Haddam forever.

Elizabeth was bringing all her essentials on the drive: her favorite trench coat over her knit orange sweater, a stick of burgundy lipstick, a capsule of Xanax, and, of course, her pistol buried in her coat pocket. She went nowhere without it. After all, her enemies wanted her dead.

The cargo bed door slammed shut before Frank made his way back and slid into the driver's seat. He tossed his latex gloves in the trash, burrow etched in the door with an inappropriately amused expression.

Wrapping her arms around herself, Elizabeth raised a brow at his reaction.

"Let's hope he doesn't scream on the way there." Frank chuckled.

Elizabeth didn't chuckle back. She shot him a scrutinizing eye.

Frank's eyes widened as an irritating grin spread across his face. "Okay—tough crowd then." He shifted the truck into reverse as they backed out of the driveway and churned past the corner, weaving into the endless forest of the night.

Elizabeth stared into the distance. The black abyss of trees danced like shadow figures as they sped past the vast stretch of them. She could still feel Sophia's words ringing in her mind. *I don't know who you are, Doctor Ainsley.* Blinking, she saw Sophia's fiery face mottled with red betrayal. That's what the truth does to someone.

"Look, I'm sorry about Sophia—"

Elizabeth waved her hand. "Do not. Let's just hurry there and be done with this already, so we can move on."

"Hey, I'm serious. I know how much she means to you." Frank paused. "But why *did* you have her mother killed in the first place? You can tell me, Ainsley. We used to tell each other everything, remember?"

Elizabeth stiffened at the question as she squeezed the belt strap around her lap. Her dry lips parted, waiting for the words to flow out. He was right. She needed to tell someone the truth.

Better Frank than no one.

"One night, I was at a dive bar," Elizabeth let out a quivering sigh, "and I tried to order a drink, but these men around me kept jeering me, laying their filthy hands on me."

She paused, staring longingly out the window, catching her pale blue reflection through the glass.

"That's when I saw her. Natalie. She stormed them away and saved me when no one else would. What a fierce, *beautiful* woman, I thought. Or maybe it was the red leather jacket she always wore that gave her that façade. We quickly became friends after the incident. I'd visit her apartment every

Friday at noon—and I found it strange there, like a black cloud loomed over that building. New Horizon," she said.

A comforting grin slipped on her face. "A little boy used to always watch me. He reminded me of my son—before my ex-husband *stole* him. Over the months, Natalie and I became closer than friends. We were lovers, and it was exciting. No matter how old you get, you never stop loving. But one day, I told her about a narcotic network I was building to launder money." Elizabeth gritted her teeth.

Frank sighed in a disappointing tone.

"That's when everything changed. Natalie thought my idea was brilliant and became invested. On occasion, she'd ask for small doses of cocaine until she started asking for larger and larger amounts each day. I should've stopped, I know, but I was in love. And after *us,* Frank, I didn't want to disappoint her. One day, I told her about the state granting me mentorship privileges and how I had a brilliant student in mind to mentor. Sophia. I did not know she was Natalie's daughter. But Natalie became furious at the idea," Elizabeth said, sniffling.

The truck rolled around a gravel corner.

"She threatened me. If I began mentoring Sophia, I would never get to see her face again. She didn't want her daughter to be anywhere near a correctional city. I mentored Sophia anyway. It would've killed me to see all that wasted potential go work at some commercial hospital when I knew she could be more. It outraged Natalie when she found out, but she really wasn't altogether there—in the end," she said.

Frank pulled to a stop at the side of a narrow gravel road.

Elizabeth continued, "She screamed at me over the phone about absurdities she'd seen, like seeing dead bodies being dragged, and how I was brainwashing Sophia to love me more than her. It was ludicrous. But that's when she threatened me to fire Sophia, or she'd tell the police about the drug networks. I couldn't let Natalie do that as much as I loved her. It would destroy everything I'd built. All the power I'd regained would be gone. I did what I had to do to protect myself and Sophia. You were right. I had someone kill Natalie."

Elizabeth's hands writhed at her side as she stared longingly out of the idle truck. The car filled with her silent sniffles and a heavy air as her shoulders sank. She waited for Frank to say anything. She narrowed her sight at her brown slippers, not daring to see Frank's reaction to everything she'd said.

Frank cleared his throat. "We're—uh. We're here," he groaned, stepping out of the truck.

Elizabeth bit her lip with regret as she crept out as well. False sympathy would've been better than none, but she should've expected that from Frank.

A long stretch of gravel road narrowed into a shadowy distance. Silver mist loomed through the air like clouds as lines of dark pine trees towered over them. To the right, a dirt path wound to a small dilapidated house with a buzzing yellow lamp hanging by a stark door. A house can say a lot about a person. Percy's parents must have isolated themselves from society, and their relationships must have been deteriorating, just like the wood panels did from the house. The boarded windows sent an unwelcoming chill up her neck.

Pulling at a loose orange thread from her sweater, Frank and she approached the ominous house. Closure, yes, this was closure for her son. Maybe she'd finally done something right.

Elizabeth turned to Frank as they stepped toward a chipped teal front door. His face was paler than usual. Not once did he glance at her since she confessed her relation with Natalie?

The silent treatment, Frank?

"Frank. Promise me what we're doing is the right thing," she said.

Frank said nothing.

Elizabeth rolled her eyes as he pressed the doorbell. Moments later, the crooked door creaked open, revealing a shifting shadow within. But what she didn't expect was to see who was waiting for them. Her brow shot in alarm as her lips parted in disbelief.

Detective Amelia Mayman.

47

Elizabeth

July 14

AMELIA TOOK A STEP forward, out the door. The moonlight cast an eerie blue glow on her face as an amused smile stretched her lips.

Elizabeth staggered back, the porch steps creaking beneath her step. Her mind stirred with hundreds of questions about why Amelia was inside the house, but all she could mutter was, "What is this?"

Panicking, her eyes fell on Frank for some sort of reassurance. She waited for him to shout obscenities in confusion as well.

But he didn't.

Frank stood still on the porch, his head tucked down, facing the floor. Not a flicker of shock overcame him when Amelia stepped out, almost as if he were expecting this to happen. "I'm sorry, Ainsley," he muttered.

Elizabeth's breaths sharpened. "Sorry? What do you mean, *sorry?* What the hell are you talking about?" The more her mind wandered, the more sure she was sure of what was happening. It appeared Frank had never changed.

"I'll tell you exactly what's happening," Amelia started. "Dr. Elizabeth Ainsley, you're under arrest for drug trafficking, the murder of Rebecca Waylow, and the murder of Percy Romano."

The air turned chilly as Amelia finished.

Murder? I haven't murdered anyone. What is she talking about? Elizabeth's beating heart rang in her ears as she shot a glance at Frank.

Not a single reaction from him. Not one damn word.

Fury twisted inside of her. "This is insanity—I didn't murder anyone! The network was all Frank! It's always been Frank, Amelia! That's why you've inquired for my help countless times!" Elizabeth roared.

"Frank Sallow is immune from all drug trafficking charges under a deal struck with the DA as of a few days ago," Amelia said contently.

Elizabeth's eyes stood unblinking as she gawked at Frank. Nothing made sense to her. Every word spoken out of Amelia's mouth was a foreign language as a lump grew in Elizabeth's throat. "Frank—you wouldn't," Elizabeth choked out. "You didn't. Frank—answer me," she stammered. Her eyes filled with tears as she'd answered her own questions by speaking them.

It was undeniably clear. Frank would.

"I had to, I'm sorry. I'm in love, Ainsley," Frank said. He placed his hairy hand on Amelia's shoulder.

The world around her spun as a silence pierced the air. It couldn't be true. The disloyal sight repulsed Elizabeth as her mouth gaped in disgust.

Moments later, shadows crept out of the trees—no, it was four police officers draped in their crooked navy. They had surrounded the area cleverly. The scene Frank lured her into was nothing more than a set-up. And the longer she glared at her two conspirators on the house steps, the clearer everything became.

Seething, Elizabeth dropped her hands in her coat pockets. "There was never a deal from the DA, was there? This has all been a ploy for me to confess to a crime since the very beginning. Tell me I'm wrong, Frank. You only stopped at my house weeks ago with that proposition to get me to incriminate myself. And you, Amelia, you were never after Frank. You knew that if I turned against him, I'd have to admit to my own dealings as well. You conniving bastards!" Elizabeth spat.

"You did this to yourself, Ainsley," Frank said, before handing his phone to Amelia.

Elizabeth smoldered with resentment, regretting not ordering the hit on Amelia and Frank instead of Natalie. She would've loved to see both of them on fire after what they'd done.

A sneering Amelia tapped a button on Frank's phone.

"But that's when she threatened me to fire Sophia, or she'd tell the police about the drug networks. I couldn't let Natalie do that as much as I loved her. It would destroy everything I'd built. All the power I'd regained would be gone. I did what I had to do to protect myself and Sophia. You were right. I had someone kill Natalie."

Elizabeth squinted her eyes furiously at her voiced confession. The entire duration Frank had been with her, he could've recorded everything she said.

A cunning smile smeared across the detective's face. "This will add criminal solicitation to your list of charges, Dr. Ainsley. Handcuff her now—"

Elizabeth swiftly withdrew the pistol from her coat pocket as she mindlessly spun around. She had no intention of going to prison. Amelia and the other officers drew their guns from the holsters on their waists.

"No one shoot. Dr. Ainsley, put down your gun. Don't do anything you're going to regret," Amelia said, creeping nearer.

Elizabeth reeled back to the surrounding forest, five guns pointed at her head. "There's been some mistake. I've broken no law!"

"Drop the gun," Amelia muttered.

But they didn't care about who was innocent or was not. It was clear the police wanted someone to shift the blame for the crimes to whoever it may be.

The thicket behind Elizabeth scratched against her coat. Taking a long breath, she dropped the gun before turning and retreating into the dense jet-black forest.

Elizabeth raced into the night, pushing through sharp branches and trampling through black foliage.

"Don't let her get away!" Amelia called from behind.

A mixture of scurrying footsteps, labored breathing, and her drumming heart filled the air. She ran mindlessly through the forest. Scratches ripped her hands as she pressed forward through a winding cover of pine trees. She gritted her teeth at the pain, careful not to make a sound.

The stampede of footsteps behind her seemed to get closer every second. She couldn't get caught. There had to be some escape.

Elizabeth's coat snagged on a thick branch as she sprinted. Panting, she jerked it with a heavy force, but the branch tore a large hole through her coat. She had no other choice but to leave it behind.

Flashlights pierced through trees like spotlights. The police were nearing in on her.

"Just surrender, Ainsley!" Frank's voice reverberated off the broad trees.

Elizabeth hastened her pace through the forest blindly, foliage crackling beneath her steps. *This can't be the end.* Branches ripped her face like thin paper as she blew through bushes.

But to her wondrous relief, a far-off engine roared as it sped down a nearby road. The grumbling loudened. She must've been near a street.

With her frail hands writhing from scratches, Elizabeth broke through a pitch-black thicket. She held her breath as she erupted onto a road, a roaring truck speeding down. There was only one thing to do.

Elizabeth flailed her hands in the air, forcing the screeching truck to a harsh stop. Relieved, the warm headlights illuminated her orange sweater, now dirty with twigs and broken leaves. She must've appeared as some lunatic, though the only lunacy was the detective's accusations against her.

Speckles of light beams flickered within the forest. She was running out of time.

Elizabeth hurried to the driver's side and smacked the tinted window until it rolled down.

A pallid, pale man leaned forward. The stench of his greasy black hair brushed Elizabeth's nose. His black, graven eyes sagged like they'd lost all life within.

"Please—you need to help me! I'm in danger! I need to get out of here now!" Elizabeth's voice quivered with pleading eyes.

The man studied her for an uncomfortably long moment, his eyes shifting to her every feature. "Get in," the man said in a low, husky voice.

Elizabeth held her breath. For a moment, she hesitated getting in the truck with a man who reminded her of the patients she used to see. An addict from the pastiness of his skin. But she conceded.

Hurrying to the passenger side, Elizabeth scurried inside the truck.

The lanky man produced a grimacing smile. "Put your seatbelt on," he grumbled.

The back of her hair prickled as his raspy voice spoke. Elizabeth gulped, her heart rushing. The moment her head turned to clutch the worn seatbelt, a heavy arm wrapped around her neck.

The man heaved her toward him with a violent force. Elizabeth let out a small scream as she squirmed in his tight grasp. But she was quickly subdued as a wet cloth fell over her mouth and nose.

His face blurred, Elizabeth's head throbbed, and blackness erupted within her regretful eyes.

48

LUKAS

JULY 14

IN THE DARKEST CORNER of Elizabeth Ainsley's basement, Lukas studied the doctor's unconscious body with a steady breath.

They say to forgive and forget your enemies, but the time for forgiveness had passed. Now, there was only time for revenge. That was the sweet taste he would never forget as he licked his lips delightfully.

Elizabeth's body twitched on the wooden chair, where he bound her with duct tape. The warm bulb overhead cast a shadowy glow on her pale skin. Her wrinkles were roughly carved into her crooked face.

Her basement was more accessible when he stole her house keys after Lukas abducted her. Someone had left a basement trap door open. For a doctor, she wasn't as smart as he'd perceived her to be. Getting into a random truck with a stranger was too perfect.

But there was something weird about her basement, Lukas thought as he fidgeted with a stainless steel kitchen knife in his hands. A small grave stood loud behind her with a white crucifix poking out of a plot of dirt. Was the basement a tomb? Either way, it was going to become her tomb next.

Elizabeth softly groaned. The faint cracking of duct tape filled the air as Lukas peered like a ghost from the shadows, his eyes wide and ready. He'd waited for this moment for so many years, and now it had finally come.

Lukas was unsure of what he'd say first, but he knew he wanted to hurt her. *Hurt* her real bad. Killing her unconscious would be no fun, and Lukas was determined to make tonight the fucking night of his life.

The doctor lifted her head, disoriented. "What?" she muttered.

A conniving smile curled on Lukas's face as Elizabeth struggled against the tape binding her to the chair. She was a trapped bug on a recluse's web, and she was about to be eaten.

Elizabeth's head spun around as she panted. She must've wondered how she ended up in her basement.

Lukas's eyes squinted in delight. Her panic was beautiful to watch.

"Help!" she screamed, uselessly.

"No one can hear you, Doctor. It's just you and me," Lukas growled.

Elizabeth's face paled white as her head turned in every direction, still struggling in the chair. "Who's there!"

"Maybe it's no one. Maybe you're just imagining my voice in your head. In the stress of a traumatic event, that can happen, right? And something like abduction has gotta be traumatic, right, Dr. Ainsley? Or should I say, The Raven of East Haddam?" Lukas crept out from the corner and into the lit area, where Elizabeth's face contorted in terror.

Sliding two fingers along the dull edge of the kitchen knife, he studied Elizabeth's fear. The sweat that dripped from her brow smelled sweet, like a sugary syrup. Her skin was delicate like butter, easy to slice. The blood that would spill was sure to be delectable.

Elizabeth's eyes fell on the knife in his hands. "Who are you—what do you want!"

"Don't you recognize me?" Lukas asked, smiling with amusement.

She stared blankly at him for a few moments.

Lukas's smile soured into a sneer. "I thought we were friends, Liz. Maybe you're making this all up in your head, but this knife feels pretty real. Do you want me to show you?"

Elizabeth shook her head, now teary-eyed, but he ignored her. Gliding the knife above her bound forearm, Elizabeth's pleas made Lukas's heart flutter with pleasure as he teased her. And with a swift motion, he sliced her forearm, leaving a narrow scarlet line. Not deep enough to be fatal.

She shrieked in pain; her bound arms writhing against the tape.

"Did that feel real, Doctor?" Lukas bent down to her eye level. "Or was that your brain playing *tricks* on you? This isn't a dream, Liz. You're in a nightmare."

At the last word, Elizabeth's brow shot up as her trembling, murky eyes met his. "It can't be," she whispered. "You're—you're Eleanor's son, Lukas?"

Lukas took a step back. Of course, she couldn't forget him. The mere memory of him was carved into the ugly wrinkles of her skin. "So, you *do* remember, then? You remember how you tried convincing me I started the fire that killed my father? Do you remember how you said I was crazy? Do you remember how you kept me prisoner in that hospital forever? And remember how they took Erica and me away from the hospital and kept us in those *cells*!" Lukas gritted his teeth with rage as the knife quivered by his side.

He wanted a response from her, but all Elizabeth could do was gawk in disbelief. "How are you here? You should be—"

"Dead? No, I got out. I survived on my rage and vowed to get revenge on the woman who ruined my life," Lukas spat. "You let us suffer in those facilities. Even your own son, Thomas."

Elizabeth perked her head. "You knew Thomas?"

Lukas's lips pulled back, exposing his clenched teeth. "I did. And you let him die in that place."

"No," she said sternly.

"You let all of us miserably suffer down there and in every cage you've created! It was all you!"

"No! I did everything I could do to free Thomas from my ex-husband's barbaric grasp! He tortured him and you in that terrible place!"

Lukas pressed his face close to hers, feeling her shaky breath on his fiery cheeks. "Doesn't matter. I'm going to make you suffer the same way you made us."

"I know you didn't start that fire in your home," Elizabeth cried.

Lukas staggered back, his heavy heart drumming. "What the fuck did you just say?"

Elizabeth shook her head. Her glassy eyes trembled with repulsive mercy. "I lied to you, Lukas. I'm sorry. I always knew you never started that fire. It was your sister. There was never anything wrong with you. I had cleared you as mentally stable during our session." Elizabeth choked on her words as she sobbed.

"You're lying!" Lukas roared, his head throbbing again with pain.

"But your mother—Eleanor. She begged me, she begged me, Lukas, not to return you or your sister. She never wanted to be your mother—"

Lukas held the knife forward, his head pulsating. "Shut the fuck up!"

"Eleanor was never fit to be a mother, she told me. Your father forced himself on her when they met, conceiving you. Then again, with your sister. Your mother was a hostage in her home! And the only escape she could see was tricking your sister into causing the fire! All she wanted was to start over in her life!" Elizabeth cried.

Molten anger flowed through him, his face mottled with red. "Stop talking! You're lying! My mother wouldn't do that! She loved me and my sister! You're a liar! That's all you do!"

"I'm not! Once you and your sister were in the hospital, she told me she'd made plans to construct a new identity someplace else," she sobbed.

Lukas howled with fury, the violent sound echoing off the walls. *Don't listen to her!* Everything was a lie. Everything was a web. Everyone was a spider. The room spun into a blur as his breaths labored. This was his last straw.

His flaring grip on the knife tightened, seething at Elizabeth's mouth. Her tongue was the root of every miserable ounce he'd endured in his life. It had created every problem in his life.

Smirking with wide eyes, there was one thing to fix that issue.

Lukas approached her and rammed his hand into her mouth, grasping her slimy tongue. The room filled with Elizabeth's stifled screams as she tried to pull her head back, but it was nothing more than amusement.

"No!" Elizabeth violently shrilled.

"You'll never speak again, bitch."

Steadying her squirming tongue out of her mouth, Lukas held the hungry kitchen knife above her chapped lips. With a rapid swing, Lukas sliced Elizabeth's tongue with an exhilarating thrill.

A clean cut.

Elizabeth writhed and screamed, blood splattering over her mouth and clothes. The air was sweet with the tang of her spilled blood. Just how he liked it.

Lukas chuckled at her agonizing sight, but he didn't want to kill her with his knife. That'd be no fun.

The bloody knife clattered to the floor as he stepped back. Elizabeth didn't deserve the delicate touch of his knife. She deserved something far worse for muttering all those lies.

Lukas wandered to a corner filled with sealed cardboard boxes and shelves with chemicals and other home-renovating materials. There, he saw it, just the item he was looking for. *Kerosene.* He grabbed the small blueish-silver can and approached her again.

Thick maroon blood spilled out of her mouth as she continued sobbing. Lukas found her loudness irritable as he opened the can and began dousing her with the bitter liquid.

"You're gonna feel my father's pain, Elizabeth. But hey, *shh*—it's okay. Maybe this is just a terrible dream, and you'll wake up someplace better. Wouldn't that be nice?" Lukas said as he pulled a silver lighter from his pocket. "I found this upstairs earlier and thought I'd take it. You don't mind if I use it, do you? I like starting fires," he finished.

Lukas flicked the spark wheel.

She's a spider.

He took a long breath, narrowing his eyes on her bloody face.

She's a spider.

Elizabeth let out one last blood-curdling scream, the chair rocking back and forth.

She's a spider.

Lukas tossed the lighter on Elizabeth's lap before she combusted into a ball of fire. The heat blasted against Lukas's face, showering his face in an orange glow. Elizabeth shrieked as her body contorted and her skin bubbled.

Art. This was art, Lukas thought, as a twisted smile smeared across him. The type of canvas Rebecca would've loved to paint. If his mother had taught him one thing, it's that violence is *always* okay.

Instead of staging Elizabeth's body like he'd done with Percy and Rebecca, he had another idea. Lukas grabbed the kerosene can and splashed the liquid along the floors and the stairs as he ascended. There couldn't be evidence if the entire house was in ashes. Continuing the trail around the living room and entrance, Lukas drenched the entire house with kerosene until he was satisfied.

A booming explosion reverberated from the basement and off the walls as Lukas flinched. The fire had expanded below, engulfing the entire basement.

Clutching the kerosene bottle by his side, Lukas hurried out of Elizabeth's blazing home and back to his stationed truck in the driveway. Everything the doctor had built would be burned to nothing, just like she deserved.

Lukas had eaten his bug.

49

LUKAS

JULY 14

BILL'S RANCH DISAPPEARED FROM plain sight like an abandoned child, invisible from the rest of the shadowy forest. But Lukas had luckily found the gravel pavement leading back to the ranch. He was running out of time. Now that he murdered Elizabeth and lit her house on fire, it was time to take action.

With the kerosene bottle in his grasp, Lukas had left a dripping trail along the road from Elizabeth's home to Bill's ranch.

Lukas rolled into the driveway before he peered at the shed in the distance. The light was still on, which meant Bill was still having *fun* with Cassandra. At first, guilt tore through him on the drive back for what he was about to do, but Bill would've done the same. A *good* friend such as Bill would understand.

Shuffling out the truck, Lukas tossed the bitter chemical can to the side before hurrying to the glowing shed. His loose-fit black tee reeked of the sour stench as a harsh wind swept through him. Dead grass and tall wheat trampled underneath his ashen shoes, sprinting across the stretch of field.

Something still propped the heavy wooden door open as Lukas carefully crept inside once again. The stifling weapon shed filled with the echo of Cassandra's whimpers and Bill's chuckling.

"Let's see what *toys* I want to play with tonight." Bill's low snicker reverberated off the wooden walls.

But Lukas ignored them as he fixated on the collection of rifles and pistols hanging on the wall in front of him. His brow twitched as he prowled toward the array of shelves, the floorboards whining beneath his step.

Lukas held his breath, hoping Bill would still be distracted. A line of sweat formed above his brow as the echo of flesh thumping continued filling the room. Sighing, Lukas gripped one of the steel pistols, similar to the one Bill gave him, but as he tugged it, the gun wouldn't budge. He tried to still his anger as he clenched his jaw, examining the gun.

To his surprise, zip ties had sturdied the pistol into place. But no matter, Lukas thought, as he gripped the gun with both hands. Taking a deep breath, he tugged the pistol with a heavy force, his knuckles flaring white. With a small crack of the ties, Lukas staggered backward with the pistol in his grasp. But as he did, he collapsed to the floor, vibrating the entire shed.

Shit!

The room fell silent as Lukas scrupulously stood up. There were no sounds of Cassandra or Bill anymore as his ears perked up, listening to the faintest sound. If Bill discovered what he was doing, he'd have no choice but to kill him. And he couldn't have that happen, not when Bill being alive was necessary.

"Don't make a single sound, Cassandra, or I'll kill you." Bill's voice rattled him.

Lukas hurried outside the shed as the stomping footsteps grew louder from behind the hidden passageway. His heart raced faster than the seconds of a clock, holding his breath behind the shed. The wet foliage crunched beneath his black sneakers before pressing himself against the prickling wooden panels.

"Hello!" Bill called into the distance

The scourging wind bellowed in response.

The shed door slammed shut

"Damn wind," Bill spat.

The rickety floorboards creaked within the shed as Bill must've descended back to the basement.

Exhaling in relief, Lukas scurried across the field back toward Seth's home, where he was supposed to be asleep in the living room. The front door was still unlocked as he slithered inside the home. A burst of wind crashed through the inside, scattering loose papers along the floor, but there was no time to pick them up.

Lukas hurried to a small dining table across the wall where Helen's portrait faced him. He caught her frozen sneer as he placed the steel pistol on the oak dining table, their eyes meeting starkly.

He pressed a finger against his lips. "Can you keep one more secret?" he whispered.

Helen didn't move. Her photographed melancholic expression remained unshifting. But the way the warm light showered in the living room almost made it seem like her eyes gleamed in response.

She'd agreed.

Satisfied, Lukas began making his way out of the house for the last time—his plan accomplished. But as he walked down the entryway, a small card stuck to his black-and-white striped sneaker. Peeling the card off his sole, Lukas held it in front of him. An ornate birthday card with different colored roses displayed in a vase with the words *Happy Birthday, Darling!* Written in elegant signage. He opened the card and read the message inside.

My beautiful Cassandra, it's finally your 21st birthday! And you know what that means? You can finally legally drink! Even though we've already done that so many times when we steal from my dad's collection. Every time he notices a missing beer bottle, I just gaslight him into thinking he's already drank it. I'm terrible, I know. But now you can do it legally, so yay! My breath trembles as I write this, love. I wish I could tell my dad about you, but he just wouldn't understand. I know you want me to be brave like you, and I'm trying to be, but I'm just not ready.

I've saved up as much money as I can now and I wanna take you out somewhere nice tonight. I know that's impossible in East Haddam, but you're finally growing up into an adult now. We can be whoever we want, don't forget that. And I don't want to think about any of the bad stuff anymore. I just want to think about you. I'm always thinking about you. That's why I chose this card, because I knew how much you love roses.

Plus, it's pretty gay since each rose is a color of the rainbow. There. I finally wrote the word. Just kidding, don't be mad. But it's cute when you get all flustered.

Happy Birthday, my darling.

Karina.

Lukas squinted at the card in his hands as his lips parted in silence. *Karina was in love with Cassandra?* But it didn't make sense. She'd never mentioned Cassandra before. Maybe he didn't know her as well as he thought. And why did Bill have the birthday card?

But as he scanned the card once more, he caught something that made his heart flash with dread. He read the words again with careful eyes.

And you know what that means?

There was something strange about the "*y*" and "*k*," like they'd been written in a hybrid of cursive and print, and there was something peculiarly familiar about the letters. And then he remembered where he'd seen those half-formed letters from as his fingertips tingled against the card. It couldn't be.

The same style of writing was on the threat note he'd received weeks ago. *I know what you did.* Lukas's breath sharpened as he dropped the letter on the floor. Karina was the sender. But he couldn't let her live knowing his darkest secrets. There was no telling what she would do with that information.

Lukas tightened his lips into a thin line as he reached into his pocket and pulled out his cell phone. Now, there was only one thing left to do. This was the endgame, and he wouldn't lose so easily. Lukas dialed *911* before placing his cell phone against his ear, his heart ricocheting in his chest.

"911, what's your emergency?"

Lukas steadied his eyes on the fallen card. "Help—there's been a fire."

50

LUKAS

MANY YEARS AGO

THE PLAN COULDN'T FAIL.

It wouldn't fail.

Lukas and Thomas had spent the entire night devising it, whispering through the hole in their dividing wall. He had told Thomas about the locked door, and the idea of finally discovering the truth buzzed in his midnight mind like swarming cicadas. He needed to know everything about *Phase Three* and where they were. And Lukas was certain, without a doubt, that their plan could not fail.

Thomas threw a meek punch at him once again. But Lukas had shielded Thomas's futile attack with his raised arms, absorbing the minor damage Thomas was making.

Lukas wasn't sure how much time had passed, but in the few weeks or months Thomas had been in The Room, he had made little progress. The hour now had been for their free training, and Lukas used the time to strategize and observe. They waited for the right moment as they both simulated another hand-to-hand sprawl with light force. Hopefully, it would deceive the director and his guards well enough.

Just wait. The timing had to be perfect. No mistakes.

Lukas's eyes wandered, launching a feeble fist into Thomas's grimy palm.

Others were paired and scattered through The Room, their punches more violent. Their hands craved blood, and their eyes could not see pain. Just like his own.

Lukas had tried to bury his bloodlust cravings after his cruel interactions with the guard and Thomas, but his hands hungered to hold that power again. Once he'd tried fear, he struggled to suppress his cravings. Blood looked tasty. Fear smelled sweet. At any moment during his sprawl with Thomas, he could hurt him real bad if he wanted to.

Hurting feels good. No—stop.

Thomas landed a soft blow against Lukas's stomach. The sudden feeling ripped Lukas away from his mind and back to the present—the plan. He needed to focus again.

Guards lined against the concrete walls, observing them while Director Miller lurked somewhere within the shadows, as if he were a shadow himself. The prickling weight of his glare shivered Lukas's neck as he continued each fluid motion with Thomas. He parried Thomas's fist with a strike to his chest, their eyes falling together in fear. They were running out of time.

A booming crack filled Lukas's ears, his heart jolting. Paling in terror, Thomas halted his blow midway. The room fell silent as Thomas's eyes widened at the sight behind Lukas. He turned around with his breath catching in his throat. The horrific sight stunned him, but it wasn't a surprise. They were in The Room, after all.

A younger boy lay still and quiet on the cold floor, his neck crooked to the rest of his body.

Dead.

The back of Lukas's neck broke into a sweat as he looked up at the girl who stood above him. Her face was stoned with no remorse and no feelings of what she'd done.

"You're not supposed to kill them, Alicia," the director's voice croaked from the shadows.

Alicia looked down at the dead boy with contempt. "He was annoying me. He talks too much."

The echo of footsteps reverberated off the walls as the director and guards approached the mess she'd made. Alicia didn't move, though. She stood perfectly still; her face indifferent about the death she'd caused.

But this was good, Lukas thought. This was the distraction they needed for the plan to work, and now that the director wasn't looking, Lukas could finally make his move. He turned back to face Thomas before they nodded in understanding. Now was the time.

Lukas slid away from Thomas and approached one guard opposite the murderous scene. He gulped. The guard squinted at him through his mask, his rifle ready at his side.

"What do you want?" the guard grunted.

"I need to pee—really badly. I can't hold it," Lukas said, gripping his groin.

The guard took a step forward, groaning. "Let's make it quick."

Lukas forced a relieved grin as he followed the guard, stealing one last glance at Thomas. This was it, and Thomas knew it. After the years in the facility, only one good thing had come out of it: their friendship. That was the one thing the director could never snuff out.

Lukas exited The Room with the guard as they traversed a narrow hallway, the grimy bathrooms on the other end. Except, he had no intention of going to the bathroom or making it all the way down the hallway with the guard.

Cold air surged into his lungs as he inhaled. Slipping the handmade shank from a pocket in his robe, Lukas smirked as he held it tight by his side. It was all according to the plan. Kill the guard, take the clearance card, open the locked door, and find the truth.

The guard led Lukas down the row of hanging fluorescent lights until they reached a pair of passageways that led to the two bathrooms. Lukas crept closer behind the guard before he could turn around.

Do it, Lukas! Now!

Lukas raised the shank in the air, ready to strike. Ready to kill.

The lights above him blared red before the surrounding walls screamed violently.

Code red.

Gasping at the shrilling sirens around him, he leaped onto the guard. He howled as Lukas began stabbing him too many times to count. Blood splurged like bursting pipes as he tried to shake Lukas off. But Lukas was on him like a spider on an insect. The guard collapsed to the floor, a puddle of warm blood forming around them.

Lukas heaved like a savage animal as he wiped his blood-soaked hands on his coarse robe. The narrow hallway had been coated in an unwelcoming red as shouting echoed from the distance. But he didn't care as he tossed the bloody shank to the side.

Maybe he was an animal, after all. No innocence. No rules. And a craving for blood.

Growling, Lukas dropped to his knees and snatched the clearance card from the man's belt. His red hands trembled as he clutched it by his side.

The sound of running footsteps from behind rattled Lukas's spine. He spun around to find a wheezing Thomas sprinting toward him, his face stretching in panic. The screaming red sirens painted Thomas's skin red and turned his eyes from the color of the sky to the color of blood.

"What's going on?" Lukas demanded, his voice deafening. He was tired of having more questions than answers.

"I don't know—but Director Miller and the guards have gone mad! They're quickly rounding us back to our cells—I was able to slip out when they weren't looking! They're going to come looking for us! You need to hurry, Lukas!"

Lukas grasped Thomas's frail wrist. "Let's go then, Thomas! I remember the way—"

But Thomas didn't budge. He remained still, like a frozen statue.

"Why aren't you moving? C'mon! What're you waiting for?" Lukas tugged against his arm, forcing Thomas to stagger forward.

Thomas threw Lukas's bloody hand off. "Lukas, stop!" He turned his head to the winding red hallway. "I—I can't go with you! I'm tired of being scared, Lukas! Someone needs to delay the guards from reaching you! I will distract them for as long as I can! This is our only chance, Lukas! Go!"

Lukas frowned as he took a step back. "You better not do anything stupid, Thomas! I'll come back for you—I promise!"

The two boys stole one last determined glance at each other.

"Hey! What are you boys doing over here!" a guard shouted from behind Thomas.

Lukas's heart raced with cold horror. They'd been caught.

"Lukas, go!" Thomas quickly turned and sprinted past the guard's heavy grasp.

The guard chased after Thomas. "Come back here!"

Lukas sprinted away, his breaths becoming sharp. He shot past a corner as he traversed the shrilling scarlet corridors, and he wasn't sure which rang his ears louder: his racing heart or the sirens. The white-tiled walls seemed to collapse closer on him as Lukas hurried past hallways full of locked rooms he'd never been in and cells.

He descended a long flight of stairs further into *hell*, where the furnaces were.

Gasping for air at the bottom of the stairwell, a series of explosive bursts reverberated off the walls. The booming noise came from above. Something was happening up there. But Lukas had no time to wonder. He gathered his thoughts back to the locked door at the end of the hallway.

Trudging toward it, he spotted the vent in the wall he'd broken through before. His fingers tingled with the cold metal clearance card in his hand. The key to the truth, just behind a white glossed door.

He examined the bold red letters imprinted on the door.

Authorized Personnel Only

Lukas approached the door, taking a deep breath. He was prepared to face whatever might be behind. He'd kill whoever he needed to get his answers. The screaming of the sirens continued as he raised the card and waved it toward the black box.

Nothing happened.

His brow furrowing, Lukas tried jabbing the box with the card.

The door remained closed.

He squeezed the card tighter between his fingers. Nothing was working. Lukas continued poking the box with the card with different angles in different directions. The stupid thing probably didn't work. Frustrated, he was ready to give until he shoved the card in from the top.

The box flashed green, and the door slid open.

A rush of simmering heat grazed Lukas's skin as he stood before the entrance. Lukas gulped as he stepped inside. It was the same type of blazing heat he hadn't touched since Erica started the fire in his home.

Lukas crept further into the dim room, where he was engulfed in a suffocating heat. The room was dimly lit, with a single overhead buzzing bulb hanging from the ceiling, casting a pale, flickering glow that barely reached the corners of the room. Grime infiltrated both the ceiling and floor he skulked on.

The imposing machine of the room was the massive furnace that lined against the wall in front of Lukas. It was a hulking, blackened metal monstrosity coated in layers of soot and grime. Its overbearing presence made the room stench acrid and bitter, like something burning. The sharp scent stung Lukas's nostrils, and he could almost taste the bitterness in the air. It brought back terrible memories, memories of the fire that had destroyed his home and family.

Lukas stepped toward the furnace, holding his breath. The furnace itself emitted a low, continuous rumble, like a growling beast hungering to eat someone. This must've been where they took the others. Where they killed Olivia.

At the mouth of the furnace was a small door that had been left open, casting an orange glow in the shadows. Lukas bent down to take a peek inside. The small latch was big enough for someone to crawl in—for someone to be fed in. As he examined the glowing embers, his eyes widened in horror at the contents inside.

Human bones were scattered around within the furnace, charred.

Lukas staggered back. His breaths sharpened as he covered his mouth with his bloody hand. He was right, after all—the director was burning them to death if they failed. But there had to be more. He needed more answers.

Lukas reeled back from the furnace until he pressed against a wall, something sharp jabbing his back. He spun around to find another door, one had hadn't opened before. It was camouflaged with the rest of the wall. Just as grimy and unwelcoming.

Holding his breath, he twisted the brass knob and creaked it open. With a soft whine, the door opened to another room—a type of filing office. Lukas stepped inside, closing the door behind him. Rows of filing cabinets on both sides stretched against a narrow wall with a desk and computer at the other end. He bit his lip at the rows of pointless documents, but he conceded this was as far as he could get.

The cold floor sent an icy chill through his bones as he approached the first cabinet. Pulling the metal drawer labeled *A-L*, he read the small labels on the folders inside.

Thomas Ainsley, Amon Anderson, Alicia Bennett, Olivia Singh.

Lukas paused. Those were the names of the kids at the facility with him, and these were their files? Without thinking, he scurried down the rows of cabinets until he found the one labeled *R-Z*. This had to be it. All the information they knew about them was inside these files. Lukas pulled the drawer open and scanned the folders inside.

Erica Retter, Lukas Retter.

His mouth parted in silence as he snatched his and Erica's file. The answers he'd been searching for must've been inside these files. It had to. It just had to. Lukas ran his fingers along the cold paper spine of the folders, his heart drumming in his ears.

With his brows furrowing for the truth, Lukas opened Erica's file and began hungrily reading. His eyes widened at the contents inside.

It can't be.

51

KARINA

JULY 1

"WHERE DO YOU THINK he goes?" Karina said, pressing her iPhone against her ear.

She gawked outside the apartment window as rain cried down the glass pane. East Haddam was always sobbing. The wrathful heather clouds looming above seemed to always have tears left to shed, just like herself.

Karina loathed every red brick and cracked road that stretched within the walls of the town, and when she'd scream at the town, it replied in silence. No one could hear her. Not even her own father listened, who was now driving off into the shimmering mist. The same time of the same night of every month. "Right according to schedule," as her neighbor's son, Jake, would say.

"*Wait, girl, who're we talking about again?*" Karina's friend Alexis asked through the phone. "*Ben keeps distracting me—hey, shut up! I love him, but I think about killing him sometimes, I swear. Oh my god, I didn't mean to say that. I'm sorry.*"

Karina held her breath at the forbidden word. Never again did she want to see, read, or hear the words *death* or *kill* again in her lifetime. Even thinking about the words shivered her skin. Too many memories.

But Karina quickly forgave Alexis, as she forgets that little rule sometimes. A tedious rule, maybe, but she intended to go the rest of her life without those terrible words in her vocabulary.

"*I wouldn't stress about it, babe. Your dad's probably just tipping back into dating again, and he's too scared to tell you.*"

Karina bit her lip. "He shouldn't be trying to replace my mom already! It's only been what, one year since she died? It's too soon, I'm not ready! And he shouldn't be either!" She turned back to her white wooden bookcase shaped like a fairytale castle.

Childish, she knew, but her childhood is where her mother lived to her fullest. Rows of different colored books stretched across its white shelves. The bookcase was the last piece of her mother's memory she treasured. The darkness inside East Haddam had taken her mother away, just like it did Cassandra and now her father.

"*Well—maybe he's not going on a date. There could be a million places he's going right now, but hopefully, it's not seeing another woman,*" Alexis's static voice said.

Karina pressed her sweaty palm into her forehead. "Maybe you're right, Alexis. But there's only way one to know for sure."

"*What do you mean?*"

Squinting at the wall with a portrait of herself and her father, she hesitated. "I mean, I'm going to follow him. It's driving me crazy not knowing where he's going every damn month. If I drive now, I can still catch up to him."

"*Do it. But be safe, girl,*" Alexis finished.

Karina hung up the call before burying her phone back into her pocket. Anger stirred within her. This night, for sure, she was going to know what her sly father was up to. But she didn't want to entertain the thought of him already meeting the other woman. Or worse—potential wives to be her new mother. The thought repulsed her as she threw on her brown leather coat and hurried out of her room.

The kitchen and living room were a mess, as always, but she didn't care. Karina grabbed her Toyota Camry keys from the white tile kitchen counter before hurrying out the apartment door.

What could her father be doing so close to midnight? She regretted asking herself as her foul mind filled in the blanks with sexual encounters he could be doing. *Please, God, no.* A jolt of rage flashed through her at the idea. Shaking the intrusive thoughts from her head, Karina hurried down the stairwell and burst through the New Horizon front doors.

Rain poured onto the streets and soaked into the back of her neck as she scurried toward the gray car. An ominous clap of thunder rattled her pale skin before she scurried inside her car and drove off.

Piercing through the heavy fog, Karina ran her shaking hand through her soaked black curls. The sky's tears fell like bullets in all directions, driving the same bleak, misty path her father did. And the blinking headlights paved an illuminated road that fled from the town to the depths of the forest. The dreaded outskirts.

Karina bit her lip as she navigated past the winding road. Black trees that swayed like shadows towered over the car. A streak of lightning shot across the sky before the car rumbled from the thunderous clap. She tried to follow the red pair of brake lights in the distance, but they distorted into a dim blur as the distance between them grew—the fog rising from the road was too thick. She'd lost her father.

Karina slapped the wheel. "Shit," she muttered.

She was driving nowhere, following a street with no direction or end. Speeding down the wet road, she gripped the wheel tightly, unsure of what she'd do now.

But to her heavy relief, she sped past a truck parked on the side. Karina slowed her car to a halt before she pulled over to the side as well. Her father must've been meeting someone inside the forest, someone discreet.

Like a woman.

There was nowhere more silent than inside the forest. That was probably why he chose it. She exited her car before creeping toward the wall of pine trees in front. Whatever her father was up to, she was determined to find out.

Karina clutched her waist as she staggered inside. She always felt more protected when someone held her, even herself—especially since there was talk about the Recluse Killer. First, her girlfriend, Cassandra, and now that poor woman, Rebecca. The horrific thought of who might've done that to them prickled her skin as she trampled over the wet foliage.

There wasn't a day that went by where guilt didn't consume her like a parasite. The ache in her heart grew each day after what happened to Cassandra. *I should've been there for her. Why wasn't I there for her?* The only conclusion she could draw was she was too weak to protect the people around her. At least she had to protect herself as she wandered aimlessly through thickets and pine. The sharp leaves scratched her hands as she pushed past thick branches. The stiff wind stormed through her hair and lungs, but there was a bitter tang in the air as she coughed.

There was a loud rustle in the distance.

Karina's heart leaped. Was it her father?

She held her breath as the rustling grew closer, twigs snapping behind a group of birch trees. The noise had to have been the wind. But Karina wasn't so sure as the rustling became rough and heavy.

Gritting her teeth, she crept forward to peek behind the trees. If the noise was her father, she could spy on him without him noticing. She took a step, her rickety breath blowing against the cold air. There was that sour stench again, like spoiled milk or rotting meat. Karina buried her nose into her jacket sleeve, and that's when she saw him.

Her black eyes throbbed in horror.

Death! Blood! Murder!

Dead!

Dead!

Dead!

The words exploded in her mind like red fireworks and the sparks in her mind formed the fractured face of her dead mother.

A grunting man dragged a corpse along the wet foliage. The man pulled him by his bloody feet like some victorious hunter who'd killed his prize animal—completely barbaric.

Karina wanted to retch her sleeve at the sight, but swallowed her horror. She couldn't risk being seen under any circumstance. Instead, she screamed silently into her sleeve.

The man dragged the bloody body further down the path, grunting with every step. If she could see who the man was, she could report it to the police, and as she took a long breath, she determined that's what she was going to do.

No more being afraid.

Karina squinted at the man, taking a slow step forward. A twig beneath her brown boot snapped. The horrifying reverberating sound echoed louder than a church bell, even in the rain. The bone-breaking sound made her heart fall to her stomach.

She was done for.

The man halted mid-step and perked his head up in her direction. His stark face narrowed against her, staring. Karina shivered at the bitter sight. But their eyes didn't meet. She wasn't sure if he had eyes or a face. The black shadows of the trees warped the man's face.

She couldn't breathe. It was as if, in that moment, she couldn't remember how to. She'd completely forgotten. She simply waited for him to launch forward and kill her like a frozen gazelle in headlights.

Instead, the sight that flashed was a crashing zip of lightning whipping across the sky. The night sky illuminated into blinding daylight for a second or two. She could clearly see the man's face now through the pair of birch trunks.

Karina's face paled as she recognized the man. Her heart burst from her chest, throbbing her skin. He was a man that lived in *New Horizon* that she'd met several times through her father's friendship with him. A reclusive neighbor, though, that she'd always had a bad feeling about, despite her father's friendly nature.

The man's name was sharp and cold, just like his pallid face.

But now, Karina was determined. Determined to make her father finally listen.

The truth about their sinister neighbor, *Lukas.*

52

KARINA

KARINA STIRRED THE BLACK coffee three times with her spoon. The acrid taste was as bitter as the feeling in her stomach after last night. There was a psychotic murderer living in the building, and her father did not know as he sat oblivious to the atrocity she had encountered.

Karina looked up from her steaming mug and shot a cold glare at him across the wooden dining table. The fluorescent chandelier buzzed above them like an incessant bug. Dimitri whisked a spoonful of sugar into his blue ceramic mug, his eyes falling deeper into the newspaper laid in front of him. They had barely spoken a word to each other since he returned home. How was she supposed to tell him she saw his tenant, Lukas, dragging a corpse?

Her father lifted the white ceramic sugar bowl and nudged it toward her. "Sugar?" he asked.

Karina pressed the sugar bowl away. "Can you please listen to me, Dad?"

His thick brows shot up. "Oh—that's right. You take your coffee with milk."

"I'm not talking about that." Karina frowned. She hesitated for a moment as she bit her lip, but when she parted her lips, the words spilled out. "Where do you keep going every month?"

Her father stared blankly at her for a few moments as if she asked some ridiculous question. "You know where I go. I have monthly business I have to take care of for the apartment. Nothing you need to worry yourself about."

"Are you seeing a woman?"

"What on earth are you talking about? No, of course not. What gave you that ridiculous idea?" Her father furrowed his thick black unibrow.

"I followed you last night into the woods. Where were you going?"

His jaw clenched. "You followed me? Do you have any idea how completely disrespectful that is to me—"

A flash of irritation rose in Karina's throat. "I followed you because I had to see Dad."

"After everything I do for you, you don't trust me?" he barked.

"I do trust you. But you're clearly lying to me because you're getting all fucking defensive right now." Karina's voice was coated with surging irritability.

Her father shot up from his chair. "Don't you dare swear at me, Karina! How dare you use that foul tongue in my home after everything I do to take care of the both of us! You do not know how incredibly dangerous that was following me last night. You're not allowed to know what I'm doing because you'll put everyone here in danger. Is that what you want? For me to get in trouble?"

A lump grew in Karina's throat as her father's stern voice rattled the surrounding walls. Warm tears filled the lids of her eyes, pursing her pale lips. "Why is it dangerous? Just tell me."

He studied her for a moment before collapsing back into his chair, sighing. "My friend, Ian, and me, you see, we're working together on a *project.*"

"What kind of *project?*"

"It's a secret organization here in East Haddam that meets once a month when the police aren't paying attention. *Libertas,* they call themselves. But we—*they've*—been planning something for a while. Something *big.* And it's only a matter of months before they carry it out," he said.

Karina squinted at him, curious. "Carry *what* out?"

Her father hesitated for a moment, running his large, sweaty hand through his curls. "The jailbreak. They're making an explosive to break the walls of this town and escape."

"*Jailbreak?*" Karina gawked in disbelief. She debated whether she'd heard correctly. She concluded she did. Unexpectedly, a wave of relief washed over her as it settled into her mind. "So, the dangerous thing wasn't Lukas then," she muttered.

"Lukas? What are you talking about?" he asked, squinting his eyes.

Karina's eyes widened with terror as she stood. "Daddy, I need you to listen to me. Your friend, Lukas, when I followed you last night, I thought you might've gone into the woods, so I wandered inside. I—I saw something terrible." She paused.

Red fireworks exploded in her mind as she pressed her sweating palm against her forehead.

Blood! Murder! Death!

The sharp words sent a rush through Karina's racing heart.

"What did you see?" he grumbled.

"He was dragging someone. Someone *dead*. And he almost saw me. I looked at him through the branches of a tree and his face—his face was so *cold*. Like there was no one sitting behind his eyes. He dragged that body so mercilessly! We have to go to the police and tell them! Who knows what else he's done or what else he'll do? I know it was him, and I'll swear an oath—"

"Stop." He raised his hand, motioning her to sit.

Karina did so, confused, waiting for him to say something back. But he didn't. He sat in silence for several moments, studying the floor, his eyes twitching up at her as the clock in the corner ticked by. Finally, he let out an exasperated breath and held his hands near his bushy mouth.

"We can't go to the police," he said.

Karina's mind stormed with endless questions as her mouth fell open. "Did you not just hear what I said? He killed someone, Daddy! He's a murderer!"

"I know that! And if what you're saying is true, we can't go to the police. Lukas is storing *something* for me, something that'll get me into serious trouble with the police if they find it. If we turn Lukas in, there's no doubt he'll bring me down with him," he said.

Karina's face pinched with frustration, her freshly polished nails dug into her palms. It wasn't fair. She felt disgusted that he didn't care about a murderer in the building. "So that's it then? We do nothing and let him get away with it!"

"Karina—"

She shot up from her chair and stomped toward her bedroom. "Just forget it."

Karina slammed her bedroom door behind her as she trudged toward her queen-sized bed in front of her. She collapsed on the white sheets stretching across the mattress.

The bed was missing a queen, though. Cassandra. Karina fixed her teary eyes on the white ceiling above, feeling her heartbeat with her hands on her chest. The bed felt emptier than ever since Cassandra was *taken*. She never even told her father the truth about her relationship with Cassandra, not until she could move at least.

Karina moved her hand to the side, hoping she'd touch Cassandra's soft hand. But she couldn't. She clutched the white sheets that screamed for her to do something. If Cassandra had been with her, she'd tell her to not sit and wait. She'd insist on bringing down her abductor, Lukas. It was him. Karina had no doubt about it. Every second that went by was another second of terrible things happening to her. But she wouldn't accept she was dead. She just couldn't be.

Karina sat up. She had to do something, even if her father objected. Walking over to a small desk tucked in the corner, Karina tore a small piece of paper from her notebook and a pen. There was no greater threat than fear. If she could instill fear in Lukas, maybe it would buy her more time to figure out where Cassandra was.

With a shaky breath, Karina scribbled the words: *I know what you did* on the scrap of paper. This had to scare Lukas into stopping whatever he was up to. She was sure of it. She folded the piece of paper and tucked it into her pocket before hurrying out of her bedroom.

Her father remained ponderous on the chair, rubbing his eyes with his thumbs. Karina hurried past him without a word and out their door. With her heart thumping in every step, she scurried to Lukas's apartment at the end of the hallway. The path of rugs that trailed to his door seemed to get dirtier the closer she approached, and the lights seemed to be peculiarly dimmer on his side than the rest of the building.

Karina took a heavy breath, gazing at the treacherous door. Trembling, she bent down and slipped the note under his door. It was finally done.

But as she turned around, she was met with an unexpected grin sitting by the stairwell. Jake, the little owl she'd babysat for many years, sat in the corner and watched as tenants went about their lives, and he was notorious for speaking about everyone's business.

"Was that a present for Lukas?" Jake beamed in his brightly colored t-shirt.

Karina stared blankly at him for a few moments before an amicable grin slipped from her face. "Can you keep a secret?"

Jake nodded.

53

LUKAS

JULY 14

"GOOD MORNING ON WRCH 100.5 FM. It's another beautiful sunny Monday morning here in Connecticut..." The static buzz of Lukas's radio rumbled inside his truck as he traversed the forest's roads.

It had been several hours since he killed the doctor, but he could still hear her sweet screams playing inside his ears. He licked his lips. The bitter stench of smoke still lingered on him, even though he'd stolen a pair of Bill's clothes and thrown away his dirty ones. A light blue button-down and a pair of dark navy jeans, which made him appear like some sort of businessman.

And after he'd made the phone call to the police, the firefighters hurried to the doctor's home to put out the fire.

Just as he intended.

Hopefully, the authorities had seen the trail of kerosene leading from the burning house to Bill's ranch. That had been the plan all along. And once they'd arrived at the house and invaded inside, the authorities would find an illegal gun in his home. It was all so beautifully perfect as Lukas tightened his grasp on the black steering wheel with delight. He was about to find out through the radio if all went according to his plan.

But there was one more hindrance he needed to take care of: Karina. Lukas couldn't let her walk around alive with whatever information she knew. It would destroy his plan. His plan to kill and gain power. And if she wanted to play this *game* with him, he was sure he would make it a bloody one with her.

Lukas cranked the volume dial higher on his car radio.

"Authorities this early morning have arrested murder suspect Bill Meyer, who they believe to be the notorious 'Recluse Killer' in the correctional city of East Haddam. Meyer was found shortly after the burning of the renowned Dr. Elizabeth Ainsley's home last night. It has been a month since authorities first discovered the body of Rebecca Waylow and since the murders of Percy Romano and Dr. Elizabeth Ainsley have tragically followed.

"And in a shocking revelation, folks, authorities have located Cassandra Holland, who disappeared three months ago. Holland was found captive in Bill Meyer's shed, where sexual torment allegedly might have been involved. But we hear she's now safe and currently being treated at Hartford Hospital, God bless. We'll keep you updated as this chilling story unfolds."

Lukas grinned, his beaming eyes glowing like never before. He wasn't the *Recluse Killer*. He heard it right there on the news radio. The killer was Bill, it always had been. Now, Amelia would get her murder suspect like she wanted and finally leave him alone. The surrounding air had never felt so light, and his heart adored the exhilaration of making a mockery of the Haddam Police Department.

Lukas was unstoppable.

Powerful.

In control of East Haddam.

He had pulled all the strings of fear in this town, and everyone feared *him*, even though they didn't know it *was* him. No longer would he be seen as a bug waiting for people to trample on. He'd trap them all in his web. Every single one of them. Lukas's eyes widened with excitement. He could almost smell the sugary scent of fear. *There's something delicious about swimming in crimson pools of your victim's blood. How savory the memory is.*

The whole town at his knees, pleading for mercy, was sure to be delectable. He'd be the shadow in the walls, striking them one by one.

A conniving grin stretched his pasty lips. And it couldn't possibly be the *Recluse Killer* that would commit murder because Bill was now in custody. And with his newfound innocence, he set his mind on his next bug to eat: Ian Addams. Karina could wait until after he took care of Ian first.

Both hands on the wheel, Lukas sped down the street, piercing through the town traffic. He weaved through cars down *Norwich St.* until he churned past a corner where the filthy hellish carwash sat taunting him. The chipping green walls greeted him like a foe, and the foldable sign that stood with the silly bubble cloud mascot chirped at him with annoyance.

Two lanes formed at the entrance of SuperShine, separated by a filing row of orange traffic cones. Lukas entered the right lane and shot a cold glare at the washer. The pathetic fucker: Ian Addams. His screams were sure to be delightful, like a harmony of tasteful chords. Producing Ian's fear would be easy when Lukas still had his *instrument* to play which was Bill's pistol stashed in his jockey box.

Lukas opened the box and swiftly pulled out the pistol before pulling his truck toward Ian. Ian obliviously beamed at Lukas through his tinted window, unaware of who he was smiling at.

"Welcome, valued customer! What kind of carwash are you looking—" Ian paused as Lukas rolled his window down. His smile sunk into an irritable frown as he sneered at Lukas's appearance. "Lukas, what the hell are you doing here? Leave right now. You're not welcome here!"

Lukas drew his pistol and aimed it between Ian's eyes. Within a second, Ian staggered back as his face paled, stricken with terror. His widened brown eyes quivered as they focused on the pistol in front of him. The humorous sight made Lukas chuckle. *The stupid fat-ass is scared of me now.*

"Wash my car," Lukas said with a sly grin.

A tear trailed down Ian's grimy cheek as he raised his hands to surrender. "Don't—Lukas, please. Don't shoot me," he pleaded.

"Wash my *fucking* truck, Ian. Now." Lukas nudged the pistol closer.

Ian quickly nodded as he slowly bent down and dipped the sooty yellow sponge in the bucket. He whimpered like a small dog, gliding the trembling sponge across the metal door. Luckily, there had been no one else around wandering with a suspicious eye. Slow morning.

Too bad Mateo isn't around right now to see this.

It was too perfect.

Ian carried the bucket by his side as he continued washing Lukas's car from the windows to the car hood. The blood in his face seemed to drain quicker every second until he became a paper-white ghost. Lukas smirked in satisfaction as he watched Ian wipe another tear from his lumpy face. It felt good. He wasn't afraid to admit it, to see Ian writhing in fear. Humiliating him was as amusing as watching a pig dance.

Just as Ian finished, he came back around to Lukas's window with the sponge and murky bucket in his chubby hand. Oil and water stained his navy blue Mets t-shirt, which was one size too small for him.

"Okay—I finished washing your truck." Ian's voice choked at the last word. His red face was mottled with tears as he slowly put the sponge and bucket on the floor. "Now, please just let me go—"

Lukas pulled the trigger. Just as the gun intended.

There was a booming explosion, and Ian collapsed to the ground. The rattling gun in Lukas's hand felt fucking amazing.

The hole in Ian's forehead formed a puddle of blood around his head and streamed down his body. Lukas had killed his prized animal, after all. He wished he could've taken Ian's body and mounted his head on a display like an antler with that dumbfounded look paralyzed on his face. But he couldn't. Lukas had to leave the scene as quick as possible.

No use lingering when people could notice him at any second.

Lukas quickly rolled the window back up, speeding away from Super-Shine for the last time. Killing Ian painted a content grin on his face. He'd never hated anyone more than Ian, and now he was dead. Dead as Lukas's spirit when he worked at the carwash.

Now that he'd satisfied his bloodlust craving once more, he could finally silence Karina once and for all.

Just as he intended.

54

AMELIA

JULY 16

FIFTY-TWO THOUSAND DOLLARS. THAT was Detective Amelia May-man's salary last year, less after taxes. Being both a detective and the *captain* of the HPD, Amelia thought she'd be making six figures, or at least a livable wage. But it seemed like other government projects had cut most, if not all, of her department's funding. Specifically for what, she wasn't sure.

Even the mayor or his city officials wouldn't tell her. Everybody's hands were apparently tied to secrecy.

Top confidentiality, my ass.

Amelia was confident that the city government was merely using that as an excuse to choke out her department. *Those fuckers,* she thought. But she knew someone had to do the dirty work around here, though, and she thought it might as well be her.

"God, when are we going to get that new coffee machine?" a lieutenant groaned.

"I'm still waiting on lab reports I requested weeks ago, Miller!" another replied.

Amelia dropped the file of Rebecca Waylow's autopsy on her desk. Things traveled slowly around her department. The medical examinations that should have been completed weeks ago barely made their way to her office at the station. A stale cup of coffee sat like a pathetic trophy next to her computer. Another homicide had already interrupted her morning in East Haddam. A middle-aged carwash owner by the name of Ian Addams.

He was shot point-blank between his eyes, lying in a pool of his own blood. Amelia found it hard to imagine that the killer used a gun, seeing that guns were impossible to purchase in East Haddam.

That made a string of four murders so far, and who knew how many more there'd be?

Sighing, Amelia grabbed a small flask from her drawer and drank. She kept a case of watered-down vodka for rainy days when the case became too heavy, and she needed to think. And right now, the Recluse Killer case was storming like a *bitch*.

The vodka soothed her storming mind as she leaned back against her chair. It was days like these that made Amelia wish she'd remained a detective at the Boston Police Headquarters, where the coffee was always hot, and cases never become cold.

But the things you do for love. For money.

She never intended to fall in love with Frank Sallow or become any means of a home-wrecker, but it happened.

They met in Boston, boxing partners at the club on Newbury Street. He coached her on how to channel her anger rather than drink it away. Their love just happened to grow in the process between punches. When Frank got sent to East Haddam for deserting his rank in the military, Amelia had to follow him, even if they'd barely see each other.

Until everything changed. The night of Rebecca Waylow's murder.

Frank had called her while he lurked in the streets that night, swearing he saw someone suspiciously dragging a large black trash bag into the St. Judas Cathedral. A dead body, most likely from how he described it, except there was one problem: he didn't catch their face. But that didn't stop Frank from telling Amelia who it might've been, who he deemed the most dangerous person in East Haddam.

Dr. Elizabeth Ainsley.

Amelia stared at the endless pile of files on her desk that had piled over the last few weeks. All the murder cases weighed both on her shoulders and her desk. She frowned, glaring at the documents.

She found it hard to believe an old woman would murder, but after another witness called into the station, it seemed possible. Frank explained to her how he had involved himself with the doctor's drug network she'd built with her status and connections with the outside world.

Amelia's first intention was to shut the network down until Frank revealed how much money they had made from their first network. Money that could save Amelia's career and department, she could regain the life she had. But if Amelia ceased the drug network spreading across the northeast coast, the money would stop coming into Frank's bank account.

She couldn't let that happen, so together, they devised a brilliant plan. Amelia could secretly take Elizabeth's place as the *queenpin* if they could take Elizabeth down. For that, Amelia needed probable cause to prove Elizabeth had been narco-trafficking and conspiring in murder. Frank was the obvious choice for getting some confession from her.

Amelia glanced over to a framed photo of her and Frank standing by a pond. She smiled at the reminiscent sight.

Frank was supposed to propose a new lucrative network to Elizabeth through Hartford as part of the plan. After she agreed, he would lure her into the East Haddam forest and orchestrate her arrest for conspiracy to commit. Problem was, she never verbally confessed to anything. Frank constantly recorded everything she said, but Elizabeth said nothing incriminating. *The stubborn bitch.*

After, Amelia had to light a stronger blaze under Elizabeth to ignite the pressure for a confession. She thought since she bluffed an immunity deal from the District Attorney's office for an inevitable confession, Elizabeth would finally talk.

The old woman did not speak a chirp, however.

It wasn't a serious matter, though, since Frank had gained proof that Elizabeth was abusing the corpse of Percy Romano. It was probable cause enough to lead to her arrest. Amelia was sure she must've been the Recluse Killer after her interrogation with Lukas.

Everything fell into place after they lured Elizabeth into a set-up where she was *supposed* to be arrested. Until her house went up in flames, and her body was found with lacerations on her wrists and tongue. Someone murdered her.

Even though she was mistaken about Elizabeth being the killer, Elizabeth's death still benefited them. Amelia could now privately take over the network, and no one would suspect a thing.

Amelia dropped the flask back in her drawer and focused her attention back on Rebecca's autopsy in front of her. The case had kept her up each night, wondering who could've done such an evil thing if not Elizabeth or Lukas. Amelia thought she finally received her answer when a man named Bill Meyer was arrested last night for the abduction of Cassandra Holland. That made him the most likely suspect for the string of murders that occurred.

Except one thing. The murder of Ian Addams.

Bill couldn't have possibly killed him because he was in their custody at the station. This time, Amelia had to get it right. There was no more room for mistakes. Another error like Elizabeth would cost Amelia her career.

She opened the autopsy file on her desk, scanning through the medical documents laid in front of her. Her polished fingers flipped through the stale pages of information, but it didn't matter. She'd already seen Rebecca's mutilated body that night. The horrific image imprinted in her mind like China on a plate.

But as she examined the autopsy, her thin brow furrowed at a certain piece of information. The cause of death differed from what she had expected. If Rebecca's death wasn't because of lacerations made on her mutilated body, that meant she was killed before she was staged inside the

St. Judas Cathedral. She read the cause of death again, squinting at the page.

Something didn't quite add up. It didn't make sense.

But before Amelia could inquire further, a policeman knocked on her glass door.

Amelia perked her head up from her desk.

"They're ready for you downstairs in the interrogation room," he said.

"I'll be right there." Amelia nodded.

She stood up from her desk with another file, firming her face into an impenetrable wall, and hurried out of her office. Amelia hurried down the flights of stairs until she reached the basement, where the interrogation room was in a narrow hallway.

Finally, the moment she'd been waiting for. It was now her time to question Bill Meyer about *everything*.

55

LUKAS

MANY YEARS AGO

ERICA'S BLACK-AND-WHITE SMILE SENT a prickling chill up Lukas's skin. The sharp yellow folder tingled in his hands as he read through Erica's file, the black-lettered words screaming from the page. He hadn't seen his sister since the guards took her that night.

In her small portrait at the top corner of the paper, she still smiled innocently, like she'd hurt no one—which was a lie. The photo must've been from when they were still at the hospital all that time ago.

Lukas scanned the document in his hand, his breath trembling. The white document had all her information, such as her age, body weight, eye color, height, and, at the bottom, PASS was stamped in large, bold, scarlet letters. A bloody shade of red, like the alarms shrieking throughout the facility. Next to the stamp, there was a record of the phases she'd passed: *Phase One, Phase Two,* and *Phase Three.*

Lukas clenched his jaw at the word. *Phase Three, what does it mean?* He glanced under the phase record and read the small status: *Last reported in Ansbach, Germany. Ready for deployment.*

The concrete walls vibrated around him, seeming to cave in on him. His ears slowly filled with ringing sirens echoing from outside, and a cold sweat formed along his brow as he read the update again, unsure if he'd read it correctly. But it was correct. Lukas stared blankly at Erica's file. It didn't make sense. How could Erica still be alive and in Germany? That was impossible. He was sure the guards had brought her down here to the furnace and murdered her in the fire, but they took her some place else? And what did it mean Erica was being deployed?

Lukas examined the file again, his eyes squinting in disbelief. He couldn't figure out what any of it meant: the files, the red sirens, or Erica still being alive. Shaking his head in frustration, he dropped Erica's file back in the cabinet and opened his own file next, his heart beating with uncertainty of what he'd find inside. The paper scratched his fingers as he flipped through the white pages.

His own portrait grinned up at him from the paper, though not with a happy smile. A forced grin that didn't do well to hide the suspicious mottled on his face. Lukas brushed his finger against his cheek. It was scratchier than it looked in his picture. In fact, Lukas hadn't seen a photo of himself in a long time. Even the suit of skin he wore felt uncomfortably wrong on him—skinny.

He scanned down the document, examining the information they had on him in black letter boxes until he reached the red stamp. The scarlet-lettered verdict read Fail in bold letters smeared on the page. Lukas held his breath at the word, unsure of what to make of it. A brief note was inscribed beside the stamp as he narrowed his sight closer.

FAIL—DOESN'T SHOW COMPARABLE LEVELS OF VIOLENCE. SET FOR TERMINATION.

Doesn't show comparable levels of violence? The director was right. He'd never intended for Lukas to live any longer since they labeled him as a *fail.* The whole time, the director was testing them for violence and killing those who weren't violent enough.

Lukas took a step back.

The whole messed up experiment reminded him of those tests he'd have to take at the hospital—each question trying to measure his violent behavior. But Lukas wondered why they were doing all this and why the director had failed him for not being violent enough.

"*Violence is never okay,*" his mother's words whispered through his mind like a soft-spoken song.

Lukas demanded an answer, and he was determined to get it. Somewhere in this wall of cabinets and endless rows of files, there had to be an answer as he fell to his knees and threw open drawers. His hands ravaged like hungry mice through walls of files, tearing through each one with no end in sight. Each cabinet only contained lost names in the system, memories of innocent kids that once existed. Now, their names haunted the facility as ghosts.

Groaning, Lukas pulled more cabinets open, ripping the files out and tossing them to the floor. There was nothing except endless piles of paper flying like kites. He grasped a heftier file from the cabinet and threw it aside. A small object clattered along the floor as he did.

Lukas spun around to the file he'd just tossed. There, lying on the cold floor, was a black USB drive that had slipped out of the file. Crawling toward the drive, Lukas held it in his hands. *Watch* was written across the plastic side in silver letters like some sort of order from the drive, so he followed its command, eager to know more.

His eyes shot back toward the desk and computer at the end of the room. Standing, Lukas trudged toward the black computer sitting on a dark wooden desk. He hadn't used a computer in a long time. Memories of computer games he played with Erica were enveloped with the shadow of their father yelling at them for playing around on it.

Lukas found his way to the computer and powered it on. He let a small grin slip on his face. The black leather chair he sat on had wheels at the bottom, so it spun.

The feeling was *fun*. He hadn't felt that way in such a long time, where he'd almost forgotten the feeling existed. *Fun*, he thought as he slid closer to the computer.

He injected the computer with the USB, and the screen went black with the word: Confidential stretching across in bold red letters. Then, finally, a face.

An older pale man fixed his red tie before staring through the screen with sharp black eyes. The man cleared his throat. "If you're watching this video, then I imagine you're already familiar with what's going on across the United States of America's criminal justice system right now." The screen faded to a picture of an unsanitary prison.

The man's low croak continued. "Prisons and correctional facilities are more crowded than any other decade in our history. Poverty, inflation, a hollow middle class—these are things that are spiking crime rates everywhere from Los Angeles to Long Island. That is why Congress passed The Safety First Act, to ensure the record number of incarcerations-per capita are dealt with appropriately and above all, humanely." Lukas was unsure of what exactly the old man was talking about, but he tried to listen closely. The screen faded to a map of America, but on the map, there were weird shapes drawn within, like states he'd never seen before.

"Under this law, each state is required to reconstruct one of their cities into a *correctional city.* And with these new systems, we hope to emphasize a more humane correction rather than the methods of the past. Inmates will receive treatment no different from citizens, with some obligatory restrictions, of course, but they cannot leave their city. We will assign a specialized police force to each city to ensure order and safety as well. In addition, we will evaluate children of criminals and children showing malice in local psychiatrists to ensure everything is all right," the man said.

Lukas stared blankly at all the diagrams being presented in front of him, full of numbers and other colorful charts. But he didn't understand a single one. This wasn't the answer he was looking for.

"Now, this is standard information that the public knows. For you, selected viewers, The Safety First Act entails a secret project for your eyes only."

Lukas sat up, glaring at the man who fixed his tie once more.

"Project Salvus has created a new beginning for the United States, free from terrorism and other global threats to our country. In order to end the war on *terror*, we must kill it in its black heart. That is why we will suggest the encouragement of violence in these children across psychiatric hospitals. That is *Phase One*. Whether they should act on their violent instincts is up to the children themselves," the man groaned.

Lukas held his breath as he widened his eyes at the screen in front of him. This was it. The answers he was looking for were all here.

"Should they pass, the children will be moved to former CIA black sites across the country and be trained under an elite Black Ops force. There, their violent nature will be nurtured until they have become military weapons. I urge you, Directors. Do not hold back on their training. They must be lethal. They cannot show any emotion or remorse for killing. Do whatever you must. You have no boundaries. This is *Phase Two.*"

Lukas's trembling breath clouded his ears, drowning the man's voice.

"Finally, if the children should prove their lethality. We will deploy them to countries of their ethnic background, where they will spark civil wars across their countries. By turning the enemy on itself, they will splurge resources fighting a never-ending battle. And they'll never have to focus on The United States again. This is *Phase Three* for Project Salvus. This *is* Safety First. This *is* the future of America," the man finished.

The screen faded black, and the voice disappeared.

Lukas stared blankly at the screen in front of him, his heart thrashing in his chest.

I'm a spider.

The sirens wailed in his ears louder than before. His head throbbed like a beating drum, almost as if the pounding were heavy footsteps inching closer to him.

I'm a spider.

The thought spiraled into his mind until it echoed relentlessly, like a cruel song. He was a spider, the same way his father was—it was true. And he loathed himself for it. But, when Lukas looked up, there was a group of bulky men dressed in black bursting through the room. They differed from the guards, but they still carried rifles.

"We found one!" a man shouted.

It happened quickly. The armed men rushed toward Lukas, gripping him with brute force and pulling him away from the desk. And before Lukas could ask questions, they pulled a black hood over his head, greeting him with the same darkness that'd touched him his whole life.

56

LUKAS

LUKAS SPREAD A DOLLOP of shaving cream across his scratchy face in his truck. His hands rattled with exhilaration from shooting Ian in the head. He wished he could've recorded the moment it happened when the trigger was pulled and Ian collapsed in his own pathetic blood.

New Horizon apartments were unusually still that afternoon. He imagined it was because Ian's death made everyone afraid to leave their home.

Lukas sharply stalked the old building from across the street as he began shaving. He swiftly glided the dull razor up and down his cheeks until they were smooth, but he kept his glare unwavering.

I need to find Karina.

The task would be like trying to catch smoke with his bare hands. Dimitri's meddling daughter could be anywhere in town, taunting him from afar. His lips thinned with annoyance that she'd thought she could beat him in his own game—trap him in his own web. He would wait however long it took for her to leave the building so he could abduct her. He longed to see her suffering for making that pathetic threat to him.

I know what you did.

The words echoed in his mind as he gripped the razor tighter.

I know what you did.

Lukas slid the razor down his neck with a heavy hand.

I know what you fucking did.

"Shit!" Lukas dropped the razor on the floor. He nicked himself on the neck as a small dot of blood began growing. *Stupid thing,* he thought.

Grabbing a dirty t-shirt from the passenger seat, Lukas wiped the blood from his stinging neck. He adjusted the rearview mirror to get a better look at his red neck, but something else caught his attention.

Lukas's little friend, Jake, was springing playfully at the small park behind him. A faint grin stretched on Lukas's twitching lips.

Since Lukas couldn't go into the apartments without being thrown out by Dimitri, Jake was his next best bet. The little boy knew everyone in the building and was sure to know where Karina was.

Lukas practiced his sympathetic smile in his rear mirror before making his way to the dilapidated park, avoiding suspicion and moving cars.

The sun hung low over the neglected park. It was uncared for, like an abandoned child or a forgotten dream. Litter scattered along the wet grass, and the playground hadn't known care in a while as missing screws made slides rattle when ridden. A large concrete cylinder sat along the edge where profanities were spray painted and huddles of shadowy figures gathered.

Lukas stepped onto the grass and was immediately hit by the filthy stench of marijuana. He held his breath as he continued.. It reeked all the way from the cylinder where the grimy beggars hid. They threw Lukas cold glares as they exchanged dollar bills and plastic bags filled with substances. The effects of Elizabeth Ainsley.

He'd almost forgotten why he was there until he spotted Jake giggling by the metal slide.

Lukas kicked an empty soda can as he hurried toward him. No Vivian in sight. *Perfect.*

"Jake!" Lukas called out.

Jake turned around, but instead of his innocent face lighting up, it widened with fear as he fell back.

"No! You want to kill me!" Jake cried as he gripped his neon blue shirt.

Lukas watched, amused, as Jake hid behind a pole that was too thin for his body, his black curls poking out from both sides.

"No, Jake, I didn't mean it," Lukas started. "I'm sorry. I was just sad because no one wants to be my friend anymore." Lukas kneeled next to the pole with a sulking expression.

Jake said nothing, but quietly whimpered.

"People are always making fun of the way I look and call me names. My birthday is coming up, and all I wanted was to throw a big party with all my friends," Lukas sighed. He hoped it would make Jake empathize with him, or at least speak again.

Jake poked his small head from the pole. "A party? What *kind* of party?"

"The best one with balloons, cake, and games. Except it won't be a party if no one shows up, but you'll show up, right, Jake? You're my friend, right?"

Jake rocked back-and-forth before nodding with a wide grin.

"I'm so happy you are, Jake! By the way, have you seen Karina today? She's supposed to help me plan the party," Lukas said. He held his breath as he waited for Jake to reply. Jake had to know something; he was sure of it.

"Jake! Honey, where are you!" Vivian called out.

Lukas furrowed his brow at her high-pitched whine. That bitch was going to ruin everything for him.

With his heart racing, Lukas grasped Jake's small shoulders and jerked him forward. "Where is she, Jake?"

Jake flinched at his touch. "I s-should go back," he said.

"No, Jake. I need you to tell me where Karina is first. This is important, remember? You wouldn't want to make your friend sad, would you Jake?" Lukas dug his fingers into Jake's small shoulders.

Jake whimpered, his dark face squirming with pain.

Lukas didn't care. He was going to do whatever it took to make Jake speak, and if he was silly enough to scream for Vivian, Lukas would make sure Vivian never saw her little brat again.

Jake's breaths became more rapid as he bit his small lip. Finally, the squirming boy leaned toward Lukas's ear. "With her friends, Ashton and Mary," he whispered.

Lukas shot up, a crooked smile curling on his lips as he hurried away from the park. It no longer stunk of the rancid drugs. Instead, Lukas imagined the sweet, sugary smell of Karina's blood and fear filling his nose.

"Lukas! Stay away from my kid!" Vivian shouted from behind.

It didn't matter anymore what Vivian said, because his web was unwinding. He could barely contain himself as his eyes widened with malevolent satisfaction.

I know what you did, Karina. You thought you could escape me. But you were wrong—you can't hide from a recluse.

57

AMELIA

JULY 16

AMELIA STEPPED INSIDE THE dim, buzzing interrogation room and shot a glance at the cold, abrasive man sitting cuffed to the table. Hopefully, Bill Meyer would be feeling cooperative enough to help solve the damn case. Either way, she needed answers, and she needed them now.

Bill shot a complacent stare as she sat opposite of him, his brown inmate uniform highlighting his ginger whiskers and venomous ivy eyes. There was something eerily off-putting about his presence, like it was her intruding in *his* space.

Why are you smiling?

She gulped.

"You seem awfully happy today," Amelia started.

Bill smirked. "I'm both flattered and disappointed the police think I'm a serial killer. I'm good at what I do, but that doesn't make me a killer," he said.

"And *what* do you do, Bill?"

"I hunt," Bill groaned. "I see the prize that I want, and I take it for my own, just like any good hunter would do."

Amelia studied his irritated gaze for a moment. "The *prize* being Cassandra Holland? Or did you mean like Helen Meyer, the wife you *murdered?* We found her body in the dungeon inside your shed. "

Bill looked up sharply. "You know what is about you women? You think you just have everyone figured out, and you just love to control everything and everyone around you. You and Helen would've gotten along great. She also loved poking her long nose into things that weren't any of her business. But God, was she the most beautiful toy.

Amelia swallowed her frustration as she quietly seethed. She wanted to slap his misogynistic face.

"Why keep Cassandra?"

"She was a one-of-a-kind. They don't make girls like *her* anymore. That's why she was the most valuable trophy in my collection." He chuckled.

Amelia squinted. "What about Rebecca Waylow, Percy Romano, or Elizabeth Ainsley? Were *they* also prizes in your collection?"

Bill stared blankly at her, his mouth stretching to a repulsive smile. "I've never killed a human before. They're not exactly *in* the market right now, and I didn't murder Helen. She killed herself after she couldn't handle all the sex I made her have."

Amelia frowned. She didn't find his humor as amusing as he did. "There was a trail of kerosene leading from Dr. Elizabeth Ainsley's home to your home, and there was a gun on your table, along with a whole shed of other weaponry. It looks to me like you're more than capable of murder and responsible for the death of Elizabeth Ainsley, aren't you?"

"Are you asking me or *telling* me?" Bill leaned forward, sneering. "It seems to me you aren't sure yourself if I killed that woman. You don't even believe I'm the *Recluse Killer*, do you? I hear the officers talking from my cell. Another man has been murdered, right? It couldn't have been me." He raised his cuffed hands. "I've been stuck here the whole time."

Amelia was losing patience. This man was clearly playing games with her. Bill's cryptic answers were becoming insufferable.

"You're right. A man named Ian Addams has been murdered. What do you know about that? Are you working with someone else?"

Bill leaned back, sighing. "Ian Addams. He owns that carwash on Boardman Road. Yeah, I've been there a few times. I even made a friend there who would tell me all these terrible things about him. If you knew how he really treated people, Detective, you wouldn't be so surprised yourself when Ian turned up dead," he said.

"A *friend?*" Amelia asked. "Who?"

"Lukas Retter." A faint smirk slipped on Bill's wrinkled face.

Amelia was glad Bill mentioned his name as she placed a file on the table. Finally, she was getting somewhere. Opening the file, she slid a picture of Lukas taken from CCTV footage from an outside building. One of the few buildings that had CCTV, even though Amelia had insisted for the last several months for the government to install more surveillance throughout the town. Of course, they didn't have the budget for it.

"Is this him?"

Bill nodded.

"Lukas has been our prime suspect since the very beginning of this case. Problem is: we don't have any hard evidence linking him to any crime, other than a motivation." Amelia folded her arms. "We even gained some leads when Percy Romano's friends came in and told me about the *hostile* encounter they had with Lukas a few weeks ago—just before Percy went missing."

Amelia slid a photo of Rebecca Waylow toward Bill. "Lukas and Rebecca were in a relationship for quite some time before Rebecca was murdered. Lukas claims he had nothing to do with her murder. But when we spoke to her mother, she told us a different story. Lukas was emotionally manipulative to Rebecca, and she constantly feared for her life in their relationship. He has bursts of anger, you see."

"Don't we all?" Bill asked.

"Well, for an average person, they aren't usually *murderous.*"

Bill took a deep breath, fixing his eyes on the picture of Rebecca, then back up. "I can't imagine what he'd do now with that gun I gave him."

"You armed Lukas Retter with a firearm? Where is he?" Amelia sat up, her heart racing. *That would explain why Ian Addams was found shot.*

Bill's face contorted into something more menacing instead of cooperative. His chapped smile stretched as he shot Amelia a complacent glare.

"You detectives always want everything on a silver platter, every answer given to you wrapped in a silver bow. Let me remind you, Ms. Amelia, you're the one that needs something from *me*. So, tell me, *woman*, what are you going to give me in exchange?"

Amelia folded her arms, scowling. *You'd be lucky if a judge doesn't sentence you to life in an actual prison.*

"This isn't a negotiation, Bill. You have no power within these four walls. What do you know about Lukas?" Amelia demanded.

Bill replied with an irritating silence.

The son of a bitch, Amelia thought as their eyes met. She refused to let him take control of the situation or let him coerce her. The more Amelia examined Bill, the more his wrinkles twisted like the scales of a snake.

Amelia's nose twitched. "What do you want?"

"Immunity." Bill smirked.

"Not a chance in hell."

Amelia stood up, trudging toward the door. She was going to find Lukas, with or without Bill's cooperation. Her fingers trembled with rage as she felt Bill's beady, snake eyes narrowing behind her.

"I wonder how many people you'll let die before coming back for my help. I always get my way, Amelia. Remember that," Bill hissed.

Amelia ignored him, but she quietly seethed under her breath. *Go to hell, you sick bastard.* There wasn't a chance she was going to surrender to Bill's conditions.

As she left the interrogation room, the haunting idea of a dangerous suspect carrying a firearm invaded her mind. But if he and Bill were friends, Bill was sure to know where Lukas was.

A line of sweat formed above Amelia's brow as she imagined what murderous things he could be doing at that moment.

Whatever it takes, I have to find Lukas.

58

Lukas

July 18

Ashton & Mary Co. The small red brick bookshop was tucked between a small, dilapidated cafe and a smaller apartment complex. For Karina, the bookstore was a type of haven for her. Lukas had always seen her carrying some stack of books in New Horizon, and when he'd asked where she got all the books from, she'd mentioned her favorite shop.

Thanks to Jake's gullibility, he now knew where she'd been lingering around. No doubt Karina would head to the bookstore today, too. She was a frequent visitor, after all. A lucky encounter was all he needed. He had to be careful, though, as he imagined the police were more on edge after he shot Ian. They'd been monitoring the streets more than usual.

He'd been watching the bookstore for the last couple of days, watching Karina entering and exiting. One day she wore a pair of light wash jeans, the other a blue mini-skirt. Her innocent facade was amusing. She was taunting him with her knowledge. He wouldn't let her spill his bloodthirsty secrets to anyone.

Lukas examined the small shop from the truck across the street. The worn wooden signage of the store's name had been half-obliterated by layers of peeling paint. The store was barely recognizable at all. In the pair of display windows, a combination of glimmering crystals, cryptic tomes and mysterious artifacts held an eerie allure, drawing the few inebriated pedestrians into its spiritual realm.

Books were never Lukas's favorite, mostly because he was a terrible reader. The last book he'd read was *Goodnight Moon* with his mother.

Lukas's brow twitched. Elizabeth was a liar. His mother was a great one, and everything the doctor said was untrue. He wasn't a mistake.

But the familiar figure quickly interrupted Lukas's thought, strolling down the street. Karina's long black curls bounced as she approached the bookstore and entered. The door closed slowly behind her.

Lukas smirked.

He didn't care that she was Dimitri's daughter; she meddled in his life—and now she needed to disappear. Lukas hurried out of his newly washed truck with a chemically dowsed gray dishrag. Making chloroform had unexpectedly been easier than he imagined. Bleach and acetone were all he needed.

He scurried across the barren street and entered the bookstore, his fingers tingling with excitement.

A fair amount of shoppers filled the space inside, and an old shopkeeper woman greeted him by a counter around a corner. Lukas forced a gentle smile back, but his eyes wandered to the shoppers creeping around the dusty floorboards. Tall rows of oak bookshelves stretched like towering walls separated by genre and category. Chandeliers of all kinds and styles hung from above, shimmering among the glossy covers of the books like tiny mirror balls. His eyes twitched at the loud lights.

There in the corner, Karina was face buried in the pages of a book in her hands. The floral blouse she wore was impeccable and his favorite color. Red. The color of spilled blood. But her beauty was no comparison to Rebecca's. No one could ever be.

Lukas crept through the bookshelves, sharpening his eyes at her through the gaps between the books. He needed to make sure he wasn't being seen by her, or else she'd know what he was up to. Karina licked her finger before turning the page. She must've been contemplating whether to purchase it. The gaps between the books thinned as he neared the end of his aisle, but he glimpsed the book she was reading: *The Dark History of Evil Nature.*

Lukas nudged into a body in front of him, a middle-aged woman covered with tattoos.

"Hey, excuse you!" the woman snarled.

He wouldn't apologize. The woman should have seen him walking down the aisle as he thinned his lips in disdain. But as they turned past the corner to the next aisle, Karina was gone. She had disappeared into the air without a trace. The musty air inside quickly became cold as his head spun, trying to glimpse the red floral blouse. If he let Karina get away, his plan would collapse.

Lukas paused. There she was, by the shopkeeper's counter, paying. This time, she'd only purchased the one book. Snatching several random books off the shelf, Lukas carried the large stack of books with both his hands. He drifted out of the tall aisle, and out of the bookstore while someone still distracted the old woman with their purchase.

Karina was mere feet down the street, her face still buried in the pages of her book.

Lukas sharpened his brow as he dropped a couple of books off his stack. "Karina!" he called.

Karina turned her head, her face paling at his appearance. The same fearful look she wore at the fire when they ran into each other.

"Can you help me get these to my truck? I can't bend down—bad knees," Lukas groaned, his face tightening with false pain.

Karina stared at him with widened eyes, not budging. "I'm actually running late right now. I'm meeting with a friend."

"Please, Karina? It'll only take a second." Lukas bent down, trying to pick up his fallen books. "Ow—my knee!" he cried in agony.

She made a double take behind her, then to Lukas, before throwing him a look of concern. "Sorry, I really am running late," she said firmly.

She's scared.

"That's okay, don't worry about me. You get going to wherever you need to, I can pick them up myself." Lukas painted a grin on his furious face. He wasn't planning on making such a disruptive, but since his truck was a few feet away, it wouldn't be so burdensome.

Karina stood motionless as she studied him picking up the fallen books. The air turned to a sweet vanilla, the scent of Karina's fear—it was insatiable.

Lukas watched her from the corner of his eye as he let out a series of groans, picking up each book. He needed to play the small man, the harmless man, the victim, to get Karina to turn her back just for a moment.

Karina stepped back before heading the opposite direction Her rugged breaths filled Lukas's ears, and her steps were quick.

She's in a hurry. This is my chance.

Lukas prowled toward her with light steps. He pulled the chemically dowsed dishrag from his jean pocket. He narrowed his bloodthirsty eyes at her trembling body as he stood right behind her.

Anybody could see it. Karina was sweating with cold terror. The mousy whimpering that slipped from her mouth like a tune was pleasurable to Lukas.

Lukas's mouth stretched with sinister delight.

Karina must've known what he was about to do because she squealed right before Lukas wrapped his arms tightly around chest.

Lukas forced the chemical rag on her nose. She squirmed in his grasp, screaming. But her sharp screams were quickly subdued as Lukas pressed the rag deeper into her face.

No one noticed a thing as he dragged his new prey to his idle truck. Karina was caught, and now unconscious, inside his truck. Just as he intended.

A crooked grin twisted his face as he hurried to the driver's side. Lukas was right. The whole thing had only taken a second.

59

AMELIA

JULY 18

ONE, TWO! AMELIA GRUNTED.

The empty gym at the HPD was dimly lit, with the relentless thud of punches reverberating against the concrete walls. The sour stench of sweat lingered in the air as the tenacious detective held her heavy fists, the worn red leather of her gloves a familiar comfort. Boxing was her outlet, a way to release the pent-up frustration and anxiety the *Recluse Killer* case had brought into her life.

"The answer is in the punches, not the bottom of a bottle," Frank had told her once. In a few years, they'd be living rich thanks to the narcotic network.

The heavy bag swung harshly in front of her. With each punch, Amelia imagined the face of every person who slighted her throughout her life, but no one angered her more than Bill Meyer's complacency over the last couple of days. She paused to catch her labored breaths. Amelia could feel the weight of the case throbbing in her heart. The unknown whereabouts of Lukas Retter fueled the fire within her.

Percy's friends had come into the station the other day, reporting his disappearance. They were shocked to discover he'd been murdered, but they were horrified when Amelia showed them a picture of Lukas and asked if they'd seen him. To Amelia's amazement and horror, they told her about an altercation that had occurred before Percy's disappearance. *How fucking convenient.*

She took a drink of watered-down vodka, centering herself in the dimly lit room.

Amelia unleashed a barrage of punches, each strike unleashing the weight of her frustrations. The image of Rebecca Waylow's mutilated body, the mysterious circumstances of Dr. Elizabeth Ainsley's death, and the chilling autopsy report about the cause of Rebecca's death stormed in her mind.

Sweat dripped down her forehead, and her muscles burned, but she welcomed the pain.

But before Amelia could continue, her phone rang from her black sports bag. She dropped the gloves and quickly picked up her shrieking phone. *Please be something good.*

"Detective Amelia Mayman speaking," she said.

"Amelia, I have a terrified father on the line saying his daughter's gone missing. He says he hasn't been able to get ahold of her in the last several hours, and he says the last time he saw her was when she left New Horizon apartments," the dispatcher woman said.

Amelia's ears perked at the familiar name. *New Horizon? Maybe he knows something about Lukas.*

"Put me on the line with him," Amelia said.

There was a static buzz on the line as Amelia impatiently waited. Her nails dug into the leather of the punching bag next to her.

"This is Detective Amelia Mayman. Who am I speaking with?"

"My name is Dimitri Pauk. Please, you have to find my daughter, Karina!" Dimitri's static cry filled Amelia's ear. *"She's gone missing! Karina said she was going to a bookstore and then coming straight back, but she hasn't, and she isn't answering any of my messages!"*

Amelia gritted her teeth as her mind raced with the potential possibilities of Karina's whereabouts, each worse than the last. But she wondered if, somehow, Lukas had anything to do with it.

"I understand, Mr. Pauk, but I need you to stay calm. My team and I will do everything we can to find your daughter," Amelia assured with a confident tone. "I need you to tell me if she mentioned anything specific about where she was going or who she might be meeting?"

There was a pause before Dimitri responded.

Why the hesitation?

"No, Detective. She didn't say much. Just that she was going to the book-store: Ashton & Mary. Please, you have to find her. I'm terrified something's happened to my daughter! I can't leave her. Not when she's already lost her mother and best friend. She was the missing girl, you see, Cassandra Holland. And now my baby is missing too," Dimitri cried.

Amelia took a deep breath, her aching mind racing toward the worst possible scenario. She imagined puddles of red everywhere with the gray skin of a corpse. But she quickly shook the idea out. She wouldn't allow anyone else to die under her watch.

"Thank you, Mr. Pauk. We'll do our best to locate Karina. Now, there's something else I need to ask you about. Have you ever heard of a man named Lukas Retter? I understand he also lived in New Horizon?"

There was another pause before Dimitri responded.

"Yes, he was one of my tenants. A strange, reserved man. I didn't feel too bad about having to evict him, especially with all the rumors of his involve-ment in the death of Rebecca Waylow and the fire started in the building," Dimitri muttered with a shaky voice.

Amelia clenched the punching bag tighter. "Did you ever witness him participating in any sort of illegal activity?"

Dimitri didn't respond, but she could still hear his shaky breaths echoing through the static.

"Mr. Pauk?"

"I didn't. But Karina did," Dimitri muttered.

Amelia held her breath as her heart raced faster.

"Karina told me the night that boy Percy Romano was murdered, she saw Lukas dragging the boy's body along the forest." Dimitri choked on his own tears as he spoke. *"Detective, the truth is, I'm scared he might've done something to her. I think Karina might've taken things into her own hands after I was too scared to report what she saw. One of my tenants, Vivian, said earlier that Lukas was asking her son about Karina's whereabouts. And he told Lukas where Karina was, Detective."*

The poor father's tears filled the line once more as Amelia connected the puzzle pieces in her mind. It was all finally coming together. Except there was still one problem: Lukas's whereabouts. Against her better judgment, it seemed the only way to get a lead on that was to talk to Bill again. *The old asshole.*

"Dimitri, I will get your daughter back. Whatever it takes. I promise."

Amelia burst through the cold doors of the interrogation room once more. This time, she wouldn't listen to Bill's cruel jokes. She was there for answers only.

Bill sat with his hands cuffed to the table. This time, he wore a tattered orange inmate uniform. In the last couple days, he seemed to have aged faster as the bags beneath his eyes only deepened, and his skin became more pallid and creased. The only thing that didn't change was his wrinkled, smug smirk.

Amelia curled her lips as she stood before him with her arms crossed, her blue vest draping just below her waist.

"Alright, Bill. You win. I spoke with the district attorney on the phone. They're working on getting it notarized right now. You'll get your full immunity if you tell me what you know about Lukas," Amelia spat.

Bill stared at her for a moment, amused. His ginger whiskers twitched as he let out a small chuckle. Somehow, his presence took up most of the room.

"What made you change your mind?" Bill asked.

"A young woman has been abducted, and she may die tonight if I don't find her. I'm not going to let that happen just because of your selfishness, Bill. So, tell me what I need to know."

Bill nodded rhythmically as he rubbed his coarse hands together. "Do you hear that? It's the sweet song of misery. It's been playing every day since they built this town. You don't even realize you're singing, do you?"

Amelia shot a cold glare at him. She was in no mood for his riddles as her brow twitched with irritation.

"The pistol I gave Lukas, it's for killing animals," Bill started. "If Lukas murdered Ian, it was maybe because Ian was an *animal*. Lukas reminds me a lot of myself, Detective. We both like our isolation, watching the lives of others pass by from the corner of a room. And just like me, he's a hunter—just not the kind that kills farm animals. But if he was, I'd say Lukas is like a farmer who's rounding his animals like that girl, Karina, back to where they belong. Back in his control, like they should be."

Amelia's eye twitched. The information that Bill was enciphering cruelly itched at her mind. "A farmer?"

"You see, Detective Lukas once took an unusual interest in my barn house. And *farmers* sure love their barns. I'd start there." Bill grinned, his crooked teeth widening.

Amelia's eyes widened with realization. Her team had already swept Bill's ranch for anything suspicious and illegal, including the barn, but they were no longer stationed. After they gathered their evidence against Bill, Amelia abandoned the property to go to the crime scene of Ian Addams. Of course, it would make sense to kill Karina in a secluded location where the police had already swept because they didn't need to be there anymore.

Amelia let out a small grin. She leaned over the table, pressing her proud face against his. "You're going to rot in prison, Bill. You aren't getting any immunity, but thank you for your cooperation." Amelia sneered.

Bill's face contorted with fury as his chapped lips thinned with anger. It was a satisfying sight to see as Amelia walked away.

"I always get my way, Bill. Remember that."

Amelia left the interrogation room for the last time with no time to waste. If she didn't hurry, more innocent blood would be spilled.

Hurry, Amelia. Hurry!

60

LUKAS

WHEN LUKAS WAS A little boy, he used to make his mother check underneath his bed and closet for monsters. Those prickly, sick creatures always hid in the darkness, lurking. And even though he never actually saw one, he could still hear them scraping along the walls of his bedroom.

But when Lukas got older, he realized there were no such things as monsters or creatures of the night—at least not the type his childish imagination thought. There were monsters all around him. Everywhere he went, they wore different suits of skin, trying to blend in with the rest of the world. Just like himself.

The hay crunched beneath Lukas's footsteps as he slid the heavy barn door shut. A waft of dust and dirt clouded his face. The filthy stench of hay was repugnant.

Now, the only monster in the still, dim coldness of the barn was him, and Karina could do nothing but accept whatever cruel fate he had planned for her.

Bill's desolate old barn was the perfect place to commit a heinous crime. Its forgotten existence was convenient in that no one would suspect a thing, and with Bill gone, Lukas didn't have to worry about his intrusion. He could be left alone to weave his web across the town in peace.

Lukas shot a twisted grin at Karina, who whimpered against the chains he'd shackled her in. He groaned. She was misbehaving and making a ruckus of noise. The slivers of pale light that slipped through the cracks of the rustic ceiling cast a mottled glow on her teary face. A small metal hook on the floor forced Karina to sit against her will. The strip of duct tape silenced her squirming squeals stretched along her mouth.

Killing his next bug was sure to be delightful. Especially since she had dared to mock him with that note.

Lukas crept toward her like a nearing predator. His gritty eyes widened connivingly as Karina continued writhing in the chains, pinning her to the floor—like the pig that she was.

Earlier, Lukas had found a cattle prod in one stable, which was sure to make Karina's torment more enjoyable. The cold metal stung his fingers as he held it in his tight grasp. Finally, the little snake would get what she deserved.

Kneeling down, Lukas clenched her flailing jaw, forcing their eyes to meet. He wanted Karina to look at him so she could understand what he was about to do to her. The sweat along her jaw was sweet, sending an exhilarating rush up his skin.

Karina's feeble eyes trembled in his gaze.

"*I know what you did.* It was clever, I'll admit, but did you really think I wouldn't find out it was you, Karina?"

Karina wailed in response, her words silenced by the tape. The only word he understood was "bug" because he scribbled it across her mouth.

Leaning forward, Lukas wiped the streaming tears off her swollen cheeks with his thumb.

"Karina, I'm sorry it had to come down to this. You were my favorite neighbor. Not so much your father anymore. I'll have to kill him, too, because I don't know what you've told him about me." Lukas took a few steps back, admiring the cattle prod in his hand.

Karina convulsed her head, sobbing. The rattle of her chains played like the soothing clatter of wind chimes.

"That mouth of yours, you know, it's really caused a lot of trouble for me lately. You have the tongue of a filthy snake, you little bitch. You'll say anything about anyone to whoever fucking listens. So, what should I do about that? Maybe I should take away your privilege of hissing another word ever again." Lukas chuckled.

A crooked smirk curled on his lips as he tightened his grasp on the cattle prod. What he was about to do to Karina made the hair on his arms rise with excitement.

Karina's censured shrills reverberated off the rustic walls. She squirmed helplessly on the floor like the animal she was. And like all animals—they must be hunted.

Lukas took a step forward, peeling the silver tape off her mouth.

"NO—LUKAS! PLEASE! I'M SORRY!" Karina screamed violently.

But her irritating shrieks were quickly silenced as Lukas thrust the cattle prod inside her mouth.

An electrifying buzz in Karina's throat muffled the *pig's* squeals. She both choked and writhed on the floor from the intense shocking.

Lukas pulled the prod out of her mouth, laughing. "Little pig can't squeal anymore, can she? Tell me, Karina, can you still say the words: *I know what you did,* now?"

A whistle of strained air escaped from Karina's pasty mouth. But for Lukas, that was a whistle too loud.

Once again, he thrust the prod inside her mouth. The electric buzz vibrated the prod in his hand.

Karina flailed in agony on the ground, her head spinning violently.

Lukas's eyes widened with enjoyment, and his twisted smile curled deeper. This was art. This was power—*beautiful* power. This was *control.*

How do you enjoy me now, Karina? Don't worry, I'll tell your father all about it when I see him later.

There was a roaring blast from behind him. Lukas flinched at the explosive sound.

The incessant shrill of police sirens filled his ears as he spun around. And the barn door had collapsed to the hay floor. The piercing flash of blue and red lights in front of him blinded Lukas. *It can't be.* How could the police have discovered him? He wondered. This meant Amelia won her precious little fucking game.

"Drop the weapon!" Amelia ordered. A row of other officers lined behind her with their pistols pointed directly at him.

There was no more point in fighting the system he'd lost. He'd lost since he was born, and he'd continue losing for the rest of his life. The country had rigged the game from the very beginning of his miserable life. Still, he unwound a web around him, trapping them all in the cage built around him.

Lukas dropped the cattle prod on the floor, holding his hands in the air. But he kept his sinister smile painted as Amelia hurried toward him and handcuffed his wrists.

Amelia forced him to walk forward. "Lukas Retter, you are under arrest for the murders of Rebecca Waylow, Percy Romano, Elizabeth Ainsley, Ian Addams, and the abduction and torture of Karina Pauk. You have the right to remain silent. Anything you say can and will be used against you in a court of law..."

Lukas drowned out the rest of her insufferable speech. He trudged past the brigade of police officers lined up outside the barn, each sneering with a disgruntled passion. The paramedics by the ambulance rushed inside the barn with a stretcher. He might not have killed Karina after all. The one witness.

The night sky twinkled with stars, stringing lines together into a web, one that stretched across the entire country. But if they knew how pleasurable it was to kill and drink the fear of their victims, they'd applaud him for his great achievements.

And that was their greatest crime. Taking away what he loved: his freedom.

Lukas said nothing as Amelia forced him into the police car and instead smiled. And he carried the prickly, sick smile on his monstrous face all the way to the end.

61

LUKAS

MANY YEARS AGO

THE ROOM AND EVERYONE that once belonged to it was gone. Through little cracks in the hood over his head, Lukas caught glimpses of the massacre that had occurred throughout the facility. They had stepped over dead guards and kids, bullet holes soaking through their bodies. Director Miller's face was unrecognizable with the splashes of thick blood painted over him.

But to Lukas's horror, there were still no signs of Thomas. *Did he escape?* He hoped Thomas might've as the piling amount of dead bodies grew.

For a while now, Lukas sat in the back of a vehicle. Armed men sat at his side, refusing to speak a word about where they were taking him. He couldn't discern much through the black hood except for little specks of light. Even his hands were bound by his side with rope. Lukas was at their mercy as his heart raced. His wet feet sent prickling chills up his skin from the puddles of spilled blood he'd walked through.

"Where are we going?" Lukas murmured once again.

None of the men responded.

The shroud of blackness over him rustled against his face. The vehicle had come to a sharp halt, and a few moments later, Lukas was pulled out of the vehicle.

He held his breath. Now, the ground had become earthy and sharp, but it was *warm*. It wasn't the same warmness that hummed from the vents in his cell. This was an unfamiliar warmth—one that felt nice. He concluded it must've been the sun that hugged him.

A brute forced pulled Lukas forward, forcing him to walk. As he did, they must've entered some building, because the floor became cold and hard. The cool air stung his arms, the yellowed filthy hospital robe he wore no longer comforting him.

There was a murmur of distorted voices around him, but he couldn't make out any of the words. A whining door creaked open and Lukas was pulled into another room before being sat on a chair.

He bit his lip as they removed the black hood from his head. The flickering light above cast a pale glow on an older man's rough face, a small table separating them both.

Lukas spun his head, examining the small, congested room they were in. The concrete walls were unwelcoming and seemed to close in on his disoriented fears.

The old man cocked his thick gray brow at him as he studied Lukas. His brutish arms folded roughly against his came-green uniform like a type of soldier. Lukas wondered what new facility they had brought him to or if they had taken him as a prisoner and planned to kill him. After all, Lukas might've been the only survivor of his training facility.

But he knew one thing for certain after the video he'd watched. He couldn't trust the government. The weapons he thought he should've been afraid of turned out not to be any gun, but themselves.

"We already found the boy they were looking for. She's with him right now," the old sergeant said to another man behind Lukas.

Lukas threw the man a look of bewilderment. "You were looking for someone? Who?"

The old man groaned and scratched his gray head. "That doesn't concern you. Someone important sent us, someone who used to be married to Director Miller. What's your name, son?"

Lukas didn't reply. A *name is something that can be used against you.* His only response was his silent breath and frowning expression.

"No name? Well, how about how long were you in that facility? I'm sure they made you do a lot of *challenging* things." The old man tried to hide his demand with simple curiosity.

"I—I don't know. I've been there for so long that I can't really remember my life before *The Room*. Maybe I was born there. I can't even remember my parent's faces. But the director made us hurt each other in terrible ways, and he threatened to hurt us if we didn't obey. So many terrible things happened there, sir," Lukas said with a raspy voice.

Terrible things that I enjoyed. I wish I could kill like I did with Amon in the showers.

There was a long stretch of silence as Lukas leaned over the table, eager for the man to answer. But the old man said nothing except sharply stare at him like he was trying to invade Lukas's mind.

Lukas sneered in response. He wanted nothing more than to be finally free from the walls built around him.

"What should we do with him, sir?" the soldier behind Lukas asked.

The old man stood up. "Well—we can't release him back into the community with how he is. We'll turn him into the state of Connecticut's hands. There isn't a home for him anymore. They'll most likely have to place him in East Haddam, considering how detrimental he's become. This boy shouldn't be around the rest of society."

Lukas spun around, his head throbbing with questions. "What? What does that mean? Where are you taking me!" Lukas's voice strained at the last words. His breaths sharpened as the soldier behind Lukas handcuffed his wrists and led him out of the room.

I just want to go home, Lukas pleaded in his mind as tears streamed down his face.

"Stop," Lukas choked out. "Just let me go."

But the man wouldn't listen as he dragged Lukas away.

A woman's sobs reverberated off the walls as Lukas was walking away. Lukas turned his head toward a cracked open door and caught a glimpse inside.

An older, familiar, pale woman clung desperately to a limp, bloody boy as she sobbed into him. The boy's arms fell to his side, unresponsive and gray.

Lukas's vision blurred from his tears. But he could still feel the piercing agony in the woman's sobs as she screamed, "Thomas!"

Many Years Later

Lukas drank his third shot of whiskey at the *Red Head*. The smooth, bitter liquid stung his throat as it streamed down. The feeling was delightful. It was the best substitute for suppressing his bloodthirsty cravings, but he knew he couldn't kill anymore. That's why every night after work, he found himself at the dive bar with a drink in his hand.

His landlord, Dimitri, was kind enough to find him a job at the carwash. Lukas hated the dull work almost as much as he hated his new boss, Ian Addams. Somedays, he'd imagine torturing the fat man in every way possible, and a smile would creep on his face as he'd wash cars.

But killing was wrong. At least, that's what society said.

Lukas looked around at all the jubilant expressions around him. The carefree air seemed to touch everyone except him. He wished he could laugh at the music like the other women did and fuck like the other men did. The sweet smell of love and alcohol floated in the air and created a blithe haze.

All Lukas wanted was to be seen, to be noticed. And one day, he'd make them all see him. He'd control them to do what he wanted. From the very beginning, the government took away his power, and one day, he'd take it back.

He'd make a mockery of them and use their very own weapon against them. Himself.

Lukas brushed his finger along the empty shot glass.

One more wouldn't hurt.

"Let me get another shot," Lukas ordered.

"You're feeling lucky tonight." The bartender woman chuckled as she poured his drink. Her auburn hair was pinned neatly into a bun, with a few strands slipping out. *How adorable*, he thought.

Lukas smirked, his cheeks flushing. "Yeah, every fucking day."

But as she waved the shot glass toward him, the glass slipped from her fingers. The whiskey spilled all over the counter and dripped down his pants. Lukas shot up from the stool, groaning uncomfortably.

"Oh my god, I'm so sorry! Let me clean that up for you!" she said.

But as Lukas glimpsed into her eyes, he found something much better. The woman's eyes were the rich flavor of whiskey, and he could drink from them all night. He even found it cute how much distress she was in, as she grabbed a towel and began wiping the counter furiously.

"Your pants are all wet now. I'm sorry. I'll get you an extra shot on the house. I'm new here, so I'm trying not to embarrass myself, but I think I just failed that." She chuckled.

Lukas smiled. Her soft voice was like an airy breeze. Cool and comforting. "Not at all. I'd say you just made my night. I'm Lukas, by the way."

The charming woman looked up and gazed longingly at him. "It's nice to meet you. I'm glad to have made your night better. I'm Rebecca."

62

LUKAS

JULY 19

"No more lies. No more secrets. Just tell me exactly what happened," Amelia prefaced the interrogation with her arms folded.

Lukas glanced up from his handcuffed hands lying on the table to Amelia's sharp face. She wore a smug smile of accomplishment, like she'd conquered some impressive feat. The irritating sight of her speckless police coat and badge made him twist with anger inside. But he wouldn't let that arrogant bitch think she got to him, so Lukas wore a sly sneer on his face.

If the handcuffs hadn't been on him, he would've strangled Amelia for his last killing.

"Let's start with Rebecca Waylow," Amelia started. She spread different folders on the table, each containing their own hearsay documents. "Walk me through that day, Lukas. The day you murdered Rebecca."

Lukas sat up, his head throbbing. He didn't have his *oxycodone* anymore, which made the last several hours completely insufferable.

"I drove to her cabin that morning. She'd texted she wanted to speak to me. When I got there, everything was just right—perfect. She was perfect, like always. But things took a different turn when I became more anxious. I asked her why, and she insisted we spoke on her father's canoe on the river."

Amelia jotted down a quick note on her clipboard.

Lukas rubbed his upper lip with his fingers. "She tried to break up with me in the canoe. I wouldn't allow it, and I wouldn't let another man have her. So, I strangled her because I loved her," Lukas said with pride.

Amelia looked up, her brown brow furrowing. "You *strangled* her? That can't be right." She pulled out a white paper from one folder and slid it across the table.

Lukas looked down but didn't dare try to interpret what any of the information he was looking at meant. The medical ciphers and charts made no sense to him as he stared blankly at them.

"Rebecca Waylow died of *cardiac arrest*, not asphyxiation, due to neck compression."

Lukas grinned, letting out a small chuckle.

Amelia narrowed her gaze, unamused. "What's so funny?"

"She *woke* up. I thought I had killed her, but I didn't. I was dragging her back to my truck when she started moving again. At first, I was relieved because I hadn't killed the one person who loved me. But I knew, after what I'd done, I couldn't let her go. I wouldn't let another man taste her body. I wanted her all to myself again," Lukas said, his smile widening.

Amelia studied him for a moment. "What did you do to her?"

Lukas leaned closer. "I pinned her down and tied her hands, then I laid on top of her, feeling her tits and skin with my hands. She tried screaming, so I covered her mouth as I fucked her. And it was the best sex we'd ever had because, finally, I was in control of her. I *owned* her body. And I fucked her until I was satisfied, even with the blood pooling from her pussy. But it must've been too much for her because the bitch died halfway through," he said.

The detective was now seething. Her fingers squeezed the black pen in her hand tighter. "Two witnesses saw you carrying presumably Rebecca's body into the cathedral that night. One of them being your neighbor, Natalie Warren. By now, we know you didn't start the fire at New Horizons. But we thought you might've figured out she was the witness and tried to kill her for it," she said.

Lukas's heart jumped. Sophia's mother was the witness. Maybe he hadn't been as careful as he thought he'd been. Still, it benefited him that the old woman burned to death.

"I turned Rebecca's body into art, just like I did Percy's. I made it into a spectacle for the entire world to see. Finally, the world would have no choice but to look at me and see what it created. You thought you could take my power away from me? I caught the country in my web." Lukas smirked.

Amelia made a note. "You enjoyed killing them?"

Lukas scoffed before violently lurching forward. He wanted to kill her too and wipe the smug expression off her face, but they cuffed his hands to the table. The only thing he barely moved was the table.

"Why do you look so surprised, Amelia? You and government take a boy from his home, put him in a cage at a hospital, move in him to another cage where he has to kill to survive, and then move him to another fucking cage where he has to be a *good boy* to survive. I know what you are, Amelia. You're a little girl playing dress up for the government while you build cages and cages for anyone that talks back," he spat. "Don't act like you don't know the *truth* about the government's real project."

Amelia stared coldly at him, fidgeting with the pen in her long, dark fingers. Her black lips thinned into a line as silence filled the room. And when their eyes met, it was in contempt. A paradox of different lives. One had to be on top, for the other to be on the bottom. She had to be powerful for him to be powerless. It wasn't fair.

"Lukas, I do not know what you're talking about," Amelia said with an irritated pitch.

He shot a cold glare at her as she scribbled more notes on her clipboard. Amelia was lying. He was sure of it. If she was in control, she could manipulate the truth however she wanted, and that's what she was doing. The detective was twisting his words to make it seem like he was a remorseless killer, but she was wrong.

Lukas thought of himself as just a man who wanted to be free.

His obsidian eyes wandered across the room until they caught something familiar: a friend. The friendly sight comforted him as he tilted his head to catch a better glance. A small brown recluse was crawling on a web it had made in the ceiling's corner. A wide smile stretched across his face, and his eyes widened with exhilaration as the spider watched longingly. He used to think spiders were the worst kind of creepy crawlies to exist, but he was wrong.

They were his friends. They'd never left him like the other bugs in his life. And with his friends by his side, Lukas knew he'd never truly be abandoned, even when he'd be moved to another cage.

"Lukas, did you hear what I said? Why did you kill the others?" Amelia leaned closer, her heavy voice laced with intrigue.

Lukas shifted his wide eyes to her. He hadn't realized he drowned her nasal voice out. But the room became sweet, like a sugary syrup. Amelia's naked fear was painted on her brown face. He could see it clearly now. The web he'd spun throughout his life had caught everything and everyone around him, including the entire country.

Lukas's smile contorted into something cold and bloodthirsty. *"I'm a spider."*

ACKNOWLEDGMENTS

First, I owe a huge debt of gratitude to *you* for taking a chance on this book. Whether you enjoyed it or didn't, I'm so grateful that you gave it a read. Writing this was always a passion project for me. I spent most, if not all, of my high school years writing this book. There were many moments throughout the process where I doubted my ability, but thanks to many people, I was able to persevere to finish writing this story.

I would like to thank my friends who cheered me on the entirety. It was their constant support that kept me from throwing my laptop into a wall. For that, I would like to thank Seth Bell, Weston Trauba, Joel Ramirez, Gwen Horrocks, Zack Lord, along with many others.

To Conner: I'm better at ax throwing.

Thank you to my amazing beta readers, who, without this book, couldn't have been completed. I owe a deep gratitude to Michael and Paula. Thank you!

Thank you to fantastic editor Maryssa Gordon. Without her feedback and notes, this book wouldn't have been finished.

Thank you to *Vice News* for bringing awareness to the public defense shortage, which inspired this book. Fun fact: I was in my freshman civics class when I first had the idea for this story while watching that video.

Thank you to the amazing team at MiblArt for designing the cover for this book.

CONSIDER LEAVING A REVIEW?

Your reviews help indie authors continue sharing their stories. If you could take time out of your day to leave a review, you would make my day!

ABOUT THE AUTHOR

Gabriel Zavala is an author with a passion for the thrilling and macabre. At just nineteen, Gabriel has already been honing his craft for several years. He's currently studying to pursue a Bachelor's in English. When not writing, he can be found at the theater, the gym, or spending time with his close friends. With a love for horror and thriller, Gabriel Zavala is dedicated to continuing his journey as a writer and sharing his captivating stories with the world.

Milton Keynes UK
Ingram Content Group UK Ltd.
UKHW012340010424
440454UK00011B/173/J